The Nightmare Was Back

How much of the night she slept away she could not tell. Suddenly the dream enveloped her. She was aware of a long corridor—an endless corridor, with doors beyond number on either side. Darkness lay about her and the doors watched her slow advance blindly, hiding their secrets.

This was the beginning of terror.

In her dream she knew it was a dream, struggled helplessly to waken and could not. The enchantment bound her and there was no escape. Always it was the same dream, always the same—as if it were foreordained.

PHYLLIS A. WHITNEY
The Trembling Hills

HarperPaperbacks
A Division of HarperCollinsPublishers

HarperPaperbacks *A Division of* HarperCollins*Publishers*
10 East 53rd Street, New York, N.Y. 10022

This book is published by arrangement with Dutton.

Cover illustration by R.A. Maguire

First HarperPaperbacks printing: April 1991

Printed in the United States of America

HarperPaperbacks and colophon are trademarks of
HarperCollins*Publishers*

10 9 8 7 6 5 4 3 2 1

ONE

Only Mary Jerome minded the closing of the house. She knelt beside an open trunk in the one bedroom where a fire burned. A welter of women's garments surrounded her as she busied herself with packing. She was a slight, small-boned woman, neat to her finger tips, with hair that had grayed becomingly and a gentle strength in her face.

From across the room her daughter Sara glanced at her now and then in sympathy. In every detail Sara contrasted with her mother. At twenty she was a big girl, well-built and handsome, though she lacked the picture-book prettiness of the currently admired Gibson girl. Her thick hair was blue-black and glossy with health and her dark eyes had a way of looking at the scene about her with eager curiosity. There was always a touch of the dramatic in Sara. The lift of her chin, the set of full lips that were not always soft, betrayed a determination that had not yet learned to be wise.

"I wish you didn't mind our leaving so much," Sara said. "I wish you could be as glad as I am to get away from this house."

The house was waiting for them to go. It stood dark and ready, its shutters closed to the January sunshine; curtains and draperies long since removed. Two days ago drays had taken away most of the furniture to be sold at auction, as Ritchie Temple had instructed. Ritchie no longer lived in Chicago, but he had come home briefly the month before to attend his mother's funeral. When he had returned to California he had left final details in the hands of his mother's long-time housekeeper, Mrs. Mary Jerome.

Sara mused on, thinking aloud. "It's nothing but a shell of a house now. It will be better to leave it." She did not add that it had been no more than a shell for her ever since Ritchie had first gone away six months before.

Mrs. Jerome sighed. "A furnished room won't be as comfortable, you know. And so far, in spite of notices I've put in the paper, I've found no position."

"There's no need to worry." Sara was confident. "After all, Ritchie paid you for a month in advance, which was the least he could do. And I have the legacy Mr. Temple left me when he died. I'll get work in an office as soon as I can. Then you can rest for a while."

But she knew that to her mother this house was home. Mrs. Jerome had lived here far longer than the few years of her marriage. Sara had been only four when Mrs. Jerome had brought her to Chicago and sought work in the Temple household. All these years

Mary had been happy here. It didn't seem fair that she must now begin all over again in some alien place. If only she were willing to let her daughter make life easier for her. . . .

Mrs. Jerome shook out a ruffled shirtwaist that belonged to Sara and refolded it into a tray. "You've no notion of money, my dear. That legacy won't go far. As for office work, I'd rather not have you struggling in a man's world."

"But this is a new century!" Sara reminded her eagerly. "I've learned to type and it's perfectly proper for young ladies to work in offices these days."

She turned to add more coal to the fire, searching for a casual way in which to ask the question that was uppermost in her mind. It was a question her mother had always met with silence, but perhaps now, in their need—

"Didn't Father have any sort of family? Isn't there anyone to whom we could turn?"

Sara spoke the words more abruptly than she intended and she knew the answer from the sad, closed look that came over her mother's face.

"There's no one on your father's side to whom I would ever turn," Mrs. Jerome said gently.

It was no use, Sara knew, beating against this blank wall. Her mother never treated her questions unkindly, or reproved her for asking, but always there was this retreat into a silent sorrow which Sara could not fully understand. When it came to her father's life, his family, where they had lived when Sara was a baby, even the city of her birth—all these things her mother had shut a door against. Sara knew only that her father had gone away one day and never been heard from again.

Always her mother's love for the husband she had lost was evident, though Sara had gathered from words spoken now and then that he had been something of a spendthrift, with grandiose schemes for making money which had distressed and frightened his young wife. She knew too that her mother believed with an unshakable conviction that her husband was dead.

Sometimes Sara wondered. She liked to weave make-believe dreams about his unexpected return. She couldn't help building a fantasy in her mind, with an exciting figure that was her father at its center. Somehow he always seemed like an older version of Ritchie, and she liked him that way. It would have been so wonderful as a little girl to have a father, as other children did. A gay, handsome father who teased and spoiled and loved her. At times faint memories of someone like that seemed to stir in her, though she could never be sure.

Jerome, of course, was her mother's maiden name. Sara knew that her married name was Bishop. But her mother's unwillingness to continue as Mrs. Leland Bishop was part of the forbidden past her mother would never talk about. Sara had grown up with the name of Jerome and no one knew that she had any other.

Rubbing her weary knees, Mary pulled herself up from the floor by the edge of the trunk. "It must be time for the postman by now. Perhaps we'll find an answer to my notice today."

"I'll go," Sara said quickly. She was glad to escape from the stuffy room and her mother's discouragement that she was helpless to relieve.

She went into the cold upper hallway and moved

toward the gloom of the stairs. As she put one hand on the rail she heard the whisper of a letter dropping through the front-door slot. The envelope made a white splotch against the dark, bare floor, and Sara ran downstairs to pick it up.

Daylight filtered through the side panes of beveled glass in the front door and she held the creamy envelope up to examine it. The postmark read *San Francisco, January, 1906,* and suddenly excitement quickened in her. The handwriting, with its black letters slanting faintly to the left, was Ritchie's. She'd have known it anywhere. But the envelope was addressed to her mother.

For just a moment old hurt rushed through her. How *could* he have gone away? How could he have followed Judith Renwick to San Francisco?

Just a month ago, when he'd returned early in December, he had stood at the foot of this stairway, his fair hair thick and shining in the morning light. And he had caught Sara's hand in his teasingly. For all that she had tried to steel herself against his touch, the old longing had run through her again, the longing to be kissed by Ritchie Temple. And by Ritchie only, always and forever.

He had not kissed her, but he'd read the look in her eyes and she knew it had pleased him. He had read that look for the first time when he had been seventeen and she twelve. Twelve and big for her age. Now, all her growing up years later, it was still, for her, like the first time he'd ever looked at her.

In those years how often he had told her he loved her, that she was his very best girl. He had looked at other girls of course. How could he help it when they always looked at him? But it was to her that he'd told his dreams. Wonderful fantasies of the fine buildings he would someday create as a great American architect. "The best architects of our time are developing right here in Chicago," he'd said. And Ritchie Temple had to be one of them. Sara's eyes would shine with her belief in him and he'd laugh and kiss her. He was going to marry her, he'd say—when she grew up.

With five years between them, growing up had been difficult to manage. When she was eighteen and surely grown, he had said that first he must be established. Always she had believed him and waited, her love never faltering.

Then, some eight months before, Judith Renwick and her mother had come to visit in this house. Hilda Renwick was an old friend of Mrs. Temple's and had lost her husband the previous year. She had brought her elder daughter with her on the trip. Ritchie had been plainly attracted to Judith and when she had gone home to San Francisco a restlessness had grown in him. There were opportunities for a budding young architect in San Francisco, he said, and since he had been invited to stay at the Renwick house until he decided what to do, there was all the more incentive to go. His mother had encouraged the trip before she fell ill.

When Ritchie left, Sara's grief had been a shattering thing which she could not hide from her mother. If only he had remained within her reach, Judith Renwick could never have exerted such a spell over him. But what could Sara do when he was half a continent away and she was trapped here in Chicago?

When he had returned for the funeral a month ago

he had not talked about Judith. Sometimes he had even looked at Sara Jerome in the old way and she could see in his eyes that he was still fond of her.

Nevertheless, when his mother's funeral was over, he had put the house and furniture up for sale and dismissed the servants. San Francisco, he had decided, was to be his permanent home, and he'd dusted his hands for the final time of Chicago. Hope died in Sara then. But love could be a hardy thing, struggling on when there was nothing left for which to struggle.

She told herself that he was gone for good and her heart must stop trembling foolishly at the mere sight of his handwriting on an envelope.

She stirred from her dreaming and carried the letter upstairs. Nothing Ritchie might write could matter now. Probably this was no more than a graceful thank-you note, removing him from any further burden of obligation. She gave it to her mother with an air of indifference which she hoped was convincing.

"From Ritchie," she said. "There was nothing else." And she went to warm her hands needlessly before the fire. Though not before she saw the sympathy in her mother's eyes.

"How nice of Ritchie to write," her mother said, studiedly casual. Her eyeglasses were attached to a metal button near the collar of her dress, and she pulled them out on their chain, pinching them to her nose with a precise gesture Sara had loved to watch as a child.

When her mother was absorbed in the letter, Sara stole a look at her face and saw in it unaccountable alarm.

"What is it, Mama?" she cried. "Has something happened to Ritchie?"

Her mother crumpled the letter in her hands. "Why, no. Nothing."

She leaned past the trunk and Sara, seeing her intent, caught the wadded paper from her before she could toss it into the fire. Mrs. Jerome's lips trembled, but she did not reach to recover the letter.

"Read it then," she said. "Of course what he suggests is impossible."

Sara spread out the crinkled paper and knelt on the hearthrug to read by the flickering light. What Ritchie suggested was indeed astounding.

"San Francisco!" Sara cried. "He wants you there. And I am to go too!"

So his look *had* meant something, and the way he had held her hand. Of course a young man must go where opportunity offered. Judith was not important after all and this was Ritchie's way of getting Sara Jerome to San Francisco.

Her mother's silence, her grave look, brought Sara back to the shuttered room in Chicago.

"But of course you'll accept, Mama," Sara said eagerly. "If Mrs. Renwick isn't well enough to manage the house, and Judith is too inexperienced—they need you. It must be quite a household." Sara had learned from Ritchie about the others—Judith's little sister Allison, and her brother Nicholas, a year older than Judith. Now of course there was Ritchie too, apparently making his home with them. "Mrs. Renwick has asked Ritchie to write to you," Sara went on, "so this is official. And it's the answer to everything!"

Mrs. Jerome's face had paled and her fine-boned

hands gripped the edge of the trunk with an intensity she seldom betrayed.

"We can't go to San Francisco. Ritchie is only trying to be generous."

No, Sara thought, and her heart did a small thump against her ribs. Ritchie wouldn't go to all this trouble just to be generous. Surely there was a purpose in this invitation which concerned Sara more than it did her mother.

"Mama," she persisted urgently, "why don't you want to go to San Francisco? I can get work in an office there, just as I could here. I don't want Renwick charity. Tell me why you're set against San Francisco!"

Mrs. Jerome shook her head. "I will never return to San Francisco. It is a wicked, evil city, and there are wicked, evil people in it."

Turning Ritchie's letter in her fingers, Sara had the feeling that she was on the verge of discovery; that if she moved carefully something might be revealed that she needed to know. She quieted the storm that ran through her blood, spoke softly.

"Return? I didn't know that you had ever been in San Francisco. Why should you hate it so?"

Mary Jerome hesitated, then made up her mind. "You were born in San Francisco. I spent the five most miserable years of my life there. I don't want to go back!"

Coals clinked in the grate and the January wind blew icily against the windows. Mary Jerome's eyes held her daughter's and there was in them that ultimate in strength which she could bring to bear when the need arose. Sara knew and respected this quality in her mother. It was her own gaze that dropped first.

She tossed Ritchie's letter on a table and ran from the room. There was no hope to be found in her mother's resolution. She must be off by herself where she might think this thing out. There must be a way—there had to be a way.

She ran through the cold hallways to her own room, took a sweater and cloth coat from the wardrobe closet and slipped into them. Then she caught up a shawl and threw it over her glossy hair. When she left her room she did not go outside, but ran up the narrow stairs that led to the attic. It was wintry cold under the eaves, but she thrust her hands into warm pockets and hurried through the gloom toward the rear of the house.

Here, a few steps up, steps she knew instinctively, was the old haven of her childhood. A pointed tower made an excrescent growth on the house and contained within its cylinder a small circular room. Sara felt for the china doorknob and opened the door. Here there were windows, smudged and clouded with cobwebs, but winter sunlight, blinding in its reflection from snowy roofs, filled the small room.

Sara closed her eyes against the pain of brilliant light, blinking until she could accustom herself to its force. A window seat of dry, splitting leather ran all the way around. She chose her favorite place and knelt upon the seat. Her breath clouded the air and the windowpane, but she rubbed the glass clear with her handkerchief and looked down upon the rutted carriage tracks of the street, upon high-heaped snow banks, and on toward the gray-blue gleam of Lake Michigan.

Ritchie had always laughed at her love for high places. He alone had known of this hideaway which had played many a role in her childhood, from crow's nest on a ship, to lighthouse tower. Once he said, "I'm sure there must be hills in your blood. Else why must you always be on top of things?"

Hills in her blood? San Francisco hills? The very name sent a prickling along the skin of her arms. An evil, wicked town, her mother said. Yet was it her father's home? The city he had loved? Who were his people? And if they knew her would they help her in this need?

She considered the little she knew of her father's people. The family was a good one. Once when she had bewailed the fact that Ritchie was above her own social plane, her mother had denied her words.

"You've good blood on both sides, Sara. Your father came of wealth and fine family. You have nothing to be ashamed of, if background is so important to you. It isn't to me. I wish I could make you understand how little social position really means."

Mama had a good many notions about individual worth that puzzled Sara. Obviously wealth and family counted more than anything else. For as long as she could remember she had yearned to be Ritchie's equal. Surely they would have married long ago if she had been his social equal.

The cotton stuffing was coming through a hole in the leather of the tower seat and her fingers plucked at it idly. As they plucked she remembered. Months ago she had pulled at this same hole, tearing at the padding with fingers that had to be busy, could not be still because of the hurt inside her. She had come here one day while Judith Renwick was in the house. How well she remembered the reason!

She had started downstairs so casually that morning, the carpet concealing without intent on her part the sound of her descent. Ritchie and Judith were in the lower hall, and Judith had been in his arms. Sara stood frozen on the stairs, not believing that he could be kissing her, that Judith's hands were clasped behind Ritchie's head.

Then Ritchie had released her and gone out the front door. Sara, not daring to move, had stayed where she was, while Judith raised lovely hands to tidy strands of pale hair, a little smile curving her lips.

Judith was within a year of Ritchie's age and she had the beauty of an exquisite crystal figurine. Her hair was ash-blond and her eyes were blue-green as Lake Michigan could be on a cloudy day. She looked as fragile as a figurine too, as if you would not dare to hold her roughly. A fine glass stick of a woman to make love to, thought Sara miserably.

She must have moved on the stairs because Judith drew a quick breath and looked up at her. There was no time for Sara to pretend she had not seen. No time to hide the stricken look which must have betrayed her. There was nothing she could say. She had turned and run upstairs, away from the girl in the lower hall. She had fled to this tower room and flung herself on the leather seat in bitter unhappiness.

Judith had surprised her. Up the narrow stairs she had come, and across the dusty attic floor, the silken frou-frou of her skirts and the delicacy of her Paris perfume strange to this musty place. She had stepped into this very room and sat right there, across from Sara. And the sunlight had touched her to dazzling beauty.

Judith had been unexpectedly direct. "What is Ritchie to you?" she asked.

Sara sat up and stared at her, recovering from her first shock and ready to do battle for her love.

"I'm going to marry him," she said. "He's always promised that. You had no right to be kissing him."

The little smile lifted Judith's lips again, and watching her, Sara felt young and awkward.

"A man may change from a boyhood fancy," Judith said, not unkindly. "But I've no desire to hurt you, or to take Ritchie away if he is promised to you. Tell me, Sara, what would you do for him if you married him?"

The question had bewildered Sara. "Do for him? Why, I'd adore him, of course. I'd love him with every bit of me."

"What if adoration isn't good for him?" Judith asked coolly. "You might sit at his feet and clap your hands over his dream castles. But if I married him, I would make him build them."

Sara had found nothing to say and after a moment Judith stood up. "You needn't worry. I'm not going to marry your Ritchie. I'll admit to his charm. I'll even admit that I'm attracted to him. But such things aren't good enough for marriage."

She had rustled silkenly away down the stairs and Sara had stared after her, silent with astonishment.

Of course, as Sara realized now, she had not needed to worry about Judith. A girl who was so pale and without warmth could never have been right for Ritchie. Certainly she had inspired him to raise no breath-taking buildings in San Francisco. Instead, as he'd admitted when he was here, he had invested in the insurance business of Renwick and Merkel. Judith's brother Nicholas was a partner in this firm, and insurance was apparently a profitable business in San Francisco.

The tower room was cold. Sara stood up and shook the stiffness from her body, blew out her breath in a great cloud of vigor. That other time when she had faced Judith she had not known what to do. But now action was possible—if only she could find the way.

As she crossed the attic she left the tower door open behind her and a finger of sunlight cut the gloom, setting dust motes dancing in its beam. When she turned toward the stairs to the lower floor, something flashed in the darkness, very close to her, and she drew back startled. Then she saw it was the oblong mirror set in the top of an old bureau discarded here in the attic. Her own reflection looked back at her out of darkness touched with sunlight, and her breath caught in her throat, her knees trembled, as sharp memory returned.

She closed her eyes and clung for a second to the edge of the bureau, aware of the sick trembling that ran through her. All in quick succession pictures flashed through her mind. A long dark corridor in a strange house. The flashing of storm across the surface of a mirror.

She picked up her skirts and fled toward the stairs, ran all the way down to her room. There she sat on her bed, clenching her hands together until the trembling stopped. She mustn't dream tonight. It was a bad omen whenever the dream came. Perhaps she could stay awake, not sleep at all. Read. Write letters. Write a letter to Ritchie to say that they'd be coming.

Because they *were* coming. Sara knew, irrevocably,

that they had to go to San Francisco. But she could not write until she had persuaded her mother, and still she did not know the way to do that.

She roamed the empty house that day, as if movement might give her a sense of meaning. In her futility she found herself remembering her childhood, recalling happy hours and sad ones between these walls. Ritchie's father had been her good friend. Mr. Temple had long ago stopped struggling with his wife and had given up his son to be raised by Mrs. Temple. He had told Sara once that he wished she were his daughter, and much to his wife's annoyance he had left Sara a bit of money when he died a few years ago. Mrs. Temple had never liked her or approved of her. Mainly, perhaps, because of Ritchie's interest and kindness.

He *had* been kind when she was a little girl. Once there had been a dance when she was ten, and she had hidden behind a door, where she could watch through the crack and observe the gaiety she could have no part in. Ritchie had found her there and pulled her out. But he had not revealed her presence to the others. He had danced her away down the hall while the music played and whirled her till she was dizzy. Afterward she hadn't minded so much going up to her own room alone.

Ritchie had taught her to dance and he'd helped her with her lessons—though he went off to private school, and she did not. She had hated her own school because Ritchie wasn't there. And somehow Ritchie's friends had always seemed so much more exciting than the few children who had been available in the neighborhood for her to play with. As long as there was Ritchie she never minded. She had been content with books and imaginative games and had never felt sorry for herself, though she knew her mother had worried about her solitary life.

Now as she looked back, remembering, it seemed a lonely life for a little girl, with only the one bright star that was Ritchie Temple to light an empty sky.

In one way or another Sara postponed the moment when she must return to her room and go to bed. The answer to her problem still eluded her and in the end the day passed. There was nothing else to do at a cold, late hour. She fell restlessly asleep in spite of herself and at once the dream she feared returned—as it had not done for years.

She was in a room in the dream. Not a bedroom. Not a parlor. But a room cluttered with furniture—a storeroom perhaps. And there was the glass—a long gleaming shaft of wardrobe mirror shining in the gloom of a stormy afternoon. Then a soft light. A candle. Moving closer, not dispelling the gloom, but making it all the more ghostly. A hand holding a tall candlestick. Then the feeling of horror that always closed her throat so that she could not scream, though she struggled to. In a moment something dreadful and completely demoralizing would appear in the glass. There was a loud crackling sound in her ears.

She awoke drenched with sweat, her throat muscles tensed, her body tightened with dread. Always she awoke before the vision in the mirror came clear, possessed by a dreadful feeling of weakness and nausea. As a child the dream had come often. "The mirror nightmare," her mother called it and could make nothing of it. But Sara had grown up with a sensitivity toward any mirror in a dark room. She knew where every mirror in the house was, and in her own room she kept a cloth flung over the one on her dresser so that it could not frighten her suddenly in the dark. A mirror in a lighted room she did not mind.

But things had been moved about upstairs in the attic during the packing, and she had not known that bureau had been turned from the wall where she had pushed it long ago.

She lay back in bed, her stomach still squeamish, and for a long while she stayed awake.

She must get to San Francisco. That was where her roots lay. Not only Ritchie, but her father's family. The Bishops of San Francisco. When she could claim her rightful background in Ritchie's eyes, how much less Judith might matter. And now she knew how she would manage. Now she knew the way to get there.

TWO

THEY ATE THEIR MEALS IN THE KITCHEN THESE DAYS, since the two of them were alone in the empty house. At breakfasttime, with the big black cookstove freshly stoked and crackling, it was the coziest room in the house. This morning snow blew across the city and Sara stood by the kitchen window looking out at the big flakes falling from a gray winter sky.

In San Francisco there would be no snow.

Her mother was making pancakes, setting golden syrup on the table and a mound of country-fresh butter. There was an odor of freshly ground coffee from the mill. Sara watched until her mother sensed her look and glanced at her, smiling.

The smile was an effort to pretend that yesterday had never been, that no letter had come from Ritchie Temple. If only she could make her mother understand how important it was to reach San Francisco. If only the thought of that city didn't worry her mother so. Perhaps it was better to plunge right away and get the words behind her. Pleading and argument had failed. Now she must take the next step.

"There's no other choice for me, Mama," she began. "I *must* go to San Francisco."

Mrs. Jerome stood with the pancake turner in her hands. "Because of Ritchie?"

"This is my only chance. If I am there, where I can be near him, I'm sure—"

Automatically her mother flipped over a browning cake. "You believe what you want to believe, Sara, not what is really so."

But she had to give this a chance to be so, Sara thought. If she sat back and passed up the opportunity, then of course what she wanted could never happen. She would have to come right out with her plan, even though it frightened her a little. She and her mother belonged together; neither of them had anyone else. Nevertheless she had to fight for this chance.

"I have the legacy," she said quietly. "If you won't go with me, then I must go alone."

"What will you do in San Francisco alone?" Mrs. Jerome asked, working at the stove, not looking at her daughter.

"I've told you, Mama—I'll find work. Perhaps Ritchie will help me in that. And then I'll look for my father's family. If I can show him that my background is just as good as his, it will weigh a lot with Ritchie. And if I am there, then everything will be as it used to be. Only I'm grown up now and he'll realize that."

Carefully Mary Jerome set the turner down on the

stove, as if it were something fragile she might drop and break.

"You're such a determined girl, Sara. Sometimes you remind me frighteningly of someone I knew long ago. Someone I disliked. Of course you can't possibly make this trip alone. We will have to go together. Now sit down and eat your breakfast."

Sara sat at the table feeling a little dazed. Her mother was like that. When necessity demanded, she could do a complete about-face and march in an opposite direction with her chin up. But the capitulation had come more quickly than expected and Sara, braced for a siege, found herself wordless.

"It's true that this solves the problem of a position for me," Mrs. Jerome went on, setting a glass of cold milk at Sara's place. "And if you must take this step it will be better if I am there."

"Truly I didn't want to go alone!" Sara cried.

Her mother smiled faintly and began to dish up the pancakes.

"Nevertheless," she said, "I can accept Ritchie's offer only on one condition."

"Anything you say!" Sara promised recklessly.

"If we go to San Francisco," her mother said, "then we go under the name of Jerome. You will have to forget what you call background. Believe me, Sara dear, I have my reasons for feeling as I do. Most of last night I went over these things again and again in my mind, wondering what was possible."

So the capitulation had not been quite so quick as it seemed. Sara waited for her to go on.

"The Renwicks have no idea that I ever lived in San Francisco. I never told Ritchie's mother and father, so he doesn't know either. They mustn't learn this now. I don't want them to discover that your name is Bishop. Will you promise me that, Sara?"

Of course she would promise. This was the thing that mattered least at the moment. To get there was everything.

"I give you my word not to tell Ritchie or the Renwicks," she said dutifully.

Nevertheless, curiosity tantalized her. *Why* did her mother want this secrecy? What was she afraid of in San Francisco?

At least the impossible had been accomplished, and now Sara began to discuss plans eagerly as they ate breakfast. Ritchie had said that Mrs. Renwick would forward their train expenses. Tickets must be purchased, a date set. Oh, this was going to be fun, really. And with Ritchie at the end of the journey, how could she help but feel excited and happy?

Her mother watched her sadly, but said nothing more.

The moment Sara had finished the breakfast dishes, while her mother returned to more packing, she went again to her room and burrowed in a drawer of possessions she had not yet packed. Laid carefully between the folds of an innocent sachet case was a small oblong of stiff photographic board. She drew it out with careful fingers so that she would not bend it at the place where it had long ago been mended with paper and paste.

It was the picture of a handsome man with fairish hair and a mustache. He was dressed in the manner of more than twenty years ago, dressed debonairly like the dandy he must have been. She had always been certain that this was her father, Leland Bishop. Even though the imprint of the photographer showed that the picture had been taken here in Chicago, she was sure.

She remembered the day her mother had torn the picture up. Sara had been no more than nine at the time. A letter had come for Mrs. Jerome which had upset her very much. She had not thought Sara was watching, there behind her book, when she read the letter, with her lips tightened and an indignant flush in her cheeks. From a drawer she had taken the picture, which Sara had never seen, and torn it in two as if she were putting a part of her life behind her, trying to forget something that made her unhappy. She had dropped the pieces in the wastebasket and gone quickly from the room.

It had frightened Sara to see tears on her mother's cheeks. Seeking the reason, she had taken the two pieces from the wastebasket and carried them away to her room. There she fitted them together and set the print up beside the mirror on her dresser to scrutinize it inch by inch.

True, the man in the picture did not have black hair like her own. Nor had Mary Jerome's hair ever been as dark as Sara's. But there must be black hair and a Spanish look somewhere in the family. The chins were different—no resemblance there. Sara's had a square, strong set to it, even as a child—a chin with a will behind it. The pictured chin was softer, more feminine in quality. A nose you could not tell about in such a picture, and the mouth was hidden by a mustache. But the eyes were enough for Sara—the width they were set apart, the shape, the vigor with which they looked out at the world.

"This is my father," the young Sara had said to herself.

She had talked to the picture as a child, and now she talked to it again.

"We're going home!" she told the bit of cardboard. She no longer restrained her exuberance, but danced about the room, whirling and dipping. Perhaps her father was out there now. Perhaps after all these years they might find each other. Though this, somehow, she did not quite believe. Nevertheless, hope was in the air, and the possible answer to many things.

Only once did the thought of Judith intrude when Sara wondered idly how she felt about this plan to bring Mrs. Jerome and her daughter to San Francisco. Probably Judith wouldn't give it a second thought, being no longer interested in Ritchie. Her presence in the Renwick house was nothing to worry about and Sara did not concern herself for long with thoughts of Judith.

In the days that followed there was so much to be done that she was kept in a whirl of activity.

The Temple house had been sold, but the new owners would not move in till the first of February. And the Jeromes would be out in January.

With her own money Sara splurged and bought herself and her mother materials at Marshall Field's Store and planned suits for them both. She had no particular skill with a needle, but she could take a bolt of cloth as if it were clay to sculpture, and bring out of it a model any lady might be proud to wear. Mama thought her a little daring, but Sara went her own way, bowing to current styles, but holding that any style must first of all become its wearer.

Mary Jerome liked to sew and she worked steadily at her sewing machine and by hand until the new garments were completed. At her insistence her own suit was black and simply cut, with only a touch of white here and there to relieve it. But Sara's was more dramatic and stylish. The bolero jacket of heavy gray English broadcloth had jet buttons, black velvet piping, and there were bands of black velvet ribbon circling the gray skirt at knee height. Mrs. Jerome thought a small train would be suitable, or at least a fullness at the back, but Sara boldly omitted the train and raised the skirt an inch so that it cleared the floor. She wanted a dress she could walk in, she said, and her mother would see—it would look just right. In the end it was, as Sara promised—perfect and quite modern.

When Ritchie sent the money, it was Sara who made the trip to the soot-blackened station to study timetables and purchase their tickets. Toward the end of their time in Chicago, Mary Jerome seemed to lose something of her courage. She had the air of a woman who walked helplessly toward a fate she had relinquished the power to fight. Often she sat idly, with her hands listlessly folded, and it worried Sara that she was able to make no contact with her mother.

There were good-bys to be said to a few neighborhood friends, but Sara found this easy enough to do. There was no one to hold her to Chicago as Ritchie drew her to San Francisco.

For all her inexperience, Sara enjoyed taking on the full management of the trip. When the tickets were purchased, Mrs. Jerome wrote to Ritchie to let him know the time of their arrival, and Sara had their trunks sent ahead. On the day of departure she summoned a hackney cab to drive them with their portmanteaus to the station. Her mother moved like a woman in a dream and Sara gave up trying to waken her. Mama would rouse herself when they reached San Francisco. She was tired now—let her rest.

Excitement, anticipation, increased in Sara during the long train ride. What lay ahead in San Francisco? The fulfillment of dreams, perhaps? Perhaps the answers to many questions which had puzzled and concerned her all her life and which now seethed to the surface of her mind, churned by her mother's insistence on secrecy.

The train trip itself was fun. Sara had scarcely taken an hour's ride in her life, yet now she was rocketing half across a continent to the accompaniment of roaring wheels, a shrill whistling and a constant rain of cinders. But she even enjoyed the discomforts of smoke and dirt, jerky starts and stops, because all these were part of the adventure.

The train trip took nearly three days, but while Mary Jerome slept badly in the Pullman and was weary by the second day, Sara never lost a wink and was bursting with energy by the time the train reached the Oakland Mole and they left it for the ferry.

Take the boat across, Ritchie had written. *Someone will meet you in the Ferry Building on the San Francisco side.*

He had been casual, but Sara knew it would be Ritchie himself. She could not sit quietly with her mother in the cabin, but walked out on deck into a whipping wind and watched the city across the bay as they neared it. How bravely the houses climbed the hills, undaunted by any height. And how tall many of the buildings seemed, clustered in the downtown section near the lower end of Market Street. She knew her San Francisco by now.

She had found a book in a Chicago secondhand store and pored over the pictures and text. Already she knew the names of the famous hills—Rincon, where the old best families had resided, and still did to some extent. Nob Hill, where Bonanza wealth lived spectacularly. Ritchie lived on Nob Hill! That must be Russian Hill there—the highest one, where the houses were smaller and there were more green spaces, more trees to be seen. And of course Telegraph Hill would be the one to the far right, with the little houses of the Italians clinging to its steep sides.

She gripped the salt-sticky rail in her excitement and there was a singing in her blood. This was where she belonged. She was aware of her mother, come to stand beside her, and as she spoke her happiness spilled over.

"There—see that big white building at the top of Nob Hill. That's where they are building the Fairmont Hotel. It's going to be one of the most luxurious hotels in the world—even finer than the Palace."

A shiver ran through the slight figure beside her and brought Sara back from her dream.

"You're cold," she said contritely. "That cloak is too thin for this wind." But the sun was shining brightly and she herself was as warm as though she had been running.

"I was always cold in San Francisco," Mrs. Jerome said.

They were nearing the Ferry Building now, with its square tower gleaming white across the bay. Mrs. Jerome stared fixedly at land, but Sara forgot her again in interest over the docking and eagerness to see Ritchie.

They followed the crowd from the boat, each with a portmanteau in hand. Sara searched the faces of those who stood waiting to meet the boat. But because she was looking for Ritchie, she did not see Judith at once. It was her mother who said, "There is Miss Renwick," and gave Sara a little push.

For a moment Sara's spirits thudded earthward, but she managed to rally in a few moments as she found excuses. Of course he couldn't come to meet them. Ritchie worked at the insurance office. It would look too eager, it would be unsuitable if he left his desk in the early afternoon. That Judith had come was only right, since she was Mrs. Renwick's daughter.

Judith had seen them, but she stood where she was, smiling serenely, waiting for them to come to her. She had lost none of her beauty. She looked no less perfect than the last time Sara had seen her. An elbow-length capelet of rich brown fur set off her fairness and she wore a toque of fur on her high-piled hair, a brown-dotted veil flattering her creamy complexion. Her furled umbrella, customary equipment for a San Francisco winter, was of brown silk and had a smart, long handle so that one might pose with it in the fashionable manner. Her brown kid gloves had an air of Paris about them.

Judith welcomed them without effusion, and shook hands with each. If she recalled her last meeting with Sara, her eyes did not betray the fact.

"The carriage is over there," she said in her low-toned voice. "Ritchie has the auto. He often uses it when my brother Nicholas is out of town on business. Nick is really the head of the family now, you know."

When they were seated in the carriage and the horses had turned up Market Street, Mrs. Jerome inquired about Judith's mother.

"She hasn't been well," Judith said, and it seemed to Sara that there was a hint of disapproval in her tone.

Sara had seen little of Mrs. Renwick when she had visited the Temples and had noted her mainly as a plump woman much less attractive than her daughter.

But now there were throngs on Market Street to watch—all San Francisco to drink in with her eyes, and she had no time for anything else.

"We have to take a roundabout way to get up the hill," Judith explained when the carriage turned north toward higher ground. "It's just as well we're not quite at the top. On Russian Hill there are rickety wooden steps to climb if you live very high, but on our hill we manage to make it to our own door."

Gusts of wind blew dust in their faces as the carriage moved along, and dust eddies swirled constantly in the street. Judith put her handkerchief to her mouth and coughed delicately.

"We're built practically on sand dunes, you know," she said with almost an air of pride. "I suppose we shall never be rid of the dust."

Sara watched the houses they passed intently. Would one of those mansions on Nob Hill strike a chord in her memory? Would there be sudden recognition if she saw the house in which she had lived as a child? Once or twice she stole a look at her mother, to see what might be reflected in her face. But Mary Jerome looked straight ahead, as if she wore blinders and could not see the houses of San Francisco.

"Here we are," Judith said. "Ours is the corner house on the next block."

Back in Chicago, Sara had thought the Temple house large and impressive, but it looked a toy beside the Renwick mansion. This was vast in size, with dormer windows and chimneys jutting from the roof. There'd be hundreds of panes to wash—but oh, what a view! If only she could have a room with a view. It appeared that every room in this house must have a view, except, perhaps, those in the cellar. Where did San Franciscans put a housekeeper, she wondered.

At the front, facing south, the house rose three stories—two full ones with tall windows which promised high ceilings within, and a third story at the top, not so high. In the center, at the very front, overlooking second-floor balconies and the steep flight of stone steps that ran up from the street, rose a square tower.

"It's the most beautiful place I've ever seen," Sara said with respectful admiration in her voice. After all, this was where Ritchie lived.

Judith laughed. "I'm afraid some of us won't agree with you. It was my father's idea of proving how important the Renwicks were. Frankly, only Nob Hill was impressed. Ritchie says it is the most awful monstrosity he has ever seen in his life."

Sara noted only that her tone was casual when she spoke of Ritchie. To her eyes this place was what she had dreamed of, and it was unbelievably marvellous that she had come to live in it.

They drove through the wide carriage entrance and went in through a side door. The woodwork was polished to a dark gloss and there were tapestries on the walls of the hallway. Through open doors as they went toward the wide, graceful stairway, Sara caught glimpses of such elegance as she had never dreamed.

Judith slipped off her cape with a languid gesture. "I'm sure you must be tired after your long trip. Susan will take up your suitcases and show you to your rooms. Ring for tea, if you like. Mother will want to see you later."

A plump, pretty young maid bobbed to Judith and picked up their bags, starting up the stairs ahead of them. "This way, please, mum," she said to Mrs. Jerome.

She bounced ahead up the wide, carpeted stairs and Sara's hopes rose. They were going *up*. Past the second floor, on up narrower stairs to the very top.

"Wait here, please, miss," said Susan to Sara. "I'll take your mother back to her room."

The depth of the house was to separate them, it seemed. Mary Jerome's room was at a rear corner and she went into it without a word or a backward look for her daughter and Sara watched her go uneasily. When Susan returned, her feet clicking against bare wood, for there was no elegance of carpets up here, her bobbing servant's manner was gone. It was quite evident she felt herself on equal terms with Sara Jerome.

"You going into service while you're here?" she asked cheerfully, leading the way toward the front of the house.

"I am going into business," Sara said with an attempt at dignity. She wanted her position to be made clear. As soon as she had work, she meant to pay for her room and board. She would not be a servant in Ritchie's house.

"Business?" Susan echoed, puzzled.

"Work in an office," Sara explained.

Susan's giggle showed a lack of respect for such an ambition. "Office work is for men. Where are the tips to be picked up? Or the dresses the rich ladies tire of? Running one of those silly writing contraptions all day! That's not for me. Here you are. It's a funny place Mr. Ritchie asked us to give you, I must say."

Susan pushed open a door into the tower itself and Sara walked in. Ritchie had chosen this! Ritchie had remembered that Sara Jerome loved high places.

The big square room was broken in the middle by a small circular stair, hardly more than a curved ladder. Windows looked out toward the front of the house, but the roof cut the view away on either side. Around the circular stairway the room had been arranged somewhat awkwardly as a bedroom. There was a brass bedstead with a tan spread, on which slept a big, tiger-striped yellow cat. A wavery, oval mirror was set in a swivel on top of a high bureau. There was the usual wardrobe closet, a battered straight chair, and a more comfortable, though shabby, armchair. A small table with a crocheted doily on its scratched top stood near the bed. The floor was bare, except for an oval rag rug, and the walls were a disconsolate tan. But after a quick glance, Sara saw only the stair.

"Nobody ever used this place to sleep in before," Susan grumbled. "Miss Allison is spitting mad that it's been given to you. It's been her playroom mostly. If Mister Nick had been home he'd have stood up for her, I'll wager. Gracious, there's that horrible cat!

Don't touch him, miss. He's possessed. He goes and comes as he pleases and there's no help for it. I do believe he goes through closed doors, he's that sneaky."

The huge tiger cat opened one yellow eye, regarded them dispassionately, dismissed them as unimportant, and went back to sleep.

Except for an amused look at the cat, Sara paid little attention to Susan's chatter. She waited only for the girl to go so she might climb to the tower itself.

Susan shivered and moved toward the door. "Drafty place, if you ask me. You can have it. Even with a fire in the grate, it's like trying to keep the whole outdoors warm. I'll come tell you when Miz' Renwick wakes from her nap and wants you and your ma."

She eyed Sara up and down, noting her fashionable traveling suit with interest.

"The lady of the house at your last place give you that? It don't hardly look worn at all."

Sara shook her head vaguely, waiting to be alone. Giving her up as a source of information, Susan went out, closing the door behind her.

When she had gone, Sara flung her handbag on the bed, took the pins from her hat and pulled it off. After a look at the sleeping yellow monster on the spread, she set her hat on the bureau. Then she hurried to the narrow curving stairway and climbed to the top, her heavy skirts clutched in one hand, the other hand pulling her around the curve.

It was drafty up here, as Susan had said, but after the bitter cold of Chicago, and with brilliant sunshine all around, Sara didn't mind. San Francisco was invigorating. She looked about in utter delight.

Glass windows completely surrounded the bare tower and she could look in every direction. Sounds of whistles tooting on the bay, of electric trolleys clanging, came to her. Out on the water a small green island floated. That would be Goat Island—Yerba Buena, as it had once been called. On the shore beyond were the towns of the bay. How wonderful to have a view of water again.

She turned next toward the valley that was Market Street, a ruled line from Twin Peaks to the water. She could see the tower of the Ferry Building at one end, and toward the other end the dome of City Hall, with a statue poised atop it. Only at the back of the house was the view cut off by mansions still higher up the hill. Even they were interesting to see. She would spend hours here, feeling strong and free and in command of her own life—as she always felt when she could reach some high spot and survey the world. Besides, there was significance in the fact that Ritchie had wanted this for her.

She climbed backward down the difficult stairway and glanced again at the tawny monster on the bed. She would deal with him later. For the moment she wanted a good wash and clean clothes. Her trunk, she saw, had already arrived and waited in a corner.

She got into her wrapper and went in search of the bathroom on the third floor. When she returned, feeling refreshed and clean again, the cat was awake. He watched her lazily, rather like an emperor surveying a slave girl, his yellow eyes neither commending nor condemning, the end of his long tail twitching faintly.

Sara found a green tweedy skirt and ruffled shirtwaist in her trunk that looked reasonably uncrushed. The cat watched her without blinking as she dressed. Once she spoke to him.

"You can't stay here permanently, you know. And I don't intend to have you as a regular visitor."

The cat yawned, revealing a pink cavern well lined with needle-sharp teeth. He stretched and began to wash his face with a well-licked paw. Sara had just buckled on a brown grosgrain belt when she heard footsteps running noisily down the uncarpeted hallway. A sudden banging on her door startled her, but before she could answer, the door was thrust open with a force that slammed it against the wall, and an angry tornado burst into the room.

Sara stared at the girl of about eleven who stood on the threshold with fury in her brown eyes. This, undoubtedly, was Judith's sister Allison, and undoubtedly, as Susan had warned, she was in a rage over the usurping of her playroom. Sara had never known many children, and she felt at a loss to deal with this one.

The girl's plain, small face was made still more plain by a bare expanse of forehead that overbalanced it. Her nondescript brown hair had been pulled back in eyebrow-lifting tightness and bound into a braid. A hair bow had been tied at the nape of her neck, but it hung loose in back in two limp streamers. She was dressed in an ugly brown jumper with ink spots on the skirt. From chin to scalp rose a mottling flush as she stared balefully at Sara.

Then she flung the strapped schoolbooks she carried to the floor with a bang and strode toward the bed.

"Even if Ritchie gave you my room," she announced, "you can't have my cat!"

THREE

ALLISON RENWICK FLUNG HERSELF UPON THE BED, AND surprisingly, the huge yellow beast sat up and began to purr. Allison put a scrawny arm about him and he climbed into her lap and began to lick her wrist. She put her face down against the yellow fur and the flush in her cheeks began to fade a little. The cat licked on steadily, moving to a fresh patch of skin.

Sara could only watch in helpless astonishment.

"I suppose you are Allison Renwick?" she asked at length.

"Who else would I be?" the child demanded. "All right—I don't care! Go ahead and say it! Say what they all say!"

"Say what? I was going to ask if this room was actually your bedroom."

"Of course not. This is the servants' floor up here. I have a bedroom of my own downstairs. But this isn't

35

supposed to be a bedroom. This tower has been mine ever since I was little. Nick would never, never have made me give it up. I hate Uncle Ritchie. I wish he'd never come here. He always plays mean tricks like this."

"Uncle" Ritchie meant he was well established as a family friend. Sara sat in the one armchair and continued to study the two who occupied her bed.

"Have you thought," she said, "that Ritchie might have been kind enough to remember how much I love high places? He wanted this room for me because he knows how much a tower room means to me."

"You'd better say *Mister* Ritchie," Allison told her, kicking off dusty shoes and pulling her skinny, black-stockinged legs up under her. "Like the other servants."

Sara tried to answer calmly. "I am not a servant. I grew up with Ritchie Temple and I shall go on calling him what I've always called him. Now do you suppose you could take that savage-looking cat away?"

Indignantly Allison hooked the great cat over her shoulder like a fur piece. "Comstock is not a savage. Next to my brother Nick he's the finest gentleman in all San Francisco."

The little girl looked comical as she sat cross-legged with the cat half around her neck. Her dignity was so enormous that Sara wanted to laugh, but she had no wish to further outrage the child.

"Comstock is an odd name for a cat," she said.

Allison looked her scorn. "I can tell you don't know much about San Francisco. The Comstock was the great Bonanza lode. Silver in Virginia City. That's where all the big San Francisco fortunes came from."

Her thin face glowed with sudden interest. "Comstock looks like a Bonanza king. I wish *I* had lived in those days. Nick does too."

Sara smiled and Allison seemed to relax a little.

"At least," the girl remarked, "you haven't said what all the others do. You haven't said, 'You *can't* be Judith's sister!' "

Footsteps sounded again in the hall and Sara looked up to see Susan standing doubtfully in the open doorway.

"Miz' Renwick's up from her nap," she said to Sara. "She wants to talk to you. I'm to call your ma too." She darted a cautious look at the two on the bed. "Miss Allison, you don't belong in here. Mister Ritchie asked me to see you didn't bother her." She nodded at Sara.

With a leap that showed surprising agility, Allison sprang from the bed with the cat in her arms and was upon Susan in a flash. She thrust the big cat directly at her, so that its forepaws clawed at her hair, pulled strands of it loose. Susan threw her hands before her face and fled squealing down the hall. Pleased at the rout, Allison looked triumphantly at Sara. She bunched Comstock up in her hands and took a tentative step in Sara's direction.

"I can do that with you too, if I like."

Sara stood her ground. "You do and I'll cuff your cat good."

"You wouldn't dare. Comstock would scratch you till you bled. And nobody in this house dares touch me."

The cat seemed to understand the tone of his mistress's voice. His ears went back and he bared sharp fangs in a snarl. But Sara was not put to the test. It was Allison who retreated toward the door.

"Come along," she said to Sara, changing her mind. "I'll take you down to Mama's rooms."

She went into the dark, windowless hallway, which had rooms all around and was lighted only by a meager bulb hung from the ceiling. At the door of the tower room Sara pointedly removed the key from inside the door and locked it from the outside, pocketing the key in her green skirt. Allison watched without comment, her gaze as fixed and unblinking as the cat's.

Susan was already leading Mrs. Jerome down the lower stairway and Allison peered over the banister after her, then back at Sara.

"I don't like that Susan. She's a sneaky one. She's sweet on Uncle Ritchie. Mis-ter Ritchie! Are you sweet on him too?"

This was certainly the most difficult child imaginable.

"Ritchie is my good friend," Sara said quietly as they started downstairs together. "As I told you, I grew up with him. Don't you have any good friends that you're growing up with so you can understand that?"

Allison shook her head. "Nobody likes me. Only Comstock and Nick." There was almost the same note of pride in her voice that Judith had used in speaking of the dust that swirled through San Francisco streets. "Besides, I don't want to be bothered with any silly children. Books are better company any day."

She paused at the landing and waited for Sara. Then she pointed.

"Any time you want to watch when they're having a dinner party downstairs, you can kneel right where the banister curves on the second floor and see through into the hall and the dining room. The way the light is, nobody's likely to see you. I've done it lots of times."

So other little girls peeped at parties just as she had done.

"Thank you," Sara said. "I'll keep it in mind."

They hurried now and caught up with Susan and Mary Jerome on the first floor. Mrs. Renwick had given up climbing stairs and had a suite of her own on the garden side of the great house. Here the main hall narrowed into an el. Allison stepped back to let Sara go ahead.

"I'm not going in," she whispered. "She's not really my mother, you know." She waited for the satisfaction of Sara's surprise, smiled smugly and went off, still lugging the great, patient, savage cat.

Mrs. Renwick held her audience from a pale blue chaise longue, heaped with pillows covered in Japanese silk. All over the walls of the corner behind her were crowded photographs, framed and unframed. Surely every friend and relative she had ever known must look out from this cozy corner collection, Sara thought.

Hilda Renwick wore a loose wrapper of no particular style and she had gained considerably in weight since that visit to Chicago two years before. Or perhaps it was just that she was obviously uncorseted. Her thick blond hair had been pushed halfheartedly into a pompadour and then tied back with a child's hair ribbon. On the small taboret beside her was a box of chocolates. As they came in, she helped herself to a cream and held out the box.

"Hello," she said with comfortable informality.

"Have some candy. Run along now, Susan. This is none of your affair."

Susan bobbed a curtsy, threw Sara a curious look and went out of the room. Mrs. Jerome refused the chocolates and took a straight chair, very much the housekeeper being interviewed by the mistress. Sara would have liked a piece of candy, but followed her mother's example, though she chose a more comfortable chair.

Mrs. Renwick licked a finger clean of chocolate and looked at Mary with faded blue eyes.

"It was a wonderful idea of Ritchie's to suggest sending for you, Mrs. Jerome. I'm very fond of Ritchie. He's always so thoughtful of my comfort. I'm delighted with the wonderful news. I can't say as much for my son Nicholas, who grows more difficult every year. But as I say, it's fine that you've come."

Mrs. Jerome murmured politely and Sara said nothing, wondering what news she was delighted about.

"You see," Mrs. Renwick ran on, "I can't trouble myself about the house any more. My heart, you know. Fluttery. The doctor says I'm to do just as I please and have no duties at all." She beamed at them cheerfully. "A wonderful man. I went through eight doctors before I found him. As a matter of fact, Ritchie discovered him for me. Ritchie knew just what I needed. Now I can read naughty French novels without being scolded, eat all the chocolates I want, and never mind my complexion! I can even turn up my nose at San Francisco society."

She laughed and looked at Mary Jerome, who was obviously bewildered. Then her quick, pale blue eyes turned in Sara's direction. Sara was beginning to like her and she smiled back.

Mrs. Renwick, however, shook her head sadly. "A pity. This girl is much too handsome for her own good. She'll be a problem to you, Mrs. Jerome. Of course all children are a problem. But the beautiful ones are the worst, except, of course, for the plain ones. Like Allison. Have you seen Allison?"

"I have," said Sara.

Mrs. Renwick moved her hands in a gesture of despair. There was nothing, she seemed to imply, that could be done about Allison.

Mrs. Jerome brought the conversation back to something more pertinent. "Now that I am here, Mrs. Renwick, I'd like to know something of my duties. About the household routine and—"

"Mercy!" cried Mrs. Renwick. "Don't bother me with such matters. The servants will tell you. Or Judith. Your duties, as far as I am concerned, are not to worry me about anything that happens. Of course you can come visit me now and then. You, especially," she said, nodding at Sara. "You look like a breath of life. I don't go out in the world any more. But I like people who bring it to me. And since you're not mine I needn't worry about you."

From the front of the house came the sound of a door opening and Mrs. Renwick's face lighted.

"There's Ritchie now! He's home early again. He'll be here in a moment. He always comes first to see me."

It was all Sara could do to sit still. She did not want to see Ritchie under her mother's eye. Or under Mrs. Renwick's, for that matter. All day she had been looking forward to this moment, but now that it drew near she felt suddenly shy, like the young girl who had once waited tremulously for Ritchie's every look and word. She didn't want to feel that way now. She didn't want to betray herself again in this first meeting. This time he must come to her.

Beside her chair glass doors opened onto a porch of red tile. Beyond she could see evidence of a garden. She gestured to it casually. "What a lovely place—a wintertime garden! May I see?"

"We have flowers all year round in California," Mrs. Renwick said. "Of course—run out and smell the posies."

Sara could hear Ritchie's voice, speaking to someone in the hall. She rose carefully, so as to give no evidence of haste, opened the doors and stepped outside, pulling them to behind her. After the stuffiness of the close, fire-heated room, the cold air was wonderfully bracing. She filled her lungs with great gusts of it and stepped to the edge of the little porch where she could better see the garden. Frequent rains had brought green to dry grass and with the sun shining it felt almost like Indian summer. A profusion of bright red and pink geraniums bordered the tile. And in flower beds beyond red roses glowed warm with color. There were marigolds, primroses, and snapdragons. An extravagantly purple flowered vine climbed against the house. In a twisted tree with a red trunk and bushy foliage, a robin twittered. All this richness in January!

Yet even as Sara breathed scented air and lifted her face to the sun, a tight core of attention was focused on what might be happening in the room behind her. She could hear Ritchie's voice again, greeting her mother. This time, she told herself, she must meet him with her guard up. She must not give everything away as she had always done in the past. Let him wonder a little. Let him not read her through and through. Ritchie might value more that which was withheld. Oh, she was older and wiser now!

She pretended interest in the geraniums as she heard the glass doors open and close. She plucked a leaf, smelling the strong, spicy odor. At home there had been a geranium or two in pots at the kitchen window —scrawny plants, dwarfs beside this riotous growth. That was it, think about geraniums, pay no attention to Ritchie, who had come through the doors behind her.

But he was so quiet, speaking no word of greeting, taking no step toward her, that she was forced to glance curiously around. He lounged with a shoulder against the brick wall of the house, his arms folded idly, watching her with amusement in his eyes. She remembered again how bright his hair could look in the sun.

"So?" he said. "That's better. For a moment I thought you had added deafness with your advancing years. May I welcome you to San Francisco, Miss Jerome?"

I will not blush, Sara thought. And all the while she could feel a pink to match the geraniums rising in her cheeks, even though she looked away and would not let him read her eyes.

"Thank you, Mr. Temple," she said, stiffly polite.

He whooped softly in laughter, but made no move toward her. "Sara, Sara! It's fun to have you here. If we weren't in plain view of the stables, I'd give you a proper greeting from an old friend."

She thrust back the trembling that would go through her, steadied herself. When she turned toward him the flush was dying, her eyes cool. Inscrutable, she thought. That was the word for what she must be.

"I don't know what you mean," she said carelessly. "But it is very nice to be here. Mama needed the work badly."

"You're looking at me like Comstock does," he mused. "Have you had the pleasure of meeting Allison's cat?"

"He was sleeping on my bed. Allison seems quite upset because I have her playroom. Perhaps it shouldn't have been given to me."

His eyes smiled at her. "You know that was my doing. That tower was made for you. Besides, Allison is a brat. Everyone else is afraid to cross her because she throws such tantrums. If she bothers you about the room, send her to me."

Sara permitted her lips to relax a little. "I love the room. I can see all San Francisco from the tower. I climbed the stair at once and looked at the view."

"It's not a stairway for a lady, of course," Ritchie said. "But I thought you'd go up it. I remember an elm tree back home. The one you fell out of when you were twelve."

She remembered too. In a rush of feeling she remembered everything about that moment. The branch had given way beneath her and she had been terrified. But Ritchie had heard the cracking and had dashed under the tree to break her fall. For a long moment she had stood there in his arms, her heart pounding with fright so that he could feel it against his chest. That was the first time Ritchie had kissed her—and after that her heart had pounded for a new reason and more pleasantly than before.

"I love to watch your face, Sara," he said, smiling. "In spite of that Comstock look you gave me a minute ago, I can read everything in it. Everything you're remembering. I haven't forgotten either."

So much for inscrutability. She had to smile at him then in the old soft way that set her lips apart.

The change in him was quick. "Don't do that," he said.

That, too, was Ritchie. The way he could gentle a girl until all the stiffness and resistance ran out of her, and then sting her with words that were like a whip across bare flesh. How many were the times when she had loved and hated him all at once. This was the old pattern and she did not want it to be like that. She must find a way to be strong against him until events turned him truly in her direction.

But before she could answer, the sound of Judith's voice came to them from Mrs. Renwick's room. Ritchie straightened from his lounging position against the wall.

"You'd better go back and get in on the domestic arrangements," he said. "I'll escape while I can."

With long strides he went off across the garden toward the stables, with no further glance at Sara. She had been dismissed in the curt manner Ritchie used with servants, and she shook herself angrily. Yes indeed, Mister Ritchie would have to learn that everything was different now. She was no longer a trembling schoolgirl to be alternately exalted and downcast because of his moods and whims.

Her mother called to her from the door. "Come in,

Sara." She looked about for Ritchie and seemed relieved not to see him with her daughter.

Sara sniffed delicately at the geranium leaf and went past her mother into Mrs. Renwick's sitting room.

"Oh, there you are," Judith said. "I've just suggested that this is a good time for you and your mother to meet the rest of the household. If you will come with me back to the kitchen—"

Whatever else she said, Sara missed. When Judith led the way into the hall Sara followed blindly. At the ferry a little while ago Judith had worn gloves. Now she wore none and there was the flash of a handsome diamond on the third finger of her left hand. So Judith was engaged. But not to Ritchie—of course not to Ritchie!

Suddenly Sara knew she could not face this introduction to the rest of the household right now. The ring on Judith's finger frightened her, even though she was already trying to reassure herself. At the place where the corridor turned, she stood her ground.

"If you don't mind, I'd like to go back to my room and do my unpacking now."

Judith regarded her indifferently. "As you please."

Sara felt something more in the way of an explanation was required.

"You see," she said more boldly, "I am not going to be working in this house. As soon as possible I want to find work in an office. Then I shall pay you for my room and board."

"That is hardly necessary," Judith said, while Mary Jerome stared at her daughter in dismay. "The arrangements we've made with your mother includes your keep. Don't concern yourself about it."

She turned away, but Sara spoke again hurriedly. She had to make her place in this household clear from the start. "As soon as I am earning I mean to pay my way," she repeated.

Amusement showed in Judith's faint smile as she paused in the hallway. "These are matters you'll have to take up with my brother Nick. We are not in the habit of taking in paying guests. Now, Mrs. Jerome, if you will come with me—"

Again Sara knew she had been dismissed, as casually as a young woman who had been brought up to take wealth and position for granted could do it. Sara picked up her green skirt and ran all the way up the two flights of stairs to her floor. She reached the top out of breath. She was *not* a servant in this household. And she would not be treated like one. It wasn't the ring that had upset her—of course not. There were plenty of men in San Francisco to whom Judith might become engaged. The sooner Sara found her own family, the better. Then she could be on a completely equal basis with Ritchie. And with Judith too.

She was far from calm by the time she reached her room, and it did not help to find the door ajar. She felt in her pocket for the key. It was still there, but someone had opened her door.

She pushed it wide with a quick thrust and strode in, meaning to pounce upon Allison and settle matters this time. She was just angry enough to do it. But there was no Allison in sight. Only the big cat washed himself contentedly in the middle of her bed.

"There's been enough of this," said Sara sharply.

From her open trunk she fished an umbrella. It was not elegant like Judith's, but a sturdy black umbrella with a crook for a handle. She took hold of it by the ferrule end and advanced upon Comstock.

"You get off my bed!" she commanded and slipped the crook around Comstock's great striped body.

He slashed at it with his claws and spit his anger at her. But though he writhed to escape, she pulled him across the bed until he leaped to the floor. He looked so much like a wildcat that she half feared he might attack her. Comstock, however, had the same illusions of superiority that marked the rest of the family. He regained his dignity at once, looked through her indifferently and walked slowly out the door. Again she had the feeling that she had been brushed aside as a social inferior. And this time by a cat!

"I suppose you're planning to use that umbrella on me too?" said Allison behind her.

Sara whirled to find the girl perched halfway down the stair, a large cigar box in one arm. For the moment Sara had had enough of the entire Renwick clan.

"I certainly will if you don't stay out of my room!" she cried.

Allison looked faintly alarmed and began to scramble down the stair. But in making the last turn she knocked the box out of her grasp and it went flying, scattering its contents across the bare floor. There were stones and shells, a silver thimble, some playing cards and other miscellaneous objects.

"Pick up your trash!" cried Sara, still trembling with reaction. "Pick it up quickly and get out!"

Allison knelt on the floor. "That's what I'm trying to do." Her hair bow was still untied and one stocking was slipping.

"How did you get into this room?" Sara demanded.

Allison reached into her jumper pocket and pulled out a bunch of keys. Her alarm was fading, since Sara had not actually reached for her with the umbrella, and she looked impish, tantalizing.

"Give those to me," said Sara. "My mother will take care of them." She took the keys firmly from Allison's hand.

"All I wanted," Allison told her, "was to get some of my things out of the tower room."

"Then you could ask permission. You could have knocked at my door and asked politely. You didn't need to come sneaking in like a little thief behind my back."

"A thief!" Allison cried. "As if you had anything anybody'd want to steal. I looked through your old trunk."

Sara stepped toward her and Allison picked up her box in a scramble and fled. Sara slammed the door after her and enjoyed the reverberation that went shivering through the house. Let them take that downstairs! At least Allison had not regarded her as an inferior. Allison had been plainly frightened.

Sara went to the bureau mirror and looked at herself. She did look rather frightening, she thought with satisfaction. Color bloomed in her cheeks again, but this time the tint was that of fury. Her dark eyes flashed and she looked thoroughly dangerous, if she did admit it herself.

They'd better look out, these Renwicks. All of them. Nick too when he got home—whatever he was like. Though she had to admit that the only one she had frightened so far was a misfit of a child who had been dispossessed of her room.

Suddenly her triumph faded. There was a hollow of loneliness in her, such loneliness as even Sara Jerome had never known before.

The meeting with Ritchie had been utterly disappointing. True, he had greeted her warmly. And he had said nothing about an engagement to Judith, as he would surely have done if it were so. Or would he?

Sara moved toward the bed, meaning to fling herself upon it. Until this moment she had not known how weary she was. But the spread bore the dent of Comstock's body and she pulled it off, threw it across a chair. As she did so a glint of bright color against the dark floor caught her eye. She picked up what looked for a moment to be some golden trinket. Then she saw that it was only paper. A cigar band—a ragged one, at that. Probably a bit of the trash from Allison's box. The medallion on the band was an impressive gold crown and there was red lettering all around.

She moved to toss the frayed scrap into a wastebasket, and then stayed her hand. If this was a childish treasure of Allison's, there was no point in throwing it away. She would return it sometime when the opportunity offered.

She dropped the band into a drawer and stretched full length on the bed, trying to think of something comforting.

If only she could remember her father. There would be consolation in a full remembering. In the little while she had known him, as a small child, there had been something warm and loving between them. There were dim memories that sometimes came to her and were surely concerned with her father. A misty consciousness of a big man with a cheery laugh and a pungent, male odor of tobacco smoke about him. There had been arms that squeezed a small person too hard, but were endured for the love behind them.

As always, however, when she tried to reach into memory and make everything clear, a curtain seemed to fall without warning, cutting off what lay in the past. It was as if such thoughts might be dangerous to remember. Yet this was all there had ever been in her life of the enveloping love she had longed for. Now, in this house, there would be emptiness again, just as there had been in Chicago.

At last, because she was weary, she slept.

FOUR

WHEN SHE AWOKE IT WAS GROWING DARK IN THE ROOM. She lay still for a moment, trying to orient herself. The door was to her right, she knew, opposite the paler splotch of the front window. Remembering the mirror on the bureau, she got out of bed to fumble toward it with averted eyes. She meant to take no chances the very first night in this house. The swivel enabled her to tip the glass toward the ceiling. It could stay that way till she wanted to use it.

Now she was conscious mainly of ravenous hunger. Judith had said they might ring for tea, but it was surely suppertime by this hour. She opened the door and stepped into the drearily lighted upper hall.

The maid Susan came out of a room toward the back of the house, looking perky and fresh in a clean apron and cap.

"Hello," Sara said, craving companionship. "So that's your room? Are all the others up here taken?"

Susan shook her head. "The rest of the help sleeps out, except the coachman, and he's got a room over the stable. This floor was so empty —I'm glad to have company up here. I have to hurry now—Miss Judith will need hooking up."

Sara wished she dared ask Susan about the ring Judith wore, but the girl hurried downstairs and Sara went to the door of her mother's room and tapped on the dark panel. Mrs. Jerome called to her to come in and she found that her mother too had been having a nap.

Sara pulled on the light by its cord—again a bare, ungracious bulb hanging high from the ceiling. Her mother's room was smaller than her own, but less haphazardly furnished. The furniture was oak and not so shabby as the pieces in Sara's room. A faded green carpet covered the floor and the air, minus tower drafts, was warmer.

"How are you feeling?" Sara asked. "Goodness, but I'm hungry! Judith told us we could ring for tea."

Mary Jerome sat up in bed, pulled down her white eyelet corset cover to meet her underskirt, retied its drawstrings. The harsh light cast brown shadows beneath her eyes and she looked worn from the trip.

"I'm still a little tired," she said. "I don't think we should get off on the wrong foot with the servants by asking anyone to carry a tea tray up two flights. Everyone seems pleasant, but of course they are sizing me up, since I'm to be in charge. Anyway, it's late for tea."

"What about supper?"

"Let's see what time it is," Mrs. Jerome said. "Please hand me my watch."

Sara gave her mother the small gold watch. It was attached to a *fleur de lis* pin which Mrs. Jerome wore fastened to her shirtwaist on the opposite side from the eyeglass button. It had been a gift from Mr. Temple one Christmas long ago.

"We can go down in fifteen minutes," she said. "The family dines at seven thirty, and we can eat ahead of them at seven."

"In the dining room?" Sara asked. Back in Chicago she and her mother, being higher on the social scale than cook and housemaids, had been permitted their meals in the dining room, though not with the family.

Mrs. Jerome folded her long cotton skirt about her legs and sat up wearily. "The dining room here is a banquet hall. No, there's a smaller breakfast room where we can have our lunches and suppers. Breakfast we'll get for ourselves in the kitchen. Suppose we dress now and I'll meet you in a few minutes."

Sara was paying little attention. "Did you notice the engagement ring Judith Renwick is wearing?"

"Yes," said Mrs. Jerome carefully. "It's very beautiful."

"That's not what I mean. Mama, you don't think—" but she wouldn't say the dreadful words out loud. She would not give them that much credence.

"No one has mentioned it, dear." Her mother's tone was gentle. "Let's not cross bridges before we come to them. But, Sara, if Miss Renwick is engaged to Ritchie, then you must be a grown woman and face whatever has to be faced."

"It's not true, anyway," Sara said. "I won't believe it."

She went back to her room, murmuring the words over to herself as she went.

By the time she and her mother went down to the breakfast room together, she had recovered a semblance of good spirits.

They found the breakfast room pleasant, with gay green paper on the walls. A cheerful fire burned in the grate and as the evening grew cool, its warmth was welcome. They were probably better off here than in some great barn of a dining hall. Sara's spirits continued to rise. She had expected too much from Ritchie at the beginning. She must be patient, give him time.

She talked enough for the two of them and set herself to please and cheer her mother. It could not be easy for her to return to this city where she had been so unhappy and Sara longed to make this up to her. Though she wished she knew exactly what *had* happened to her mother.

Once Allison came to the door and looked in on them. She had tidied up in a fresh dress, still an unbecoming dark color that did nothing for her sallow skin, and had a stiff black hair ribbon tied at the back of her head.

"Good evening, Miss Allison," said Mrs. Jerome pleasantly.

Allison mumbled, "Good evening," and went away after a moment, having said nothing else at all.

"What an odd child," Sara said and described her experiences of the day.

Mrs. Jerome shook her head in sympathy. "She's lonely, I expect."

Perhaps she could make friends with Allison, Sara thought, though the prospect did not seem too promising.

After supper she returned to her room to finish unpacking. The question of Judith's engagement remained unanswered, but she knew no one well enough to ask pointed questions. It was maddening to be in a houseful of people who knew, and yet not be able to ask. But she would surely find out tomorrow.

For a moment she felt busy and hopeful. Tomorrow she would begin to *live* in San Francisco. Tomorrow there might be a better chance to talk with Ritchie.

During the evening it began to rain. The sound made a great rush and clattering in her room, and cool gusts of wind were sucked down the stairway. Sara heaped more coal on the fire, slipped into a warm wrapper and did not mind at all. Before she went to bed she climbed into the tower itself and there in the noisy darkness she felt a sense of exhilaration. She had always loved storms. Even as a child she had exulted in them. Let thunder roar and lightning slash black skies —Sara Jerome felt no fear, but only a mounting stimulation. A restoring of life forces. Even the mirror dream had given her no fear of storms. It was something else she dreaded in the mirror.

Tonight gusts of wind flung rain in wet swirls against the windows of her tower. This smaller, higher room seemed to tremble in the wind and she loved the stormy feeling of movement. She stood beneath the dome of the wind-shaken tower and watched the drenched lights of San Francisco swim and waver in the rain. If only Ritchie could share such a moment with her. Where was he now in this great house? She did not even know the door of his room.

A sudden memory returned to her. When she and her mother had been with Mrs. Renwick in her sitting room, Judith's mother had talked about how much she liked Ritchie. And she had spoken of "wonderful news." What else could she have meant but that Ritchie and her daughter were engaged to be married?

The rain was only rain now and the tower chilly. All Sara's exhilaration faded and she went downstairs to bed in the square, unlovely room, trying to shut out thoughts of the ring on Judith's finger and the possibility of her marriage to Ritchie.

All the next morning it rained. After breakfast, Mrs. Jerome commenced her new duties and Sara, now unpacked and well ordered, ready for life to begin, had nothing to do. Once, roaming dejectedly down the stairs from third floor to first, she heard the familiar silken rustle of Judith's taffeta petticoats and saw her opening a middle door off the corridor that ran parallel with the western side of the house. Judith noticed her and paused.

"I've been thinking about your plan to look for work, Sara. I believe it's an excellent one. You'll need something to occupy your time. I'll speak to my brother about it when he returns from his trip in a day or two. In the meantime, if you'd like something to read, there are magazines in the library. And of course books, if Allison has left any on the shelves. She has to be kept from moving the whole library into her room."

But Sara was staring at the ring on her left hand, hardly listening. She was able to hold back her question no longer. Judith herself could tell her.

"You've become engaged since you were in Chicago," Sara said flatly.

"Why, yes," said Judith. "Didn't Ritchie tell you? He gave me my ring just a week ago."

It was as if her breath had been snatched away.

"I thought," Sara faltered. "I mean you said—" But there was no use in going on. What was there to say? She had a sense of unreality, as if none of this mattered very much.

Judith watched her. "Sara—are you all right?"

"Of course!" Sara said. She had no intention of betraying weakness before Judith.

She would have turned away, but the older girl put a hand on her arm and her eyes were not without sympathy.

"I know how much love can hurt, Sara. That's why I was afraid this time. Even now I'm not sure—"

Sara moved back from her touch. "If you're not sure, how can you marry him?"

"I'm not sure I won't be hurt," Judith said quietly and went toward the stairs.

Sara found that she was standing alone in the front hall. She opened the nearest door and stepped into the Renwick drawing room. She had the queer feeling that nothing had happened. After that first moment of shock she felt perfectly all right. Her life had been completely smashed and she couldn't feel anything. Sometimes a wound was like that, she remembered. The throbbing began later. For the moment she could only stare numbly around the vast room, noting its detail impersonally.

It was an amazing room—big enough for a ball, surely, but so crowded with furniture and bric-a-brac that it looked smaller than it was. This, presumably, was further evidence of Mr. William Renwick's old-fashioned tastes. Every inch of wall space was hung with valuable paintings, one above another, each touching the frame of a close neighbor. There were small rugs running diagonally over larger rugs, lush with Oriental color. Chairs and sofas were silk-fringed, and mirrors decked with velvet drapery. An enormous crystal chandelier hung from the center, reigning in splendor over the conglomeration of colors and shapes. At the far end stood a grand piano and beside it on the floor was a huge vase filled with long-stemmed roses. In every corner were the marble busts of gentlemen whom Sara did not recognize.

She took inventory carefully, postponing the moment when she must face her own feelings. How very elegant, how fashionable must be the ladies and gentlemen who gathered here. As Ritchie's wife she might have attended elaborate parties in such a room. But now she would never be Ritchie's wife.

She closed the door and went out. Down the hall was the dining room and, moving without direction, she crossed the threshold and looked in.

This room was, as her mother had said, a banquet hall. The long table set in the center had acres of wine-red carpet space all about it. The great buffet gleamed with an elaborate silver service, and the chairs had brocaded seats. Everywhere, hung against dark wood paneling, were pictures, sometimes painted scenes, sometimes portraits of the Renwick family.

If only she could have reached San Francisco sooner! If only she could have found her father's family so that Ritchie could see her in a new light. But now it was too late. She would never sit with the others in such a dining room, facing Ritchie down the length of a table.

She found the library next on the east side of the house. It looked cold and dark on this rainy day, with no fire in the grate. A gloomy room, in keeping with the mood that was slowly enveloping her.

Sara turned on a lamp and searched idly through titles until she found the shelves of California history. The thing to do was occupy herself, keep busy. She took several volumes down and piled them on a table beside the big green leather chair near a window. The chair had the feeling of being much used and the leather was no longer new, but veined with faint cracks. Somehow Sara could not imagine the elegant Judith sitting in it. Judith was too slight for such a chair. And Ritchie had never been a great reader. The chair would lose Allison in one corner, and probably did. But it was not here for Allison alone.

A book rested open on the velvet table runner beside her and she picked it up. It was by some Roman philosopher, Marcus Aurelius. Next to the book lay a pipe and Sara picked that up too, weighed the smooth bowl in her hand. It had no feel of Ritchie about it and she set it down, smelling her fingers afterwards with distaste. Ritchie smoked cigarettes, not a pipe. So this chair and the pipe beside it, the book, must belong to the unknown Nicholas Renwick. Nick, they called him. Allison claimed him for her champion, the servants deferred to him, his mother, Hilda Renwick, resented him, and Judith spoke of him often as if the household revolved around him, ran at his bidding. Ritchie had never mentioned him at all.

She mustn't think of Ritchie. She didn't dare.

She found a book which told the story of the great Comstock Lode, and began to read. Hazy figures that she could imagine were her own people came to life and moved through the Bonanza excitement, taking part in it, becoming powerful and wealthy. But though she watched always for the name of Bishop, she did not find it at all. And if she had found it, it would not have mattered. It would come too late.

Finally the book slipped from her knees onto the floor. She reached for the lamp chain and turned off the light. The chair was big enough to hold her like two great arms as she curled herself into it. She drew up her knees and rested her head upon them, but her eyes were dry and burning. A storm of weeping might have helped, but she could not cry.

This was worse than when Ritchie had gone to San Francisco the first time. This was more final, more irrevocable, and it hurt all the more because it had been preceded by a period of brave hopes.

Her mother found her there and tried to draw her out of the cold, dark room. But Sara stayed curled in her chair and would not move. Mary Jerome had learned the truth by now too, but she knew Sara well enough to realize that no offer of consolation or comfort could help her. She would have to work this out in her own way.

She made only one quiet remark. "I wonder," she said, "how much of your feeling about Ritchie grows out of old habit, out of determination, and how much of it is truly love."

Sara threw her an anguished and indignant look and she went off, returning only to bring Sara a bowl of soup for lunch, standing over her, mother-fashion, until she finished it.

In the late afternoon the rain stopped, the sun suddenly flashed through scudding clouds and pavements shone like wet satin. Sara, wearied at last of cold and gloom, slipped into an old jacket and skirt and went outdoors with no word to anyone.

She went through the big front door, finding its iron grillwork heavy to move, and ran all the way down the long flight of stone steps to the street. The windows of the house stared at her all the way, but no voice questioned, or summoned her back. She climbed to a higher rise of hill and looked again at the spread of the city.

The bay, she found, was always changing in color and the texture of its surface. It was ruffled today and tinged with gold. Everything sparkled so, looked so clean after the rain. For once there was no dust blowing and the air was something to drink—like a heady champagne. She drew great deep breaths and some of the fever went out of her spirit.

She hardly knew which way to turn—there was so much to explore. But she carried a map in her head and she knew that Chinatown lay down the hill toward the east. Not that she would visit it alone, with all its dens of iniquity which people talked about. Perhaps Ritchie would take her—no, not Ritchie! At least she could walk in that direction.

The hill was even steeper than she expected, but she did not mind the thought of climbing back. As she went down the houses grew disappointingly shabby. Bishops would surely have been hilltop people—she'd not find their house down here. No matter—she was seeing San Francisco.

Then, at a place where the hill inclined more gradually, she paused to watch the most exciting of events. A clanging of bells broke the afternoon quiet. The doors of a bright red firehouse half a block away sprang open and from its yawning mouth leaped three powerful gray horses, heads held high, feet lifting proudly as they pulled a glittering nickel monster into the street, swung in a turn and galloped away toward the lower section of town. Bells clanged wildly and black smoke poured from the mouth of the steamer. Away sped the fire chief's carriage, and the long red truck that carried the aerial ladder, then the bright red hose wagon.

Off they dashed with a roar and a clamor, and Sara, who had drawn as close as she dared, felt the wind of their passing stir her skirts. She turned to the empty interior of the firehouse—surprisingly quiet after the uproar—to see if there was anyone left. Yes—a man sat at a roll-top desk, his chair tilted back, his feet against the wall.

"Please!" Sara cried. "Where is the fire? Do you suppose I can get to it?" A fire would suit her right now. It would gratify a need that was growing in her to become angry and smash something.

The man was young, with sandy hair and a freckled face. He tilted his chair to earth and stood up. The look he turned upon her was an odd mingling of interest, disapproval and sympathy.

"I know just how you feel, miss, but the best thing any citizen can learn about fires is to stay away from 'em. Especially young ladies. Sure and you'd get in the way and faint and—"

"I never faint!" Sara cried impatiently. "And I love fires. I wouldn't get in the way."

"The people who are getting burned out don't like 'em so much," he said dryly.

"But where *is* this fire?"

The young man pointed. "Down that way, miss. It's not a neighborhood a young lady like yourself should be going into. In fact, when I saw you coming downhill just now I thought somebody ought to tell you that you were walking the wrong way on the wrong street. Could be you're new to these parts?"

Plainly this was a fire Sara couldn't catch, and the young man was pleasant, with a fascinating occupation. She stepped to the wide doorway and peered again into the hollow that was a firehouse with all its equipment gone. At least a distraction was something.

"Are there many fires in San Francisco to keep you busy?"

He nodded proudly. "Quite a mint of 'em, miss. We have a lot in the general run of things, and then of course there're always fires after a good quake. But our laddies are the best trained you'll find in the country! It's a good one, the job we do."

"I'm sure it is," said Sara politely. "But tell me—what do you do when houses catch fire on top of the hills?"

"Ah, now you have me for sure, miss. That's not so easy. Sometimes we get up, sometimes not. Depends on the hill. Have you noticed the burned ruin of that restaurant on top of Telegraph Hill? Only one engine made it to the top that night."

"But then I should think a whole hilltop could get away from you and set everything around on fire."

"Indeed, and that's a sound notion. But most of the danger lies south of Market, not on the hills. The shacks over there are like tinder. One poof of fire and they're all likely to go. San Francisco used to burn down regularly. Good parts of it, at least."

Sara shivered, not unpleasantly. "I should think that would be exciting."

The young fireman did not smile. "Depends, I suppose, on what you like for excitement. Now Chief Sullivan has a plan for quartering the city, so we can save a good part of it at least and hold any fire to one section."

"How would he do that?"

"Down there lies Market Street." The fireman pointed toward the south. "It's wide for a fire to jump and the Chief would make a stand along it. Then to the west there's Van Ness Avenue, another wide street that just about divides the city the other way. With Chief Sullivan in charge, the citizens of this town can sleep easy in their beds of a night."

Sara thanked him and turned in the direction from which she had come. But the young fireman seemed reluctant to lose her company.

"You'll be interested to know that insurance rates are high as they come in San Francisco. Just a little while ago the underwriters put the city down as a bad risk. But we'll fool 'em—the Chief and his laddies."

"I'm sure you will," said Sara. Since nothing further that was exciting promised, she told him good-by and climbed back toward the Renwick house.

She felt stronger than when she had descended the hill. Hope had been drained out of her then. But she couldn't drink this air and feel entirely despairing. Rising in her was a groundless, but somehow heartening feeling that she could yet do battle for her love. How, she had no idea. But Ritchie wasn't married yet. There was at least that straw to cling to.

When she reached the steps she saw Allison sitting at the top with Comstock beside her. The little girl looked smugly triumphant.

"Are you ever going to catch it!" she cried happily. "Your mother's in a tizzy and half the servants are out looking for you."

"But I went down the street only a few blocks away," Sara said.

"Pick the right blocks and the neighborhood gets awfully tough," Allison said. "At night there're always footpads out and holdups. Nick carries a pistol any time he goes walking alone at night. All gentlemen do in San Francisco. This is a very wicked city."

San Francisco, Sara was beginning to note, took considerable pride in extremes of reputation. But she could not feel that she had been in the slightest danger. Nor did she intend to stay indoors of an afternoon because of anyone's fears.

"All I did," she told Allison, "was to stop at a firehouse and watch the engines go out to a fire. Then I chatted for a little while with a fireman left on duty. After that I came home. So it's nothing to be in a tizzy about."

Allison's expression turned suddenly respectful. "You went to a firehouse and talked to a fireman! How exciting! Will you take me sometime?"

"Without a pistol?" Sara asked. She went past Allison up the last step and put a hand on the heavy door to open it. Then, on sudden whim, she turned back to the girl, who still watched her. "Allison—since you've lived in this city all your life, perhaps you'll know. Have you any knowledge of a family named Bishop?"

Allison thought a minute, then shook her head. "I don't think we know any Bishops. Are they Nob Hill people?"

"They might be," Sara said and went into the house.

Ritchie, again home early from the office, met her in the hallway. He looked more disapproving than pleased to see her.

"Better not run around without telling anyone where you mean to go, Sara. Your mother is really upset, though I assured her that you could undoubtedly hold your own with anyone who might accost you."

It was the wrong moment for criticism from Ritchie. Sara stared at him, taking several deep breaths before she could speak.

"May I offer my congratulations," she said stiffly. "I hope you will be very happy in you marriage to Judith."

She had the satisfaction of taking him aback. He looked suddenly less sure of himself, even a little wary, as if she might prove difficult. She brushed his self-conscious thanks aside and went on almost casually, a little surprised at her ability to hide what she really felt.

"I've been wanting to ask you about getting work of some kind. Office work. I can run a typewriting machine and I want to find a position as soon as possible. Do you think there might be a place for me in your office?"

He recovered himself quickly. "It's hard to imagine you in an office, Sara. At the moment we don't need anyone at Renwick and Merkel, and I'm afraid hiring is not in my hands anyway. However, I'll keep you in mind if anything turns up. Perhaps Nick will have an idea when he gets home."

Behind her cool air, behind her smiling lips, unspoken words were surging. *Ritchie, how can you marry someone else! How can you have forgotten, Ritchie!* But she held them back, thanked him impersonally and went upstairs. Without looking down she knew he stood there watching her and that he was not in the least comfortable.

In her room she made herself face what must have been the truth all along. In writing to Mrs. Jerome to ask her to come here as housekeeper, Ritchie had been doing exactly that. He had been trying to find someone as suitable for Mrs. Renwick as he knew Mary Jerome would be. He had known she would not come without her daughter, so of course had included Sara. That was all his invitation had amounted to. All the rest she had read into it herself.

Nevertheless, now that she was here he could not be entirely indifferent to her. The faint hope that had risen earlier began to take hold again. Sara Jerome knew Master Ritchie a great deal better than Judith did, or probably ever would. And she could not give up yet. What, exactly, she might do, she could not tell as yet. But the way would open for her. It *had* to open.

When she went down to the supper table that night with her mother, she had bounced back to an almost cheerful mood.

Unexpected company joined them at the table. Judith and Ritchie had invited guests to dinner and the meal was to be served at a later hour. When there were guests, Allison was considered too young to eat with the family. Obviously she resented this. But tonight, after she had tasted her soup without appetite and pushed it back, she announced that she was glad not to be with tonight's company.

"That old silly Jenny-Geneva is coming for dinner, and I can't stand her," said Allison.

"Don't you want to finish your soup?" Sara's mother asked gently.

"I hate soup," said Allison. "Pass me the crackers, please. Her name's just Geneva, really. But when Nick gets sappy he always calls her Jenny. Ugh! Here's what she's like."

Allison pushed back her chair, sat forward on the edge of it, and looked at them with a cow-eyed, girlish expression of sweetness. She became so astonishingly like another person that Sara rocked with laughter. Pleased at Sara's appreciation, even though Mrs. Jerome did not smile, Allison pulled her chair back to the table and began to spread butter on a cracker.

"That was clever," Mary Jerome said quietly. "But a little unkind. Especially if this young lady is someone your brother cares about."

Allison ate the cracker, undismayed by her reproach. "She's the one who cares. She dotes on Nick and I'll bet she'd marry him in a minute if he asked her. But he has better sense. Some people like marshmallows, but not me. They're too sticky and sweet. Isn't it funny the way most people are like some kind of food?"

"What do you mean? What food am I like?" Sara asked.

"Oh, onions and vinegar. And peaches," Allison said.

This time Mrs. Jerome smiled. "That's rather a good description, Allison. But I'm glad you added the peaches. Do I dare ask what food you'd pick for me?"

The child munched another cracker and thought a moment, wrinkling her expanse of forehead. Then her face lighted. "You're easy. You're like toast with hot milk and lots of butter."

Mrs. Jerome looked puzzled, and Allison went on. "That's what they bring me when I haven't been feeling well. It warms me to my toes and makes me feel sort of good and comfortable."

Mrs. Jerome reached out and touched Allison's square, ungraceful hand. "That is the nicest thing anyone has said to me in a long while. Thank you, my dear."

Sara looked at Allison wonderingly. The child had put it very well.

Allison took her hand away at once, but she looked as if she might smile.

"Do the others," Sara said. "Do Judith and Ritchie."

"Judith's easy too. I thought her up ages ago. She's like a candied violet that has been put away in the ice chest. Uncle Ritchie was harder. I couldn't figure out something for him for months. But now I know exactly. The grownups were having a party and somebody left a glass with a long stem and some amber stuff in it on the hall table. It looked so nice when I held it up to the light. It was very clear and golden amber. But when I sipped it the taste was so bitter I spat it right out."

"My dear child!" cried Mary Jerome. "That was undoubtedly an intoxicating liquor you were tasting. You must never take the chance of drinking something when you don't know what it is. And of course you must not drink from the glasses of others."

"Oh, I knew what the stuff was all right," Allison said airily. "But I won't want to taste it again."

The main course had been served and Sara cut her meat with an air of preoccupation. Allison had put her finger exactly on Ritchie Temple, bitterness and all. But Allison was too young to understand that some people might like the surprise of a bitter taste—especially when all the rest was golden amber.

Not until the meal was over and she was back in her own room did Sara recall that Allison had not given them a picture of her brother Nick. She would have to ask the child to do him sometime.

The wind blew around her tower tonight, but there was no rain. Sara poked up the fire and got into her warm wrapper, slid her feet into the sheep's wool slippers which had kept her warm on icy nights in Chicago. Then she brushed her long black hair and bound it into a single heavy braid down her back. When she had plumped the pillow on her bed she sat up against it, pulling the quilts to her chin. This was a lovely evening for reading in bed. Since there was a dinner party going on and she could not roam about the house, she had brought more California books upstairs from the library.

Due to the obstruction of the tower, the ceiling bulb had not been suspended from the middle of the room, but dangled not far from her bed. Its light was dim, however, for reading; and after a while her eyes grew weary.

Something would have to be done about this uncomfortable room. A screen around the foot of the bed might give some protection from drafts. And a reading lamp would certainly help. She wondered what furnishings the rest of the unoccupied rooms on this floor might have. Why not explore?

Slipping her feet back into woolly slippers she got out of bed, opened her door a crack and looked into the hall. All was quiet up here. A thread of light showed beneath her mother's door. Susan's door was dark—she'd be downstairs helping with the dinner. Circling the hallway tentatively, Sara listened to the sound of voices and laughter, the clatter of dishes that rose from below. She forgot her mission and leaned above the rail to see if she could glimpse what was going on. But these narrow upper stairs were set away from the main stairway and she could see nothing but the floor below.

On the second floor all the doors were closed and all was silent. She remembered Allison's words about the view that was possible from the curve of the second-floor banister and mischief began to stir in Sara. Allison had said she would read in the library till bedtime, so as not to see "Jenny-Geneva." Judith and Ritchie were safely with their guests at the dinner table. Mrs. Renwick never came upstairs. So why not? Perhaps she could catch a glimpse of Geneva and see if she matched Allison's caricature. Perhaps she could see Ritchie too, when he was not on guard against her. There was a loneliness for Ritchie in her tonight. For the old Ritchie who could not have disappeared entirely.

Soft slippers made no sound on the stairs as she stole down, her wrapper clutched about her, the dark braid swinging down her back. Voices were nearer now. She reached the banister curve and dropped to her knees where she could look between two of the plump balusters.

Only part of the dining table was visible. Ritchie sat near this end. There were lighted candles in silver holders and their gleam touched his fair head, softening his face, so there was no malice in it, no dissatisfaction. Sara's heart yearned over him. Why could he not look at her in as kindly a manner as that?

Next to him on his left sat a girl and Sara noted her with a sense of recognition. This was surely Allison's "Jenny-Geneva." She was facing this way—gently pretty and young. Soft brown hair curled in tendrils about her face, and she listened to Ritchie with the same attention Allison had imitated. But now Sara did not feel amused. There was an appeal about the girl that roused her sympathy. Geneva apparently felt about Nick as Sara did about Ritchie. And from what Allison said, Nick did not return her interest. Poor little thing, Sara thought, regarding Geneva as she would never have regarded herself. She, at least, was not gentle and helpless, but Geneva looked as if she could never stand up to life with any great force or courage.

"It's rather fun to watch them, isn't it?" said a man's voice behind her. "More fun than being down there."

Sara froze in her ignominious position on her knees. She turned her head slowly and saw his legs first—long legs encased in well-cut gray trousers. Her braid swung over her shoulder as her eyes traveled upward. A very long way upward. This man was tall. Tall enough to make even Sara Jerome seem small, had she been on her own feet, instead of kneeling at his. He was rather thin too. The bones in his cheeks stood out, spoiling any claim he might have had to being handsome. His hair was dark and straight, not softly waved like Ritchie's, and he had gray eyes which seemed to see clearly and with penetration. His straight mouth was barely smiling. Yet he did not seem angry as he looked at the huddled figure at his feet.

"You're the new housekeeper's little girl, aren't you?" he asked.

Sara choked and tried not to laugh out loud.

He went on, kindly and reassuringly, evidently taking her lack of reply for confusion. "I am Nicholas Renwick. I expect every child who lives in this house will find that particular vantage post sooner or later. I used it myself as a boy. But now, if you'll excuse me, I'll have to go down and join the party. I slipped in by the side door and they don't know I'm home ahead of time."

He nodded to her and went down the stairs. Still suppressing her desire to laugh, she watched him all the way down. When he reached the last step he glanced toward her dim post and waved before he vanished into the dining room. Sara sat rigid until he was out of sight. Then she jumped up and ran upstairs to her room.

She kicked off her slippers and hopped into bed, put her head down on drawn-up knees and smothered her laughter in the bedclothes.

"Little girl," he had said. And she had probably looked that, crouched small in the shapeless robe, with her hair down her back. She really ought to regard the matter seriously, decide on what she might say and do when next she faced Mr. Nicholas Renwick.

But in the end she could only cover her face with the quilt and shake with laughter. It was good to laugh. Somehow—laughter was a relief and a release. It pushed tears that much farther away.

FIVE

THAT NIGHT, LONG AFTER SHE HAD GONE TO SLEEP, SARA was wakened by the distant sound of piano music. The diners must now be in the drawing room, and someone was playing for them. Nick's Jenny-Geneva? No, Sara thought not. She remembered having heard music like this before. It could be no one but Judith.

When Judith had come to Chicago on that visit with her mother, she had sometimes played the piano in the Temple parlor. Sara knew little about music except through her own emotional response to it. But everyone said Judith's technique was perfection itself. The most difficult passages tripped without error from her fingers. But always, Sara felt, it was chill music, music that did not satisfy the listener. Whether the tempo was swift or slow, whether she played crescendo or diminuendo, there was no heart behind her touch. It was the sweet, clear sound of glass set ringing, but it was not music that could make you laugh or cry.

On a few special occasions in Chicago Mrs. Jerome had taken Sara to concerts at Orchestra Hall. Once they had heard a famous pianist play an all-Chopin program. For a long while afterwards Sara had not been able to get the stirring measures of the *Polonaise* out of her mind. Now Judith was playing it—a tinkling thing without the spirit the composer had written into his music.

Poor Ritchie, Sara thought with unexpected pity for him. Why had he not seen that Judith was like that— empty, emotionless? Why did he want her instead of Sara who brimmed to overflowing with the need to love warmly and to be loved with equal warmth in return. What need had Judith for love?

Yet something about this cool, remote music brought tears to Sara's eyes before she fell asleep.

The first thing in the morning Allison, ready for school, came pounding on Sara's door. At least she knocked now, though with a somewhat heavy hand.

Sara got up and opened the door sleepily. "It's practically dawn," she protested.

"Dawn!" cried Allison in scorn. "I've been up for hours. I just wanted to tell you before I left for school that my brother Nick is home. And the very first thing today when I see him I'm going to ask for my room back. *He* won't let you stay here."

"Well, you could at least let me sleep till I'm put out," Sara said. "But now that you're here, wait a minute. I have something of yours."

She went to the bureau and opened the top drawer,

fumbled among handkerchiefs and gloves, while Allison waited curiously.

"Why do you tip your mirror back like that?" the child asked.

"Because I like to see the ceiling," Sara muttered. "Here—I think this cigar band belongs to you. I found it on the floor after you spilled all your truck."

Color rose in Allison's sallow cheeks. She made no effort to take the band, but stood where she was, staring at it.

"What *is* the matter?" Sara asked. "You look as guilty as though you'd been smoking cigars. I won't tell if you have."

Allison snatched the band from her and ran out of the room. Sara could only shrug the incident aside. Whatever the association that band had in Allison's mind, it was one which embarrassed her.

Breakfast was the meal Sara liked least, since it must be eaten in the kitchen, the family having taken over the breakfast room for its proper use. Sara ate hastily, alone at the kitchen table with the servants busy around her, paying no attention except when she was in their way. Having eaten, she roamed the halls again, wondering if she would run into Nicholas Renwick. She rather looked forward to the next encounter with him. However, he had apparently gone early to the office and was not to be seen around the house.

During the morning Mrs. Renwick sent word that Sara and her mother were to have lunch with her that day. This, at least, promised an interesting change of routine, since Sara had liked Mrs. Renwick and found her unexpected and amusing.

At noon Mrs. Jerome came to her daughter's room

and they went downstairs together. In Mrs. Renwick's suite a scrawny little woman, evidently the dressmaker, was bundling up her sewing, getting ready to leave after the morning's work. A Singer sewing machine stood out from the wall and there were threads and snippings of cloth all over the carpet.

Hilda Renwick, corsetless and comfortable in a frilly negligee, greeted them cheerfully from her chaise longue.

"Good morning, Mrs. Jerome. Good morning, Sara. I'm glad you came in time to meet Millie. This is Miss Millie Matson, who is very busy these days with Judith's trousseau. Without her, I'd never know what was going on in San Francisco. Millie, this is Mrs. Jerome and her daughter Sara, who are making life more comfortable for us in this house."

The sour grimace Miss Millie turned upon them was meant, Sara decided, to be a smile. The woman nodded curtly and her bright eyes, like beads of black jet, took in every inch of the gray suit which Sara had put on this morning, on the bare chance that she might meet Mr. Nicholas Renwick in the halls. She wanted to restore her young-lady status and prove her dignity after last night. "You didn't make that yourself," Miss Millie stated flatly, her eyes upon the fashionable bolero jacket.

"No, my mother made it," said Sara. "But I cut it out."

"Whose pattern?" Miss Millie asked.

"Well, I planned it," Sara said diffidently. She had no desire to set her talents up for professional comparison.

"Humph," said Miss Millie, and there was no knowing whether she implied praise or blame. After telling Mrs. Renwick she would be back in a couple of days, she went off with a scant nod for Sara and her mother.

Mrs. Renwick laughed comfortably. "I won't say, 'Don't let her frighten you,' because she is a positive terror. No San Francisco secret is safe within three blocks of our Miss Millie. I couldn't do without her. Well, come along—I have my meals served in my own little dining room. Then I can see people or not as I please."

She hoisted her bulky person up from the chair, pulled her robe around her and slapped toward the door in loose bedroom slippers.

The dining room was small and had been done in pink rosebuds which looked like bedroom paper. There was not a heavy, dark note in it. Decorative Oriental plates of red and gold china graced a rack about the wall. The chairs were painted gray, with pink satin seats, and the gleam of silver serving dishes added a further bright accent.

Mrs. Renwick looked about proudly. "The only mahogany piece in here is the table and I keep that hidden under a pink tablecloth. All my life I've eaten in mahogany-heavy dining rooms. Pink's good for the digestion. My doctor says so. Of course I gave him the idea, but he's delighted with it. Says he'll pass it on to his other patients. Here, Sara, next to me. I like young people, even though the modern generation alarms me. Will you take the end place, Mrs. Jerome?"

They sat down and Mrs. Renwick lifted a long-stemmed silver bell at her place and rang for the butler.

"Light the candles, Jonsey," Mrs. Renwick directed. "I do like candles for company."

The room was brightly pink and sun streamed in the windows, but Jonsey solemnly lit the candles in their branched candelabrum at each end of the table. Mrs. Renwick regarded room and guests happily.

"I suppose Judith has told you that I've gone to pot? It's wonderful to be irresponsible and do as I like. William Renwick was as fine a husband as any woman could have. But he knew exactly what he wanted in a wife. I shall always be glad I was able to give him what he expected. I dressed stylishly and kept my figure at the size he thought most ladylike—thank heaven he never cared for ladies who were puny. I spoke only to the right people—those, that is, who would speak to me. Old San Francisco snubbed us, of course. They put no stock in money, but only in blood, and while ours is healthy, it's more red than blue. But we had lots of Bonanza company up here on the hill, so we weren't lonely."

The butler moved impassively, serving the rich luncheon Mrs. Renwick had ordered.

"Now that I've let down I do only what I like. I have let down, haven't I, Jonsey?"

"Yes, madam," said Jonsey politely, serving Sara from a platter of salmon creamed with a luscious egg sauce.

Sara stole a look at her mother once or twice and almost smiled at her expression of bafflement and disbelief.

Mostly during the luncheon the guests said little. Mrs. Renwick enjoyed the sound of her own voice and required few responses. She had been rather a timid and suppressed child, she admitted—it was pleasant to be over that. Never, never would she go back to being young. Her one regret was that she could not seem to be a better mother to Allison. This was what Nick couldn't forgive her. But how did one go about being a mother to a child like Allison? She rolled her eyes heavenward and shrugged expansively.

"The girl won't be touched, she won't be talked to, she won't be loved," Mrs. Renwick said, and for a moment there was no laughter, no outrageous joke in her eyes.

While they were finishing lunch, Nicholas Renwick came into the room. Sara knew his voice, though he stood behind her in the doorway. She smiled and waited.

"Darling!" Hilda Renwick cried. "How nice to see you! Did you have a good trip? Do let me call Jonsey to set another plate so you—"

"Not today, Mother. Thank you. I promised to lunch with Judith and Allison. They're going into the dining room now. But since I had no chance to see you last night or this morning, I wanted to pay my respects. The trip went well enough. Good morning, Mrs. Jerome."

There was a brief silence and Sara could almost feel his eyes on the back of her head.

"This is Sara," Mrs. Renwick said. "Miss Sara Jerome."

Nick came around the table for a better look. He said, "How-do-you-do," politely, but with surprise and a hint of amusement.

Sara smiled and acknowledged the introduction. Nick Renwick would not give her away, she sensed.

"I'm afraid Allison is disturbed because I've been given her playroom," she told him. "Ritchie must have remembered how I loved towers when he suggested it. This tower is wonderful. I hope I won't have to give it up."

Nick seemed surprised. "Why, yes, Allison mentioned the room to me just now when I came in from the office. She says she likes you and she thinks you ought to keep it. Thank you, Miss Jerome, for being so kind to her."

He kissed his mother lightly on the cheek and went out, while Sara looked after him in astonishment. He had surprised her more than she had surprised him.

"How very nice that you've befriended Allison," Mrs. Renwick said. "I know the child is lonely, though she won't admit it."

"I—I didn't know that I had," said Sara frankly.

Mrs. Renwick nodded. "I understand how that can be. And I wouldn't put too much stock in it anyway. Likely as not she'll be screaming to have you out of the room by tomorrow. Children *are* a problem! Thank heavens Judith is settled at last. I'm delighted over her engagement to Ritchie and I can't think why she has postponed it for so long. Of course she had a heart-breaking experience a few years ago with a young man who proved to be a roué and a rascal—a mere money-seeker. Judith was desperately in love with him. If William hadn't shown him up and sent him packing she'd have thrown her life away. The poor girl has been fearful of her own judgment and distrustful of men ever since."

Sara winced inwardly, but the revelation surprised her. She wouldn't have thought Judith could step out of her shell long enough to fall in love.

Clearly Mrs. Renwick had no inhibitions when it

came to talking about family affairs. The fact that those she talked about so readily might have preferred more reticence on her part never occurred to her.

"Now if Nick would just make up his mind about Geneva," she ran on, "everything would be perfect. Goodness knows the child is mad about him. And I do like having her around. She goes out of her way to visit with me and make me comfortable. In fact, I expect it's more at my invitation than Nick's that she comes here so often. A dear child, really. Well, since we've finished our ices—"

Her sentence was interrupted by a shiver that seemed to start underfoot and run through the house. Sara saw the painted china dishes on the wall rack tilt forward, then settle back. The sensation quieted in seconds, but it was startling while it lasted.

Mrs. Renwick's laugh was cheerful. "There, Sara, you've had your first earthquake. Though I can't say it was a really good sample."

"I've wondered what one would feel like," said Sara.

"That's the spirit." Mrs. Renwick approved. "No good San Franciscan ever regards a quake as anything but a joke. Mercy, Mrs. Jerome—you're not frightened?"

Sara saw that her mother was dabbing at her lips with her handkerchief.

"I'm afraid I—I shall never become accustomed to earthquakes," she said.

"You'll be all right in a minute," Mrs. Renwick assured her kindly. "I imagine it seems a nasty feeling to strangers. Sara, I saw you watching my Japanese plates. But you needn't worry—I've had them wired into place. William treasured them and I'd feel terrible if anything happened to them. He brought them home from one of his trips. I've never lost one even in a good quake. What we just had was a mere vibration. But as I was about to say, do let's go back to my sitting room and be comfortable."

She rose and Sara glanced at her mother as she left the table. Mrs. Jerome had recovered, but Sara knew she must be remembering other quakes. An earthquake was no new experience to her.

Mrs. Renwick chattered on as she returned to her favorite chair with a sigh of repleteness. "Do stay and visit me. After all, I haven't a single tidbit about you to report to Miss Millie when she comes next time. Not that she needs any help. She can take one look and ferret out a whole family history. Undoubtedly it will be all over San Francisco by tonight that a gentle-woman named Mary Jerome has come to work as housekeeper for the Renwicks. And that her daughter is a handsome young thing who dresses like a Paris model."

Sara saw her mother wince. Perhaps Millie Matson might be the right one on whom to try the name of Bishop.

As they sat down in the sitting room, Mrs. Renwick nodded toward the picture-crowded walls behind her chair. "There is my husband, Willie. The double pictures of us in the middle. They were taken during the first year of our marriage. Wasn't I pretty then?"

Two old-fashioned photographs, somewhat yellowed by age, had been mounted in a wide, forget-me-not painted border and framed beneath one glass. The man looked a little like his son Nick, with the same high cheekbones. But obviously William Renwick had been built more of iron than of flesh. His eyes were cool as Judith's, his mouth undoubtedly set grimly beneath the usual bushy mustache.

"Of course," said Mrs. Renwick fondly, "I never called him 'Willie' while he was alive. But I'm afraid he has let down too, lately, poor dear. I keep him there behind me so I can't see when he disapproves of what I say or do."

Mrs. Jerome sat on the edge of her chair, again uncomfortable and at a loss. Sara knew that her mother wished they could escape from Mrs. Renwick's bewildering company. She liked people to stay in proper pigeonholes. But Hilda Renwick's pigeonholes had jumbled all their contents, so you never knew what she would pull out next.

"How do you like my son?" she asked now of her visitors.

"He seems a fine man," Mrs. Jerome said. "Responsible, sober. A kindly man, I should think."

"He can be when he pleases. But like my husband, he is a man of high principles. It is somewhat difficult at times to live with high principles. I do wish he had a family of his own to give his attention to. If he'd just marry Geneva Varady, I'd be relieved."

Sara had been watching her mother and she saw exactly what happened. As Mrs. Renwick spoke the name "Varady" a shock went over Mary Jerome's face, blanching it, leaving sallowness behind. She did not move or start, but her color betrayed her and Sara did not take her eyes from her mother's face. Here was more than the response she had been waiting for.

"Varady, did you say?" Mrs. Jerome repeated the name with an effort.

"Yes. Geneva Varady. Very old San Francisco family. I've been snubbed by them often in the past. But times change and the young must be considered."

Mary Jerome spoke softly, and again with an effort to steady her voice. "What branch of the Varady family is this?"

"Branch? I thought you didn't know San Francisco? Though I'm sure one begins to pick up the names quickly enough. The blood is a bit thin in Geneva, I suspect. She was no more than a convent waif when Miss Hester Varady took her in to raise as a child. Nick met her because of all the real estate Miss Varady owns —and insures with Renwick and Merkel. Of course she'd never have looked twice at Nick as a suitor for her niece in the old days, since the insurance business is not regarded as one of the suitable professions for a gentleman. Miss Varady herself always sends regrets when we invite her here. But she permits Geneva to come and she has not opposed her going about with Nick."

Mary Jerome put a hand to her forehead, and Sara went to her quickly.

"Mama, you're ill! Would you like a drink of water? Or to lie down?"

Mrs. Jerome stood up shakily. "I—I shall be all right. If you'll excuse me, Mrs. Renwick, I'll go upstairs for a little while."

"Of course," Mrs. Renwick said. "It's probably all that rich food. Few stomachs but mine can take it. Run along with your mother, girl. I'll send Susan up with some of my stomach medicine."

Mrs. Jerome leaned heavily on Sara as they climbed the stairs. Back in her own room, she lay on her bed and closed her eyes, while Sara unlaced her high shoes and pulled them off, rubbed her cold feet in their white lisle stockings.

Susan tapped on the door with Mrs. Renwick's medicine, but Mrs. Jerome sent her away and would take no more than a few sips of water. She clung to Sara, keeping her near. After a little while the spasm, whatever it was, seemed to pass and she quieted. But her fingers tightened more strongly on Sara's hand until the girl winced.

"Mama, you're crushing my fingers. What is it? What's wrong with Geneva Varady that the name upset you so?"

Her mother turned her head from side to side with an air of desperation. "I knew we should never have come to San Francisco. But I thought we might be safe in this house. That we would not move in the same circles, that—"

"*What* circles?" Sara asked. "If you'd tell me what this is all about—"

"A Varady visiting here! And then there's that sewing woman. Goodness knows what word she will spread."

"What *is* it that she can spread? Anyway, I'm not likely to meet Geneva socially, goodness knows."

Her mother raised herself on one elbow and looked at Sara almost fiercely. "Listen to me! Miss Hester Varady is a monstrously wicked person. She is dangerous to us—to *you*. Under no circumstances are you to go near her. Avoid this Geneva when she comes here. The girl may be harmless. It is her connection that is dangerous."

"I'm sure you're upsetting yourself over nothing," Sara said, bewildered. "Mrs. Renwick told us the aunt never comes here, that she is too snobbish. And I'm sure I don't care for snobs."

Mary Jerome closed her eyes. "I can't argue with you. I should have been prepared for this. Somehow I'd lulled myself into a hope that we might go unnoticed in San Francisco. Now I'll have to be on guard. I'll rest a few moments now, Sara, and then return to my duties."

Sara went uneasily from the room. She wished there were some way in which she could reassure and comfort her mother, but she could not really believe in any cause for alarm. What had happened, however, made the whole mystery all the more tantalizing and provoking. What was Hester Varady to her mother and herself?

At least she had something with new possibilities to think about now. Perhaps "Bishop" was not the key name for which she must search. Perhaps the important name was "Varady." Perhaps the Varadys would lead her to the name of Bishop. The Varadys at least were known in San Francisco. Mrs. Renwick might even be persuaded to talk about them.

Somehow Sara had to know the answers. Somehow she must find her father's family and establish herself before it was too late. With every passing moment Ritchie seemed to move farther out of her reach. Yet she could not accept what seemed to be happening. There must be a way to stop it.

She went back to the books she had taken to her room, determined to look through them for the name of Varady. Certainly she would seek an opportunity to meet Jenny-Geneva if it was possible. Her mother's fears were not for her. This was the year 1906 and melodrama in San Francisco belonged to the past.

SIX

THE RAINS CONTINUED INTO FEBRUARY. THERE WOULD be a stretch of weather in which torrents came down and the hills of San Francisco ran with water. But grass and flowers drank refreshment and bloomed beneath the downpour. Then would come a few sunny days and the deserted streets would flood with people. Now and then when the sun brought warmth as well as brilliance of a Sunday, trolleys and cable cars filled to the brim as the city's multitudes poured toward Golden Gate Park and Ocean Beach.

Sara's life went on in a routine she was beginning to find monotonous. Nothing had developed in the way of a position, though she had gone to several firms to apply. She and her mother went downtown shopping a single time and Sara had been delighted with Union Square. She had coaxed her mother to walk with her through the corridors of the St. Francis Hotel, and she had loved exploring counters of goods in the White House and the City of Paris. She could probably get a job as a saleslady in one of these stores, but that was not the sort of work she wanted.

At home Ritchie still eluded her. Sometimes she did not see him for days. Sometimes he passed her in a hallway with no more than a nod. How childish she had been to think that merely by coming to San Francisco something of their old relationship could be regained.

Yet she would not give up hope. Even though the house buzzed with preparations and plans for the wedding, still Judith held back and did not set the date. Sometimes, it seemed to Sara that Ritchie was not altogether happy in his engagement to Judith. He did not always have the manner of a joyful young man about to be married. And in this too there was hope.

Though now, Sara knew that even if he should turn to her again, the innocence of their young days would be gone. Ritchie was a man, not a boy new to kisses, playing at first love. Yet Sara wanted nothing clandestine and shabby. What she wanted was a miracle; the happy ending to a fairy tale. And there seemed no immediate way for that to be.

Nor had she made much headway in making the acquaintance of Geneva Varady. Geneva's relationship with Nick seemed to be of a tenuous sort. True, he saw her frequently and took her out, but he also moved in a casual social life of his own that did not always include Geneva. The girl came to visit the Renwicks once or twice a week, usually at Mrs. Renwick's invitation. Sometimes Nick went to fetch her. Sometimes she arrived in a moth-eaten carriage, driven by a coachman in a shiny black coat. The Varadys, Mrs. Renwick pointed out, had no need to prove anything to San Francisco, so they did not trouble with matters of front like the carriage they rode in, or the clothes they wore. She always said "The Varadys," as though the clan was extensive. But from what Sara could gather, there remained only Miss Varady and the poor relation, Geneva. So far Sara had been unable to figure out a plan for getting Geneva alone in order to talk to her.

Even if she managed a meeting with Geneva, what could she say? "My mother has a horror of the name Varady. Will you please tell me why?" Geneva would only look at her in sweet astonishment.

At least in the days following her discovery, she had one thoroughly satisfying experience. Perhaps it answered no questions with certainty, but it pointed so clear a finger that Sara prickled with excitement over the revelation, sure now that she was right; sure in her very bones.

She found the Varady name in a book in the Renwick library.

It was the usual rainy morning. Allison was in school. Judith had gone shopping with a friend, and Mary Jerome was busy with household affairs. Sara had the library to herself, except for Comstock the cat. A curious relationship had begun to develop between Sara and Comstock. When Allison was home the cat had eyes for no one but his favorite child. As Allison said, he thought he was her mother. He supervised her meals, her dressing, her study. He was even known to cuff her with velvet sheathed paws on occasions when he disapproved of her actions. And no one else cuffed Allison. At night, of course, he was a gay bachelor and roamed abroad, coming home in the light of gray dawn like other San Francisco blades. Mrs. Renwick said he was the terror of Nob Hill. More than one elegant young lady cat with a pedigree longer than her tail had disgraced herself by presenting her household with a batch of yellow, tiger-striped kittens. But Comstock slept well by day, and disowned all responsibility toward these offspring. There was nothing domestic about him except when it came to Allison. Then he turned into a fussy old mother tabby.

In Sara, however, he had discovered another lone wolf. She was neither afraid of him like Susan, nor did she dote on him and lug him around like Allison. He could sleep comfortably in her presence, feeling a certain human companionship nearby which he apparently liked. Sometimes she would address a remark or two in his direction. Then he would open the yellow shutters of his eyes and listen with remote courtesy. She had the feeling that there was a good deal of wisdom piled up in Comstock's head, if only one could tap it.

This morning it was chilly and she had lighted a fire in the library grate, closed the door into the hallway. Comstock lay upon the hearthrug napping and Sara curled into Nicholas Renwick's green leather chair with a tome about California in her lap. She turned the pages idly now, merely looking for names. And suddenly VARADY seemed to leap to her eyes. The name of Julian Varady I.

She read eagerly, breathlessly.

He had come to the Spanish regions of California from the East, sailing the long trip around the Horn. His Boston family was a good one, but his pockets were empty. Nevertheless, he had managed to ingratiate himself with the great rancho-owning family of the Oliveros. And he had married the youngest, most beautiful of the six Olivero daughters, Consuelo. She had borne him a son, Julian Varady II; but two years later she had died at the birth of her daughter. The baby had lived only two days longer than Consuelo.

The elder Julian, brokenhearted, had not married again, but with the Olivero name and fortunes behind him, he had furthered his own position to an extent that made him a power in California, with an influence not usually exerted by Americans at that time. In turn the second Julian had married and fathered two daughters, Hester and Elizabeth. When Hester was about six Mexico had ceded California to the United States and the budding community of San Francisco had become an American city. In two generations the Varady name had gained eminence. In the third there was no son to carry it on.

That was as far as the story went. The book was an old one, dated. There was still no mention of anyone called Bishop. But Sara had her lead when she came upon the name of Consuelo Olivero.

She dropped the book with a thump that roused Comstock to a quiet stare. Across the mantlepiece ran a strip of narrow mirror and Sara pulled over a hassock to a spot before the fire screen. Comstock got out of her way and settled at a distance, recognizing in distaste a female with a purpose.

Sara stood upon the hassock and peered at herself in the strip of mirror. Black hair and eyes so dark a brown they were nearly black. A faintly olive tint to her complexion, and warm southern blood coursing in her veins, as well she knew. It must be true! Somehow, somehow she was a throwback to the Olivero family—to Consuelo herself. A true daughter of old California.

She jumped to the floor and stood proudly before Comstock. "Look at me! Can't you see how right I'd be if my hair were done high with a comb and a mantilla?"

Undoubtedly she was related to Miss Hester Varady. And even to Jenny-Geneva. A second or third cousin, perhaps? Though how Geneva's name came to be Varady, she wasn't at all sure. There must have been more relatives than the book had mentioned. Later ones, of course.

For days after that she carried herself with something of an air about the house. Once Allison asked who she thought she was, acting like Queen Victoria. Sara said, "Don't be foolish—I'm Isabella of Spain," which had left Allison gaping. Several times her mother spoke to her worriedly, inquiring if she felt well. And when she went past Ritchie in the hall with her nose in the air, even he was startled.

Nick, too, seemed to note the change in her and she hoped he was impressed. It still rankled that he had once taken her for a child. She'd had few encounters with him since, never really talked to him, but she knew he noticed her in a puzzled, faintly amused way, which annoyed her. But at least Nick seemed to regard her—though neither Ritchie nor Judith did—as an individual in her own right.

At length, however, her effort to keep up the make-believe role of a Spanish belle began to be a strain. Gradually she lapsed into her usual self, waiting without theatrics for the opportunity to prove her distinguished inheritance.

One mild February afternoon when the windows stood open to a few hours of warm sunshine, Sara came running downstairs from her room to find that Judith's door was ajar. She had never before had so much as a glimpse into this room and she slowed her steps, lingered, so she might look in. She could hear Judith downstairs talking on the telephone. There was no one to see if she satisfied her curiosity by pausing at the door. So why not?

The room looked like Judith. It was done in cool blue-grays, with here and there a pale touch of gold. The draperies were made of fold upon fold of gauzy blue material. The quilt on the bed was of blue satin with a pale gold pillow upon it, and the padded seat of the dressing-table bench was also blue quilted satin. Several furry blue rugs lay about the shining floor. The wallpaper was pale yellow with a faint blue flower pattern running through it.

The room was the most beautiful Sara had ever seen. Her own poorly furnished tower seemed all the more harsh and unlovely by comparison. Drawn by physical beauty as she always was, Sara forgot precaution and stepped into the room. There was the fragrance of Judith's perfumes in the air and luxury at every turn. She could not resist a peep through the bathroom door. A fine big tub stood on claw feet and the fittings looked like gold. The bath towels were huge and deeply piled, and the scent of perfumed soap was delicate.

When she turned back to the bedroom, meaning to leave at once, the dressing table caught her eye. Soft gray-blue chiffon looped about the tall mirror, framing it. And upon lace doilies placed to save the beautiful rosewood top, lay a silver toilet set more magnificent than any Sara had ever seen. The mirror had a long, slender handle. Even the glass hatpin case had a silver top.

The entire room seemed to breathe the very spirit of Judith and a curious realization grew in Sara. Judith was not a cool glass figurine whose existence she could forget or ignore. She was a woman engaged to marry Ritchie. In some queer way Sara had avoided facing that fact; really facing it. She was not, she felt, without conscience. But a conscience could sleep comfortably if you shut it off from the facts of what you were trying to do.

Now in this room Judith had become real to Sara as she had never been before. Judith was a woman who could love and be loved. She could be happy, or suffer pain. This was not something Sara wanted to face because it weakened what she felt were her own rights, made her own plans more difficult. She turned from the dressing table unhappily.

In the doorway Judith stood watching her. For a moment Sara could not speak. It took an effort to recover herself.

"I know I have no business in your room," Sara said. "I have no excuse for being here. I was passing the door and I was—curious." But even as she spoke the words something in her was whispering, *the girl Ritchie wants to marry.*

Judith came into the room, a faint aura of roses about her. "Do you like it?" she asked calmly.

Sara nodded. "It's a—beautiful room. It fits you."

"Does it? I've never thought so." Judith went to the dressing-table stool and sat down, her skirts swirling gracefully about her. "Stay a minute," she said to Sara, gesturing toward a quilted chair.

Sara, wanting only to escape, took the chair and sat as her mother did, on the very edge.

"I've been wanting to talk to you," Judith went on. "A few days ago I had a discussion with Nick about you. I told him you wanted a position in an office and he said he would look into the matter. Last night he said at dinner that one of the girls at his office was leaving and there would be a place for you. You can go to work next Monday if you like. He will tell you about the salary and other details himself."

Sara stared at her. A position. Something to do with herself. Money that would be her own. She could not sit here mooning when an opportunity like this was offered her. She jumped up, barely missing the protruding handle of the mirror as she moved.

"How wonderful! Thank you for telling me. I'll run find my mother now and let her know." She was glad of an opportunity to escape this room.

When she ran upstairs to the third floor to look for her mother, she found Comstock and Allison waiting for her in the hall.

Allison said, "There she is!" Comstock picked something up from the floor and came trotting toward Sara. In the dimly lit hall she did not recognize what he was carrying until he laid at her feet a small gray mouse and sat back to look up at her with pardonable pride.

Sara did not care for mice—especially dead ones. It took all the will she possessed not to vent her dismay in a yelp. But there was something about Comstock's air of having offered treasure, about the fixed way in which Allison was staring at her, that made Sara choke back the sound that rose in her throat.

Hastily she looked away from the offering at her feet. "Thank you, Comstock," she said in a voice that quavered slightly.

Allison smiled at Sara for the first time since she had come to this house. The effect was astonishing. One forgot all that naked expanse of forehead, forgot the freckles and the snub nose. Allison's smile came from the heart and it was warmly beautiful. Sara felt a sudden urge to do something about Allison's appearance. Really, it wouldn't take much.

"He likes you, Sara," Allison said. "He brought it right up to your door and sat down to wait for you. Tell him what a fine hunter he is."

Sara felt a nervous tendency to giggle. "Somehow I'd have expected Comstock to bag an elephant at the very least." She tried to look at the attentive cat without seeing the mouse. Fortunately Comstock would not expect her to lean over and pat him. "I think you're a fine hunter," she told him dutifully and then turned back to Allison. "What am I supposed to do now?" No matter what these two expected, she was not going to touch that mouse.

"Oh, he doesn't want you to keep it," Allison said, and spoke to Comstock. "It's all right, darling, you can take it outside now. Run along."

Comstock, having proved his competence, picked up the mouse and carried it at a leisurely pace down the stairway. Sara hoped he wouldn't meet Susan on the way.

"Have you seen my mother?" she asked Allison. "I

want to tell her that I have a business position. Your brother Nick is going to let me work in his insurance office."

"What fun!" Allison cried, her smile lingering. "Your mother's downstairs talking to old Jonsey. You'd better wait. I wish I could do something like that when I grow up. Work in an office."

Sara started toward her room and Allison came along, walking prissily, as if she swished a full skirt behind her, very flat in front in the straight-front-corset manner. With her neck stuck high and slightly forward, as if propped by a starched collar, she was the picture of a genteel young lady working in an office. Sara couldn't help laughing. She still had an urge to do something about Allison's appearance, but she didn't know how to manage it.

Pleased, Allison stayed right at Sara's heels when she opened her door.

"Don't you lock it any more?" Allison asked.

Sara shook her head. "I don't need to. Do I?"

"No," said Allison. "But maybe Judith does. I saw you go in her room just now. So you aren't any better than I am, really. What did you do when she caught you?"

Ignoring the question, Sara said, "Come in, Allison, and unbraid your hair. I can't stand seeing you wear it that way a moment longer. Close the door and keep still. Now where did I put my scissors?"

Allison was startled into closing the door, but she stood with her back against it. Her interest in Sara's misbehavior had vanished at this distraction.

"Wh-what are you going to do?"

"Nothing that will hurt. Come over here."

Sara tipped down her mirror and stood Allison in front of it. "Look at all that forehead! You have a lovely smile and nice eyes, but nobody can see anything but your forehead. You're topheavy and all wrong."

Allison gaped at herself in the mirror. "But all the girls wear their hair like this."

"What does that matter? You're a special girl. You're you."

Since Allison was making no move toward her own hair, Sara untied the hair bow and pulled the soft brown strands free.

"How fine your hair is. Like your mother's, isn't it? And don't tell me she isn't your mother. What sort of talk was that anyway?"

Allison stood helpless, half terrified by what Sara's swift fingers were doing to her, yet too fascinated to pull away.

"We'll just try a thin fringe to begin with," Sara said, running the rat-tailed comb across the front of Allison's head to part the hair.

"F-f-fringes are old-fashioned," Allison stammered in fright. "I heard Miss Millie say so."

"Nothing is old-fashioned that makes you look right," said Sara. "Don't wriggle."

Now she turned the girl so she could no longer see the glass. Strands of long hair came away in Sara's hands as she ran the scissors across Allison's forehead. She combed and evened, took a few more strands, stood back to get the effect. Allison was no longer a freakish child with a too high forehead. The soft brown bangs gave her face its proper proportions. Sara smiled in pleasure at her own handiwork and turned Allison so she could look in the mirror.

Allison looked at the stranger in the glass. Once more the warming smile stirred her lips, spread outward, lighting her face.

"It does look better," she whispered, as if to speak loudly might break the charm.

Sara narrowed her eyes, seeing more than was to be seen in the mirror. "In a few years you are going to be a very stunning young woman. You'd better get ready to live up to it."

Allison could not take her gaze from the mirror. "I don't know what you mean."

"I mean a lot of things. Untied hair ribbons. Stockings that wrinkle. Tears and spots. Though I know my mother has been taking care of those. And you shouldn't wear so much brown. I believe I'll talk to Mrs. Renwick about some new dresses for you. Something brighter."

"But I don't like clothes. I don't care how I look."

"Stop saying such things. You only say them to make people stare at you. It's the wrong way to be important. You don't care how you look because you don't have to look at yourself. Others do."

Allison regarded the mirror again and pushed the bangs back for a second, then brushed them down into place.

"But what's the use?" she asked, suddenly gloomy. "When I have Judith for a sister? Everybody thinks I'm homely beside her. And I can never look like she does."

"You don't need to. You shouldn't want to. You must look like *you*. The sort of you that is going to have much more to look at than Judith ever had. Because you're alive and Judith isn't. Judith's a glass figure on a shelf." The words echoed in her mind, but she would not listen to the echo. She must think only of Allison.

A mingling of wonder, disbelief, and hope had come into Allison's eyes. She leaned over and pulled one ribbed black stocking straight on her leg, fastened it more tightly with a garter. Watching her, Sara was moved.

"Sit down a minute, Allison," she said gently, "and tell me why you wanted me to think Mrs. Renwick wasn't your mother."

Allison sat on the bed, squirmed a little, grew pink in the face and began her confession.

"It was that gold cigar band. When I was little I used to pretend that I couldn't be my mother's child. Or Papa's either. Papa was very stern and he didn't approve of children being like children. He thought everybody should grow up right away. And Mama always did everything he said."

Sara listened, feeling a new gentleness toward the girl. "What about the cigar band?" she prompted when Allison gulped and came to a halt.

"I guess I was around seven when I found it in a wastebasket. It looked so beautiful, with that big gold crown and all the red lettering. So I pretended that I was a lost princess and that was my secret crest. That way I could feel I was better than all the people around me. Even better than Judith—who was always so perfect and just the way Papa thought she ought to be. But not better than Nick. I used to pretend that my king father would be like Nick. Of course all this was when I was small. I don't believe such things any more. I only said that about my mother to make you jump."

"And you certainly did. Now I'll tell you something. I've played that same game most of my life. I'm a lost princess too. Wait—let me show you something."

She hopped off the bed, pulled open a drawer and rummaged in it for a lacy white scarf that had been a Christmas gift from her mother. Then, tongue between her lips as she pondered, she looked around the room. Yes—that small book would do. She picked it up and posed before the mirror, held the book at the back of her head and flung the scarf over it. Then she turned around to face Allison.

"There now! What do I remind you of?"

"The way they dress at a fiesta?" Allison said promptly. "You'd look fine in Spanish dress. You really do look Spanish."

"You see?" Sara laughed. "I'm a lost princess of Spain. Or anyway a daughter of the dons!"

Allison, on the verge of growing up, yet still a little girl, looked both delighted and puzzled. Sara was presumably too grown-up for fantasy.

Sara laughed at her expression. "Make-believe," she said, snapping her fingers. It would be just as well not to have Allison claiming that Sara Jerome was a lost Spanish princess. "And now you'd better go look for Comstock. I'll run down and tell my mother about my new position."

Mary Jerome's reaction was mixed. She agreed that it was a good thing for Sara to do something with her empty time. But there was an uneasiness underlying her attempt to seem pleased. Sara suspected that her mother could not bring herself to approve anything which would take her daughter into what she regarded as the dangerous outer world of San Francisco.

Monday, to Sara, seemed a long time away. She helped the hours to pass by checking over her wardrobe, deciding which skirts and shirtwaists would be most suitable for a young woman in business; making sure they were clean and well pressed.

Yet these distractions could not keep her mind from Ritchie's marriage to Judith, and the fact that Judith had the rights of a young woman engaged, while Sara Jerome had no rights at all.

She broke a length of thread with her teeth and sat idle for a moment, trying to fix her thoughts upon Allison. But now no distraction served.

She flung aside the shirtwaist and let a button roll across the floor as she rose. Under the handkerchiefs in her bureau drawer was the picture of Leland Bishop. She took it out and studied the face, but now when she looked at it she could feel no flood of feeling rise in her. This bit of cardboard no more stood for real life than did Allison's cigar band. It was as much make-believe as her dream that Ritchie might someday be hers.

She could hardly wait for Monday and a new life. If she were busy enough she wouldn't have to worry about loneliness. Anything might happen to a girl who worked in an office.

SEVEN

Long after she had gone to bed that night, Sara woke to hear a distant clock chiming three. But she knew it was not the clock which had awakened her. There had been another sound much closer at hand. As if someone were walking in the hall outside her door. She had not bothered to lock it, feeling quite safe here at the top of the house.

She propped herself up in bed, listening intently, her heart thudding a little. Yes—there was plainly the sound of a step. Not the firm step of one who walked without heed for any who might hear him, but a softened, stealthy sound. Then she heard clearly the opening of a door and knew it was the door of the empty room next to her own. What mystery was this? Who prowled the house at three in the morning?

Never a timid girl, Sara did not hesitate now. Something was amiss in the Renwick house and she had better find out what it was. Allison's stories of footpads returned to her. But she had a good pair of lungs and she would keep her distance, scream mightily, if the need arose.

Again her wool slippers served her well, making no sound upon the floor. And her wrapper was warm against the chill of San Francisco's night air. Her own door had been oiled recently and opened without a creak. The dim light in the hall burned all night and in it she could see that the door of the room next to her own stood open.

She did not want to appear silhouetted against the light, so she slipped softly along the wall till she was at the edge of the door opening. Then she listened again. Yes, there was definitely someone in the room. She heard small fumbling sounds, then a sudden click and a sharp draft of cold air as a window was opened. But why open a window on the third floor of the house?

She ventured a careful peep around the edge of the door. The open window across the room showed a star-filled, deep blue sky. Against it was the smudged outline of a man. The outline merged with the shadows of the room and she couldn't tell who it was.

She could see the dangling light cord against the light from the window and she darted in to pull it. The overhead bulb came to life and the man at the window looked around without alarm. It was Nicholas Renwick.

"Good morning, Miss Jerome," he said in quiet amusement. "Were you looking for me?"

"I was looking for footpads. And—and thugs," she admitted.

"I've disappointed you." He smiled. "I'm sorry I

wakened you. I did try to be quiet. The rest of the family know my habits. Often when I'm sleepless at night I come up here to Allison's tower to watch the city. Since the tower is no longer available, I thought I'd slip in here and look out this window instead."

"Next time I'll know better," Sara said.

She turned to go, but he spoke again. "Turn off the light and come here."

His voice carried authority and it never occurred to her not to obey. She tugged the light cord and crossed the dark room to stand beside him at the window.

"Have you seen it like this?" he asked softly.

A strange fog glow lay upon the sleeping city. The mist was not thick enough to blot out the lights, but only to blur them into a pale shimmer in the night. From a distance came the clang of trolley cars, and the deeper, warning voices from the bay.

"I'll take San Francisco on a foggy night to any place I know," Nick said.

Sara nodded wordlessly. The spell was upon her too and she scarcely felt the chill night wind. But as she watched the drifting wraiths of fog she could not help wondering about the man who stood beside her. Why should Nicholas Renwick, who must have everything in life he wanted, find it hard to sleep at night? Why was there a stamp of loneliness upon him that set him apart from the others in this house?

He breathed deeply of the cool, damp air. "Somehow it clears my wits to come up here and watch the city at night. The things that irked me by day seem to matter less up here."

"I know," Sara said. "I feel that too."

Nick glanced at her quickly and then closed the window. "Better run back to bed. You're not dressed for this night air. Next time I'll try to be more quiet."

She hesitated. Perhaps this wasn't the time, but no matter. "I haven't had a chance to thank you, Mr. Renwick. Your sister told me about the position in your office. I'm very grateful."

"That's fine," he said. "You'll have to see that you do me credit. I've assured Mr. Merkel, who was my father's partner and is the senior member of the firm, that you are a whiz at the typewriter."

"I'll do my best," Sara said. "I'm very anxious to pay for my room and board here as soon as possible."

"Judith told me that too. Good for you! We'll respect your wishes. Now do go back to bed, or you'll be down with a cold and unable to poke at the keys of that Oliver."

She felt suddenly foolish, conducting a dignified conversation at three o'clock in the morning, while dressed in a woolly robe and slippers. But at least he had not laughed at her.

Back in her own bed, she found herself still wondering about him. Here was a man who could not be easily read by the exterior he presented to the world. There were depths behind in which unknown emotions stirred, seldom flashing to the surface. But though she had no knowledge of what drove him, she had the feeling that perhaps she had a friend in this household.

Though slow in coming, Monday finally arrived. Sara drove to work with Nick and Ritchie in the automobile, a veil tied over her sailor hat to shield her from dust and winds, high anticipation in her heart. Ritchie seemed to regard the whole thing as a joke, pretending to believe that Sara would be completely helpless in an office. She ignored him and discussed her duties seriously with Nick.

In bright daylight it was hard to believe that she had stood beside this tall, grave man only a few nights before, watching trolley lights pick out San Francisco. The incident had taken on the unreal quality of a dream. But her confidence in Nicholas Renwick had grown, her feeling that the entire household—and that included her mother and herself—was secure in his hands.

Renwick and Merkel were housed in one of the tall buildings downtown near Market Street. The offices looked like those almost anywhere. A small waiting room with several stiff chairs and a bench against one wall was separated from the office by a low wooden partition. A framed photograph of Mr. William Renwick, mustache and all, overlooked the scene sternly and gave it a no-nonsense air. A girl with an ink smudge on her nose and a pencil stuck into her high-swept tresses pecked at one of the two typewriters. A gangling young clerk whose hair grew long on his neck shuffled through papers at a filing cabinet, and let his eyes linger upon Sara.

The private offices of the partners opened off this section, and through one door Sara glimpsed a large mahogany desk and deep leather chair. It was this room Nick went into.

The other girl was introduced to Sara as Miss Dalrymple, and she stood upon her senior dignity, a bit superior and cool. In a distant, condescending manner she showed Sara her desk and her supplies. Sara could be cool and dignified too, however. She felt very correct in her dark blue skirt and pin-striped shirtwaist, with its man's starched collar. Miss Dalrymple had fastened paper cuffs over her wrists to protect her sleeves from grime, but Sara decided that she would prefer to do up a clean shirtwaist for herself every day.

Almost at once she was called to Mr. Merkel's office for an interview and some dictation and she went rather nervously. Mr. Merkel, however, did not alarm her. In fact, he reminded her of Mr. Temple. Ritchie's father had been a peppery little man like this, but he had been absolutely just and could be counted on. Mr. Merkel gave her the feeling that if she did her work well he would approve of her and stand by her.

She sat with her shorthand tablet propped against her knee, her pencil poised. He dictated with consideration for her novice state and went at a speed she could handle. After giving her three or four short letters, he sent her away to type them.

Back at her desk, Sara ignored Miss Dalrymple and the attentive file clerk, feeling very competent and professional. The keys of the Oliver clicked under her fingers and she transcribed Mr. Merkel's dictation without understanding much of what she wrote. The language of insurance was still a mystery to her, but that took nothing away from the glamour of working in a real office.

Once during the morning, when Miss Dalrymple was away from her desk, Sara looked up to see Ritchie in the doorway of his own office, watching her steadily. To her surprise she saw that he was not laughing at her. Instead there was unexpected affection in his eyes. She dropped her own gaze hurriedly. Her fingers slipped on the keys and she had to stop to make an erasure. She had not seen Ritchie look at her like that since she had come to San Francisco. It was unsettling, disturbing. She had almost convinced herself that his old feeling for her had died completely. This opened the door again and set her emotions in a turmoil.

When she raised her eyes he was gone. But his look had been as personal as a caress and it warmed her all morning in the drafty office. It was hard now to remember Judith.

Since Nick and Ritchie did not always leave at the same time, and sometimes one, sometimes the other, had the automobile, Sara went home at the end of the day by cable car. She found herself lucky to get an outside seat where she would face outward with her back to the gripman as she clung to a metal post. Passengers stood on the steps crowded against her knees, but Sara hardly saw them. She loved the cable cars and the way warnings were shouted as they swung around curves, or went uphill or down.

At home her mother hung over her solicitously, plied her with a second bowl of warm soup as if she were an invalid, and expected her to be bone-tired. Sara was merely exhilarated. It was wonderful working in the outside world. She had needed to get away from this dull, dark house! And besides—there was the way Ritchie had looked at her.

That evening, remembering her promise to Allison, she went downstairs to tap on the door of Mrs. Renwick's sitting room. She heard voices before she was told to enter, but she had not expected to find the room so full of women.

Judith stood in the middle of the floor, while Miss Millie, her mouth filled with pins, knelt at her feet arranging a hem. Mrs. Renwick lay back in her favorite chair, giving directions, and in a straight chair nearby sat Geneva Varady. If it had not been for Geneva's presence, Sara might have withdrawn and returned another time to speak about Allison's clothes. But here, at last, was her chance to meet Geneva, and she went in eagerly.

"Hello, Sara," Mrs. Renwick called to her. "Come join our party and tell Miss Millie what you think of Judith's new dinner dress. You know Geneva Varady, don't you?"

"How do you do, Miss Varady," said Sara and took a chair near the girl.

Geneva acknowledged the introduction with a smile that was half shy, half friendly. As Sara was to find, she looked at everyone like that in the beginning, almost as if she expected to be rebuffed for a show of friendliness. It was a look that made Sara want to reassure her and she gave Geneva a warm smile.

Miss Millie merely grunted at her entrance and remarked that she needed no advice to do her work as it should be done. As Mrs. Renwick well knew, it was not her habit to work evenings. Her poor eyes took beating enough. And this was an extra on top of the trousseau things. It was only as an extreme favor that she had come here tonight at all.

Mrs. Renwick said, "Nonsense, Millie. You know you'd be disgraced for good if Judith had to go to the Riorden dinner in an old gown. Sara, tell us what you think. You know, Judith, Sara has quite an eye for fashion."

Sara had no desire to say what she thought. The gown was black lace over shining Nile-green satin, with a low square neck. Except for the neck, which Sara did not like, it was lovely. But on a sheet of tissue paper beside Miss Millie lay a heap of jewel-and-sequin-embroidered butterflies. Sara felt suspicious of any use which might be made of those butterflies.

"There," said Miss Millie, sitting back on her heels. "It's right now. Turn slow, Miss Judith. Real slow."

Judith turned obediently. As always she seemed a little remote from the scene about her, as if her thoughts were elsewhere and she had no interest in what was happening to her. The black lace flattered her fair skin and that shade of green went well with her ashen hair. But now Miss Millie rose from her knees and gathered up the butterflies.

"Turn toward the light, Miss Judith," she directed and began to pin glitter across the bodice of the gown.

In spite of herself, Sara gave a cry of distress. Everyone except Judith stared at her; Miss Millie with a distinctly sour expression.

"What happened to you?" Miss Millie asked. "Sit on a pin?"

Sara decided to speak her mind. "Miss Renwick doesn't need those butterflies. They'll spoil the effect completely."

For the first time Judith glanced across the room at her reflection in a tall mirror.

"What do you mean, Sara?" she asked.

Sara addressed herself solely to Judith. "Remember what you said about your room—that it didn't fit you. Those butterflies don't either. People want to look at *you*. That glitter is distracting. And you shouldn't wear a square neck either—"

"Square necks are being worn in Paris, if I may be

allowed to speak," said Miss Millie tartly. "And so are sequined butterflies. Appliquéd glitter is all the rage."

"That doesn't make it right." Sara left her chair and picked up a piece of extra lace. "Look—see how it would be if you put the lace in a heart-shaped scallop over that square of green. Place it so the edge of the lace is against her skin."

Mrs. Renwick applauded. "Good! She's right, Millie. I like that. Judith, you don't need that butterfly trash. You're enough in yourself."

Judith looked into the mirror for a moment, then nodded. "Yes, I like it that way. Do you think you can manage it, Miss Millie?"

The little dressmaker wrapped up her butterflies angrily. "I must say—when my customers begin taking the advice of an inexperienced chit, it's time for me to go elsewhere. You can finish the dress yourself, Miss Judith. I'll send my bill, for the hours of work I've put in so far."

She folded her bundle together, gave them all a stiff good evening and went out, offended pride bristling all about her. Sara stared after her in dismay. She had not meant to take work away from the little dressmaker.

Mrs. Renwick, however, seemed in no way perturbed. "She'll come back. She's been getting altogether too bossy lately. But she's not going to let anyone else take over for Judith's wedding."

Geneva said, "Do you mind if I talk to her?" and ran after Miss Millie.

"She won't be back in time to finish the gown," Judith said. "Now Ritchie won't want to take me to the dinner tomorrow night."

"I don't care about the Riordens," Mrs. Renwick

said. "But we can't disappoint Ritchie. Sara, don't you sew at all?"

"I'm no good at sewing," Sara said. "But perhaps my mother—"

Geneva had come back from her vain effort to placate Miss Millie. "I'll finish the dress for you, Judith," she offered. "If Miss Jerome will tell me what to do, I'll go to work on it right now."

"There you are!" Mrs. Renwick cried. "The matter is settled. Do get out of the dress, Judith, and let the girls have it."

When Sara had pinned the lace on the bodice of the gown, Judith went into her mother's bedroom to change. When she came back she looked breath-taking in a chrysanthemum-yellow flowered kimono, with long Japanese sleeves.

"I left the gown on the bed," she told the girls indifferently. "If you need me for another fitting, I'll be upstairs."

Mrs. Renwick agreed. "Run along, Judith. You're decorative, but no help. You can work in my bedroom, if you like, girls. I've a new novel I'm anxious to get to."

Sara went into the bedroom, filled with a sense of anticipation. Here, unexpectedly, was her opportunity to talk with Geneva Varady. As the other girl threaded her needle and went to work, Sara sat in the bay window and wondered how to begin.

"Have you always lived in San Francisco?" she asked at length.

Geneva, sewing in a chair pulled over to the bed where the gown rested, nodded without looking up from her work. Sara studied her thoughtfully. The girl had a small, pointed chin that gave her face the look of a valentine. Her brown hair grew down in a peak on her forehead, adding to the effect. It was a face too wide at the cheekbones for beauty, but her eyes were dark brown and expressive, and the general effect was one of mild prettiness. Indeed, everything about Geneva was mild. She was not the sort of person you could ever imagine losing her temper.

Sara decided to hesitate no longer. There was no need to be cautious with this meek little person.

"Have you always lived with Miss Hester Varady?" she asked directly.

This time Geneva looked up from her sewing, plainly startled. "Why—yes," she said hesitantly. Sara's very intensity seemed to force her on. "Aunt Hester took me into her own home and raised me when I was very little. I owe everything to her. But why are you interested in me, Miss Jerome?"

"I'm interested in San Francisco," Sara said. "But I know very little about it. I understand the Varadys are an old family. I was reading about them in a book lately."

The explanation seemed to satisfy Geneva. Her attention returned to her careful sewing. But she did not warm to the subject of San Francisco's old families.

This was getting her nowhere, Sara thought, and tried an even more direct course. "Do you know of anyone on your family tree named Bishop?" she asked.

Geneva's head was bent above her sewing. "Aunt Hester's younger sister Elizabeth married a man named Bishop."

Excitement prickled through Sara. "Did they have any children?"

Geneva considered for a length of time that made Sara jumpy. When she spoke, her words had nothing to do with ancestors.

"Do you think these stitches are small enough? And am I getting the lace in the right place?"

"Yes, yes, you're doing lovely work," Sara said. The delay was maddening.

Geneva held up the bodice of the dress and looked at it thoughtfully. "I do hope it's right. Children? I don't believe so. Both my Aunt Elizabeth and her husband were lost at sea. Of course Aunt Hester, and Elizabeth too, are really my great-aunts. Aunt Hester is in her sixties."

So again, Sara thought, her search had led to nothing. A blind alley. Except that there really had been a man named Bishop connected with the Varadys. To what branch of the Bishop family had Leland belonged? Plainly there was nothing more to be extracted from Geneva for the moment. Sara ceased her questioning and gave her attention to directing the work on Judith's gown.

More than once she saw the other girl glance at her curiously, but she did not discover why until the work had come to an end. Geneva fluffed out the dress, patted the rich material wistfully.

"Wouldn't it be wonderful to wear clothes the way Judith does? Have you seen some of the things in her wardrobe? She took me up to her room one time and let me look at all her gowns. I felt like a child in a candy store. Just to touch those lovely materials! And such beautiful styles. Though no more beautiful than she is."

This was not a topic which engrossed Sara. But she

wondered why Geneva Varady shouldn't have whatever clothes she desired. Geneva's frock was a dark bottle-green and old-fashioned in cut, but Sara had attributed the fact to a simple lack of taste on Geneva's part.

"Why should any Varady envy a Renwick?" Sara spoke her thought frankly.

"Oh, of course I don't envy her," Geneva said, and all but glanced over her shoulder as if she expected to be overheard. "It's just that my aunt doesn't believe in ostentation. She says a true lady can wear what she pleases and still be accepted."

Geneva's valentine face lighted with a surprising imp of mischief. This time she really looked over her shoulder toward Mrs. Renwick's sitting room before she spoke in a whisper.

"Aunt Hester does, too! Wears what she pleases, I mean. And no one respects her the less. But I'm not like that. I feel shabby in old clothes. Not that this dress really is shabby. The material is quite fine. But it lasts such a very long time."

"I expect it will be different when you marry," Sara remarked idly.

A look of such softness, such gentle love came into Geneva's face that all her affection for Nicholas Renwick was plain.

"I hope it will be," she said, "—if I marry."

Sara envied her a little. Geneva, at least, could wear her feeling for Nick openly. He was promised to no one else.

Geneva was watching her again. "Do you know— you remind me of someone. There's something about the way you tilt your head—a look in your eyes—something. I've been wondering about it all evening. It's tantalizing because I can't place it."

Sara leaned toward her. "Think! Think hard and tell me who it is!"

"I'm sorry," Geneva said, gently surprised by her eagerness, "I really can't remember. I'll tell you if I ever do. But now we'd better go upstairs and show Judith her dress. Nick had to go to a business meeting tonight, but he said he'd be here in time to drive me home. I want to be ready."

"Of course," Sara said, controlling her disappointment. She followed Geneva back to Mrs. Renwick's sitting room. The girl probably had the answers to all sorts of questions right in her head. But how was one to get them out?

Geneva held the dress up for Mrs. Renwick to see. But before they could take it to Judith, Nick came into the room.

Sara saw the look he gave Geneva. His lean, sensitive face, the gray eyes under dark brows, took on a softer expression at the sight of her. Allison, it seemed, was wrong in her notion that Nick did not return Geneva's affection.

"Happy about something, Jenny?" Nick asked.

"About seeing you, of course," Geneva admitted shyly, but without being coy. "And because Sara Jerome and I have had such fun tonight." She let Nick see the dress. "Look at the way we've fixed Judith's gown for the dinner tomorrow. Miss Jerome made some wonderful suggestions and Miss Millie went away mad, poor thing. So I did the sewing and Miss Jerome directed."

Nick smiled at Sara, his eyes friendly, approving. "It

seems you're going to be a welcome addition, Sara Jerome. Mr. Merkel reports that you did an excellent job
on the work he gave you today."

It was gratifying to earn Nick's approval and Sara
was pleased. But when she followed Geneva upstairs to
Judith's room the little glow of pleasure died. Ritchie
was lounging in the hall not far from Judith's door.

"I heard there was going to be a style show," he said.
"And I don't want to miss a thing."

Sara hardly looked at him as she took the dress from
Geneva's hands and carried it into Judith's room.
When she had explained a detail that Judith would
have to watch in getting into the gown, she said good
night quickly and went out of the room. Again her
glance went past Ritchie. She had no desire to stay and
watch Judith parade before his eyes. That moment
when he had stood watching Sara today in the office
had been something warm to hold to. She did not
want it so quickly erased.

Not until she was back in her own room did it occur
to her that she had completely forgotten the matter of
new dresses for Allison. Never mind—she would get to
that soon. It would be better to talk to Mrs. Renwick
alone. Indeed, this would give her an excuse for talking to Mrs. Renwick about other matters besides Allison.

As she undressed for bed she thought about this
further muddle of her possible relationship to the
Varadys. Every new thread that came into her hands
seemed to be as tenuous as all the others. They wound
about one another in a gauzy knot, but none of them
led clearly and simply to the center.

Her room was a little more comfortable now,

though hardly luxurious. She had found a small bed table in one of the other rooms and had made the purchase of a lamp with a china shade on her trip downtown with her mother. She lay in bed with the lamp burning for a little while, staring at cracks that streaked the ceiling, puzzling over her bits of knowledge.

If Hester's younger sister Elizabeth had married a man named Bishop—there lay the trail to her own heritage. But if these two had, as Geneva seemed to think, been lost at sea and left no children, then where did the trail lead?

If only she could talk to Miss Varady! How, she wondered, could one go about meeting Hester Varady? Through Geneva, perhaps? But though she and Geneva had worked pleasantly together tonight, there was no reason why she should invite the daughter of the Renwick housekeeper to meet her aunt.

Just as she went to sleep she began to think again of Ritchie. Of the way he had stood in the door of his office watching her with the old affection in his eyes. She was too sleepy to struggle against the picture. In spite of everything it was comforting and she was smiling as she fell asleep.

She still smiled when she wakened later to hear footsteps in the hall. But this time she did not stir beneath warm covers. Now she knew Nick's nocturnal habits of roaming the house. She was drowsing back to sleep when the tap sounded on her door. She propped herself on an elbow, turned on the lamp.

"Yes?" she called softly. "Who is it?"

There was no answer, only a second tap, more sharply insistent. Was Nick ill? Was there something he needed? She reached for her wrapper and bundled it about her. Then she went to the door and pulled it open.

Ritchie Temple stood in the hallway. He looked a little imperious, even annoyed that she had not come more quickly. Her heart began a deep, painful thudding in her breast.

EIGHT

"WH-WHAT IS IT?" SARA FALTERED.

"Obviously I can't talk to you standing in the hall like this," Ritchie said. He stepped past her into the room and closed the door behind him. The haughtiness went out of him and he spoke her name softly.

"Sara," he said. "I've missed you, Sara."

Sara moved quickly away from him across the room. She meant to trust neither Ritchie nor herself.

"In this house," he went on, "it seems as though I never have a chance to speak to you alone."

"This room isn't the place to speak to me," Sara said stiffly.

He moved then, came toward her impatiently. She had backed to the corner that held her bed and she reached out shakily for the brass bed knob. Her hand closed upon the same weapon she had used once before to rid herself of an intruder. It was the black umbrella with the crooked handle which she had hooked about Comstock. Ritchie was only a few steps away. In a moment she would be in his arms and she would be lost for certain.

She caught the umbrella up in her hand and bounced barefooted into the middle of the bed. Ritchie stared at her in blank astonishment. Then he dropped into the one armchair, choking with laughter.

This was not what she had intended. Sara lowered the umbrella and regarded him angrily. "Now what's the matter with you?"

He went into another paroxysm of mirth. "Lady defending her honor!" he choked. "Sara, you look so funny posed up there with that umbrella. Put it down so I can stop laughing."

Sara hooked the umbrella handle over the end of the bed and went to sit in a chair across the room from Ritchie. She felt miserable. From her position of grown-up young woman she had been reduced to the stature of a ridiculous child. She hated herself and hated Ritchie.

"That's better," he said.

"Don't talk so loudly," she snapped and threw an uneasy glance toward the door of the room.

"You needn't worry. Susan's room is on the other side of the house, and you know how soundly your mother sleeps."

She stared at him in distaste.

"It's hard to talk to you across the room like this," he went on. "Your reception isn't exactly what I'd pictured. Sara, what's wrong between us? Why don't we know each other any more?"

"I should think," said Sara, "that the reasons are obvious. Perhaps Judith is the most important one."

He seemed not to hear her. "Do you remember the talks we used to have at home in Chicago? On winter Sundays in the library? You always had your nose in a book and I could be sure to find you there. Such a lively, curious, eager little girl, you were, Sara."

She made a sound of displeasure, but he went right on.

"Such a bundle of stormy emotions! I used to love you very much."

"You were grown and I was a child," Sara said coldly. "I remember very well."

"No—you were always both older and younger than your years. But at that age the years mattered. My mother and yours would both have objected if we'd tried to marry at twenty and fifteen. But you were the only one I could talk to. The only one who would listen. Have you forgotten all that?"

"I've not forgotten," she said and held herself stiff in resistance against him—though he sat across the room. It was he who had forgotten.

When he moved from his chair her unruly heart began to thud again, but he went to the big central window and looked out upon the city.

"February!" he said. "Though you'd never know it. Roses in the garden and the grass as green as summertime."

"Don't you like it that way?" Sara asked.

"Like it? I detest it! I'd like to look out there and see snow on the rooftops and heaped in the streets. Icicles hanging from the eaves. Good winter snow that belongs with February. And a good old-fashioned elm tree, instead of those spooky eucalyptus trees. Sara, come here."

There was gentleness in his voice and he was no longer mocking her. When he was like that she could never resist him. She went to stand beside him at the window, though not too close, and he made no move to touch her.

"Do you know something, Sara? I hate this city!"

"But it's a beautiful, exciting city," Sara protested. "No one could hate San Francisco."

"I do. There it stands sliding down its hills in all its ugliness. Look at those houses with their gimcrack trimmings—carpenter's Gothic! The most horrible taste in America. Bow windows like fat bellies. Lath and jigsaw monstrosities. Even the downtown buildings are ugly. All wrong for a city like this."

"I thought *you* were going to build beautiful buildings out here," Sara said.

"It could be done. Back in Chicago Richardson and Sullivan have been preaching that form should follow function. And there's a young fellow named Wright who is doing things in terms of this country and time."

Sara could not suppress a small surge of triumph. "Judith said she could make you build your dreams. But she hasn't, has she?"

"Judith doesn't listen to me," he said.

She was surprised at the hurt in his voice and she couldn't help reaching out in the old way. "I'll listen—tell me."

He talked then as he used to do. A fog had crept in from the bay during the night and as Ritchie built with words, great shafts of steel and concrete seemed to shimmer tall in the mist. Sara, listening, made the discovery that Ritchie the dashing, the self-sufficient, the confident, did not entirely believe in himself. Was that what Judith had done to him, so that he needed a friend in this household, just as Sara Jerome needed one? They had reached out to each other tonight, without so much as a touching of hands between them.

He turned from the window, away from the fog. "Wait till you see how thick it gets later on. I hate the beastly stuff. There's something hushed and creeping about it. I feel smothered when the fog comes in. It's not like mist from Lake Michigan. Listen to those moaning horns on the water!"

Sara made no denial, but in her heart she knew she would love the San Francisco fogs as she loved all else about this city. She could stand endlessly by the window and watch the fog envelop the city in its embrace. But here was Ritchie beside her, and there was no mockery in him—only a need for her in his eyes. She forgot San Francisco and the fog, forgot Judith and the fact that Ritchie was going to marry her. She swayed a little toward him and her black, heavy braid swung forward and touched his hand.

The touch seemed to waken him from some dream. He lifted the heavy thickness and let it slip through his fingers wonderingly. And she had the sudden intuition that he was thinking of Judith's pale gold hair.

He turned abruptly away from her and went across the room to the door. In a moment he had closed it after him and she heard his light step moving toward the stairs.

She could only stare blindly after him while the throbbing in her blood quieted and a sick revulsion rose in her against her own body. Against her black hair and olive skin and all about her that was not fair and blond and pale. And against her own willful longings which made her want the forbidden.

Sara Jerome had never been easily given to tears. When she did cry it was in no ladylike manner. Now she flung herself down upon the bed while sobs shook her wildly, so that she had to stifle the sound with her pillow, lest somehow she be heard in this angry grief.

Tonight Ritchie had come back to her for a little while. He had needed her to talk to of his dreams, of the sore things that were in him. For a while he had loved her again and wanted her. Then her own black hair had swung between them, parting them. Judith still came first. He had never really turned away from her. Now, too, there was the thing she had only recently faced—that Judith had a right to come first.

Always before Sara had rushed headlong at life when an opportunity offered. She had been able to close her eyes blindly and reach out with stubborn hands for what she wanted. But now she had recognized Judith as a person and she could not rush in blindly. Who was to know what Judith thought and felt behind that cool exterior? Hating to consider her, Sara knew that she must do just that. There was no other way in which she could live with this unwelcome new self that had begun to stir within her and would not let her be again the child she wanted to be. If Ritchie broke his engagement to Judith, that was one thing. But unless he did, there was no step she could take.

Her tears dried at length, leaving her limp and helpless. She did not want to stand aside and let life wash over her head, submerging and defeating her. She

wanted to swim courageously against the current. But
how could she swim when she had no direction? How
could she do anything but strive to keep afloat?

By the next day she had steadied herself a little. The
only goal she could find was one of escape from this
house and the nearness to Ritchie. She might even seek
a new job so that she would no longer be near him at
the office. But she was still helpless when it came to
making the first step toward a change. She did not
know where to turn.

That evening on her way to the Riorden dinner,
Judith looked very beautiful in her gown of Nile-green
and black lace. Sara, coming downstairs, saw Ritchie
helping her into a long flower-embroidered opera cape
of black velvet. Judith's feet were hidden in carriage
boots, and she tucked one hand in a white kid glove
into the crook of Ritchie's arm. He smiled at her
proudly as they went out the door.

Sara turned away. She must think of other things,
forget those two, keep busy somehow. There was still
the matter of Allison's dresses. Here was a chance to
find Mrs. Renwick alone. Sara had seen little of Allison
in the last few days, but when she did see her, Allison's
bangs were still in place and her stockings were sometimes pulled quite straight.

Mrs. Renwick received Sara with pleasure and liked
her suggestion. "But of course the child shall have as
many new frocks as she wants. If you can work the
miracle of getting her to take an interest in her appearance, we'll all be grateful to you. Nick and I are both
delighted with her new bangs. All this is most generous of you, Sara."

Sara listened in embarrassment. "I think she would

look well in a dark shade of red," she suggested. "Some shades of blue too. Do you suppose Miss Millie is coming back to work for you after what happened?"

"We could never keep her away. But I think we had better give her free rein on the first dress she makes for Allison. You and I will decide on the goods and the color."

Sara pursed her lips. "Miss Millie is just the sort to pin butterflies on Judith, who doesn't need them, and make everything plain for Allison, who needs something to liven her up."

Mrs. Renwick reached for a box of opera mints on the table at her elbow and broke the seal. "Have some, Sara? Really, you know—you're rather a disrupting element in this house. I'm not sure I approve of you. I like having Allison's appearance and disposition improved. But I don't want to be drawn into controversies. I will not fight any battles for you and you might as well accept that fact. I don't want to be disturbed."

Sara took a green mint and bit into it, smiling. "I can fight my own battles. And you'd have a box seat."

Mrs. Renwick sighed and rubbed her temple with her fingers. "I wish Geneva were here tonight. She always brushes my hair when she comes and it helps my poor head." She looked plaintively at Sara, who rose readily to the occasion.

"Let me brush it. Sometimes I brush my mother's. She says I have a surprisingly gentle touch. Somehow Mama always expects me to bang things around."

"I can well see how that might be," said Mrs. Renwick dryly. "However, I'm happy to give you a try. Run in the bedroom and get my brush, there's a dear."

Sara came back with a silver-backed brush in her

hand. When she had pulled the pins from Hilda Renwick's heavy blond hair, she pressed her strong fingers on her scalp until Mrs. Renwick purred with pleasure.

"You make me feel just like Comstock, Sara. Geneva's little fingers could never manage this."

Sara went on, alternately massaging and brushing until the long strands shone like gold. And as she worked she talked.

"I've been reading some books I found in your library," she said in a conversational tone. "About California. I love this part of the country. I want to know all about it. While I was reading I came on the name of Geneva's family—the Varadys. And the Oliveros."

"There—right at the back of my neck," Mrs. Renwick said. "Mm—wonderful! Yes, California is full of romantic stories."

"It's too bad the Varadys have petered out in Miss Hester, isn't it?"

Mrs. Renwick laughed. "Petered out is not a term one uses about Hester Varady. Probably if the truth were known, her story's the most romantic and dramatic of the lot. The way she built that big house out on Van Ness Avenue when she was engaged to marry Martin Bishop. So they would have a place to live after they were married. And furnished it with all sorts of truck she imported from abroad. Then living in it all alone after Martin turned around and married her sister Elizabeth."

This was more than either book or Geneva had told.

"Have you ever been in the house?" Sara asked.

"Hardly. Miss Varady looks down her nose on vulgar Nob Hill. I can remember the way she snubbed William and me at the opera one night. I laughed for days afterwards, though only to myself. Poor Willie was so disturbed. Nobody had ever put him in his place before. He'd always had the notion that money could buy anything. He would really carry on now if he knew that his own son is seeing so much of Geneva Varady. Willie never forgave anyone who offended him."

"But then how does it happen that Miss Varady permits Geneva to see him—if she disapproves?"

"It's probably the hope of getting Geneva off her hands."

"But if her niece is a Varady and Miss Hester takes so much pride in the Varady name and blood—"

"Ouch!" Mrs. Renwick cried. "Remember about being gentle, Sara. I fancy the blood has thinned out with poor little Jenny. Though we don't really know what her connection is with the family. The matter has always been peculiarly hush-hush. Frankly, I don't think the child knows herself. Miss Varady chooses not to discuss the matter with her, and has even led the girl to feel that it would be better if she did not ask too many questions. I've wondered at times if Geneva really is a Varady. Not that it matters. We're extremely fond of her."

Sara, however, was less interested in Geneva's connection than she was in her own. "What happened to Elizabeth after she married Martin Bishop?"

"Oh, that's the saddest part of the story. They went on a voyage around the Horn to New York. But the ship was lost at sea and none of the passengers was ever heard of again."

"So Hester Varady lost her lover twice over," Sara mused.

"Don't waste any pity on her. She is made of nails and granite, I'm sure. She probably thought it a fit punishment for them both and reveled in it."

"And since they left no children, that was the end of their line?" Sara asked.

Mrs. Renwick's words surprised her. "Who says they left no children?"

"Why—Geneva did."

"I'm afraid Geneva has had her head filled with a great deal of nonsense. And since she believes anything a body tells her, it must be easy enough for Hester to stuff her with what she pleases."

Sara held the brush still. "You mean there *were* children?"

"One. I understand he was a handsome little boy. Fortunately—or perhaps not, depending how you look at it—his parents left him at home when they went off on their fateful voyage. Miss Varady took him in and raised him from babyhood. Leland, I think his name was. But I gather he grew up a rather bad lot. Went in for gambling his aunt's money away and getting into scrapes of one sort and another. Of course we didn't know the family, so this is all gossip of the sort Miss Millie likes to spread. Sara, you are forgetting to brush."

Sara recovered herself and lifted the brush again. "And this boy, Leland Bishop—what became of him?" she asked, trying not to sound as breathless as though she had been running for a long time.

"What a one you are for stories! I gather Hester disowned him a couple of times. But he kept showing up like a bad penny. Married some girl of no consequence and brought her home to his aunt's house.

There was a baby, I think. But in the end Hester packed the lot of them off and washed her hands of her nephew. And that's the last San Francisco saw of the Bishops. It was then that Hester took this poor relation, Geneva, out of the Sisters' hands and decided to raise her as an heir."

Sara brushed with slow, regular strokes, her thoughts far away until Mrs. Renwick told her she might stop. When she said good night, Sara ran upstairs and climbed to the high post of her tower. There was no fog tonight, but it was raining again. She looked out upon the drenched city, feeling a greater kinship with it than ever.

The pieces of the puzzle were falling into place now. Leland Bishop was her father. Elizabeth Varady Bishop her grandmother. And Miss Hester Varady was her great-aunt. Where Geneva fitted as a distant cousin, did not matter.

And there was a house. A big house on Van Ness Avenue. That was the street her friend the fireman had mentioned as a place where a stand could be taken if there were every again a really bad fire in San Francisco. The Varady house on Van Ness Avenue had been the place of her birth. It was part of her heritage. She must find some way to visit it.

She wondered what would happen if she should confront her mother with the details of her knowledge. But no—she knew what would result. And she had to have the answers to these mysteries, without interference from her mother.

She stayed in her tower so late, lost in her dreams, that she heard Judith and Ritchie come home from their dinner party. She looked down upon their carriage as it turned into the driveway at the side of the house and felt a little superior toward them. Who, after all, were the Renwicks and the Temples, when *she* was a Varady? But the feeling, she realized, was an empty one and far from satisfying.

The rain and stormy winds kept on into March, but the hills were green and flowers bloomed with a lush growth Sara had never seen in Chicago.

Her work at the office went on, and so far Sara had taken no step toward the house on Van Ness Avenue. When she met Miss Hester Varady she wanted to know exactly what she would do and say. This time she would not rely on impulse. But how to accomplish her purpose was a problem to which she had found no answer.

As the weeks passed, the office lost something of its early glamour for Sara. She discovered that there was a certain monotony about the insurance business. She couldn't blame Ritchie for the boredom he betrayed and for his constant absences from his office. She continued to type the letters given her with care, but now she yawned over them a little. She was yawning absentmindedly when she carried a batch into Ritchie's office one day for his signature.

He looked up at her, smiling. "Don't yawn, Sara. You'll get me started too. Sit down and tell me what a wonderful businessman you think I am. Maybe I can even dream up more letters to write somebody. Just don't go away and leave me to this solitary confinement."

He crossed the room suddenly and closed the door. Sara knew this restless mood of Ritchie's. It could be dangerous. She opened her tablet in a businesslike manner and got her pencil ready. She had been on guard and carefully impersonal ever since that night he had come to her room. But Ritchie ignored her preparations for work. He leaned over and kissed the nape of her neck.

"No umbrellas around today," he said. "So you can't do a thing to me. Sara, Sara, come here!"

Tablet and pencil scattered as he pulled her none too gently into his arms. The breath went out of her in a long sigh and with it went all her intended resistance. She had wanted for so long to be in his arms. Her lips remembered his and responded with joy.

He laid his cheek against her and laughed softly in her ear. "Where is all that outraged resistance you led me to expect? What a fake you are! I can feel your heart thumping right under my own. It's giving you away, Sara. I'm glad you love me, even if Judith doesn't!"

His flippant words made her head stop whirling and she pushed away from him. Mr. Merkel could walk into Ritchie's office easily through adjoining doors and find him making cheap love to his secretary. It was better not to answer at all, better not to trust herself with so much as another look in Ritchie's direction. She retrieved her notebook and pencil and walked quickly out of the office.

A dowdy-looking woman sat in the anteroom and Sara gave her a careless glance as she returned to her desk. There were some letters for Mr. Merkel which required typing and she rolled paper in the machine, went furiously to work, hoping no one would notice that her color was high, her breathing quick. She must concentrate somehow. Somehow she must forget

Ritchie's arms, the way his lips had felt upon her own. She was angry with herself that all her resolute decisions had fallen to nothing at his first touch. When she tried to work she made mistakes and had to erase. What had he meant about Judith not loving him?

She was hardly aware of what went on around her until Miss Dalrymple at the next desk spoke under her breath.

"Don't look now, but you seem to be the center of attention."

Sara, her thoughts still whirling so that she hardly knew her left hand from her right, looked at once. And she couldn't help jumping. The dowdy woman had left her bench and come to stand beside the wooden partition that separated waiting room from office. Her interest seemed focused upon Sara, who could only stare at her in surprise.

This, she realized, was not dowdiness, after all. It was merely that this tall woman with the iron-gray hair was dressed in garments of ten or fifteen years ago. She wore a bold, rich costume of dark red, handsomely banded with wide black velvet. Her sleeves were huge and puffed—long out of style, and there were impressive rows of jet across her bosom. On her head she wore a small bonnet of dark sable and velvet, old-fashioned in every detail, yet somehow distinguished.

It was the woman's eyes, however, which held Sara's. They were dark and set deep in their sockets. The lids were heavy and when she blinked she did so slowly, as if nothing would ever ruffle or hurry her, if she chose not to hurry.

"Stop staring, girl," the woman said unreasonably, since she herself had fixed Sara with the steadiest of stares. The heavy lids blinked once and the intent gaze turned upon the openmouthed Miss Dalrymple. "You," she said and it was as if she had snapped her fingers at a lackey. "Go and tell Mr. Merkel that Miss Varady has been kept waiting long enough."

"Yes'm," said Miss Dalrymple and all but dropped a curtsy before she scuttled away.

Sara sat with her fingers frozen upon the typewriter keys. This was the woman she had dreamed of facing, but her appearance was too sudden, too dramatic. Sara felt like a schoolgirl, confused and at a loss.

"Stand up," Miss Varady said. "Let's have a look at you."

There could be no disobeying that autocratic tone. Sara pushed her chair back and stood, her own gaze held completely by Hester Varady's.

"You're the Jerome girl," said Miss Varady.

It was a statement, not a question, and Sara bristled at the tone. Suddenly the compulsion under which she had been held was gone. Her own will revived and she faced Miss Varady coolly, almost insolently.

"No," she said. "I am not the Jerome girl. I am Sara Bishop."

NINE

EVEN ON A BRIGHT DAY THE VAST RENWICK DINING ROOM was a gloomy place. Dark wood paneled the walls, and the furniture too was dark, reflecting no color or light. Judith stood before the sideboard arranging roses in a silver bowl. Sara was helping her. Sara, Judith had found, had a way with flowers, and she had asked her to do the centerpiece. In the doorway Nicholas Renwick stood watching them. As always his lean face had a faintly saturnine look about it.

Judith was giving a dinner party tonight. As Nick had commented, "Another one!" Whenever it was possible he avoided these social affairs. But Geneva would be coming this time so he had to put in an appearance.

"Don't you ever get tired of social rounds?" Nick asked his sister.

Judith shrugged, not looking up as she clipped the stems of the roses. "Ritchie enjoys them. And we owe so many dinners because of invitations we've accepted. Besides, what else is there to do?"

"A very good question," Nick said and he sounded so irritable that Sara glanced at him in surprise.

Nick had always seemed to her an equable, good-natured person. This afternoon at the office he had come out to placate Miss Varady without becoming annoyed or toadying to her. Ritchie had stayed in his office to avoid her. But Nick had explained calmly that Mr. Merkel had been called away unexpectedly. He himself would be glad to go over Miss Varady's business in Mr. Merkel's place. Hester Varady looked at Nick as if she had never seen him before and remarked coldly that she preferred to do business only with the firm's *senior* partner. Nick walked to the door with her, his dignity unshaken, and Sara had felt quite proud of him. She had not particularly liked it when Ritchie had put his head out the door of his office when he was sure Miss Varady was gone and remarked that the lady was an old harridan.

Sara managed to get little done the rest of the afternoon. She was keyed to a high pitch of excitement, and there seemed to be no way to let off steam.

It had been frustrating to have Nick come out of his office at the very moment when she had made her dramatic announcement to Miss Varady. He had not heard her and Hester Varady had not so much as blinked her heavy-lidded eyes. She had looked at Sara as if the name "Bishop" meant no more to her than "Smith." She had said, "Indeed?" and turned at once to Nick as he came toward her. And she had not glanced at Sara again when she left the office.

Just the same, thought Sara, arranging pink and

white phlox in a low white wedgewood dish, Miss Varady had known who she was. She would not have asked a complete stranger to stand up for inspection. And she had used the name "Jerome" with knowledge. But what her conclusions had been there was no way of telling.

Judith stood off to get the effect of the roses she had prepared for the piano in the drawing room. "Just what would you suggest instead of parties?" she asked her brother.

"I suppose that requires no answer," Nick said. "I doubt that anyone in this house will take up my drastic solutions. Except perhaps Sara." He threw her a half-amused look. "Sara at least is always ready for something new—such as running off to interview firemen."

"Did you do that, Sara?" Judith asked.

"I suppose Allison has told on me," said Sara.

"With a great deal of admiration," Nick admitted. "She has been coaxing me to take her down to the same firehouse ever since."

Judith sucked at a finger she had pricked. "And what did you learn. Sara, talking to your fireman?"

Sara leaned over the long, damask-covered table to set her centerpiece in place. The shades of pink and white went well with the silver.

"He's not *my* fireman," she said. "I came on him just after the engines had gone out to a fire. I wanted to see the fire too, but he discouraged me. Since he was ready to talk, I stayed a while. He says San Francisco is considered a very bad insurance risk."

"A sound opinion indeed," said Nick. "I'd hate to think what would happen to Renwick and Merkel if the city went up in another blaze. That's why we charge high rates."

"Well, let's not have a fire tonight," Judith murmured. "It would spoil my party. Thank you, Sara. The flowers look lovely. Now I'll have to hurry if I'm to bathe and dress and be ready in time."

She went out of the room with her usual grace, not hurrying in the least. Nick stared at the beautifully laid table with its candlesticks ready, its silver and napery and crystal shining, and drew down his brows in a frown.

"Sometimes I think it would be fun to take hold of a corner of that cloth and just walk off, holding onto it. A most satisfactory mess it would make. Don't you think so, Sara?"

Sara felt shocked and a little troubled. Nicholas Renwick was the one strong center about which this household revolved. The rest of them might do foolish things—except Judith, of course—but Nick was serious and sound and clear-sighted. He worked hard in the insurance office, as Ritchie did not, and he didn't go around with impossible dreams in his eyes. Guiltily she darted away from this faint disloyalty to Ritchie.

Nick laughed at her expression. "Don't look so astonished, Sara Jerome. Have you never wanted to make a really fine mess of things? Have you never felt it would be gratifying to stop doing what you're supposed to do and do what nobody ever expected you to?"

"I don't know," said Sara. "I'm afraid I hardly ever do what I'm supposed to do. I quite often make a mess of things."

"At least that might furnish variety," he said. "Now

take Judith and me. We grew up under my father's rule and neither of us ever managed to squirm out from under his thumb. Don't misunderstand—I had the greatest admiration and respect for my father, but I'm not sure that I ever loved him. After his death, when I was ready to strike out for myself, sink or swim—circumstances prevented me. So you see I've been a pretty tiresome fellow, Sara, always doing what I'm supposed to do, and accomplishing nothing that really matters."

The circumstances, Sara knew, had been a houseful of women who needed him. She thought him admirable, not tiresome, but she didn't know what to say in response. By the faint twinkle in his eyes she judged that he expected no answer.

"Anyway," she said, "I don't want to smash things just for the fun of it. And I can't imagine you doing that either. Besides, what could be more fun than to go to dinners like this? To dress up as Judith does and talk to clever people who are so rich they can have anything they like. All the clothes and jewels and lovely homes—"

Nick shook his head. "Wake up, Sara! You've got things badly twisted. As a matter of fact, you have more yourself than all this put together."

Sara went past him through the door and then turned back. "What have I?" she demanded.

"Life," he told her without hesitation. "You're brimming with it. It's the thing we all sense when we look at you, Sara. A quality that makes us more than a little envious."

She thought this nonsense. What good was it to brim with life when she could do so little living? No, it took money, possessions, position, to make living possible. She was learning that more than ever here in the Renwick house.

"I haven't anything," she said as she went toward the stairs. "I haven't even one silk taffeta petticoat to my name, while Judith has dozens."

Nick laughed out loud and she knew she had sounded like a child again. She did not look back as she ran up the stairs.

But his voice stopped her at the landing. "Sara—if you want to look down through the balusters tonight I won't say a word. And you'll have the second floor all to yourself."

She did not answer, hating the fact that he thought her so young. Up to the third floor she hurried and shut herself into her room. Across the bed lay a cambric petticoat—the source of her impatient remark to Nick. She had sat up late last night sewing a false border of taffeta clumsily around the hem in a dust ruffle that she hoped would make her rustle silkenly like Judith. Now she picked up the skirt and tossed it into her wardrobe closet to get it out of sight. She didn't want a single ruffle. She wanted a whole dozen rustling taffeta petticoats of her very own. Or at least she wanted to believe that was her desire. The things Nick had said were confusing, and she did not want to be unsure, confused.

That evening, lonelier than ever, she picked up some Bret Harte stories she had found in the library and went to tap on her mother's door. At home in Chicago they had sometimes spent happy evenings reading aloud to each other. But her mother worked hard in this house—it was so much bigger than the Temples', and there were so many more matters to supervise that she had been going to bed as early as she could.

Tonight she had stretched out on her bed and when Sara went in she found her lying there wearily with her eyes closed.

"Would you like me to read to you for a while?" Sara asked, pulling up a chair beside the bed. "I've found some interesting stories in the library."

Mrs. Jerome was pleased and Sara settled down in her chair, turning pages to find a story. From downstairs the flurry of guests arriving drifted up to them—the laughter, the high voices of the women, the lower tones of the men, all gay and carefree. Quickly Sara started to read, to shut out the festive sounds with her own voice and the words of the author.

Her mother listened contentedly and Sara began to relax and enjoy these moments of an interest shared. At length Mrs. Jerome began to drowse and when she fell asleep, Sara returned quietly to her own room.

Dinner was over by now and she could hear Judith's music coming from the drawing room. Someone always asked her to play and she always complied. Again it was her usual perfect, emotionless music and tonight it made Sara angry to hear it. She thought with sudden sympathy of Nick's remark about the mess he would enjoy making of that whole beautiful table. Judith's music put her own teeth on edge like that and she began to walk nervously back and forth across her room.

The tap on Sara's door stopped her restless prowling. Ever since the night Ritchie had come here, she had been half afraid he might return. He must never come in again, of course. Being so close to him that afternoon in the office had been dangerous to the cool head she must keep. She knew Ritchie. He would be willing to have his beautiful Judith and Sara Jerome too, if it could be managed without inconvenience to himself.

The tap came again, sounding faintly anxious. Ritchie did not rap like that. Besides, Ritchie would be downstairs. He could hardly disappear while his fiancée was playing for their guests.

Sara opened the door to find Geneva Varady turning away.

"Oh," said Geneva, "I'm glad you're in."

Surprised at finding this particular visitor at her door, Sara stood in the doorway staring.

"May—may I come in?" Geneva asked hesitantly. "I'd rather not have anyone know I've come up here."

Sara stepped back. "Of course. Do come in. I'll put some more coal on the fire. I don't mind the drafts up here the way some people do. We had such cold winters in Chicago."

Geneva waited until Sara had closed the door. Then she seated herself in the one straight chair and regarded her clasped hands uncomfortably. Sara glanced about the room in distaste. Its appearance did not matter too much to her, since she regarded it as a temporary station on her journey to something else. But she disliked having Geneva, who bore the Varady name and probably knew great luxury, see how Sara lived in this house.

"I don't know what you'll think of me for intruding on you like this, Miss Jerome," Geneva ran on. "This is not something I would have done if—" She broke off and moved her hands apart helplessly.

She seemed so distressed that Sara's own confidence began to return.

"That's quite all right," Sara said cheerfully, though still at a loss as to the reason why Geneva was here. Unless Miss Varady—she looked at the girl sharply. "Did your aunt send you?"

Geneva's pointed chin came up, her pale little face turned toward Sara in surprise. "How did you know?"

"I guessed," said Sara. She put a shovelful of coal on the fire, her back to her guest.

"I'm so bewildered," Geneva said. "Though of course I never question Aunt Hester." She shivered delicately at the thought. "She has been quite indignant because I first mentioned your name and presence in this house to her only recently. She feels I should have told her long before. But how was I to know she would have a special interest in you? Since she knew I was coming here to the dinner tonight she sent you a message. She was very particular about saying that no one else in the house was to know, so I've not even told Nick. Aunt Hester would like you to come to tea at our house next Sunday afternoon. That's day after tomorrow."

Sara left the fireplace and walked about the room again. This was the beginning. It was the first step and it had come from Miss Varady! Nevertheless, she felt faintly nettled by the tone of command behind the invitation. There had been a time when Hester Varady must have treated Mary Jerome very badly. Mary's daughter did not want to capitulate too quickly.

"This Sunday?" she murmured. "I'm not sure that I can. I had some plans—"

Geneva gave a chirp like a frightened bird. "Oh, but

you must! Aunt Hester doesn't ever take 'no' for an answer. You know it really is a compliment she is paying you. She hardly ever has guests any more. She only asks Nick to tea or dinner once in a while, and no one else from this house."

"I don't believe I can accept," Sara said, though she knew perfectly well that she meant to eventually.

Geneva looked as if she might burst into tears. "I'll never dare go home and tell her that. She'll say I didn't ask you, or that I offended you. Have I offended you, Miss Jerome?"

"No, of course not," Sara said. "If you put it like that, I suppose I'll have to agree. But please make it clear to your aunt that I wasn't sure at first that I could arrange it on such short notice. How am I to get to your house without the family knowing?"

"Aunt Hester thought of that. You might take a walk of a Sunday afternoon, mightn't you? I can wait for you in the carriage a few blocks away. And I'll bring you home again. You needn't be gone for more than an hour. Surely you can manage that?"

Sara nodded, still pretending hesitance as Geneva set the time and exact place. Aunt Hester was not going to have everything exactly her way with *this* niece.

"Did your aunt suggest any reason for this invitation?" Sara asked.

"None at all. But that's like her. She often does surprising things. I happened to tell her about the way you stopped Miss Millie from putting those dreadful butterflies on Judith's dress the other night. And about your working in Nick's office. She doesn't go out a great deal herself and she always wants to know what's going on. But why she wishes to see you, I haven't any idea." Geneva shook her head and rose from her chair.

"Do you have to go back right away?" Sara asked. She had more questions she wanted to ask Geneva about the house on Van Ness Avenue. But the girl was already moving toward the door.

"It wouldn't do to have them miss me downstairs. Everyone is listening to Judith's playing, so it was easy for me to slip out. I want to get back before she stops."

Sara stood in the doorway watching Geneva hurry down the stairs. Somehow, now that the meeting was set, she felt a little uneasy. There was a disloyalty to her mother involved which did not rest comfortably on her conscience. Yet she knew she must take this step and that she did not dare to tell her mother about it.

TEN

BY GOOD FORTUNE THERE WAS NO RAIN ON SUNDAY AFTER noon, though a fog was rolling in from the bay. It drifted at hilltop height, but did not envelop the streets. Sara, who had already shown a liking for foggy days, told her mother she was going for a good long walk, and left the house on the downhill side. No one mentioned the threat of footpads any more, providing she confined her excursions to the daytime.

At the appointed corner Geneva awaited her in Miss Varady's shabby, old-fashioned carriage. She appeared relieved to see Sara and signaled the coachman to drive off the moment her guest was settled.

"I was afraid you might not come," she murmured nervously, as Sara settled down beside her. "How very nice you look."

Sara had worn her best gray suit again and a small hat with a silver-gray feather curled along the brim. It was an old hat which her mother had retrimmed for her and she wore it tipped slightly toward her nose.

Geneva sat back in her corner of the carriage, at a loss to make conversation with someone she must regard as an odd visitor to her aunt's house. The carriage rolled downhill toward Van Ness, passing the tightly packed houses of a poorer section, all with the fat bow windows which Ritchie had decried.

"Have you recalled who it is I remind you of?" Sara asked Geneva when the silence grew long.

The other girl shook her head. "I've checked everyone I could think of and I haven't found a clue. But now the first feeling I had of recognition has gone, so I'll probably never remember. I mentioned it to Aunt Hester and she gave me the queerest look."

Geneva hesitated, glancing up at the wreathing of fog as it drifted above them, blotting out the highest turrets.

"I wonder if you'd mind if I say something," Geneva went on.

"Anything you like," said Sara.

"It's about Aunt Hester. You seem to be rather an independent person, and—and it might be that you could easily irritate her. She is really a very remarkable woman and I am grateful to her for all she has done for me. But she can be—terrifying when she becomes angry. She doesn't like to be crossed in any way. So—whatever it is she wants of you this afternoon—may I suggest—"

"I'm not afraid of Miss Hester Varady," Sara put in firmly.

"That's exactly what *I* am afraid of," Geneva said with a quick sidelong look at Sara. "Aunt Hester enjoys having people afraid of her. I don't think she can help it. But it's not good for her to become too excited. Last year she had a dreadful row with one of her tenants and she was so ill afterwards she had to go to bed."

"Are you really fond of her?" Sara puzzled. She could imagine feeling kinship and respect for Hester Varady, but she could not imagine feeling an affection toward her.

"She is all the family I have, except perhaps Ah Foong."

"Ah Foong?"

Geneva relaxed in her corner and a smile dispelled her worried expression. "I still say 'God bless Ah Foong' in my prayers every night, just as I used to as a little girl. He has been with Aunt Hester since long before I was born and I expect he is her very best friend, even though she is the mistress and he the servant. Ah Foong cooks and serves our meals. And he scolds our maids—when we have one, since they never stay for long."

"I've heard about how wonderful Chinese servants are in San Francisco," Sara said. "Will I see Ah Foong today?"

"If I know him he'll be right there to look you over. If Aunt Hester has told anyone why you're coming today, it would be Ah Foong. He's very old and wise. I don't know what I'd have done without him as a child. He's the one person who isn't ever afraid of Aunt Hester, and he can take her in hand when she goes on a rampage and get her quieted as no one else is able to."

Once more Sara felt drawn to Geneva as she had been the first time she had seen her. If ever she were established with Aunt Hester, she might be able to stand up for Geneva, as the girl was unable to stand up for herself. As yet Geneva didn't know of the blood relationship between them. She couldn't know that she did have someone else who was "family." How odd it was that Miss Varady chose not to tell her.

The carriage had turned a corner and Geneva glanced out the window. "Here we are on Van Ness Avenue."

Sara gave her attention to the wide residential street, with handsome houses lining both sides. Van Ness, though it boasted its own slope, was a valley between high hills. There was little view here except of hilltops around. But apparently it was an avenue of worth and dignity. Its houses were not as big as the mansions on Nob Hill, but they had an air of being old and respected citizens with none of the show-off manners of the Bonanza rich. Family meant more than money here. Sara fixed her attention on house after house as they passed and a sense of anticipation grew in her. Would she have a feeling of recognition about the house of her birth? Would it speak to her in any way?

But when Geneva said, "There's Aunt Hester's house —the big brown one on ahead," Sara had no conviction that she had ever seen it before. No chord of memory reverberated.

Hester Varady's house looked like something out of a fairy tale, with its gloomy turrets and peaked roofs. Vines grew heavily over the front windows as if the house wanted to hide its secrets from the street. Undoubtedly Ritchie would have thought such architecture horrible, but Sara loved the structure on sight.

This was a house Miss Varady might wear as fittingly as she wore her handsome, old-fashioned gowns.

At one side grew two tall eucalyptus trees and Sara felt that they too belonged in this setting. The carriage stopped at the concrete block before the house and Geneva got out first, waited for Sara. As they went up the steps together Sara felt a certain tensing in Geneva's manner. For a while in the carriage, when she spoke with affection of Ah Foong, she had seemed relaxed and at ease. But now, approaching her aunt's presence, she had tightened as if in instinctive self-protection. Sara pitied her and was determined not to let Hester Varady frighten her.

Ah Foong answered their ring. He was small and shriveled, with the fore part of his head quite bald, though the back hair grew into the conventional long pigtail. His face was leathery in texture and color and amazingly wrinkled. Out of this network looked a pair of eyes as black and lively as any Sara had ever seen in a young person. He wore the usual blue trousers and tunic of the Chinese house servant.

Geneva he ignored as they came in, though she spoke to him. All his attention was fixed upon Sara and she smiled at him warmly, sensing the need to win him as a friend, to have him on her side. He would have known her father. That was why he looked at her like this.

He did not, however, return her smile. He said, "Missy Valady this way. You come." Then he looked at Geneva and shook his head as if he spoke to a small child. "Missy Valady no wantchee you. Jus' Missy Sala."

"I understand." Geneva smiled apologetically at

Sara. "I've been banished for a little while. I—I hope everything will go well."

The big hallway was dimly lit. Sara could just make out a wide stairway toward the rear which ran up several steps to a landing, then turned right to the upper floors. In the wall above the landing was set a circular window of stained glass, permitting faint, colored light to filter through.

The door to which Ah Foong motioned opened on the right—the side of the house where the eucalyptus trees stood. Sara stepped to the door and found this room brightened to some degree by lights in a crystal chandelier. A fire, flanked with big brass andirons, had been lighted in a grate beneath the marble mantelpiece, and Miss Varady sat before it, erect in a stiff chair with a high, ornately carved back.

As Sara crossed the room she was aware of a musty, airless odor and masses of heavy dark furniture, carved and uncomfortable-looking.

But it was the woman by the fire who held her fullest attention. Miss Varady wore her iron-gray hair in a frizz of bangs across her forehead, and wound into a chignon on the back of her neck. She was gowned in heavy watered silk of kingfisher blue. Apparently Hester Varady did not hold with the notion that older women should wear black. Color became her, suited her bold, vigorous air of authority.

Today she seemed more gracious than she had been that time in the office. When Sara reached her she rose and held out her hand. Something which passed for a smile softened a mouth carved against ivory.

"How do you do, Sara Bishop," said Hester Varady. Sara put her own strong hand into Miss Varady's and found that lady as large of bone as she. Her aunt's hand was cold and dry, however, and Sara was glad to be released from its chilly clasp. She took the chair Miss Varady indicated; a stiff chair with a leather seat, that looked to be Spanish in origin. Ah Foong performed an odd little bob in Miss Varady's direction and went soft-footed from the room.

After her first response to her aunt's greeting, Sara sat as silent as her hostess, suddenly less sure of her wisdom in coming here. She looked about, trying to pretend a casual manner as she waited for Miss Varady to speak. Over the mantel hung a painting of a woman and Sara wished she could see it more clearly. Vine-grown windows, heavy velvet draperies shut out the daylight, and the distant chandelier did not reveal the picture's detail.

Miss Varady stirred in her chair. "There's a candle-stick on the piano. Fetch it here."

Sara glanced at her, startled. Then she walked the length of the drawing room to the closed grand piano at the far end. A tall side window nearby, unshrouded by vines, let misty daylight through. Sara saw that the music rack on the piano was not entirely free of dust, that its carving showed traces of cobweb. Apparently this room was not in frequent use. She picked up the tall silver candlestick and returned to the woman by the fireplace.

"You can light the candle at the fire," Miss Varady said.

Sara held the candle's tip to a red coal and awaited her aunt's direction.

"Well!" said Miss Varady. "You wanted to see the picture, didn't you? Then look at it!"

The candle flame flickered in a draft, then flamed high. It did not cast sufficient light to fully illumine the painting above the mantel, but at least Sara could see that it was the portrait of a young girl. A beautiful, striking girl with haunting dark eyes and teeth that flashed white in her smile. Her gown was the color of sunshine, her black hair almost hidden beneath a white lace mantilla draped over a high comb.

Sara felt a sense of recognition. This was Consuelo Olivero. Consuelo Varady. The smiling face looked oddly familiar, but Sara could not think who it was she resembled.

"Do you know who she is?" Miss Varady asked.

Sara answered at once. "Yes—my great-great-grandmother, Consuelo Varady."

Hester made no denial. "You look like her. Geneva has been trying to remember who it is you remind her of. She did not think of this picture, which is just as well. I prefer that for the moment Geneva should know nothing about why I wished to see you, or who you are."

With a minimum of words Sara had come a long way in this house. She had been accepted without question, she had been allied to some extent on her aunt's side. The future promised to be exciting, yet her first uneasiness remained. If only she knew more of what had happened to her mother in this house. She set the candlestick on the mantel, where it threw a faint light on Consuelo's small feet. Apparently Sara's good-sized bones did not come from the Oliveros. Judging by her aunt, they must be a Varady heritage.

Once more Sara seated herself in the embossed leather chair and waited.

"You seem to be better acquainted with the Varady side of your family than I had expected," her aunt went on. "Did your mother tell you these things?"

Sara shook her head. "Only my father's name, and that I was born in San Francisco. She has never answered my questions. Lately I've been searching through books of California history. First I found the Varady name and then Olivero. And Mrs. Renwick told me your sister had married a man named Martin Bishop, that they had a child whom you raised—Leland. Mrs. Renwick doesn't know why I am interested."

"At least you show some enterprise," said Miss Varady. "Geneva accepts what I say and asks no questions. Geneva is a timid fool."

Sara said nothing. She was not yet in a position to stand up for Geneva.

"Your father proved a great disappointment to me," Miss Varady continued. "He had no sense of family worth, no pride in the name of Varady which was his mother's. With every opportunity given him he threw his chances away, got into one disgraceful scrape after another. I sent him out of town and hushed things up more than once. He had charm, but was without scruples."

Sara stiffened at these words against her father.

"I wish my father were here to speak for himself. I don't remember him at all. I have only an old picture of him."

Miss Varady looked at her niece without rancor. "At least you say what you think. You don't tremble and trip over your tongue. It may be that you will do."

"Do?" Sara echoed the word.

"This is not the time to explain. I don't know you yet. And I have been disappointed before. Do you realize that if your mother had not run away, taking you with her, you might have been raised in this house? Then perhaps I would not have bothered with Geneva, whose blood is not as good as yours."

"My mother wanted to get away from San Francisco and what she calls its wickedness. She didn't want me to come back at all."

"Mary Bishop was always a ninny," said Miss Varady flatly.

Sara did not like that. "My mother is not a ninny," she told Miss Varady. "If she was afraid of this town, perhaps there was something here for her to fear."

A faint pinkness tinged Miss Varady's cheekbones. Her lids lowered over dark eyes for a moment and then raised again. It was her only show of emotion.

"I know what she feared," she said. "If you had grown up in this house you would have belonged to me. Mary Bishop was scarcely strong enough to stand against me. She was afraid to lose her daughter."

"Then perhaps she was wise to escape," said Sara.

"Escape—escape! As though I held her prisoner! What brought you back to San Francisco?"

"I wanted to come," Sara said. But she changed the subject quickly. "I have always wanted to know what became of my father. Can you tell me?"

Miss Varady's blue-veined hands tightened upon the arms of her chair. The tinge of pink turned to red in her cheeks. "That last time he disappeared without a trace. As far as I am concerned he is dead. We do not discuss the matter in this house. Never ask such a question again."

For an instant Sara felt chilled. Though her aunt had not moved, or raised her voice, there was cold venom in her tone and Sara was conscious through all her nerves of a force of personality so strong, so ruthless, that nothing could stand against it and win. What this woman wanted she would have. What she chose to do she would do. All who did not run away must yield to her will. So Martin Bishop had run away with her sister Elizabeth. Leland had fled this house never to be heard from again. Mary Jerome had taken her four-year-old baby and escaped to another city.

For a shaken moment Sara too had felt an urge to escape, to save herself while there was time. But she would not be like the others. Already she recognized that there was something of Hester in her own character. Sara Bishop would be the one who did not run away, the one who stood up to her.

Her aunt waited and the driving force that burned in her was almost a tangible presence in the shadowy room.

Sara moved to a more comfortable position in the stiff chair, made an effort to relax.

"Why did you invite me here today, Aunt Hester?" she asked directly.

"I do not recall having granted you permission to call me 'aunt,'" Miss Varady said. Then she glanced toward the closed door of the drawing room and clapped her hands. "Ah Foong! Stop listening at the keyhole and come here!"

Unabashed, Ah Foong opened the door at once and shuffled into the room, performed his bent knee bow in Miss Varady's direction. His wrinkled face was expressionless, but the lively eyes noted Sara, so obviously uncowed. It seemed to Sara that there was approval in Ah Foong's look. Perhaps he would be the one to tell her truly what her father had been like.

"You may serve us chocolate here," Miss Varady told him. "And tell Miss Geneva she is to join us now."

"Yes, Missy," said Ah Foong and went quietly away.

Miss Varady turned again to Sara. "What do you think of Nicholas Renwick?" she asked abruptly.

"I admire him very much," Sara said readily. "Everyone in the Renwick house looks up to him and depends on him." She hesitated, thinking of certain facets of Nick Renwick's character which puzzled her. But these were not something she could put into words for her aunt.

"You have reservations?" Miss Varady asked with quick perception.

"No—not really. It's just that he seems dissatisfied at times. He doesn't care a great deal for the social life of the household."

"The more credit to him. The Renwicks have money, but no real family. Nevertheless, I shan't object if Geneva marries him. Though I'm not sure she'll have the gumption to manage it. Of course I don't know him very well. It has seemed to me at times that Nicholas Renwick has hardly shown me the proper respect. Which makes me doubt his intentions toward Geneva."

"I think he wouldn't be afraid of you," said Sara.

Miss Varady's tone was suddenly cold. "I can see that you have been badly brought up. It is a growing habit in this low-mannered century for the young to express themselves as no young lady of my day ever did to her elders."

Sara merely stared, wondering if there had ever been a day when Hester Varady had been too young to express herself.

Her aunt went on, warming to her lecture. "Had you grown up in this house as you should have done, I would have seen to it—"

"You could never treat me the way you have others," said Sara, finding herself a little breathless.

"Do not interrupt me!" Miss Varady snapped. "I will not tolerate rudeness." She would have said more, but Geneva stood in the doorway. "Come in—don't stand there. Bring another chair here by the fire."

Geneva looked about with an air of being on unfamiliar ground. She smiled faintly at her aunt and started to lift a heavy chair. Sara went quickly to help her, paying no attention to her aunt's remark that Geneva could manage well enough alone. Geneva was slight and frail, while Sara carried the chair easily, placed it where her aunt indicated beside her own.

When they were settled, Ah Foong brought frothy cups of Spanish chocolate, hot and spicy with cinnamon. Sara sipped the strange flavor with pleasure, as Miss Varady explained that this was a drink of old California. Those who continued the Spanish heritage had the duty of keeping up some of the old customs.

As they drank their chocolate it was Miss Varady who talked, the girls who listened. She spoke of the Oliveros and of the first Julian Varady. The Olivero family had wanted no American suitor for their youngest daughter. Americans were outsiders. But Julian had apparently had a way with him and he had been a brilliant, well-educated young man. He had a dream for the future of California as United States territory and knew that the day of the Spaniards would end. It was clever of him to be, in a sense, on both sides of the border at once, a friend with both races. The Oliveros had been proud enough of him, had loved him well, once they had decided to make him one of themselves. By the time the change came, the elder Julian was ready to step in as an influential American.

Miss Varady paused and Geneva, draining her cup, asked politely if Sara Jerome was still interested in these stories of old California.

Sara said she was and exchanged a quick look with her aunt. The flicker of a smile passed between them, leaving Geneva out. Whether Aunt Hester admitted it or not, Sara thought, she had begun to accept her. Satisfaction flowed through her in a warm flood.

Miss Varady set her cup on a table inlaid with mother-of-pearl, and rose. "Since you've finished, Sara, come with me. I want to show you something. You might as well get into your things, Geneva. It is past time to take Miss Jerome home."

As she crossed the room Miss Varady made a bright splash of color in her kingfisher-blue. Sara went quickly after her, eager to see something of this house. Dismissed for the moment, Geneva went to put on outdoor things and Hester Varady led the way toward the dim stairway at the rear of the hall, where it rose beneath the stained-glass window. She held herself more erectly than many a younger woman, her strong chin lifted at a proud angle that allowed no folds of flesh to gather at her throat.

Sara started after her up the stairs, and now, staring at the bits of blue and amber of the circular window, she had for the first time in this house a sense of the familiar. She knew that window. It was part of some childhood memory. Perhaps it had seemed a thing of marvellous beauty to the baby Sara who had lived so briefly in this old house.

Hester Varady gave the window not a glance. She mounted quickly from the landing to the second floor and here Sara found herself in a long dim hallway that was surely the hall of her old dreams. This hall was of normal length, and in spite of all the closed doors facing upon it, it seemed not at all strange. In the dream the hallway stretched into obscure distance, with seemingly countless doors bordering it. Had that been the way the real hall had looked to very young eyes?

What an exploration could be conducted in this house, Sara thought. Would it ever be possible to wander this corridor alone, to find herself unattended and able to explore?

Miss Varady turned toward the rear of the house, where a few steps led upward to several small rooms. Sara glanced hastily about, but nothing else spoke to her as the stained glass and the corridor had done. Hester opened a door upon a small balcony. The fog had descended now, creeping along this valley between the hills. Sara could feel its droplets wet against her skin and she lifted her face eagerly to the caress of San Francisco.

"So you like the fog?" said Miss Varady. "Come out here—this is one of my favorite spots in the house."

The balcony, which opened from a small room, overlooked a courtyard at the rear of the house. Below the balcony was a flagstone walk, and beyond were the remains of what had once been a little garden.

"Look!" said Miss Varady and never took her eyes from Sara's face.

There was very little to see. Here grew another eucalyptus tree, raising its branches skyward. The flower beds were weed-grown, long neglected. Brown paint on the balcony's wooden rail had peeled, so that rotting wood showed beneath. Sara gazed about with a puzzled air, wondering what it was her aunt found significant.

"On a sunny day this is a lovely place to sit," said Miss Varady. "We are secluded from the street and no other house overlooks this part of the courtyard. Sometimes as a child you used to play here, Sara. Do you remember it?"

Sara shook her head. "I remember the stained-glass window on the stairs. But not this place."

Hester nodded carelessly and turned back to the dark corridor. Sara longed to see the rest of the house, but Miss Varady led her downstairs to the front door, where Geneva waited.

Again her aunt extended a hand, and Sara felt the cold touch of her strong clasp. Then she was in the carriage again and no word had been spoken of another visit, of any future plans.

Sara was quiet on the way home, and Geneva asked her nothing, though she must have been curious about her visit to Hester Varady's. Since Aunt Hester had asked for silence, Sara was willing to comply, and was grateful for Geneva's consideration. Perhaps it might mean something to Geneva as well, if ever Sara Jerome came to live in that house.

ELEVEN

WHEN SARA GOT HOME, ONLY ALLISON WAS SITTING ON the stairs, with Comstock beside her. She remarked wistfully that she wished Sara would let her go along sometime when she went walking. Sara promised that she would another time, and went upstairs to her room.

She was too excited, too keyed up to risk talking to anyone. Allison would be sure to sense that something out of the ordinary had happened. Sara needed to be alone, to compose herself before she could face the others in the house.

In the tower above her room she sat on a window ledge and watched the drifting fog. It was not so heavy that it blotted out the city completely. Here it thickened like a heavy veil, there it thinned to transparent gauze, so that it was fascinating to watch the ever-changing aspect of rooftops and towers. From the bay came the bleating of water craft, the continuous hoarse warnings of foghorns, but otherwise the city seemed utterly still.

Sara could think with less turmoil now of her visit to Aunt Hester, of the significance it might hold for the future. There were sure to be more visits. When she had left with Geneva, she had been disappointed because no mention had been made of another meeting. Nor had there been any real indication of how Sara had measured up in Aunt Hester's eyes. But all this would come in good time. She had the feeling that she had done well to be herself and stand up to her aunt. The one thing which still nagged at her conscience was the fact that she must keep her visit secret from her mother.

During Sunday-night supper Sara thought of this uncomfortably as her mother chattered about household affairs. Susan, Mrs. Jerome reported, had been rude to her and she was upset about the matter. She had done no more than make a necessary suggestion and Susan had resented her direction. The girl was not always reliable and responsible.

"I'll talk to her," Sara promised. "You can't have her being rude to you. One of these days everything will be different and you won't have to stand for such things."

Mrs. Jerome heard only her first words. "No, please! There's no use making her give notice. I was just talking—I don't mind, really."

Sara wished she could blurt out the truth and assure her mother that a change might be due in the very near future. But that would upset her more than any pert words from Susan. It was better to wait until the thing was accomplished. Now Sara felt all the more eager for the time to come when Mary Jerome could take her place properly as Mrs. Leland Bishop.

That night, long after she had gone to bed, Sara went on building dream pictures. Perhaps she and her mother would go to live in the Varady house again, as they had long ago. If they went there a new existence would begin for them all, and for the house too. Sara would persuade her aunt to have the vines clipped away from the front windows, to open up the drawing room for more comfortable use, banish the cobwebs, perhaps bring in more comfortable furniture. They would begin to entertain and both she and her mother would be established in San Francisco.

As she fell asleep she thought again of the little balcony at the rear of the house, which her aunt had somehow expected her to remember. And of the door-lined hallway upstairs. She did not want to remember that hall now.

How much of the night she slept away she could not tell. Suddenly the dream enveloped her. She was aware of a long corridor—an endless corridor, with doors beyond number on either side. Darkness lay about her and the doors watched her slow advance blindly, hiding their secrets.

This was the beginning of terror.

In her dream she knew it was a dream, struggled helplessly to waken and could not. The enchantment bound her and there was no escape. Always it was the same dream, always the same—as if it were foreordained.

Without warning she was no longer in a corridor, but in a dark room crowded with unarranged furniture. There was a fury of storm outside, the threshing of trees in the wind, rain against the windows. Then the mirror—tall and narrow and black—and gradually, silvering the glass, the gleaming approach of light. Candlelight.

Sara knew her body was bathed in cold sweat, felt the trembling run through her limbs. She wanted to scream, to rush wildly away from this place, to escape whatever was to come. But horror held her, closed her throat, locked her muscles. The candlelight came closer, and a pale hand showed in the mirror. Once more came the sharp sound of a strange crackling, the overwhelming sense of an evil so great that her mind could not endure it and must at last bring her shudderingly awake.

For a moment she did not remember where she was. The room about her was strange, unknown. She had forgotten where the door lay, or upon what scene the windows opened. Her hands were wet, her trembling uncontrollable. The unknown room seemed to spin about her, as if at length it would tumble out into space and take her with it. Then it steadied and she saw the windows against a sky less dark than the room, saw the faint light which came through the opening of the circular stair.

Fear shook her again. But now it was fear of the reality about her. Above her head an empty tower looked out upon a frightening city which held for her only the threat of evil. Something crouched in the tower above her, something that might steal down the stairway at any moment and seize her in its frightful grasp.

Sara flung herself from the bed and fled toward the door. She scarcely felt the cold boards of the floor beneath her feet as she stumbled toward the stairs. Somehow she must escape that tower, reach a place where evil could not touch her. Not her mother's room. These dreams had always frightened her mother. If only she could find Ritchie. Ritchie would remember from her childhood. He would hold her close and comfort her.

On down the carpeted stair she ran to the first floor, her damp palm slippery on the banister, her night-gown sticking to her skin. Ritchie *had* to be up—still downstairs. She could not return to that frightening tower.

When she reached the lower hall she saw an edging of light beneath the library door and ran toward it, flung open the door. Within was lamplight and warmth. A man sat in a big chair before the fire. He looked around as she burst into the room. It was not Ritchie, but Nicholas Renwick sitting up with a book in the cozy quiet of the library.

He crossed the room and took her trembling hands in his. "You're shivering, Sara. Come here by the fire."

From the back of his chair he caught up an afghan made of varicolored squares and wrapped it snugly about her. Nick was so tall that Sara had again the sense of being small beside him, like a child in his hands. He put her into the big chair, brought a foot-stool for her feet and wrapped them gently in a corner of the bright afghan.

"There now," he said. "You'll be warm soon. And you needn't talk unless you want to. Will you be all right if I leave you alone for a few minutes?"

"Don't be long," she pleaded.

His smile reassured her as he went out of the library.

She leaned her head against the chair's leather back and watched the glow of the dying fire. Gradually the frenzy of fear slipped away, leaving her weak, but no longer terrified. Here in this room, with Nick soon to return, she was safe. No fearsome thing could reach out and grasp her here.

In a little while he was back with a glass of hot milk on a tray, and a plate of crackers. He sat on the rug before the fire and held the tray for her. The liquid was so hot she could only sip it at first, but it went down her throat soothingly and something of strength and peace began to seep back into her veins.

"It was a dream," she told him. "A dream that has come again and again all my life. There's always a mirror in it and the feeling that I'm about to see something so terrible in the glass that I can't bear it. But I wake up before it happens. And then I'm terrified and shaken for a long while afterwards."

Nick did not cluck sympathetically as others had done. "It's too bad," he said, "that you can't hold onto the dream long enough to see it through."

"See it through?" Sara was startled.

"Dream it through. Live through whatever was about to happen. Then perhaps you could be free of it. Have you any knowledge that might help you to the meaning of your dream?"

"No." Sara shook her head, shivering again. "None at all."

"Do you know what brings it on again?"

It was surprising to have someone consider her dream in so quiet and objective a manner. Surprising and somehow reassuring. When she considered, she knew what had made her dream tonight. She had vis-

ited the house of the dream. But she could not tell
Nick that, so she said nothing.

He knelt before the fire, put fresh fuel on the red
coals, speaking to her over his shoulder.

"Perhaps something frightening happened to you as
a child. Something that terrified you so that you put it
out of your consciousness, refused to remember it. I've
read of such things. Yet the knowledge of what happened is still there in you, and until you face it again, it
will always torment you."

She sipped her milk, nibbled at a cracker, and
watched him kneeling before the fire. She was beginning to feel a little sleepy and she could not entirely
comprehend what he was saying. But how wise he was.
And how kind, how gentle. She could not remember
that she had ever before known a truly kind man.
Women could be kind, but never men. Ritchie had his
gentle moments, but there was little of kindness in him
now. Nick was someone to trust and lean upon. He
would always be fair. She could imagine him angry,
but he would never be cruel.

"What sort of food does Allison think you are like?"
she asked drowsily.

He looked around at her, startled. Then he chuck-
led. "You mean that game she plays of likening everyone to some sort of food?"

Sara nodded. "She has done us all. Everyone but
you. I want to know what she picked for you."

"I shan't tell you," he said, still smiling. "It was too
uncomplimentary. What did she choose for you?"

"I won't tell either," said Sara.

He finished with the fire and turned about to sit
crosslegged on the hearthrug, looking up at her. "I've

wanted to thank you for your kindness to Allison. You've given her a bit of pride in herself that she has never shown before. She's turning from a hoyden into a young lady. And she's not nearly so prickly as she used to be."

"I like her," Sara said.

"I have the feeling," Nick went on, "that of all the Renwicks, it's Allison who matters most. Mother no longer wants anything but ease and pleasure. I can't blame her after those years of patterning herself to Father's slightest whim. She deserves to do as she likes. But she has lost touch with Allison. Judith I'm concerned about. I'm not at all sure of this marriage to Ritchie. I hope *she* is sure of it."

"There's you," Sara said softly. "You matter. You matter to all the others."

He did not look at her. "I matter least of all. I managed to be born in the wrong age. What do I do with my life that counts? I play harder at the insurance business than Ritchie does, but it's still play. There's nothing to stretch me out, or make real demands on me. Allison has more than all of us put together. If she finds a direction, she'll make something of her life."

Sympathy for him and a glimmer of understanding began to grow in Sara. A sense too of confidence in Nick. He was a person who might listen; someone she could trust.

"Ritchie could have had a direction." She roused herself from drowsiness, sat up in her chair so that she could watch the black skyline of coals in the fire. Coals with shapes that reminded her of the buildings Ritchie had wanted to create.

Nick listened, saying nothing.

"Has he ever shown you any of the plans he's made on paper?" Sara asked. "Why hasn't he gone on with his work in architecture? Why is he in insurance when he cares nothing at all about it?"

"The answer's simple enough," Nick said. "Ritchie would have had to work to become an architect. His plans are impractical. Insurance rates are too high in this town for the sort of buildings he wants to raise. We have to remember that San Francisco is built mainly of wood and that when there is a fire wood burns. His expensive buildings would be hemmed in by the inflammable. They would go too. No, there's too much for Ritchie to battle here. He went into insurance because it was easy, because he can continue to be a playboy and do no real work. He's a dreamer, not a worker. Don't you see that, Sara?"

Now she doubted her wisdom in speaking to Nick. He had not, after all, the perception to see the truth.

"You don't understand Ritchie," she said. "He needs others to believe in him and encourage him. He only pretends the self-confidence he puts on. *I* know what he could do if only he had the chance."

Nick was looking at her oddly now, in some surprise, and she settled back in her chair, pulled the colored squares of the afghan about her. She had said too much, let too much of her own emotion creep into her words. She had forgotten that Nicholas Renwick was Judith's brother.

"Like the rest of us who fail," Nick went on quietly, "Ritchie needs to make his own chances. And I'm afraid he'll never do that. I've never been happy about his engagement to my sister. You seem to think quite a lot of him, Sara."

She nodded, on guard now, wary. "We grew up together. I've known him all my life." She yawned widely. "I do believe I'm getting sleepy again."

"That's fine," he said. "Would you like to go back to your room? If you like, I'll walk upstairs with you."

But that she did not want at all. The thought of the tower waiting above her in the dark, like something ready to pounce, made her shiver again.

"Please," she said, "could I stay here? I believe I'll fall asleep right in this chair. And you needn't wait. You must get your own sleep. Before daylight I'll go back to my room. But for now—please, Nick, let me stay."

The kindness was back in his eyes. "Of course, Sara. Nothing can hurt you here. I'll turn off the lamp, so there'll be just the firelight."

She was drowsily aware of him somewhere in the room behind her. He had not gone away. His presence was comforting. The pink glow from the coals flickered on the ceiling. The room held no frightening darkness. She was so warm, so soothed, and sleepy.

If she dreamed again it was of quiet things. She had no nightmare memory to trouble her when a hand touched her gently awake. The fire had gone out long ago and a faint gray light painted the tall library windows, seeped into the room. Sara looked up into Nick's face, felt the warmth of his hand on her arm. He had not gone away. He had stayed.

"It's dawn, Sara," he told her. "You must go back to your room now. Then no one need know about your fears during the night."

She yawned, stretched to her toes like Comstock. The room was chilly now and she shivered, though no longer from fear. At once Nick wrapped the afghan more tightly about her.

When she was on her feet, he did not turn her toward the door at once, but led her gently to a long window facing east. Here the hillside dropped steeply away and there was nothing to cut off the view. Sara looked and caught her breath.

The bay glistened brightly. Over the hills to the east of the sleeping shore towns the sun was coming up. Long pink streamers stained the sky, with a few stray clouds floating black against them. In the west, edging the gray, dissolving the night, were tinges of blue morning.

Nick stood with one arm about her, holding the afghan in place so she would not be cold. There was no need for words. They watched the sunrise together until it was truly morning and the bay had turned to gold. Then she moved within the shelter of his arm and looked wonderingly up at his face.

"There's no way to thank you," she said softly. She felt the sting of tears in her eyes. She did not know how to meet such kindness.

He put a hand beneath her chin to tilt her head, and there was tenderness in his eyes.

"You remind me of the first time I saw you, Sara—kneeling there above the stairs. You have the same look of a little girl this morning. A child who still has her Christmas packages to open. I remember how I wanted to reassure you, so you wouldn't be disappointed because the wrappings were only tinsel."

She moved uneasily from his touch. "I'm not a child and I know about the tinsel."

"Do you? When it comes to Ritchie?"

He had seen too much, yet he was not condemning her as he might have done. He seemed more regretful than critical. But he couldn't help her. No one could.

He spoke again before she could slip away from him. "It's natural, Sara, to be fond of someone you grew up with. But the time comes when you must accept reality, face it."

"You don't need to tell me that!" she cried. "I know it already. I don't want anyone to feel sorry for me. I—I'm all right!"

She ran out of the room, not daring to look at him again, for fear she might burst into childish tears.

TWELVE

MARCH SEEMED A MONOTONOUS MONTH TO SARA. THERE was no return of her odd moment of companionship with Nick. He was friendly when he met her about the house, businesslike at the office. But there was no hint that he remembered that night in the library. Nor did he again offer his counsel or sympathy. And that was the way she wanted it.

She tried to avoid Ritchie as much as possible. This was most difficult to do in the office. Now and then she had the experience of catching his eye upon her as if he were puzzled. It would not occur to Ritchie, she thought a little scornfully, that she might be willing to give him up altogether.

Geneva came and went in the house as usual, but she had not again sought Sara out, and before the others there was no betrayal of the secret that lay between them. In any event, Geneva's chief interest lay in Nick.

She turned love upon him with every look, hung upon his words, glowed in her own quiet way whenever he was present. And Nick showed plainly that he enjoyed her company, was openly fond of her.

Most tantalizing of all was the fact that no further word came from Hester Varady. Sara, so sure at first that all had gone well that Sunday afternoon, now began to doubt, to look back and question her own behavior. Had she, after all, been wrong to stand up to her aunt? But she knew she could not, would not, do otherwise.

By now the one satisfying thing about her work at the office was the fact that she could pay something for her room and board out of each week's salary. The work itself she found tiresome. She couldn't blame Ritchie for his frequent escapes, for his love of parties and balls, theaters, concerts. She had only the resource of books to take her out of the dull days of her existence. And there was a limit to what could be found in books when her own unquiet emotions cried out for life itself.

Then, late one morning when Nick stood at her desk giving instructions on a letter, the unexpected happened.

Neither she nor Nick glanced up when the door to the waiting room opened, though later Sara recalled Miss Dalrymple's faint gasp. There was a silence while Sara pored over her notes. Then Miss Hester Varady's voice broke in upon them curtly.

"I would like some attention, if you please!"

Sara started and Nick looked around at the woman who stood beside the partition. Miss Dalrymple gaped openly.

"I'm sorry, Miss Varady," Nick began, "but Mr. Merkel will not be in until three this afternoon. If there is anything I can do—"

"There is, indeed," said Miss Varady. "Will you please release Miss Bishop from her work? I wish to take her to lunch with me."

"Miss Bishop?" Nick echoed blankly. "I'm afraid—"

Miss Varady was obviously enjoying this bit of drama. "Miss *Sara* Bishop. My niece. You are talking to her, so I presume she is visible to you."

Nick seldom looked astonished, but there was obvious surprise in the look he turned upon Sara. She could only nod at him helplessly. At least she had kept her promise to her mother. The truth was not out because of her own doing.

"Miss Varady is my great-aunt," she told Nick. "My father's name was Leland Bishop. Jerome is my mother's maiden name."

Again there was a stifled gasp from Miss Dalrymple.

"Then why—" Nick began, only to have Miss Varady cut him short again.

"Come along, Sara, come along. I don't choose to wait here all day. You can explain matters to Mr. Renwick later."

Sara threw Nick a glance of apology and ran to get her hat and wrap. When she returned she saw that Nick looked a bit red. The expression he wore as Sara joined Miss Varady beyond the partition was less kindly than usual. Undoubtedly he considered Sara's "masquerade" inexcusable. But Nick would have to think what he liked for now. Later she would find an opportunity to explain the true situation. What a hubbub this was going to cause back at the Renwicks'. Sara could hardly wait for evening to come. It was a hub-bub she would enjoy. All except the part that concerned her mother.

The shabby carriage waited outside the door and Miss Varady got into it regally, motioned Sara to the seat beside her.

"Well? How did you like that?" Aunt Hester asked, sitting up with her usual ramrod stiffness.

Sara, remembering Nick's expression, Miss Dalrymple's stare, laughed out loud. "It was wonderful. And certainly unexpected. I wish Mr. Merkel and Ritchie Temple had been there to hear."

The sable bonnet that belonged to an older generation of great ladies nodded in Sara's direction. "I have decided to acknowledge you as my niece. No more than that, for the moment. I have not made up my mind about you. But I shall be better able to see you if the relationship between us is known."

The carriage had turned down Market Street in the direction of the ferry. When it reached Montgomery Sara hardly noticed, being too excited by the possibilities which had suddenly opened before her. Not all of them pleasant.

"Mama will be fearfully upset," Sara mused. "I don't know how I'm going to break this to her. I wish she didn't mind so much."

"I'm sure I don't care whether she minds or not," Miss Varady said. "Any arrangements I make which concern you will not necessarily include your mother."

Sara stared at her angrily. What sort of daughter did this woman think she was? The time had come to make her own feelings, her own loyalty to her mother entirely clear.

"My mother and I belong together," she told her aunt, meeting her look squarely.

"We'll see about that when the time comes." Miss Varady's tone was tart. "Your mother has no love for me, any more than I have for her. Well, do let's get out of the carriage. We can't sit here all day."

They would return to the subject later, Sara thought. This autocratic woman was not going to make her back down on this. But now she looked about and saw that they had stopped before the entrance of the Palace Hotel. Above them rose the famous structure, its many bay windows shining in the sunlight.

"But—I'm not dressed for—" Sara began in dismay.

"Do stop chattering and get out," said her aunt. "You are a Varady. You may dress as you please."

The doorman ushered them in with a bow and Miss Varady swept royally ahead of her niece into the great court. All around were chairs and tables and a great many potted palms. Columned galleries ran around the court for several stories above, ending in a vaulted, glassed-in roof.

Miss Varady sniffed as though the scene displeased her. "Once my carriage would have driven into this court. It has been closed in because the noise and fumes of motorcars disturbed the guests in the rooms above. As I should think they would. Come along, Sara, don't gape like a bumpkin. We'll go directly to our table in the dining room."

Never had Sara stepped into a room so filled with mirrors, with crystal and silver. The linen was shining white and there were flowers on every table. A frightening array of waiters stood about, or carried trays to and fro.

The head waiter addressed Miss Varady by name and included Sara in his bow. Much was made of the ceremony of ushering such distinguished guests to their table and at once a waiter hovered beside them.

The menu was printed on a large stiff card and the dishes were for the most part in French. Sara glanced at it fearfully, but her aunt made no pretense of consulting her wishes. She ordered for them both and sent the waiter off at once.

Miss Varady had been helped out of her wraps and Sara saw that she again wore a rich, old-fashioned gown. This frock was of golden brown gabardine, with touches of burnt orange to lend color and distinction. Whether in style or not, Miss Hester Varady was the best-dressed woman in any room and she carried herself as if well aware of the fact.

"I love your gowns," Sara said frankly. "I'm glad you wear what suits you and pay no attention to fashion."

"What I choose to wear *is* the fashion," said Miss Varady complacently. Nevertheless, she looked pleased.

If Sara had hoped the conversation would take something of a personal turn during the meal, she was disappointed. Her aunt spoke of San Francisco, of life as it had been in the days when she had lived in her father's house in South Park, near Rincon Hill—then a fashionable section. All of which was interesting to Sara. But Miss Varady said nothing at all about possible plans for the future, or what moves she might now make, having acknowledged Sara as her niece. Apparently she planned no immediate change. Sara had imagined that she might be asked to give up her work at the insurance office, invited to move at once to her proper place in the Varady house on Van Ness. But none of these things seemed about to happen.

The meal was rich, but Sara's appetite was good and she ate with relish, right through to the *bombe glacée*.

When the waiter had brought a demitasse of coffee for each of them, Miss Varady opened the old-fashioned reticule she carried and drew out a tissue-wrapped packet.

"See what you make of this," she said to Sara.

Opening the tissue on the table before her, Sara found that it contained a handsome tortoise-shell comb. The shell was a smoky amber color, touched with traces of golden light. The prongs of the comb were long and into the spread of the fanlike back had been set a pattern of rhinestones.

"How beautiful!" Sara said in a hushed voice. "It's a Spanish comb, isn't it?"

Aunt Hester nodded. "You can catch only a glimpse of it in the painting because of the mantilla. But it is the comb *she* was wearing when she posed for her portrait."

Sara touched the satiny smoothness of the tortoise shell and the stones sparkled as she turned the comb.

"Consuelo's comb! Aunt Hester, was it truly hers?"

"I've just told you so," said Miss Varady, but she looked pleased at Sara's respectful reaction. "I hoped that you might value it. That comb has been in the family through generations. But I did not choose to give it to Geneva."

"How I'd love to wear it," Sara mused. "How I'd love to dress up in a mantilla."

"Yes, you are the type. All that black hair, your dark eyes and olive skin. I too was the type when I was younger. My sister Elizabeth was not."

There was scorn in her tone as she spoke of her sister and Sara remembered what Mrs. Renwick had told her —that Elizabeth had run off with the man who was engaged to marry Hester Varady. She wondered if her aunt could ever be brought to talk about her sister, Sara's grandmother.

"What was Elizabeth like?" Sara ventured.

For a moment she thought Miss Varady might not answer. This was an old hurt, an old anger, yet clearly it still had the power to wound. Hester Varady had never forgiven.

"As a matter of fact, Elizabeth was much like Geneva," she said at length. "Too soft, too gentle, too pallid."

Nevertheless, thought Sara, Martin Bishop had chosen Elizabeth in preference to Hester.

Miss Varady said nothing more of Elizabeth and they were both silent as they left the dining room. Hester spoke only when she ordered the coachman to drive back to the office. There she left Sara, without any word concerning the future. Sara thanked her for the comb and the luncheon, and went into the office, again baffled and a little disappointed.

Ritchie stood at Miss Dalrymple's desk and the reedy young file clerk hovered in the background, his ears fairly stretched from his head. All three looked at her as she came in and Sara braced herself, fearing for a moment that Ritchie might be as displeased about what had happened as Nick had seemed.

But Ritchie's eyes were dancing. He turned to her

desk and pulled out her chair in an exaggerated gesture.

"If you please, Miss Bishop! May I sharpen your pencils, Miss Bishop? May I pick up your handkerchief, Miss Bishop? To think we've been harboring an heiress of one of San Francisco's best families all this time! Sara, why didn't you confide in me—the old friend of your childhood?"

He was clowning, of course, but she sensed an excitement in him, knew that he was surprised and more than a little impressed.

"I couldn't tell you. I didn't know," she said. "Not until a few weeks ago. And you mustn't leap to conclusions. I'm not anybody's heiress."

"You will be!" Ritchie cried. "I can see that poor Geneva may be left quite out in the cold."

Nick spoke quietly from the door of his office. "I'm sure that Geneva will be well taken care of."

Ritchie waved a careless hand in his direction. "No offense, Nick. It's just that I can't imagine a dramatic old girl like Miss Varady leaving the bulk of her fortune to Geneva when there's someone like Sara on the family tree. Sara might even live up to the colorful Varady tradition."

Sara glanced uncomfortably at Nick. He must feel that she had deliberately deceived them, and she wished she could explain the truth to him. But it wasn't possible with everyone gaping and listening.

Ritchie perched himself on a corner of Sara's desk. "This is one day when I'll certainly knock off early. I can't wait to get home and drop this bombshell. What a stir it will make! To think that the Renwicks, who can't hold a candle socially to the Varadys, are harboring a Varady heiress under their roof."

"I would suggest," Nick said, and Sara had never heard his tones so clipped, "that you say nothing at all at home until Sara herself chooses to tell the others."

"Oh, come now—" Ritchie began.

Nick went curtly on. "I mean that. This is only a matter of fun for you, Ritchie. But I am wondering how it will affect Mrs. Jerome. Will you come into my office for a moment, Miss—Bishop? I imagine you'd like to tell us a bit more about this. You too, Ritchie, if you will."

They left the curious file clerk and Miss Dalrymple to struggle with unsatisfied curiosity. Following Nick meekly to his office, Sara felt more like a schoolgirl who had been caught cheating at her exams, than like an heiress.

Nick gave her the chair opposite his roll-top desk, while Ritchie lounged against a bookcase. Nick stood at the window, staring out into the street, not looking at Sara, but obviously waiting for her to speak.

Sara, having somehow been put in a position of guilt, began to grow faintly indignant. She told her story in as few words as possible.

"I don't know what became of my father," she concluded stiffly. "Mama made me promise to tell none of you about my San Francisco connection. When she found that Geneva was Miss Varady's niece, she was terribly upset. Her feeling seemed unreasonable to me, but I was bound by my promise. However, I'd made no promise not to see Miss Varady if she sent for me. I don't see why I must be blamed for this."

"I'm beginning to understand." Nick spoke more

kindly as he turned from the window. "This is a strange situation, but I can see that you would, under the circumstances, be helpless to deal with it in any other way. We must consider your mother's feelings, however, and that means Ritchie had better not blurt the news out impulsively when he gets home. Will you agree to wait, Ritchie?"

"I suppose I'll have to," Ritchie said and Sara was startled by the resentment in his tone. She had not realized that Ritchie so disliked Nicholas Renwick.

"It's right that I should talk to Mama first," she told Ritchie gently. "Perhaps I can make this a little easier for her. I don't know why she is so disturbed by this connection with the Varadys."

"I shall," Ritchie promised lightly, "be as silent as the grave. Once your mother has been told, however, you might give me the fun of springing it on the others."

Nick ignored Ritchie's notion of fun. "There are further matters to be considered," he said to Sara. "Just what are your plans for the future? I presume you will be leaving this office, leaving our house?"

"I haven't any plans." Sara shook her head helplessly. "My aunt has made no suggestions of any kind. Will you let me keep on with my work here? And of course not make any change just now at the house?"

"If you wish it that way," said Nick.

Sara rose from her chair. "I'll go back and type those letters—" She started toward the door, but Nick's voice stopped her and he was smiling in the old, friendly way.

"I know this is exciting and perhaps a little frustrating to you just now. But I'm glad you're willing to go right on with your everyday affairs. That's the best way to keep your balance."

"What else can I do?" said Sara, and went back to her desk.

It was difficult, however, to concentrate on her work for the rest of the afternoon. She ignored, but could not forget the continued interest of her companions in the office. Her thoughts kept returning to the luncheon with her aunt. Once, when she had a moment to herself, she unwrapped the Spanish comb to re-examine it. Never had she possessed such a treasure.

From time to time she worried about the coming interview with her mother. In her mind she tried first this way of telling her, then that. No plan seemed easy and she no longer looked forward to the coming of evening.

Ritchie was true to his word and the Renwick house was as calm as usual when Sara got home. Allison followed Sara up to her room, with Comstock padding lithely after her, but the child was brimming with her own affairs and knew nothing of Sara's secret.

"Sara," she announced the minute they were in the tower room, "I have something to tell you. But you must cross-your-heart-and-hope-to-die you won't tell."

Sara made the required sign. "What is it?"

"The grocer's boy likes me!" said Allison. "Today when he carried the potatoes down cellar I waited for him to come up. And he looked at me. He really did. And he said, 'Oh, you kid!' before he went out to his wagon. Don't you think that's significant, Sara?"

Sara managed a sober expression. "Yes, of course. Very significant. But isn't he a little old for you?"

"Oh, I don't know," said Allison airily. "I expect

he's fourteen. But I think my bangs and my new dresses make me look older, don't you, Sara? Bernard really looked surprised when he saw me today."

"Were you—doing anything special when he saw you?"

"Not really. Of course I did have one of Ritchie's cigarettes in my fingers. I wasn't going to smoke it, but I'm sure I looked as if I might any minute."

Sara no longer felt like smiling. She gave the little girl a quick hug. "Don't count too much on Bernard, honey. The people who like you won't do it because you astonish them. You *do* look very nice these days and we're all proud of you."

Allison's sigh was the long one of youth. "Someday I'll be grown up. Then everything will be wonderful."

Sara did not add that she'd better not count on that either.

Not until her mother was free from her work, did Sara seek her out. Then she went into her room and offered to brush her hair.

Mrs. Jerome surprised her. "Never mind the hair-brushing, Sara. Tell me what is troubling you. I've seen your concern all through dinner. What has happened?"

At least this made it easier. Her mother wore the braced look which meant she must prepare herself for the worst.

Sara plunged in at once. "I know who Hester Varady is. I've seen her. She sent Geneva to bring me to her house Sunday afternoon a few weeks ago. And today she came to the office and took me to lunch at the Palace Hotel. She told Nick who I am. I'm sorry this has to be such a shock to you. I didn't expect it would come out like this."

Her mother had seated herself to remove her shoes. At Sara's first words she paused, a shoe in one hand. Her eyes did not leave Sara's face. She uttered no protest, however. It was as if she had dreaded this for so long, suffered its possibilities for so many years, that now she had no emotion left to deal with the moment when it came. The shoe dropped from her hand and she leaned back in the chair.

Sara knelt beside her, put her arms about her mother's slight body. "You mustn't worry, Mama. Surely this is the best way for us both. If Papa left an inheritance that should be ours, then there isn't any reason why we should live as we do. You can have a home and luxuries. Nice clothes. And I can—I can *be* somebody."

Mrs. Jerome spoke without emotion. "Hester Varady will not give you one penny unless she buys your soul in the bargain."

"Oh, Mama, that's melodramatic—buying souls! Besides, she hasn't asked anything at all of me. All she did was to give me Consuelo Olivero's Spanish comb as a gift. For the time being nothing is changed. We'll go on just as we are."

"She won't leave it at that," her mother said. "She can build the most fantastic plots. She's cooking something up right now, you can be sure of it. Something to destroy us both."

Sara sat back on her heels. "She doesn't want to destroy me. She likes me. She likes me better than she does Geneva, in fact."

"Sara"—her mother leaned forward and clasped thin

fingers about her daughter's wrist—"who is Geneva Varady? Where did she get the name? There's no possible connection she can be descended from. Believe me, I know that family tree as well as I know my own face. It was preached at me again and again in the years I lived in that terrible house. There can't be anyone named Geneva Varady."

Sara moved from her mother's grasp. "I don't see how that matters to us. The important thing is that you mustn't believe Hester Varady can take me away from you. I've already told her that what happens to me happens to you too. We stay together, no matter what."

Her mother looked at her for a long moment. "I'm glad you feel that way. My only wish is to stand between you and something which might injure you. Perhaps between you and yourself, Sara. You are a strong-willed young woman, but to be strong-willed is not always to be strong."

She held out her hand and as Sara put her own in her mother's the words seemed to echo through her mind. There was something in them she would need to think about.

THIRTEEN

It was Nick, after all, who told the family quietly the next night at the dinner table, before Ritchie had a chance to dramatize the situation. Later in the evening Sara had a full report of what happened from an enraptured Allison.

Even Mrs. Renwick had chosen to dine with the family that night, so they were all there. In turn Allison mimicked the reaction of each person at the table, and Sara, bubbling with laughter, could see the picture.

Mrs. Renwick's first thought had apparently been of the news she would now have for Miss Millie Matson. This was something that she would know, for once, before the gossipy little dressmaker. Imagine having Varady relatives working here in her own house! If only William could have known about this, having been so richly snubbed by Hester Varady!

Judith, however, Allison reported, had been no more than coolly amused. The revelation seemed not to matter to her very much, one way or another.

"Except," Allison said, "that she kept watching Ritchie in a funny sort of way. Of course Ritchie thinks it's wonderful, just like I do. You really are a princess in disguise, Sara. Comstock, bow to the princess. Pay your respects."

Comstock, in Allison's lap, his tail curled about him, gave his mistress's hand a cuff, like a mother chiding a child, and yawned in Sara's face. Of all the household, Comstock was the least impressed by Sara's Varady blood.

Geneva's reaction had been one of pleased surprise. If any concern about sharing her inheritance entered her mind, she had apparently not revealed it. Allison, who had little patience with Jenny-Geneva, being jealous of her interest in Nick, nevertheless seemed to understand how she felt.

"I guess she grew up lonely in that old house. And now she might have another girl there for company. I think she likes that."

Sara was touched. She had been drawn to Geneva from the first, even though they were so different. Now she was anxious to see her alone, so they might acknowledge this newly found relationship.

She had the opportunity a few days later when she was arranging flowers for the dining room. This pleasant duty Judith had lately delegated entirely to Sara. It was fun, Sara discovered, to create new effects with unusual combinations of color and form. Today she was working with geraniums—scorned for indoor use, since they were so common in this climate. But Sara found that rose geraniums with their accompanying leaves could be effective in a black vase. Set on the sideboard they would dispel the gloom of the dining room. The pungent odor of the plants pleased her as she snipped and arranged.

Geneva, glancing in the door, saw her and smiled uncertainly.

"Come in and talk to me," Sara invited.

Geneva looked pleased as she came into the room. "Isn't it exciting, Sara? Our being cousins, I mean. Of course Aunt Hester hasn't said anything to me as yet. She doesn't know that Nick told us at dinner the other night. I wasn't even aware there was such a person as Leland Bishop. Aunt Hester has told me so little. I've never had a close relative except my great-aunt. Certainly not anyone near my own age. I'm twenty-two, Sara. How old are you?"

"I'm twenty," Sara told her, feeling that she was in reality years older than Geneva.

"Do you suppose you'll come to live at our house now?" Geneva asked. "I do hope you'll come soon. It's such a lonesome place. If it weren't for Nick and visiting here, I don't know what I'd do."

"Aunt Hester hasn't invited us to live with her," Sara said, her hands busy among blooms spread over newspaper on the sideboard. "So I'm glad you come here often. What a good thing it is that she hasn't opposed your going out with Nick."

"She didn't like it at all in the beginning," said Geneva.

"And you stood up to Aunt Hester?" Sara regarded her with new interest.

"Well, no. Not exactly. I just behaved like water."

"Like water? What do you mean?"

"Have you ever read the Chinese philosophers?" Geneva asked.

Sara shook her head. She liked to read, but she knew little of China or its philosophy.

"I wouldn't have learned about them myself if it hadn't been for Ah Foong," Geneva went on. "I found there had been English translations of some of the great teachers he talked about. This man, Laotse, believed in what he called the strength of the weak. He wrote that water is gentle and soft. It escapes through your fingers when you try to pick it up. But water, gently dripping, can wear away a rock."

Sara listened in delight. "No wonder Nick is so fond of you," she said impulsively.

The flush that swept Geneva's cheeks was almost painful. "Do you really believe he is? Nick's so far beyond anything I can ever live up to."

"Don't be so humble," Sara said. "No man's as impressive as all that. And it's obvious that he's very fond of you. I wouldn't be surprised if you found yourself getting married before Judith and Ritchie."

Geneva picked up a geranium leaf and sniffed it, trying to hide her confusion. When she spoke again, it was not of Nick.

"Lately I've been concerned about Judith and Ritchie. I know he's provoked because she won't set the wedding date. I couldn't help overhearing them in an argument about it just the other day. I can't understand why Judith wants to wait."

"Perhaps she's not really in love with him," Sara said, the old hurt stabbing through her guard.

"Oh, but I'm sure she is!" Geneva cried. "Though

perhaps not as much as I am with Nick." She dropped the leaf on the floor without noticing. "How strange that I'm saying such things to you, Sara. Do you know —I've always been a little afraid of you before."

"Afraid of me! But how very foolish!"

Beside small Geneva, Sara felt herself overly large and clumsy. As if she stood near something so delicate that it might shatter into fragments at the touch of a rough and heedless hand. Moved again by impulse, she touched Geneva's shoulder lightly, as if she were a child, and bent to kiss her cheek in a sudden fleeting gesture. It was possible to guess the tenderness Nick must feel toward this girl.

"It's very nice to have a cousin," Sara said. "I've had no relatives either, except my mother. Will you loan me that book by your Chinese philosopher sometime?"

Geneva's eyes thanked her and her laughter tinkled. Geneva did not laugh aloud often, but when she did the sound was like windbells stirring in a breeze.

"I'll be happy to loan it to you, Sara. But you're already strong the way a torrent is strong. I'm only quiet water."

Nick's voice called to Geneva from the hallway, and she smiled at Sara before she went quickly out of the room. For a sober moment Sara looked after her. Geneva *was* quiet water. But unexpectedly deep. There was in Sara a new stirring—a desire she had never felt before to be somehow more than she was. Not just to *have,* but to *be.*

"What are you mumbling to yourself about?" asked Allison from the doorway, and added nastily, "My, what a tender scene with Geneva just now!"

The words broke through Sara's wistful mood and

she spoke impatiently without looking around. "When will you learn that it's bad manners to spy and listen to other people?"

"I like to be bad-mannered," said Allison. She came into the room and stepped deliberately on the leaf Geneva had dropped, grinding it into the carpet. "I'll spy whenever I please."

Sara glanced over her shoulder at the girl. "Your left stocking is coming down. And you don't have to stamp that leaf into the rug."

"I know. I just unfastened my stocking so it would slip. I like it that way. Strong like water! I never thought you'd listen to Jenny-Geneva, Sara. I thought you had more sense."

"That sounds like jealousy," said Sara. She eyed her arrangement of bowls and vases without enthusiasm. Proper attention had not been given to this task and the result was not her best.

Behind her Allison was unexpectedly quiet and Sara glanced around again to see what she was doing. To her surprise, there were tears in the child's eyes. She had never before seen Allison cry.

"What is it?" Sara cried in dismay.

"I've had the most horrible day!" Allison gulped. "And now you say I'm j-j-jealous!"

"I'm sorry," said Sara more gently. "Tell me what's happened, honey."

"I only wanted to show Bernard one of Mama's Japanese plates. It was such a little thing to do. And then I—that is, the plate slipped. And—I'm an outcast, I'm never to set foot in Mama's dining room again!"

"Begin at the beginning," said Sara, "and tell me

what happened. Why in the world did you touch one of those plates?"

The story emerged gradually between gulps. The grocer's boy, long Allison's ideal, had hardly noticed her until that day with the cigarette. Then he had looked at her in surprise and had even spoken to her. But the next day he had paid no attention again.

Whereupon Allison had worked out a new scheme. She discovered that if she took some beautiful and valuable object outdoors with her and placed it beside her on the bench near the back door, Bernard would stare at it and say, "What's that?" Then Allison would weave an elaborate story to which he would actually listen. She had worked this successfully for the last three days. Today she had thought of the valuable plates which her father had brought all the way from Japan and which had probably been eaten from by the Emperor.

Sara remarked that this detail was doubtful, but Allison said she thought it would interest Bernard and make his eyes pop.

"You know the way Mama has those plates wired to the rack?" Allison said. "So an earthquake won't shake them off. Well, this afternoon, while Mama was having her nap, I climbed on the sideboard to get one of them unfastened. And just as it came loose and everything was fine, Jonsey popped in and started to shout at me. He scared me so that I dropped the plate."

It had, said Allison sorrowfully, "smashed to smithereens." It couldn't even be glued back together. "And Mama acts as though Papa lives up on that shelf with the plates. She even talks to them sometimes. So when she got up from her nap, Jonsey told her and her heart started fluttering like anything. She even cried over the old plate. Though I'll bet she wouldn't cry over me! She told me I was incorrigible and I was never to touch anything of hers again. I won't either. I don't care if I never see her again. If it weren't for you and Nick, Sara, I might even run away."

Sara found herself at a loss. "I think you're exaggerating a little," she soothed. "Your mother will feel better about the plate in a few days. Then everything will be all right again."

"Nothing will ever be all right," said Allison. "Not until I'm grown up. Then I'll boss everyone and be mean to all the people around me." Her face puckered again. "Everything was lovely until today. Nick is going to take us to Sutro Heights, Sara. Just you and me. Not old Jenny-Geneva. I made him promise I could have whoever I wanted. We're going the first bright Sunday."

"This is news to me," said Sara, "but it sounds like fun."

"Nothing will be fun ever again." Allison shook her head gloomily and disappeared to brood by herself in the library.

Sara went down the hall to Mrs. Renwick's door and tapped lightly.

"Come in," Hilda Renwick called and there was a note of strain in her voice. "Oh, it's you, Sara? Really, I'm not up to talking to anyone now. Just look at what that child has done!"

She waved a hand and Sara saw that the gold and red bits of the Japanese plate had been collected in the cover of a chocolate box on the table beside her.

"You've still five plates left," said Sara, reasonably.

"But William valued these plates so highly! You've

no idea the trouble he took to get them safely home from the Orient. He said they were practically museum pieces. Yet he gave them to *me*. Now the set is ruined."

"What about Allison?" Sara asked. "What about how she feels?"

"The child didn't care in the least. She was rude and indifferent."

"I wonder if she's really indifferent," Sara said. "She came to me crying just now."

"Of course. She always cries after the milk is spilt. But she will go right ahead and do something equally dreadful next time. I don't know how to manage her. My other children were never like that."

"Anyway," Sara said, "I thought I ought to tell you that she seems pretty upset about it."

Mrs. Renwick wiped her eyes. "I do believe you're scolding me, just the way Nick does. Please hand me my smelling salts, Sara. There on the table."

Sara gave her the small green bottle and went off, feeling that two such different people as Allison and her mother could never come together.

Things simmered down all around, however, and while an undercurrent of resentment remained, there was no further open outbreak between Allison and her mother. The household grew accustomed to the revelation about Sara and everything went on as usual. For the time being, Miss Varady made no move at all.

The first week in April the world was shocked by the news of the most terrible eruption of Mt. Vesuvius in modern times. Everyone talked about the disaster—on the cars, at home, in the office. Why, men and women asked one another in bafflement, did people continue to live knowingly on the slopes of a volcano where they might be blown sky-high at any moment?

Nick said dryly that it was probably for the same reason that everyone went right on living in San Francisco. The rest of the household assured him, however, that it wasn't the same thing at all. Earthquakes there had been in San Francisco, and would be again—everything from tremors to good solid shakes. But they could be laughed off and really did very little damage. As for fires—they belonged to the past. The present fire protection was admittedly the best in the country and San Francisco had no need to worry.

The day after this discussion Sara came back to the office from her lunch hour—she had walked to Portsmouth Square and sat on a bench watching the Chinese children play. She returned to her desk to find an extraordinary bit of construction upon it. The object had been built of white cardboard and she did not see until she picked it up that it was a miniature office building. The tower was unusual—a straight shaft which did not taper at the top, but was nevertheless graceful and uncluttered in line. Sara knew, even before she found the card on her desk, who had made it.

The card said simply, *A tower for Sara.*

This was the sort of thing Ritchie used to do sometimes when she was a little girl, and an old tenderness swept through her. The rest of the staff was still out to lunch, but she had seen Ritchie go into his office a few minutes before. She picked up the little cardboard tower and went to the door of Ritchie's office. It stood ajar and she entered without knocking.

"It's a beautiful tower," Sara said as Ritchie glanced up. "I can see the way it will look out there on Market

Street, making the other buildings seem old-fashioned."

Ritchie smiled, but he shook his head. "It was only a bit of make-believe for you, Sara. Because you like towers. You'd have a wonderful view from this one. But you'll have to pretend you're seeing it. It's not for real."

"Why not, Ritchie?" she asked earnestly. "Why can't you make others see how sensible a building like this would be? Why can't you and Nick build it yourselves?"

He took the shaft of cardboard out of her hands gently. "Don't take it so seriously. It's nothing but a paper dream."

His indifference made her impatient. She too knew how to dream, but a dream was no good unless you made it real.

"Stop dreaming, Ritchie!" she cried. "*Do* something about this! It's all there in your mind—but you've got to make it real. And you can. Oh, I know you can!"

A light she remembered from long ago came into his eyes. "All right," he said. "I'll stop dreaming." And before she could move away, he had pulled her into his arms and kissed her in the old sweet way. A lethargy seemed to flow through her body. She wanted only to stay where she was and let her lips quiver into softness under his. Yet in her, too, was some new strength which would not follow the old course, which would not be denied.

She turned her head from his kiss, put her hands up to push him away. But he moved first and released her abruptly, looking past her with a devil-may-care light in his eyes. She had not heard the door to the adjoining office open, but watching Ritchie she knew with a sinking heart what she would see when she turned her head. Nick Renwick stood in the doorway.

"That is all for the moment, Miss Bishop," said Ritchie lightly. His eyes, his mouth, his tone mocked them both.

Nick said nothing at all. There was a remoteness in him—as if they were two people he did not know, and for whom he had only a cool contempt. He stood there for a moment and then went back to his own office.

It was the contempt Sara could not bear. The reaction of hot anger shook her. Anger and resentment. Nick had no right to set himself up as a judge, no right to condemn. She stormed into the office after him, stood by his desk as he sat down paying no attention to her.

"You listen to me, Nicholas Renwick!" she cried.

Still he said nothing, did not look at her. He picked up a brass paper knife, toying with it idly. His very silence angered her all the more. If he meant to give her no benefit of the doubt, then she might as well accept the guilt he implied and use it as her defense. She no longer cared in the least whether he thought her innocent or guilty. She wanted only to wipe the contemptuous indifference from his face.

"Perhaps you don't know that Ritchie belonged to me before your sister ever came to Chicago. If Judith hadn't met him, I'd be his wife by now. It was what we always planned. I'm the one he loved first of all!"

Nick looked at her now, and while his mouth was straight and stern, there was a certain compassion for her in his eyes. But he did not speak. She turned away, still shaking with futile anger. Ritchie stood in the doorway, watching in wry amusement. He looked like a young man who attended an entertaining play.

A sudden recognition of the difference between the two men impressed itself unexpectedly upon Sara. Even now, when he was so coolly remote, so out of reach, there was a sensitive strength in Nick's lean face. A strength that was wholly lacking in Ritchie. Nick was a man, with a sense of responsibility for his own conduct. Ritchie was a boy with a heedless disregard for the result of his actions. She did not want to realize the difference between them, or rate one above the other. She wanted only to dislike them both.

Angrily she returned to her own desk. It was just as well that the little cardboard shaft had been left in Ritchie's office. If it had been within reach she would have ripped it to bits and flung the pieces to the winds of Market Street. She wasn't sure which man she hated most—Nick or Ritchie.

FOURTEEN

THE SECOND SUNDAY OF APRIL WAS THE BRIGHT DAY FOR which Allison had been waiting. The rains would not fully cease until May, but now and then there could be a glorious warm day when all San Francisco poured into trolley cars, carriages, automobiles, and headed for the beaches.

But on this particular Sunday Allison went into sackcloth and ashes. She was still upset about the incident of the plate and this last straw was, she announced, "The end." She plastered her bangs back from her forehead with Vaseline, put on an old brown jumper with a tear in it, and let both stockings slip. It was possible that she rubbed her shoes through a flower bed to achieve so scuffed and unpolished a look.

Sara, breakfasting in the kitchen with her mother, was treated to a display of Allison's despair before the rest of the family gathered in the breakfast room.

"Nick says we can't go to Sutro Heights today, even if the weather is fine. It's the *most* beautiful day! I think I shall run away. Or perhaps I shall throw myself out of the tower window."

"Don't behave like a baby," Sara said, disturbed herself, and without sympathy. "Besides, I don't want to go anyway."

"But you said it would be fun—" Allison wailed.

"Never mind. I've decided against it. And if you have to dress yourself up like a fright, please go away so I needn't look at you. You're spoiling my breakfast."

Allison, outraged, took herself into the dining room, where she could nibble ahead of time from the buffet and thus show a languid lack of interest in food when the others came down.

Mrs. Jerome shook her head. "You were too sharp with the child. It really is a disappointment to have her promised holiday taken away. Nicholas Renwick doesn't usually do things like this. You can at least be kind to her."

Sara knew well enough why Nicholas Renwick had changed his mind about the outing. Nothing had been said at home about the scene at the office with Ritchie. Nick had put on a pretense of being just as before when others were around. Obviously he wanted to spare his sister knowledge of what had happened. But no such pretense was needed with Sara. He did not ignore her, but his manners remained cool and remote. He would hardly consent to her company on a trip to Sutro Heights.

During the morning Sara went to church with her mother as usual. When she came home she settled herself boldly in the library, where Nick himself was likely to be. She would not allow him to frighten her away from this one comfortable room that was open to her. She gathered a pile of books on the floor at her feet, usurped Nick's own chair and began a pretense of reading. Her thoughts, however, went right on whirling about the center of her concern.

If it was to be like this in the Renwick house, then she would have to resort to Aunt Hester. Surely Miss Varady would not want her niece to be subjected to contemptuous treatment. Perhaps she could now be persuaded to take some step that would free Sara from working in the office, or sleeping one more night under this roof. This very afternoon she would call upon Aunt Hester and make the situation clear.

She heard Nick when he came in the door, and pretended intense concentration on a page she had already read three times without being aware of its contents. His silence was tantalizing and she knew he was watching her, but she would not look up. Let him order her out of this chair if he wished. She wondered what would happen if she refused to move.

"Excuse me, Sara," Nick said. "May I have your attention for a moment?" His tone was courteous, mild. He did not sound as if he wanted to put her forcibly from the room.

She looked at him, very proud and outwardly calm. Haughty—that's what she would be.

"I am listening," she said.

It seemed to her that there was a faint quirk at one corner of his mouth, but his tone remained serious as he went on.

"Thank you, Sara. The fact is that I am in the awkward position of having to ask a favor of you. If Allison didn't have so much right on her side, I might be tempted to ignore her words and her dress. But she is already upset over breaking that plate, and this new disappointment isn't her fault. She's taking it very hard."

He paused and Sara waited for him to continue.

"I suggested to Allison that perhaps she and I could drive out to Sutro Heights by ourselves. We could leave in a half hour, take a lunch and spend the afternoon there. Once this would have pleased her sufficiently. But now she has the notion that the day will be nothing unless you go along. Do you suppose we could declare a truce for one day, Sara, in order to give Allison a happy time?"

"Certainly not," said Sara flatly. "After your behavior at the office the other day, I shall go nowhere in your company."

"After *my* behavior!" Nick echoed. Then he affronted her by laughing out loud. "Strange how things can look from different viewpoints. However, I am still asking this favor of you, Sara. Not for my sake. For Allison's."

"Very well," she said, still haughty. "Since you put it in the light of doing something for Allison. I'll go change my clothes." She left her chair and moved toward the door.

"Good," he said quietly. "Dress warmly. In spite of the sun there will be a wind."

She chose a starched boating suit of pale blue linen with a fitted jacket. A bow tie graced the glazed collar of her shirtwaist and she pinned a small sailor hat atop her dark hair. She felt she looked very neat and sportsmanlike as she stood on a chair in her room to glimpse bits of herself in the bureau mirror. This suit too had been of her own designing and she knew it was exactly right.

The fleeting thought crossed her mind that there was no need to look exactly right for Nick Renwick, whom she detested with all her heart. But she dismissed this at once.

Allison had been unable to get all the Vaseline out of her bangs, though she'd rubbed them strenuously with a bar of Pears soap. But while they still had a tendency to plaster, she had at least pasted them down the right way on her forehead. The rest of her costume had been transformed accordingly. She wore a new dress of pale blue and she was beaming with happiness as they got into the carriage. Ritchie, as usual, had gone somewhere in the car.

"You know," Allison said as the carriage started west toward the beaches, "I'm really very glad it happened."

"Glad what happened?" Nick asked cheerfully.

"I mean," Allison said, "that you frightened me first when you said we couldn't go. So I mussed myself up in that horrible way I used to look. And now it feels extra good to stop looking like that and to have everything right after all."

Nick's laughter was understanding. "Maybe you've found the secret of happiness, my dear," he said. "Everything is comparative."

With the sun shining so brightly the long drive was pleasant. The carriage rolled along oiled red roads past Golden Gate Park, and the wind was not too cold.

"Sutro Heights is out near the Cliff House, isn't it?" Sara asked. So far she had not seen this famous spot.

Allison nodded. "The heights are right above the

Cliff House and the Seal Rocks. I like the heights best. It's so queer up there—like something out of a storybook."

"The park was Adolph Sutro's estate," Nick said. "When he died the ground was deeded to San Francisco."

"Wait till you see!" Allison cried. "All those deer and lions and goddesses and things!"

"Deer and lions?" said Sara. "You don't mean *alive?*"

"No, of course not. Wait—you'll see."

The carriage left the lower road and climbed to the heights above. At the entrance to a wide carriage drive was an ornate white arch. Two lions crouched on pedestals at its base, guarding the way.

"This used to be the vehicle entrance when Mr. Sutro was alive," Nick said.

They left the carriage and Allison saluted the lions as old friends as they walked past the arch. A variety of trees from every climate lined the straight drive. There were northern pines, cypress, and tropical palms from the south, meeting at this California borderline. The pines had been thickly planted—to make a windbreak, Nick said—and their branches all leaned away from the sea-borne wind.

The most startling feature of the lushly planted drive was the collection of Grecian gods and goddesses, copies of classical statues, which rose from the shrubbery and peered unexpectedly from behind almost any bush.

Now Allison wanted to fly in every direction at once and could not fit her steps to the slow pace of adults.

"Wait for me in the summerhouse," she beseeched Nick. "I want to visit all my friends. I'll find you there."

Nick let her go and led Sara toward the shelter. The summerhouse was a small wooden structure with a slanting, shingled roof. Its windows and door stood open, and Sara sat down on the bench within. Nick was content to lean in the doorway, breathing deeply of the bracing, pine-scented air. This was a lonely place. Most of holiday San Francisco chose the lower level of the Cliff House, Sutro Baths, the beach. This was a spot lost to the past, where few chose to wander.

"We'll go on in a little while," Nick said. "Then you'll see the view."

Sara listened, saying nothing. All turmoil seemed to have drained from her on the quiet drive out here. She wanted to be nothing but a creature of the moment. She loved the brisk wind blowing from the ocean, loved the sunlight on her face. It was good to feel somnolent, quiet, ready to listen to Nick, or not to listen. She wanted to feel strongly about nothing.

He stood tall in the narrow doorway of the summerhouse, his dark head in shadow, and she knew that he was watching her. But in this quiet mood she did not care. Let him condemn her or not, as he chose.

"Sara," he said, "I am more than sorry about what happened in the office the other day."

She held to her sense of remoteness. None of this mattered very much, one way or another.

"I feel," Nick went on, "that I should try to understand your viewpoint. I suspect that Ritchie was to blame for what happened."

She turned her face to the sun and wind and closed her eyes, relaxed, indifferent. When she did not answer, he continued.

"I have been trying to understand what you seem to

believe, to understand why you believe it. I mean that your right to Ritchie comes before Judith's."

She did not really believe that. Not any more. She had said in anger more than she meant that day in Nick's office. But she could not explain. It would be no use.

"Why should it be difficult to understand that another person can be in love?" she asked.

There was a hint of pity in his eyes, and she turned away from it. Pity might make her sorry for herself. It might make her angry again.

"Now Judith is in love with Ritchie," Nick said quietly, "though I can remember when she was in love with another man. Not so guardedly and fearfully then, but with all the generosity and belief that was in her. She was badly hurt that time. I always thought my father brutal in his handling of the affair. I've little use for Ritchie, Sara, but I don't want to see Judith so deeply wounded again. Now do you understand a little better how I feel?"

Sara nodded wordlessly. She could understand, but understanding would not help her in her own soreness and confusion.

Nick went on in the same quiet tone. "However, I'm not forgetting you, Sara. In fact, I've thought about you quite a lot. I hate to see waste and there is so much of it under our roof. Don't take a wasteful course yourself, Sara. There's something better ahead for you."

"What?" she asked blankly.

"What is it that you want from life?"

Answers were easy, cheap, she didn't have to think.

"I want more dresses than I can wear. A fine house. A dozen taffeta petticoats."

"Those petticoats again!" He laughed, but without derision. "I won't take such an answer. What is it you truly want, Sara?"

He had a way of drawing out the truth, whether she wished to speak it or not. She gave him the answer evenly. "All I have ever wanted was to be Ritchie Temple's wife."

"But, Sara," his voice was gentle, "no human being can cling blindly to something that is lost to him. You have to face life as it really is."

He still didn't understand that she was trying to face it. But if she could not have Ritchie, she must find something to put in Ritchie's place. And what was there left except *things*? Once she had wanted material things to make her Ritchie's equal. Now she knew the fallacy of such a wish. But still, what Aunt Hester might give her could fill her life with glamour and excitement. But she could not explain this to Nicholas Renwick who had never known what it was to lack for anything.

"I only want to be happy," she said at last. "Isn't that what everyone wants?"

"I suppose I've never given happiness much thought," Nick said. "As a goal in itself I don't think it's very real or important."

"Not important!"

"It's not something you can take in your two hands and wring from life, Sara. Considered that way, it's only a mirage on the horizon. More likely happiness is a by-product of other things. The small things as well as large that one meets every day. Perhaps it's most apt to come when we're not even looking for it."

She listened wonderingly. This was not an aspect of happiness she had ever considered.

"Here comes Allison," Nick said. "And it's just as well. There's been enough of long talk for one day."

She agreed with him, but she was glad that he no longer condemned her, or felt contemptuous toward her. Indeed, she had an odd sense of having, for this little space of time, someone to lean upon and trust. Someone she might be able to talk to, if only she dared, as she had never talked to anyone before. She could understand what it was that Geneva loved in this man, and for a moment she almost envied Geneva.

Allison's voice broke in upon them from the doorway. "I'm most horribly hungry, Nick. Do let's eat. But not in this damp old place. Out in the sunshine."

Nick had brought the lunch hamper from the carriage and now he spread a checked tablecloth on the grass, while Allison and Sara set out sandwiches, cold chicken, chocolate cake, fruit. The day had apparently gone to Allison's head. Sara had never seen her so gay, so free of all sullenness. Her quick wit and flights of imagination kept them laughing.

Sara felt completely relaxed and tranquil. This world, this afternoon, seemed to exist apart from the rest of her life.

When they had repacked the remains of the lunch in the hamper, Allison announced that the best still remained to be seen. They walked toward the edge of the cliff, where it dropped away to the road below. Through the trees the square white lookout tower of the Sutro house was visible. Allison skipped and danced ahead and back, covering the distance several times over. When she reached the terrace, she ran up a flight of steps and stood at the top, waiting for them.

"You're such slowpokes! Hurry, Sara. It's wonderful up here."

They followed her up the steps and out upon the level top of a rocky promontory around which had been built a curved wall like a battlement. At intervals in the castellated granite were set more white urns and classic statues.

Far below rose the turreted wooden structure of the Cliff House, and below that jutted the Seal Rocks. White froth curled at their feet, and beyond rolled the great Pacific.

"The brown spots on the rocks are the sea lions," Allison pointed out. "They're not seals, really. But look at the beach. Isn't it beautiful?"

A long stretch of golden sand lay beside the ocean, with the water curling and creaming along its edge. There were hundreds of people down there, driving in carriages, or sitting on the sand in the sun.

The holiday clatter that must be going on below could not reach them in this high, remote spot. Here there was only sea and sky and wind.

Sara's interest was held by the endless stretch of ocean and sky, interrupted only by the Farallons. The sunset must be magnificent here. She wished they could stay.

"The Sundown Sea," Nick said, almost reading her thoughts. "The Costanoans called it that."

Then, without warning, the earth stirred, quivered under their feet. A white urn on the wall seemed to tip toward them and then back. Allison was out of reach, but Nick caught Sara's arm and pulled her away from the wall. The tremor was gone in seconds and she laughed out loud.

"My second earthquake! Did you think I was going over into the sea?"

"I took no chances," Nick said, looking around to make sure Allison was on safe ground. "I see you've learned to laugh like a good San Franciscan. Just the same, don't forget that this is earthquake country and the ground can do nasty things on occasion. Don't laugh so hard that you stay in a dangerous spot."

"Oh, pooh!" cried Allison, dancing toward them. "That was a silly little shake. I wish we could have a really good one and show Sara what we can do."

They left the terrace and wound their way through the rest of the lush growth Adolph Sutro had planted here. There were lawns and gardens and bridle paths. And only an occasional human being to be seen. There could hardly be a more tranquil spot in the area.

The drive home was quiet too, and they were all a little sleepy from sun and wind and exercise. How differently this day had ended, Sara thought, from the way it had begun. She felt soothed, renewed. Strength was flowing back clear to her finger tips. Nick was wrong about happiness. It *was* something you could work for, attain as a goal in itself. Somehow, somehow —she would find it.

FIFTEEN

THE FOLLOWING SUNDAY WAS EASTER AND SAN FRAN-
cisco dressed in its finest and turned out to attend its
many churches. Sara suspected that the city was well
satisfied with itself these days. Real wickedness lay in
the roaring past and could be regarded with tolerant
pride. In this prosperous and more orderly era, the
town felt itself still colorful and distinctive—a city men
lost their hearts to like no other city in the country.

It was exhilarating, Sara found, to be a part of this
San Francisco of a new century. The Victorian days
were over, the future bright, and there was a great deal
to give thanks for on this Easter Sunday, the fifteenth
of April, 1906.

The days following Easter were gay and busy. On
Tuesday night Caruso and Olive Fremstad were to sing
Carmen at the Opera House and the diamond tiaras
and dog collars of the Bonanza rich would be out in

full force. It would be a night of after-the-opera parties and festivity. The Renwick household was in a buzz of preparation.

Judith looked more beautiful that night than Sara had ever seen her, with a diamond butterfly in her ash-blond hair and diamond drops in her ears. Her gown had come from Paris and was a concoction of pink chiffon, steel spangles and chiffonné roses, of lace and ribbonwork in intricate layers. Paris or not, Sara did not like it. But Judith transcended the conglomeration and made the dress itself seem beautiful.

Allison and Sara, of an age tonight, knelt in the second-floor hallway and watched beneath the banister as the opera party left. Ritchie was more handsome than ever in a silk hat and opera cape, and even Allison, who disliked him, had to admit that no gentleman in San Francisco could touch Ritchie for gallant appearance. Nick was going too and had brought Geneva earlier from her aunt's house. Nick looked himself as always. He never seemed to take on the coloration of his surroundings as other people did. Geneva wore glowing wine-red satin and the rubies about her throat must have been given her by Hester Varady.

Sara watched and ached with longing. Even though she couldn't go to the opera at Ritchie's side, she should have been there tonight in her own right. Geneva had told her that Miss Varady had for once come out of seclusion and taken a box. She had invited some old friends from Rincon Hill. Geneva said she would sit there, lorgnette in hand, and look disdainfully upon the tiaras, which she regarded as being in inexcusable taste. One wore fine jewelry, of course. But a lady did not drape quantities of it on her person until she sparkled like a Christmas tree.

Why couldn't Aunt Hester have taken *her*, Sara wondered, and ate her heart out with longing.

It was hard to sleep that night. She kept waking up and listening to see if she could hear them coming home. They were attending a supper party after the performance and it must have been after two o'clock when they came in. Everywhere lights burned late on Nob Hill and the echo of music and laughter drifted through the spring night. Eventually, however, the Renwick household settled down to what hours of rest remained.

Sara felt that she hardly slept, yet she must have dozed off for she heard no sound of footsteps on the bare floor of the hall outside her door. She heard nothing at all until the faint tapping began in her dreams. Then she roused herself and sat up in bed.

Yes, someone was tapping at her door. She slipped into her wrapper and went to unlock the door, pulled it open a crack.

"Sara," Ritchie said softly, "I must talk to you. Let me come in for just a moment."

Her first impulse was to shut the door in his face. She had not forgiven him for his behavior that day at the office and she distrusted him completely. But she had drawn his laughter once before by leaping onto the bed and brandishing an umbrella. Since she did not want him to laugh again, she would hear with dignity what he had to say, and perhaps tell him a few things herself before she sent him away.

He came into the dark room, shivering a little. "Light a candle, Sara. So I won't bark my shins. Not that ghastly electric bulb. What a drafty cave this is. But never mind the fire—I won't stay long."

That was reassuring. She humored him by lighting the candle she always kept on the dresser, since power lines could blow down in a high wind. She had forgotten to tip her mirror up last night and for a startled instant her face looked palely back at her from the glass as the candle flame sprang to life.

Ritchie stood with his back to the door, while candlelight sent long shadows up the walls behind him, touched his face and hair with light, softening, gentling. She turned away, not wanting to remember his appeal.

"How was the opera?" she asked casually.

"Fine enough, I suppose. Certainly the evening wound up to a grand climax."

She sensed a nervous edginess about him, something that was queerly like defiance. He walked to the middle of the room and stood for a moment looking up the shaft into the tower above. Almost, it seemed to Sara, that he was listening. But for what? What was there to hear up there in the windy dark?

Then he turned, startling her. He reached a hand into his pocket and drew something out, balanced it on his open palm so that she could see. Sara caught the dazzle of a diamond in the candlelight. It was the stone in a ring. She had seen it a good many times on Judith's third finger.

"You see what I mean by a climax?" Ritchie said. "We've finally had this out. I'm tired of hedging and postponement. I told her we would be married next month, or not at all. You can see her answer."

There was a bright excitement in his eyes that Sara

knew of old. Pity for him stirred in her. Judith had not brought him happiness after all.

"I'm sorry," she said gently.

He closed his fingers over the ring, returned it to his pocket. "Sorry? Why should you be? And haven't I come directly to you, now that I'm free? Haven't you always been my girl, Sara?"

He came toward her so quickly that she had no chance to move away and his hand was cold beneath the sleeve of her wrapper. For the first time she was frightened, less sure of her own control of the situation.

"Let me go," she said. "It's too late to start over, Ritchie."

He almost flung her aside and dropped into a chair, where he sat watching her mockingly. "So that's the tune you mean to play? But you're not the stiff-necked sort like Judith. Relax and come talk to me, Sara."

The brief pity she'd felt for him had vanished and she remained stiffly where she was.

"I've nothing to say to you, Ritchie. Not now or ever again. There's nothing you can say that I want to hear. I'm truly sorry about you and Judith. But I can't believe that you'd turn so quickly from her to me. And I wouldn't want you if you did."

There was satisfaction in speaking the words, in telling him off at last. But the bright kindling in his eyes gave no hint that he understood what she was saying. There was still a strange listening quality about him. Almost as if he waited for something to happen.

He began to talk quickly, nervously, not troubling to lower his tones. His words were disconnected, as if he paid little attention to what he was saying. He spoke of Caruso's great voice, and of how wonderfully Fremstad had sung. But Sara knew he was merely uttering words, that he did not really care. And this was even more frightening.

"Hush," she whispered. "Don't talk so loudly. Why have you come here to tell me these things?"

He laughed at her caution. "Who is there to hear? I remember how soundly your mother sleeps. And Susan's room is at the other end of the house. There's no need to whisper. Is there, Sara?"

There was a tension in him that was dangerous. She must get him out of her room at once. She took a step toward the door, and then she too began to listen. The sound came from the next room and she knew at once what it was.

Someone in that empty room was opening a window to the cool night air of San Francisco. It could be no one but Nick, again on his night vigil, unable to sleep. She held up her hand to silence Ritchie. When she spoke it was so softly that no one but he could hear.

"Nick is in the next room. He has just opened a window. You must go downstairs at once before he hears you. Quickly. Don't make a sound!"

Ritchie's laugh had an ugly ring and he made no attempt to hide it. What he said might not be audible in the next room, but the sound of his voice would be.

"That's why I'm here," he said. "I followed him upstairs, though he doesn't know that. The time I kissed you in the office was an accident. It was a rebound from Judith's coolness. I hadn't planned for his interruption. But it gave me an idea, if ever I chose to use it."

She wondered if he had gone completely mad.

"What are you talking about? You must leave quickly before he finds you here!"

Because she was pulling at him, he rose from the chair, but in the candlelight she saw his kindled elation and he made no step toward the door.

"That's exactly what I want!" he cried. "Let him find me here. Let's see what the mighty Nicholas Renwick can make of that. Let's see what sort of fine scene he will make. Let's see how his sister will feel about this!"

Sara could only stare at him in dismay. His purpose made no sense, but his hatred of Nick was plain. Something else was plain too. Not for an instant was he considering her in any of this. She was an instrument for some twisted purpose of his own and it did not matter to him what harm might come to her from the scene he promised.

It was a chilling thing to see him like this—in the harsh light of a man completely centered in himself. No, not a man—a heedless boy who would not grow up.

He reached out to grasp her arm again and she struck him sharply across the face.

"Get out!" she told him rigidly. "Go back to your own room and don't make a sound on the way."

The slap startled him and he looked at her in genuine alarm, moved toward the door.

"But Nick—" he began, making one last try.

"If he has heard you, I will deal with him."

She pulled open the door and stood watching as Ritchie went toward the stairs. Once he looked back at her, but her will commanded and he continued on his way. She did not move until she heard the soft closing of his door downstairs. Only then did she turn her head and look toward the shadows of the other door.

Nick stood there, watching her. When he knew that she saw him he crossed the hall and pushed her unceremoniously back into her own room, came after her and closed the door behind him. In the candlelight she could see once more the contempt in his eyes, but increased now a hundredfold.

"You heard me and sent him away, didn't you? But not soon enough. How many times has he come here?" Nick's tone was quiet, knife-edged. "No—don't trouble to lie. You'll do that skillfully, I'm sure. I have only one thing to say to you. No word of this is to reach Judith. I will deal with Ritchie myself. As for you —tomorrow morning, *this* morning—you pack your things and leave. And I wish I could send Ritchie after you."

She could feel the trembling run through her as she faced him. In this unwelcome moment the truth she had not seen flashed upon her. It was not Ritchie and a childhood love that mattered to her. It was Nicholas Renwick. Nick—who held her only in contempt.

Shaken by the realization, she floundered for something to say. "Judith has broken her engagement to Ritchie only tonight. He—he told me just now—"

"So you've achieved your aim! I hope it gives you satisfaction." He turned from her and the doorknob squealed as he wrenched it, but he steadied the door and did not slam it as he went out.

He made no sound crossing the hallway. Sara stood where she was for a long moment, staring dazedly at the dark panel of the door. She felt stunned with shock, unable to comprehend what had happened.

Now there was no feeling in her, nothing. Had she held her hand above the candle flame she would have felt no pain, she thought. Once, she recalled wryly, she had enjoyed a slight bitter flavor. But now bitterness lay in her mouth, in her very spirit, and when she came to life again she would have to taste it, swallow it.

Because there was nowhere else to go she closed the door and turned toward the bed. In the middle of it sat Comstock, calmly washing his face. Comstock looked well with candlelight shining in his yellow eyes.

It was the presence of the cat that released hysteria in Sara. She flung herself upon the bed and sobbed with laughter, not troubling to stifle the sound against her pillow. There was no one to hear now. No one but Comstock. And Comstock had seen young hysterical females before. He drew himself out of the hollow which his big body had made in the covers and arched his back languidly, unimpressed by this outburst. After a long stretch to the tip of his forepaws, he came to sit beside her and began to wash her cheek with his sandpaper tongue. Comstock, the gayest Lothario on all Nob Hill, was happiest when he could mother some benighted human female.

The rasping touch of his tongue quieted Sara. She reached out and pulled the big cat close to her. She was crying now, but softly, and she no longer wanted to laugh. It was still not possible to understand all the facets of what had happened, but she knew that she had lost something forever tonight. Perhaps she had lost two things. First, the dream-Ritchie whom she had loved for so long and could never love again. Though now the fading of a dream seemed not to matter as it had before.

Far more important was the loss of Nick's respect and liking, the loss of friendship which had grown up between them. There were times, she knew, when Nick had liked her warmly. But he would not again understand and forgive. And this was the deepest loss of all.

Comstock purred steadily and the sound was soporific. He stood guard over her while she slept, and took care not to disturb her. Not until a little after five in the morning, when daylight was pressing against the windows, did he stir uneasily.

SIXTEEN

SARA SAT UP IN BED AT THE TOUCH OF COMSTOCK'S PAW, sharply, clearly awake. The look of the sky against her windows was somehow terrifying. It was steel-blue in the dawn, glittering. If you tapped it with a metal rod it would surely ring. The utter quiet was ominous. It seemed the quiet that must surely precede chaos.

She had a few minutes in which to think of getting out of bed and going to her mother's room. But it was too early to waken her mother for a foolish whim. At least she could get up and start the fire, begin to dress. Painful realization swept back upon her. This was the morning when she must pack and leave the Renwick house. Whether Miss Hester Varady liked it or not, she would have to take her niece without further delay. And that meant Sara would have to tell her mother. This would be a difficult day.

She had just pushed back the covers in order to get

out of bed when the underground roaring began and the room commenced to shake. The sound was like express trains tearing at full speed through the earth beneath her feet. The room rocked so that she was flung across the bed. As if waves rolled beneath it, the floor moved and the furniture danced about. All through the house there was a multitude of crashings. In the tower a vast shattering of glass sent jagged bits down the stair shaft. And all the while the rocking and roaring of the earth went on. Once or twice it lessened, only to commence again.

Sara and Comstock clung together, the cat yowling in terror. The underground monster would surely have its way, Sara thought; the entire Renwick mansion would be swallowed by the earth. Nothing could withstand this force that shook the world.

The span was only seconds—forty-eight, she learned later, but it seemed a lifetime. The final crash of a falling chimney, shattering against the roof near her windows, was merely one more noise in a disintegrating world.

Then the movement stopped. Vibration and sound ceased. From the ceiling across the room a great path of plaster slithered down the wall and crumbled into bits while Sara watched it. This time Comstock leaped spitting and snarling out of the bed and landed in the middle of the floor, every hair abristle. Only later did Sara find how badly he had scratched her arms.

She sat up and put on her slippers, because that was the thing you did when you got out of bed. Her clock lay face down on the floor, its face broken. The hands had stopped a little after thirteen minutes past five. This, Sara thought, must have been one of those real shakes that Allison had spoken of. She must go at once and see about her mother and how the rest of the house had fared. But when she tried to pull open her door it would not budge. It wasn't locked—she tried the key and it turned easily. Somehow the frame had jammed and though she threw herself against the paneling, while Comstock watched her, mewing, she could not jar it loose.

After a moment of fright at the discovery that she was trapped, Sara quieted. Surely if the house had come through a shaking like this, it could survive anything. Sooner or later she would be remembered and rescued. Perhaps if she climbed to the tower she could call to someone in the street. Besides, she wanted to see what had happened to San Francisco.

As she turned to the stair, Comstock's yowls at the door grew louder, more protesting. He had other responsibilities in this house, he wanted her to know.

"I'm sure Allison is all right," Sara told him. "We'll both have to wait a while to get out."

She climbed the narrow stair to the tower. It was a cold, clear morning, without wind. She still wore her wrapper and she turned the collar up about her throat, stepped gingerly over broken glass. Every window up here had shattered, but the tower stood intact. She looked out toward the south upon a city curiously changed. Where there had been chimneys and spires, many were gone. Here and there walls had collapsed outward, or a roof had caved in. Over everything a thin dust was rising, engulfing the city even as she watched, like a peculiar, choking fog.

Yet most of San Francisco seemed to be standing, unharmed except for those chimneys and steeples. The business district stood as usual. Sara waited and as the dust cloud lifted, she could see the town again. Everyone was in the streets now. As far as she could see pavements were black with people who had rushed outdoors. In front of the Renwick mansion several had gathered. She saw Ritchie with a dressing gown flung over his night clothes, and Judith shivering in a lacy negligee. There was Allison in a long nightgown, jumping up and down while her mother sought to quiet her. Susan came running out sobbing, and no one told her to stop. Only Nick and her mother were missing. Had they been hurt?

She called down to the others in sudden alarm. "Have you seen my mother? And where is Nick?"

They all tipped their heads back and stared at her, like dolls pulled by a string.

"Nick went to find your mother and you," Mrs. Renwick shouted. "You'd better come down from that tower, Sara. There's no telling what may happen if there's another shake."

Allison began to scream that she must go inside for Comstock.

"Comstock's all right—he's with me," Sara assured her. "But my door's jammed and we'll have to wait for Nick."

Those in the street ceased craning at her and Sara felt strangely remote in her high tower. An enchantment lay about her through which reality could not for the moment penetrate. What was happening seemed distant, as if it did not affect her.

To the south, beyond Market Street, a dozen or more wisps of smoke were drifting skyward. Sara remembered the young fireman's words: "There's always fires after a quake." It looked as if the fire department would have its work cut out for it this morning. Undoubtedly fires had already been lit in the shacks south of Market. Probably stoves and lamps had been knocked over. People there rose earlier than they did on Nob Hill.

From the room below she heard a sudden pounding, heard her mother's voice calling her name. Quickly she went downstairs and tried the door again.

"I can't get it open," she called to her mother. "But I'm not hurt. Are you alright?"

It was Nick's voice that answered her. "She's perfectly all right. I'll find some tools and get you out of there."

Sara looked at the distraught Comstock. "We'll have to be patient," she told him.

At least this would give her an opportunity to dress more suitably than those who had rushed out in the streets. She put on her gray traveling suit and even her gray hat and veil. Then she pulled her suitcase from beneath the bed and began to pack methodically, calmly. This was the day when she must move to Hester Varady's, and she would not give Nick a chance to mention it again.

A slow, dull ache began in her at the thought of him, and she turned her mind quickly to other things in order to shut it out. Her trunk would have to be sent later, but she could take the more important things now. She packed Consuelo's Spanish comb, put in her father's picture, her toilet articles and some wearing apparel.

It helped to keep busy. She was glad of any distraction that kept her from really thinking, from living over what had happened during the night.

Nick was working on the door now, using a metal instrument. Comstock moved back a little, but continued to give mewing advice.

When Sara had packed she climbed again to the tower. From Nob Hill down to the valley of Market Street, people gathered fearfully in clumps outdoors. But the Renwicks seemed to have gone to dress in warmer clothes. The fires in the distance looked more serious than they had before. In fact, some of them seemed to have combined and she could see spurts of flame. How lucky that there was no wind. She wondered if Chief Sullivan would have to follow his plan to make a stand at Market Street. But surely not. Every fire engine in the city must be at work by now, and the fires would soon be under control.

In the room below the door burst open with a bang and her mother called to her anxiously.

"I'm coming," Sara said and managed the stairs again.

Comstock had vanished and Nick Renwick was picking up his tools. He gave her no more than a glance and a cool good morning. She fancied that if her mother had not been there he might not have spoken to her at all.

"Why—you've packed your suitcase," Mary Jerome said.

"I had time, so why not?" Sara told her lightly. "There're some fires around town. And there might be another earthquake. I thought I'd get ready to move."

Nick said he wanted a better look at those fires and climbed to the tower. When he came down a few moments later his face was grave. He spoke to Mrs. Jerome.

"I believe I'll go down to the office. It's on the south side of Market and there's no telling whether those fires will get out of hand. I suggest that you fill every bathtub in the house with water, while it's still to be had. Sometimes a main breaks when there's an earthquake and we don't want to be left without water."

He went off to dress and Sara helped her mother fill the tubs. Ominously the water gave out halfway through the second tub.

Before he left, Nick gave orders that no fires were to be lit in stoves or grates. Some of the chimneys were damaged and no risk must be taken. By now Susan had gone to take the ferry to Oakland where her family lived. And the other servants hadn't come to work. Only the coachman had stayed with his horses. Mrs. Jerome and Sara managed to serve a cold breakfast, which they all ate together at the table in the kitchen.

Judith seemed like a sleepwalker today, as if what was happening to San Francisco was a dream from which she expected to waken. Her left hand was bare of any ring, though this was something Mrs. Renwick had apparently not yet noticed. Ritchie had found that by giving all his attention to Mrs. Renwick, he could ignore both Judith and Sara.

In the kitchen Mrs. Jerome moved with a calm capability, restoring order out of a chaos of pots and pans and broken crockery. She had the air of a woman who knew how to meet trouble, and the others in the house had begun to lean on her.

There had been two or three mild temblors since the

big shock, and now any stirring of the earth made them fly to dubious outside safety, only to troop sheepishly back indoors when the shock had passed. As time went on, however, everyone began to take the after quakes somewhat more for granted and find them less terrifying than at first. Though more bricks fell from the chimneys from time to time, no further serious damage was done.

After a hurried breakfast, Ritchie went out to stand on the front steps, watching the smoke cloud in the valley. Nick had not suggested that he come along to the office and he was plainly bored at being left behind with the women. After a time he decided to see for himself what was happening, and went down the hill toward Market Street. Judith hardly appeared to know that he had gone.

All over Nob Hill people stood in upper windows, in towers, even on the rooftops, watching through field glasses as the fires spread through the low area. Sara and her mother and Allison climbed to the tower to watch the spectacle. Judith stayed in Mrs. Renwick's sitting room, while her mother moved from door to window, wanting to miss nothing. Mrs. Renwick remained confident that all would soon be well.

From the tower Sara could see that the lower end of Market Street was hidden by smoke and all the Mission district looked to be on fire. The clouds, boiling straight up on the windless air, pulsed with light on their under side and the roar and crackling could be clearly heard.

"It's out of control," Mrs. Jerome said without emotion. "This is more than the fire department can handle."

Streams of refugees had begun to leave the danger area and pour toward the hills. They made a black tide along the streets as they turned toward the west and north for safety. Once Sara ran downstairs to talk to some who had climbed Nob Hill in their anxiety to put height between themselves and the fire. Then she went back to the tower with her disquieting news.

"They say the water mains were broken by the quake," she told the other two. "There's no water to fight the fire except close to the bay. All electricity went off at once and the fire stations didn't receive orders as quickly as they should. People are saying that the whole section south of Market will burn before nightfall."

"Will the fire come up here?" Allison asked.

"Not right away, dear," Mrs. Jerome said. "I think we can stay where we are awhile longer."

At least there was the heartening news that General Funston had brought in his men from the Presidio and they were helping to get people out, setting up fire lines. Union Square, one man said, was so crowded you could hardly get through. Somebody had seen the great Caruso there, sitting on his trunk like any other refugee.

It was Allison who first spied Nick climbing toward the house, burdened by a huge wastebasket filled with ledgers and papers. Sara and Allison hurried downstairs to meet him, while Mrs. Jerome followed more slowly. Allison called to her mother as they went out, and Mrs. Renwick and Judith joined them on the front steps.

Nick set his burden down on the sidewalk and rested on the steps.

"Of course no one showed up at the office," he told them. "Merkel lives across the bay and probably couldn't get in. The ferries are still running, but they're only taking people out, not in. This stuff is all I could manage to carry of our records and papers. I'm afraid our side of Market Street will go like the rest."

"But won't the firemen make a stand and keep the fire from crossing Market?" Sara asked.

He glanced at her wearily. "They're doing their best, but there's no water to be had except from the bay. Lines of hose are being stretched the length of Market, but the pressure weakens to a trickle at that distance. And it all takes time. Time is what we lack most, along with water. At least I brought some records out. They're more important than ever now. People are going to need insurance money when this is over."

Judith seemed to come momentarily out of her trance. The look she exchanged with her brother was filled with some grim meaning which Sara didn't grasp. She hoped Nick would stay with them now, but already he was rising from his brief rest on the steps.

"Keep an eye on this stuff, will you?" he said, gesturing toward the basket. "I'm going back. Every hand is needed. You're all safe enough up here—don't worry."

"You—haven't seen Ritchie?" Judith asked.

"No. I probably wouldn't see him in the crowds. People are streaming both ways down the middle of Market—going toward the ferries and toward the hills, depending on which appeals most. And there are hundreds more turning up the side streets."

Allison pointed suddenly. "Look! Here comes that Chinese servant from Geneva's!"

Ah Foong had evidently come all the way from Van Ness on foot. He bobbed a silent greeting to the group on the steps as he handed Nick an envelope.

"Geneva has been worried about us," Nick said, opening it. "Her aunt sends word that we are all to come to her house if there's any danger." He smiled wryly. "I can see that the role of host to refugees might appeal to Miss Varady's sense of the dramatic. I've never known her to miss a chance of playing the *grande dame.*" But he shook his head at Ah Foong. "Tell Miss Hester we're a lot safer up here than where she is. One of the fires got across Van Ness near the Market Street end. Though I believe it's under control by now. Tell Miss Geneva we're safe, Ah Foong, and if their house is in danger she and Miss Varady must come here."

"Miss Valady stay," said Ah Foong calmly. Today he had bound his pigtail in a neat coil at the back of his head where it would not get in his way. His only concession to disaster, apparently.

When he had gone an officer rode up on a horse, looked them over and spoke to Nick. "You got an automobile here? We need volunteers to haul dynamite."

The women stared at him, but Nick said quietly that he did have one and he would drive it if he was needed.

"Not dynamite!" Mrs. Renwick cried. "Surely you won't take dynamite into the fire area, Nick?"

"We'll do what has to be done," said Nick. "I'll get the auto now."

"What are they going to do with dynamite?" Allison demanded, beside herself with excitement.

The man on horseback gave her a lopsided grin. "Blow up a few buildings maybe. If they can ever agree which ones to sacrifice. That's one way of fighting a fire. But it will take a lot of dynamite to do the job."

Sara looked toward the tall buildings of Market Street, standing strong and high, with the fire bright behind them. In only a few minutes, the scene seemed immeasurably worse. The air was growing warmer from the heat.

"Could be we'll need your horses too," the officer said to the women. "We'll use all the help we can get to pull and haul. They're plenty of earthquake injured lying on the grass in Portsmouth Square. We're setting up refugee camps in Golden Gate Park and the Presidio. You folks better start trekking out there if the fire comes this way. But go on foot. We need cars and carriages for those who can't walk."

"The fire won't climb Nob Hill," said Mrs. Renwick stanchly.

Nick had driven the auto into the street from the side drive and he heard her words as he stopped at the curb. "The laws of gravity don't impress fire very much, Mother. Better keep a lookout posted. I'll get back when I can."

Sara stood up to watch them go—Nick toward the Presidio for his first load of dynamite, the officer toward the fire. She felt both excited and alarmed. She wished that she could volunteer for some useful job as a man had the right to do. When you worked you could forget worry. When you did nothing, anxiety ate at you, wouldn't let you rest. She wouldn't be at ease again until she saw Nick safely returned from his assignment.

Before Nick left he told the coachman to take the horses where they could be used, and drive the carriage as a rescue vehicle if he wished. The man was eager enough to be a part of what was happening and he had gone shortly after Nick. So the women were alone.

So far the one thing in favor of the fire fighters had been the lack of wind. But now a breeze stirred from the southeast, rising to a wind, blowing strong. The clouds of smoke and flame began to billow as they had not done before, rolling eagerly toward new fuel. The wind dropped cinders and bits of char on Nob Hill, and now they could feel the fierce heat of the fire on their faces. The smell of it was hot and choking.

When the first blast of dynamite came, it startled them all. A flash ripped the smoke canopy, there was a roar and a shower of sparks. Then black bits of the building which had blown up dropped back to earth. A new tide of refugees said the fire fighters had had to retreat from Market Street. The wind had sent the fire bearing down upon them, driving them back with its heat. Hundreds of feet of hose were being sacrificed because the fire was too close, too fierce.

Again the women in the Renwick house managed a cold meal. Then they went inevitably back to watch the fire from either windows or tower. The roaring was closer now and the furnace heat flushed their cheeks. They dipped their handkerchiefs in water and kept applying it to their faces to ease the burning.

All about the Palace Hotel the fire raged, but the building withstood until late afternoon. Then, with the last defender fled, flames broke through every bay window so that the entire structure flared like a torch. No one spoke now as they watched. Even the refugees in the streets were silent, dazed, the mark of horror in their eyes.

Never, Sara thought, would she forget the sound of those crowds pouring away from the fire. Not only the steady drum of feet, but the constant rattle, the scraping noise of possessions being dragged across cobblestones. Anything on wheels had been put to use, from doll carriages to wagons. Trunks bumped along on roller skates or wagon wheels, or scraped harshly as they were pulled by the handles. There was no panic, no tears, no wailing. Just this vast, stunned exodus.

Still Mrs. Renwick said, "It won't touch Nob Hill. This is William's house. He would want us to stay."

By evening, when the sun was red in the west—red as the sky and the sea beneath—Ritchie came home, blackened, weary but strangely alive, as Sara had never before seen him. Market Street was lost, he said. And the refugees would have to get out of Union Square and Portsmouth Square too. The fire was already eating that way. But there was no hurry here on Nob Hill. He was going to drop into his own bed and sleep till the fire wakened him. Mrs. Jerome took him some food, but he fell asleep, too weary to eat.

A man who identified himself as a member of the Citizens' Patrol came around and warned them to light no fires, no candles. The Mayor had ordered those citizens who had not been evacuated to stay at home when night fell. Looters would be shot without mercy. The Mayor's Committee of Fifty was in charge—made up of leading citizens—and the city could count on a continuance of rescue and patrol work.

With all telephone and telegraph services out, San Francisco might be isolated from the world, but law and order was being maintained. A great tragedy and handicap had been the injury of Fire Chief Sullivan, who was said to be near death due to the collapse of the fire station where he had his living quarters.

While there was still daylight, Mrs. Jerome suggested that they get packed and ready for the worst. They should be prepared to leave at a moment's notice if the time came. She had taken over the guardianship of Nick's wastebasket full of papers and she placed it in the hall near the front door so that it could be saved first if necessary. Sara found herself in the role of aide to her mother and she did her bidding without question.

Once, when Sara went into Mrs. Renwick's rooms to see how she was managing, she found Nick's mother standing on the sideboard in her small dining room, taking the Japanese plates down from their rack on the wall.

"What are you doing that for?" Sara asked.

Hilda Renwick clasped a delicate gold and red plate to her bosom. "I really must save these plates, Sara. If William's house burns, this is all I will have that he treasured."

"Perhaps you could let Allison carry the plates when the time comes to leave."

Mrs. Renwick stared. "Allison? But it was Allison who broke one of these very—"

"But don't you see," Sara tried to explain patiently, "it would be good for Allison to be trusted with them."

With a cumbersome effort Mrs. Renwick sat down on the sideboard. But it was not the subject of Allison which most interested her.

"Sara, have you any idea what's happened between Judith and Ritchie?" she asked. "When I noticed that she wasn't wearing her ring, I pointed it out, thinking she might have laid it down somewhere. But she told me Ritchie had it and after that she wouldn't say another word."

"Then perhaps you'd better ask Ritchie," Sara suggested, moving toward the door.

"Wait, Sara! Ritchie won't talk about it. He looks like a thundercloud if I mention Judith. And usually he's so sweet."

"I don't know anything about it," Sara said and escaped from her questioning.

No one slept very much that night. Not wanting to go upstairs to lonely bedrooms, the women gathered in the library, clearing a space among hundreds of books which had been jarred from the shelves. They napped uneasily on the leather couch, and on mattresses dragged down from their beds. The room never grew completely dark because of the fire glow in the sky. Dynamite blasts shattered the air with their constant recurrence, and began to seem frighteningly close. Orders had been given for all windows to be left partly open so that concussion wouldn't blow out the panes. This made the night hotter and more noisy than ever. The after tremors continued and added to the general uneasiness, though now no one rushed outside when they occurred.

Mrs. Renwick had wrapped her precious plates in pillowcases and brought them into the library with her. Somehow, to his wife, they seemed to embody the strength and decision of William Renwick, and there were moments when she regarded them with an expectant air, as if they might speak with his voice and direct them all.

Mrs. Jerome and Allison shared a mattress, with Comstock at their feet. It was Mary who finally got Allison to settle down and go to sleep. Judith spent most of the night at the tall southeast windows, staring at the fire. Her crown of pale hair took on a reddish hue in the glow and she seemed like a woman in some spell of enchantment. Sara, stirring now and then from her own fitful sleep, saw her and wondered what she was thinking. Why must she stand without cease, watching the fire? How did she feel about Ritchie?

In the red, glaring dawn, Sara climbed once more to the tower to see what was happening. All the sky was hidden by smoke and flame. She held her ears against the roaring, winced at the blistering heat. Now fire lapped the low streets below Nob Hill. Chinatown was burning. All the downtown area had been swept to skeleton ruin. In the red light she could see the Chinese making their way uphill in an endless line—differing from other refugees in their bright costumes and the strange burdens they carried. She saw one old man who moved haltingly, bearing in his hands a porcelain statue of some Chinese goddess. And there were those with tiny cricket cages, others with lacquer boxes. Here were not only servants in their blue linen, but mandarins in handsome robes, and gaudily dressed women tottering along on tiny "lily feet," leaning on attendants.

"Sara!" That was Allison calling. "Sara, come down. I'm frightened."

No longer was this an adventure for Allison. She still lugged Comstock, and while he rebelled now and then and pushed her away, he always returned to comfort her. Sara climbed down to the glass-strewn room where Allison waited. The little girl drew her at once from this high place where the fire lit every corner. The upper hallway of the house was dark, comparatively cool. Allison shut the door upon the fire glare, groped her way to the top step. The distant sounds were muffled here, the darkness soothing to smarting eyes. She slipped her hand into Sara's and they sat in silence for a few minutes, each comforted by the human touch of the other.

"This house is going to burn too, isn't it?" Allison whispered.

"I'm afraid so," Sara said. "Mama says we must leave soon. I keep hoping Nick will come and tell us what to do." The thought of Nick and his dangerous work had never been far from her mind through this long night. He had said he would come back when he could. And he had not come. If he had been hurt, even killed, they might not know for a long time. She dared not let her mind follow that frightening path.

"Nick is all right," Allison said with an air of confidence. "We don't have to worry about him."

"Why are you sure?"

"Nick's careful. He's not like Uncle Ritchie. Uncle Ritchie would take a stick of dynamite and see how close he could get to the fire. But Nick won't take foolish chances."

They sat in silence again and Sara, who had begun to lose her sense of courage and strength, felt oddly comforted.

Allison said, "Nick's like bread, isn't he?"

For a moment Sara didn't know what she was talking about. Then she remembered the game Allison had played long ago, before the city of San Francisco had begun to burn. Yes, she thought, Nick *was* like bread. Something to live by, to depend on. She remembered that he had thought Allison's term unflattering.

"With butter?" Sara asked, smiling a little in the dark. "Don't you think we ought to add butter?"

"No," said Allison. "With Nick you don't need any butter."

It was still early morning when they heard someone pounding on the front door. Allison flew down the stairs and reached the door first, with Sara right after her.

In the doorway, bowing with his usual formality, stood Ah Foong. When he spoke his words permitted no contradiction.

"Miss Valady say you come now. She wantchee you Valady house, Missy Sala. Also fam'ly of Mista Nick."

"There's nothing else to do," Sara said. "I'll tell Mama and we'll come at once."

When she saw Ah Foong, Mrs. Jerome was disturbed. "We need not go to Miss Varady's house," she told him. "We can go to the Park as others are doing."

But this time Mrs. Renwick objected and the rest bore her out. There was no point in camping in a park if a house waited for them in a safer area. So Mrs. Jerome dropped her opposition and went silently to oversee the last-minute things that had to be done. Sara watched her mother uneasily. She was not at all sure what would happen when she and Miss Varady faced each other.

The women put their hats on and gathered up their various bundles. Until the last minute, Sara hoped that Nick might come. But when they were all outside and he still had not appeared, she gave up looking for him.

As her mother pointed out, Nick would know where to find them.

There was a moment when Ritchie spoke directly to Judith before they left. "I'm going to see you to the Varady house before I go back to help in the fire area," he said.

Judith did not look at him. "That's not necessary. I'm sure you can do more good somewhere else."

But Ritchie, though he flushed angrily, did not leave them.

Mrs. Renwick had apparently heeded Sara's suggestion, because Allison, her face red from heat and pride, clutched Comstock under one arm and two of her mother's plates, carefully wrapped, under the other.

Ah Foong marched ahead, carrying Nick's basket of papers, and Sara and Allison followed close on his heels. Ritchie helped Mrs. Renwick, and Judith walked on the other side of her mother. Mrs. Jerome came last, making sure their little group stayed together.

As they turned west the steep drop of the hill shielded them from the withering heat at their backs. And hats were fine things for catching cinders. But the fire was on their left too, roaring at the foot of every street. The Nob Hill mansions stood serenely, indifferent to their doom. And always the dynamite blasts crashed along the nerves, shattering in their unexpectedness. No matter how you braced yourself, you weren't ready for the explosion when it came.

California Street looked safe enough and along it the endless stream of refugees stumbled. Once in a while there was a burst of song and even laughter. One old man, resting on a washbasket filled with his possessions, called to them as they went by.

"Wait till you see the city we build next time!" And again there was laughter.

Sara began to feel a pride and a kinship for the strangers around her. She too belonged to San Francisco. These were her people.

Now and then they rested, but always they picked up their burdens and went on again. Ahead lay Van Ness and the house of Hester Varady. But to judge from the way the wind was blowing and the way the fire downhill seethed toward the west, it might be that Van Ness Avenue was doomed too.

SEVENTEEN

When they reached Van Ness they saw water being used for the first time. Here some of the mains were still intact and soot-blackened firemen and civilians worked with lengths of hose. Someone said there was a fireboat as well, down at the end of the street pumping water from the bay. If necessary, one fireman claimed, they'd blast every house on the avenue to hold the line here.

Toward the Market Street end, some of the houses on the east side of Van Ness were already burning, but here the western houses stood bleak and waiting, their façades dripping wet where firemen had hosed them down to help resist sparks.

They reached the Varady house to find it had suffered little outward damage from the earthquake. Ah Foong led them inside, where the usual broken bric-a-brac, cracked mirrors, fallen plaster were in evidence.

Only Mrs. Jerome remained near the doorway, reluctant to meet Miss Varady.

Geneva greeted them eagerly, but looked only for the absent Nick.

"He said he'd get back to us when he could," Sara told her. "He—he's helping where he is needed."

"Of course," said Geneva. "Nick would do that. Do come in, everyone. Aunt Hester is waiting for you in the drawing room."

The great room was dim, and Sara blinked to accustom her eyes to the gloom. Miss Varady waited for them as calmly as though nothing untoward were going on outside. The crowding vines sheltered the room to some extent from both heat and red light. A great bowlful of roses stood on the piano. So long had the refugees breathed smoke and dust that the scent of the flowers seemed astonishing and unreal.

Miss Varady left her high-backed chair and came toward them. She wore cool pale green today and one had the feeling, looking at her, that no disaster could ever ruffle a hair of her head, or cause the slightest change in her demeanor.

Though the others went into the drawing room, Mrs. Jerome remained in the hall. She had not wanted to come to this house at all, and had done so only to remain in the party. Ritchie bowed as charmingly over Miss Varady's hand as if the occasion had been a party, and Hester Varady seemed pleased.

Of all the group, Mrs. Renwick had rallied most surprisingly. Not once on the walk from Nob Hill had she mentioned her fluttering heart. Having rescued her plates and William's picture, she had apparently resigned herself to the loss of all else. Now she regarded Miss Varady with an open and lively interest.

Miss Varady's attention, however, had been caught by the little girl who stood in the doorway with an unhappy Comstock in her arms.

"Take that cat out of here," she ordered. "I cannot abide cats. Put him outside at once."

Allison, who had set her mother's plates down to struggle with the uneasy cat, stared at her.

"If my cat has to go outside, I will too," she said.

Sara drew her quickly into the hall, out of her aunt's sight. "You needn't put him outside, but perhaps you'd better keep him out of her way for a little while. I'll try to explain that he's one of the family."

"Comstock doesn't like her either," said Allison.

And indeed Comstock was showing a remarkable antipathy for this house and its mistress. With a final struggle he leaped from Allison's grasp and landed lightly on the hall carpet. Then he rose to the tips of his toes, while his tail bristled and every hair on his body stood on end, until he was a monstrous size.

Mrs. Jerome watched him in sympathy. "That's exactly how I feel in this house," she admitted.

"It's because he's not a witch's cat," Allison said. "He likes *good* people." She let Comstock stay where he was, but kept near lest he dart away.

"Don't let Aunt Hester hear you say such a thing," Sara warned. Then she turned to her mother. "Please come in, Mama. You mustn't stay here in the hall."

"Not now," Mrs. Jerome said. She was tired after the long walk, but she held herself erect and somehow remote from these surroundings. "I don't want to go near that woman until I have to. Perhaps we won't stay here after all. You go back if you like, Sara. I'll keep Allison company."

Pulled two ways, Sara's curiosity won out and she returned to the drawing room to find the others sitting about uneasily in stiff chairs. Miss Varady dispatched Ah Foong to make tea with the aid of a spirit lamp in the kitchen.

"You are all quite safe here," she assured them. "My house will not burn." But her assurance was to be contradicted almost at once.

They heard steps outside and a man came through the front door, walked into the drawing room without ceremony.

"Who's in charge here?" he demanded, looking at Ritchie.

Miss Varady answered him. "I am in charge. What do you wish?"

"Orders," he said. "You'll have to leave. Everyone out of the house. Fire's blowing this way. You can start for Golden Gate Park, if you want. Or if you don't care to go so far, there're a lot of folks camping in Lafayette Square. But don't take more than ten minutes to get out of here."

"What if we do not choose to leave?" Miss Varady said.

He stared at her. Then he slapped a holster on his hip. "You'll leave. We don't waste time arguing. I'll be back in a bit to see that you've cleared out."

He went out and Sara could see that her aunt's eyes glittered with anger.

"Well," said Ritchie, "I suppose we'd better start. I'll see you as far as the Square, and then come back to the fire lines here."

Miss Varady stood beside her chair, watching Ritchie follow them from the room. Geneva hovered beside her aunt anxiously. Sara stayed where she was.

"Stop twittering!" said Miss Varady to Geneva. "You'll go with the others, of course. And you, Sara. Don't go any farther than Lafayette Square. When it's over you can come back here. All of you. I shall be happy to make you welcome and as comfortable as possible."

As Nick had expected, Hester Varady was enjoying her dramatic role.

Geneva hurried after Mrs. Renwick, eager to ask about Nick, but Miss Varady made no move toward the door.

"Aren't you coming with us, Aunt Hester?" Sara asked.

Miss Varady shook her head. "I shall not leave my house. Ah Foong and I will remain here."

"Then I'll stay too," said Sara.

The decision surprised her a little. She had made it without thought. But now that the words were spoken, she knew this was what she wanted to do. There had been enough of tame retreat. The women were in no danger, and her mother would not need her for the moment.

Miss Varady, however, had other ideas. "You will go with the rest," she told Sara and her words were a command.

For a moment Sara thought of rebelling. Then she turned away. There was a better means of staying than to oppose her aunt openly.

She went to the door where Mrs. Jerome still

waited. The man from the Citizens' Patrol had gone on to the next house and was paying no attention.

"If it gets too bad here, I'll come to find you in the Square," she whispered to her mother. "But for now I'd like to stay. This is where everything is happening."

Her mother looked at her sadly, but she did not protest. It was as if she had done all she could do. Now what lay between Sara and Hester Varady was out of her hands. There was dignity in the way she drew Sara to her, kissed her cheek lovingly, and then turned away to join the others. For an instant Sara felt as she had as a child, seeing her mother go away from her on some errand, being uncertain of her return. But now she was grown and she could not cling as once she might have done.

She returned softly to Miss Varady's hall. She could hear Ah Foong talking to her aunt in the drawing room, and she ran toward the stairs. Up she went to the dark third floor, dropped the suitcase and pillowcase of tinned goods she had carried inside a bedroom door and stole back to the head of the stairs to listen for what happened below.

It was very still within the house. Outside the fire sounds, the shouting, the noise of blasting made an ugly chaos. She wondered how her aunt meant to deal with the patrol fellow when he returned. Before the time was up she heard Miss Varady and Ah Foong cross the lower hall, heard the quiet opening and closing of a door downstairs.

The man from the patrol was back in ten minutes as he had promised, calling out to know if everyone had left the house. No one answered. He banged about a bit, opening a door or two, slamming it shut. Then he came up to the second floor, while Sara retreated from the third-floor rail. He called again, listened, then ran downstairs and out of the house. Sara crept back to the stair well.

A door opened softly, there were footsteps close enough for her to hear. Her aunt's voice called to her up stairs.

"Very well, Sara. You may come down now."

She went down, astonished, and a little shamefaced. Her aunt waited for her in the dim lower hall.

"How did you know?" Sara asked.

There was no softening of Miss Varady's expression, but she was not angry either.

"You did what I would have done at your age. Since you've chosen to stay, we are in this together. Fortunately the fellow didn't look for us in my medicine closet under the stairs. Come along to the dining room and we'll have that cup of tea and some food. If the patrol returns I shall deal with him."

The dining room, off the lower hall at the rear of the house, was dusky behind closed shutters, and a few degrees cooler. Ah Foong brought tea and a plate of sandwiches and Sara found she was hungry. Miss Varady did not talk as they ate, and Sara wondered what thoughts went on behind her aunt's stern calm.

When they had finished the meal Ah Foong spirited away the dishes, cleared the table. But the two women sat on in the dim room, lost at one end of the great table, with the heavy, forbidding furniture standing about in dignified array.

Once Miss Varady raised a finger as if to hush Sara, who had not made a sound. Beneath the outside noses came the clear echo of footsteps at the front door.

Miss Varady rose swiftly, but before she could move Nick's voice called from the hall and Ah Foong darted out to greet him.

Into the dining room he came, blinking to accustom his eyes to the gloom, after the fire glare outside. He stood at the far end of the table, his hands gripping a chair back as if he needed to hold to something in order to stand. His face was haggard, soot-streaked; he was utterly weary. Sara looked at him with her heart in her eyes and was glad he would not notice.

"You are all supposed to be out of this house," he told Miss Varady. "They'll be dynamiting across the street in the next block and this is no place to stay."

She ignored his words. "When did you sleep last?"

Nick drew a hand over his face as if to rub away the weariness. "I had an hour or two during the night out at the Presidio. What does it matter?"

"Are you still carrying dynamite for the fire fighters?"

"No." He shook his head again, shaking away the haze. "The auto finally broke down for good. I've had tire and engine trouble several times. The streets are rough going because of earthquake debris."

"Then go upstairs and get some sleep," Miss Varady said. "You're no good to anybody in the state you're in. We're not leaving this house unless we are driven out by the fire itself. Ah Foong, bring more tea."

"I've told you we can't stay here," Nick said dully. He could not seem to rouse himself to give a real order.

It was Miss Varady who gave the order. "Sit down. Before you collapse. Your family has retreated safely to Lafayette Square and Geneva has gone with them. Sara chose to remain with me. And I have no intention of turning my house over to looters, or to be dynamited."

There was plainly no arguing with her, and Nick was too tired to try. He pulled out the chair and dropped into it, leaned his head against the back and closed his eyes. In a moment he would probably have been sound asleep, but Ah Foong came with tea and food. Sara ran to take the tray from Ah Foong's hands before he could object. She poured a cup of tea quickly, added a little sugar.

"You'll feel better if you drink this," she said, and set the cup beside Nick's blackened hand, the sandwiches before him.

The hot liquid seemed to revive him as he drank. Sara, moved by a new tenderness, watched him. If only the time need not come when he would look at her again as a person and remember what had happened that night with Ritchie.

Miss Varady left her place to look more closely at Nick's hands as he raised the teacup.

"Your hands are burned," she said. "They need care. Ah Foong, bring me my kit."

Ah Foong scurried off and was back in a moment with a professional-looking tray of bandages and salve. Nick allowed her to smooth on the ointment, bind his hands. She talked the while, as briskly as she worked.

"If I'd been born a man I'd have been a doctor, I think. You didn't know that, did you? Sometimes I'm sorry I didn't study for the medical profession in spite of the prejudice against women. Of course my father would never have forgiven me. At least I've learned all I could through books—and that's a good deal."

Nick thanked her and revived enough to question

Sara. "How are the others doing? Mother? What about her heart?"

"She seems to be fine," Sara told him. "I think she forgot about her flutters completely. But she wouldn't leave those Japanese plates behind, no matter what. I think she felt that bringing them along was a little like saving your father."

Nick winced as Miss Varady touched a raw place. "And Judith?"

"She's in a sort of daze. She stood at the library window most of the night watching the fire as if it fascinated her. We all watched it, of course. But not so steadily. And she doesn't show any emotion about what's happening."

"Poor Judy," Nick said gently. "It's time she came to life. Though I'm not quite sure what will happen when she does."

It was the first time Sara had ever heard him use the nickname and it did not seem to suit the magnificent Judith. She went on to tell him about Allison and how keyed up with excitement she had grown. Her chief concern had been for Comstock, who had proved himself quite a handful.

Nick listened without comment and when she had finished Sara got restlessly up from the table.

"Aunt Hester, I'm going to the front windows to see what is happening outside."

Her aunt made no objection. Sara crossed the hall to the drawing room, where hot red light now glowed behind the draperies. How close the fire was! It seemed impossible that this house could escape. She was aware of tall gilt-framed mirrors reflecting light and shadow, and of Consuelo's picture watching calmly from above the mantel. The picture was askew, a mirror was cracked and there were bits of plaster strewn across the carpet.

Before Sara could part the draperies to look out, the explosion came. The flash was brilliant and the house rocked with the impact, echoed with the crash of sound. Draperies billowed as if in a gale and if the windows hadn't been open the glass would all have blown to bits. As it was, glass crashed about Sara's feet from the window nearest her and she jumped back, glad of long skirts which saved her from the jagged slivers. Almost at once debris began to rain on the roof, clatter against the wall of the house.

Nick came into the room quickly and Miss Varady followed him. They stood at the windows, watching the sea of flame lapping the very shores of Van Ness, with only dynamited ruins standing black against it.

From behind vines shriveling now in the heat, they could look without being seen. But they could not stand at the windows for long. It was as if a gigantic furnace door had been opened and its breath blew heat that fairly scorched the skin. Yet the house did not burst spontaneously into flame, and back within its dim hallways and rooms it was cool by comparison.

No one came to see if the house was empty, and after a while Nick lay down wearily in the library and went to sleep. Miss Varady moved restlessly from window to window about the house, upstairs and down, watching for fire within as well as without. Ah Foong kept his own alert vigil. Sara at length fell asleep with her head on the dining-room table.

In a few hours Nick was up again, this time to work with the fighters who held the line, in spite of his burned hands. Ritchie was out there too. All that long day and into the night the struggle continued. Now and then Ah Foong went out to gather news and see what was happening to the rest of the town. He climbed to Lafayette Square and located the Renwick family. From the vantage point of that height he watched the mansions burning like great torches on Nob Hill. Sara and Miss Varady had spread mattresses on the floor in the dining room and they wakened quickly when Ah Foong came to tell them what was happening.

The fire was eating all Nob Hill and blowing toward Russian and even Telegraph Hills. But the change of wind was a blessing for Van Ness. The fire had turned back, and was rolling like a juggernaut upon all it had missed before.

By morning it was certain that the western boundary would hold. There could be no return of the fire, for there was nothing left to burn. At least a part of Chief Sullivan's plan had saved what remained of the city.

Paint on the houses on the western side of Van Ness had bubbled and scorched into odd patterns. Cinders and char lay everywhere and the wind stirred clouds of brick dust. A canopy of yellow smoke lay over smouldering ruins that would be long in cooling, and there was no air to breathe that was free of the smell of smoke. Now refugees who still had homes in the evacuated section began to return. Their number was tiny compared to the thousands who were homeless.

Early in the morning of the third day Ritchie brought the Renwicks back to Miss Varady's and they trooped down the hill with him, looking untidy, dirty, and thoroughly weary. Miss Varady held a council at the long table in the dining room. She had changed from her green gown to one of rich purple and there was nothing about her to indicate that she had been through a major disaster. She ruled at the head of the table, disregarding debris and cracked plaster. Sara was placed at her right, as she waited for the others to join her about the table.

Mrs. Jerome, white and tired, had greeted Sara with the joy of a mother who had hardly expected to see her child alive again, and Sara's embrace was equally warm. Now at length Mary Jerome brought herself to step into the same room with Hester Varady.

Miss Varady gave her a long look and remarked that the years had hardly been kind to her. "You would have fared better if you'd stayed in this house where you belonged," she told her.

Sara would have spoken indignantly, but her mother's hand tightened on her arm, silencing her.

Mary Jerome did not flinch. "My daughter is still my daughter," she said with quiet meaning.

Miss Varady ignored her words and inquired about Nick's hands. He looked more like himself this morning, with some of yesterday's grime removed, and his bandages renewed.

Mrs. Renwick and her plates seemed to have survived the night, and Allison was as lively and keyed up as ever. Too keyed up, Sara thought. When she came into the house she was still lugging Comstock and her wrapped-up plates. But mindful of Miss Varady's dislike for cats, she set Comstock down in the front hall and he whisked himself off at once on a trip of exploration about the house. Goodness only knew, Sara thought, whose bed he would now turn up on. She hoped it would not be Miss Varady's.

Of them all, Ritchie seemed the most flippant. He had come out of his black mood and was quick with mocking words. Sara, appraising him with new eyes, felt that he might at least take disaster seriously. His gaiety had a false ring and he and Judith still seemed to be ignoring each other. Judith was very quiet, taking no part in the discussion, but apparently attentive and no longer dazed.

Miss Varady led the talk. It was, she said, evident that the fire would now burn itself out across town. It was up to San Francisco to think about the future.

"We have a tradition," she said. "We look ahead, not back. And we spend no time bemoaning our losses. You are all welcome to stay in this house for as long as you wish. I have sufficient room and apparently I will not be without servants. Ah Foong has been taking in a few refugees of his own in his cellar quarters and it seems that we will have a full staff of uncles, cousins and nephews."

Ritchie laughed and was not abashed when Miss Varady gave him a sharp look.

"I have already told Ah Foong to get rooms ready upstairs," she went on. "He and his staff are at work on them now. As soon as they are prepared I will show you to them. On the first day of the fire I sent to Fillmore Street to buy what provisions we could and we are well stocked for the time being. In any event, I fancy that San Francisco will be taken care of. The rest of the world will be sending help. And our own organizations, military and civic, have not collapsed. We can begin to plan at once for the future."

Sara had never admired her aunt more. Hester Varady was obviously in full control of the situation and her air of confidence gave assurance to those at the table.

"We have all lost a great deal," Miss Varady said. "You, the very house you lived in, all your possessions, and your business offices. I have my house, but many houses I own about town have been burned down. Of course the real estate is always good and if the insurance companies pay up, I will suffer very little. Fortunately many of my investments have been made in the Western Addition, where the income will remain intact. Mr. Renwick, what plans have you to carry on your father's business?"

If she had expected to catch Nick unaware, she was disappointed. He sat near his mother and Allison at the far end of the table, with Geneva beside him.

"Would you consider renting us front-room space in this house for an office?" he asked directly.

Sara half expected an indignant reply, but apparently Hester Varady could accept the realistic quickly and calmly when she had to.

"If the library will do for your purpose, yes," she told Nick. "I fancy that business establishments will be opening now in many an unlikely place. Will your company have the funds to meet your insurance debts, do you think?"

Nick did not hesitate. "Of course not—if you mean with cash. What company could be ready to meet a disaster like this? Especially since we have no out-of-town affiliates. Nevertheless, I hope we can raise the necessary money, even if it takes every penny the Renwicks have."

Mrs. Renwick stared at her son. Judith made no move, but she looked wide awake now and she was watching her brother with new interest. Even Ritchie had sobered.

"Look here, Nick," Ritchie said, "I've put most of what I have into the business. Do you mean to say—"

"I mean to say that before the year is out we'll all be flat broke," Nick told him. "We'll be lucky to have a roof over our heads. And it won't be a Nob Hill roof."

Ritchie sank back in his chair, his flippancy gone, looking too stunned for words.

Judith, however, reached a hand across the table. "Papa left me a considerable amount in my own name, you know, Nick. You can have that of course."

Nick gave her a warm smile and covered her hand with his own bandaged one. "Thank you, Judy. And don't worry. It won't hurt the Renwick tribe to go to work for a change."

"Maybe," said Allison, "I could sell newspapers. Do they ever have girl newsboys, Nick?"

Everyone laughed except Hester Varady. Her attention had been suddenly caught by Allison.

"What did you do with that cat?" she demanded.

Allison stiffened into a poker of resistance. "I put him down in the hall. He is probably looking at your house."

Miss Varady left the table, more disturbed than she had ever seemed since the start of the fire. She went to the sideboard and picked up a padded stick. Then she struck the Chinese gong on the sideboard a firm blow. The sound went booming through the house. While those at the table waited in uneasy silence, Ah Foong came soundlessly into the room.

"Yes, Missy?" he said.

"There is a cat in this house," said Miss Varady. "You are to find the creature at once and put him outside. I will welcome refugees from the fire, but I will not take in a cat."

Ah Foong did not so much as blink. He said, "Me go topside, fixee looms. Busy. You no botha. Cat all lite."

"What do you mean?" Miss Varady asked sharply.

Ah Foong went out, paying no further attention. Miss Varady had called him from important duties and he was plainly annoyed. Allison slipped from the table and ran after him into the hall. Sara could hear the child's questioning tones as she followed Ah Foong upstairs. Apparently she had found an unexpected ally.

The pinkness of anger tinged Miss Varady's cheekbones, but she had the good sense to know when she had lost a skirmish. Nevertheless, Sara suspected, she was not one to give up a battle. Comstock would need a strong friend in this house.

EIGHTEEN

THE BIG MASTER BEDROOM AT ONE FRONT CORNER OF THE house belonged to Hester Varady. Its door was kept carefully closed and so far not even Sara had been invited into its private precincts. Other of the numerous bedrooms on the second and third floors were distributed among the guests. Geneva, Sara found, had her room on the third floor at the rear. A curious arrangement in an empty house with two women rattling around on a floor apiece.

When their room on the second floor was ready, it was Ah Foong who escorted Sara and her mother upstairs. Mrs. Jerome stopped on the threshold with a cry and drew back.

"Not this room, Ah Foong. Please put us somewhere else."

The Chinese looked at her without expression, his

seamy face bland as a moon. "Miss Valady say you stay this place." And he padded off on further duties.

Mrs. Jerome glanced unhappily at Sara, then seemed to steel herself to face whatever awaited her within these walls.

"Was this your room when you lived in this house?" Sara asked gently.

Her mother nodded. "Your father and I planned this room and bought its furnishings when I came here as a bride. Hester hasn't changed it. You were born here."

Sara linked her arm through her mother's and they went through the door together. The soft green damask draperies and mossy rug were still lovely, though faded. There was a double bed with green draperies hung from a hoop above the head. The dressing table had folding mirrors, so a lady might see herself from all sides. Earthquake damage had been slight here, and Ah Foong had apparently cleared away most of the evidence.

For just a moment Mrs. Jerome covered her eyes with her hands. Then she walked to the chaise longue and sat down, while Sara watched her in pity. She could imagine how it must be to return alone to a room which you had long ago shared with someone you loved. This was too painful an experience for her mother to bear.

Sara moved decisively toward the door. "Wait here, Mama. I'll go speak to Aunt Hester and ask her to move us somewhere else."

But her mother sat up very straight on the edge of the seat. "No! I'm not so weak a woman as that. A night or two in this room won't hurt me. There's no need to trouble her now when so many must be settled. Later I'll ask her myself."

Sara moved about the room with the wistful feeling that she had truly come home. This was the place where life had begun for her. A delicate rosewood desk stood out from one wall and above it hung a water color of a San Francisco scene. Sara paused before the picture, studying it. The painting showed the windy corner where Lotta's Fountain stood. All those buildings must be rubble now. Yet this room had stood intact, waiting.

"It's as if the room has been holding its breath all this time," Sara said softly, "waiting for us to come home."

Her mother saw her interest in the water color. "Your father painted that. Perhaps he could have been a real artist, if only he had been willing to work at it. *I* believed in his talent, even though Hester always belittled it."

"Tell me about my father," Sara said softly. In the past it had always been painful for her mother to talk, but here in this room there might be release in speaking of him.

Mrs. Jerome lay back in the chair, while Sara went to sit on the floor beside her. Her mother's fingers touched Sara's hair, lingered on its dark thickness.

"You look a little like him," she said. "Though you're more striking in appearance, and dark where he was fair. You're like him in other ways too—you have the same vigor he had. The same gift for being alive. He was always gay and laughed a lot. Sometimes he would make Hester furious by laughing right in her face when she wanted to talk of serious matters."

She could almost see him, Sara thought, as her mother went on.

"Sometimes he could be very tender and kind." Mrs. Jerome sighed. "I think he never meant to hurt me, but Hester was too strong for him. Perhaps if he had been willing to leave this house and give up the ease with which his aunt surrounded him, we might have had a happy life. Hester didn't like his schemes for making quick wealth, but she encouraged what I felt were wastrel ways. And she was forever trying to turn him against me. Perhaps she succeeded. When he left without a word, she told me he had been called out of town and would write to me later. But no letter ever came and I knew he was dead. I think she believed so too, though she would never admit it."

Sara reached for her mother's hand and held it tightly.

"He might not have returned for me, Sara, but you meant everything to him. The best thing about him was his love for you. If he had been alive all these years he would sooner or later have tried to reach you. I waited as long as I dared for him to return. Then I took you and ran away one night. I was terribly young then and I had a feeling that she might have prevented my going if she knew what I meant to do. She is capable of going to great lengths to exert her will."

The dam had broken now and words poured out. Sara waited, listening with all her being.

"I took only a few things, left most of our clothes and possessions here. Not even Ah Foong heard me leave. He would have stopped me—because you were Leland's child and he'd have felt you belonged in this house. He doesn't always do what Miss Varady says, but he has a strong sense of family. I felt we'd be safe in Chicago, which was my home, though my people were dead. It was in Chicago that I had first met Leland, when he was there on one of his business schemes. There was no way for her to bring me back. Not that she didn't try. She found out where we were at the Temples' and wrote to me frequently for several years. She tried everything—threats, flattery, bribery. I remember one letter that came after a long silence which told me all too convincingly how little I could have meant to Leland. It upset me so much that I tore his picture in two and threw it away. As if I could escape from pain by an act of anger."

Sara looked up at mention of the picture and her mother nodded.

"Yes, I remember. When I went back to retrieve the pieces, I knew you had taken them from the wastebasket and mended the picture. I never tried to take it away from you. You had a right to that much of your father if you wanted it."

Sara laid her cheek against her mother's hand, feeling closer to her than ever before. "But why did Aunt Hester keep writing letters?"

"She wanted you. She has some sort of terrible compulsion to continue the Varady blood and to rule as head of a great family. She turned this compulsion on Leland and ruined his life. She would have turned it on you too, but I burned her letters without answering. I would never have gone back."

Mrs. Jerome closed her eyes wearily.

"At least," Sara said, "she can't do anything to us now. I'm grown up and she can't make me do anything I don't want to do. She can't hurt you any more."

"You don't know," her mother said. "You've no idea of her strength." The release of words seemed to have relaxed her, made her drowsy. "Let me sleep for a while now, Sara. I'll feel stronger after a nap."

Sara took a quilt from the bed and tucked it around her tenderly. For a little while she waited, until her mother fell asleep. Then she left the room and stepped into the hall. Allison was stealing down the stairs at the far end.

She looked around at Sara and beckoned. When Sara reached her she whispered, "I've got to find Comstock. Come help me. I've poked into every room I dared, but he isn't anywhere. And Ah Foong wouldn't talk to me about him at all. He's such a queer old man. Don't make any noise, Sara, or the witch will catch us."

"Miss Varady isn't a witch," Sara said. "You mustn't call her that. I think I know where to look for Comstock. Come along."

Downstairs she found the way to the kitchen and stepped into the rear garden, overlooked by the balcony above. A nearby door opened upon stairs to the cellar and a volume of chattering sound reached them.

Allison went down a few steps and called for Comstock. For a second the chatter ceased and the big yellow cat came bounding up to her, leaped into her arms. Sara reached out to scratch him behind the ears and found that he smelled strongly of fish. Apparently he had been well and recently fed.

"What am I to do?" Allison wailed, carrying him up the steps. "You know I can't leave him. I just won't stay in this house if I can't have Comstock with me."

"Where will you go?" Sara asked. "Back to Lafayette Square?"

They crossed the flagstone path and walked into what had once been a small garden. A few roses still bloomed untended, but no one had cared for the flower beds in years. A stone bench waited beside weed-grown earth and they sat down, while Allison and Comstock purred to each other.

"I have a friend," said Allison in answer to Sara's question. "A girl who lives in a *tent* up in the park." Her emphasis on the word "tent" implied palatial quarters. "We had only umbrellas, but she and her mother had a tent. All the children around us were boys, except for a few babies. So Miranda and I are friends. Her mother is very nice too. She says I am a skinny little thing and need feeding up. I ate practically a whole liverwurst while I was in their tent."

"What is Miranda like?" Sara asked curiously.

"Miranda Schultz is her whole name. And she is very beautiful and fat like her mother. Her father is in prison and her mother runs a delicatessen store that got burned out by the fire. But they saved quite a lot of food. Sara, I've never known anybody who had a father in prison before. It's interesting, isn't it? And Miranda likes me. I gave her all the spare hair ribbons I saved from the fire. She likes my stories too. She'd never heard of King Arthur until I started to tell her about the Round Table. I've a lot more stories to go. We haven't even reached Sir Galahad yet."

The implication seemed to be that this friendship would last as long as the Round Table could supply heroes—which was probably a very long while indeed. Somehow Sara could only smile at Allison's pleasure in her new friend. She was afraid to ask why Mr. Schultz was in prison, but Allison supplied the information without prompting.

"Miranda says he strangled another man. With his bare hands. But of course the other fellow deserved it, only that isn't what the judge decided. It was a good thing the man didn't die. Miranda says the judge was very prejudiced and her father didn't have a chance. Anyway, what I was going to say was that if the old witch won't let me keep Comstock, then I can move in with Miranda Schultz. I'm sure she and her mother will be happy to have me. Her mother likes to feed people."

Sara reached out and hugged Allison hard, cat and all. Comstock yowled at this indignity, but Allison seemed not to mind too much.

"Do you think we could possibly get along without you?" Sara asked the little girl. "Nick and your mother and Judith would be terribly unhappy. They always look for you the minute you're not around. And remember how your mother let you carry those two plates all through our escape from the fire."

Allison looked suddenly stricken. "That's something else I have to tell you. I broke another plate. I don't know just how it happened last night, but in the dark I sat on them and the top one broke. Mama doesn't know it yet. She went right to bed and didn't even look at them. But I know she'll start counting plates the minute she wakes up. That's another reason why I need to leave home."

"Never mind about the plates," Sara said firmly. "I need you here, Allison. You're my best friend. You can't go off and leave me now."

Thus appealed to, Allison agreed to postpone her departure for a day or two at least. Though Sara wondered what would happen when Hilda Renwick found that a second of her precious plates had been broken.

All went well, however, for the rest of that day. A man from the Citizens' Patrol came around to let everyone know that the fire was under control in this section and those who still had beds could sleep in them without fear tonight. The remaining flames had nowhere to go except into the water. He said all but a little patch of Russian Hill had burned, and most of Telegraph Hill. The Italians had managed to save some of their homes and it looked strange to see their tropical gardens filled with flowers and parrots in cages, blooming out of the ruins. Still no fires or candles were to be lighted. Not a chimney must be put to use until they had all been repaired and officially inspected. No further chance of fire must be risked.

Ah Foong, his second cousin and third nephew built an outdoor kitchen on the curb in front of the house, using bricks from a fallen chimney. Nevertheless, linen and silver were laid for the use of guests in the Varady dining room, and the meal, though mainly stew, was served with all the flourish Ah Foong could give it. Only Mrs. Renwick stayed wearily in her room and went right to sleep again when she had finished the bowl of stew Nick took up to her.

At dinner Judith seemed to be burning with some inner unrest that was entirely unlike her. Once Nick, passing behind her chair, touched her lightly as if to quiet her. She was flushed and animated in a nervous way, as Sara had never seen her. Even Ritchie looked at her, puzzled, though she paid no attention to him.

When she had eaten her dessert—stale pound cake which Ah Foong had baked the day before the fire— she suddenly put both hands on the table and pushed herself away, as if she could not sit still for a moment longer. Her voice reached a pitch when she spoke, as if she were on the verge of hysteria.

"Do you realize that San Francisco is gone?" she cried. "Here we sit at this meal as if nothing had happened. Already we're taking it for granted. Every bit of Nob Hill has been wiped out. Every bit of the life we're used to is gone."

Nick said, "Judith," quietly, but she rose and went to the door. There she turned for an instant.

"It's done and it will never come back. Not as it was before. And I am glad! I hated it all. I'm glad it's burned out for good!"

They sat in astonished silence while her footsteps echoed sharply in the hall. A moment later they heard the sound of her hands on the keys of the grand piano in the drawing room. She was playing great crashing chords that fairly shook the house. Chords that were like sobs. This was not the insipid, emotionless music she had always played before. There was both suffering and elation in the sounds that poured from the piano. Only three nights ago great voices had sung *Carmen* at the Opera House, and now Judith played the *Habañera* with an excitement running through the music. Without pause she went into Chopin's *Polonaise,* and it was no tinkling finger exercise this time, but music with a stormy spirit behind it, ringing through the house.

Those in the dining room sat as if frozen. Only Sara, drawn by a magnet she could not resist, left her place and stole into the hall to be closer to the music. She had felt these things too—the storm and turmoil was in her blood as well.

The drawing-room door stood open and Sara slipped through it. The woman at the piano sat shrouded in evening gloom. Her flashing hands were a blur of white against white keys, her face hidden in shadow. Sara went to the piano and leaned upon it, listening. If Judith saw her she gave no sign. Before the *Polonaise* had come to a stormy end, her fingers crashed into discord on the keys and she suddenly put her head down upon her arms and began to cry.

This was more alarming than the transformation in Judith's music. Sara could not touch her comfortingly as she might have done with Allison, or her mother. There had never been any liking lost between them and Judith would not welcome comfort offered by Sara Jerome. But something must be done to stop what might become hysteria.

"If you're glad San Francisco has burned, why are you crying?" Sara asked, trying to sound matter-of-fact and calm.

Judith raised her head from the keys, her pale hair luminous in the dusk. She gave no sign that she found it strange to see Sara standing beside the piano.

"I suppose it's natural to mourn when something comes to a cruel end. Something you've lived with all your life. Even though I'm glad I need live with it no longer."

More had come to an end for Judith the night of the fire than a manner of living, Sara thought. She waited and after a moment Judith went on, her voice steadying.

"Sara, I was wrong about Ritchie. That's gone too,

along with San Francisco. Perhaps it has been lost before this, but I've only just faced it."

Sara said nothing, filled with unexpected pity for Judith, but helpless to offer comfort.

"Do you know what sort of woman Ritchie wants, Sara? He wants a doting mother who will always think he is wonderful. Who will see him as he wants to see himself. Then he can go on dreaming and playing, doing nothing. He can be happy loving only himself, providing someone else gives him confidence by loving him that way too. But he can't stand a woman who expects him to prove himself. He wants to be thought perfect as he is, without lifting a finger in effort."

Sara spoke gently. "Yes—that's the way it is with Ritchie. It's the way he has always been."

A sound near the door made Sara turn. If Judith heard she did not look around. Nick and Ritchie were there and Sara wondered how much Ritchie had heard. All of this, she hoped. It might be good for him.

Judith pushed back the piano stool and stood up. Emotion had been drained from her in the playing. She walked toward the doorway as if she did not see the two men who waited there. Ritchie put his hand on her arm, but she went past him as if he did not exist. When she had gone upstairs Ritchie swung about without a word and went out the front door, out of the house.

Sara did not look at Nick. She returned to the dining room where the women still sat at the table.

Miss Varady wore an expression of displeasure. She did not like other people's storms.

"I trust the crisis is over?" she asked Sara coldly.

Sara nodded, but there was nothing she wished to

explain to Hester Varady. Geneva was bewildered and uncertain, with no notion at all as to what Judith's stormy playing signified. Only Mrs. Jerome looked as if she had understood.

San Francisco kept new hours these days. Tomorrow would mean not only a new day, but the beginning of a new life. So many pieces to pick up—pieces of a shattered city and transformed lives. When they left the table, the women went straight to their rooms and to bed.

Mrs. Jerome might face the room, but nothing could bring her to sleep in the big mahogany bed she had once shared with her husband. In spite of Sara's pleading, she went to sleep on the chaise longue and left the big bed to Sara.

With darkness which could not be dispelled shadowing the old house, Sara would have felt more comfortable with their door locked. There was, however, no key and none to be found in any of the drawers of the room. She was not frightened, nor had she any impending sense that her nightmare would come again when she went to sleep. But she could not help wondering what would happen in this house if it did. Would she rise in her sleep and follow the course of the dream to some terrible ending? A key in the lock would make her less uneasy.

Wondering if she dared tap on her aunt's door and ask for a key, she went into the gloomy hall. Hester Varady's room was a corner one at the front of the house. When Sara fumbled her way toward it in the dark, she struck against some low object in the hall near the door. It seemed to be a cot with bedding upon it, and at once a shadowy figure sat up and peered at her questioningly.

"You Missy Sala?" said Ah Foong.

Sara was relieved to hear his voice. "Yes. Do you have a key to our room, Ah Foong? With all the lights out, there's no telling who may be prowling around tonight."

In pidgin English that Sara sometimes found it difficult to follow, Ah Foong explained. There were keys, yes, but Miss Varady kept them locked in a drawer in her room. She never permitted anyone in the house to lock a door. The front door and back door were locked and that was enough, she said. Besides, as Ah Foong assured Sara, he himself slept every night on this cot near Miss Varady's door. If anything was wrong he would know at once. And he seemed to imply that he could deal with whatever emergency might arise.

Sara went back to bed, somewhat reassured, but curious as well. How odd that the invincible Miss Varady, who allowed no one else a key, should feel the necessity of a bodyguard when she went to sleep at night.

In spite of the room and its memories, her mother fell asleep first. Sara lay awake, lost in the huge bed, thoughts whirling through her head.

Events had come so quickly since the earthquake that she had scarcely taken time to think. With anxiety and stumbling weariness engulfing her, there had been no energy left for facing the problems of the future. One lived from one moment to the next, and if there had been occasions when her eyes rested on Nick more tenderly than before, she still had not faced what had happened to her.

Now, with her body at rest, and the immediate danger of the fire past, her mind turned of its own accord to thoughts of Nick and what he meant to her. Her feeling was no sudden thing, as it had seemed in her first moment of recognition. Just as the taut thread which had held her to Ritchie and a childhood love had stretched unnoticed to the snapping point, so the heavier cord that drew her to Nick had been gradually strengthening without awareness on her part.

Perhaps her feeling for him had begun that night in the library when he had surrounded her with his strength and kindness. Or perhaps even before when she had stood at an upstairs window beside him and watched lights move across the sleeping city. It had increased in a flash that day when Ritchie had kissed her at the office and she had been suddenly aware of the contrast between the two men. She had wanted to hate Nick that day, but only because of her own hurt pride when he had looked at her in contempt.

The feeling in her had grown constantly deeper, though she turned instinctively away from it and would not accept its portent. Now she could escape recognition no longer. She loved Nick and he felt only scorn and distaste for her. The fact that what he believed was not true gave her little comfort, since there seemed no way to make him know the truth. And there was something else which stood between herself and Nick. Someone she could not overlook or ignore. There was Geneva.

Sara moved restlessly on her pillow, seeking release from the torment of her own thoughts. Now she began to listen to the startling stillness of the night. At first she did not realize what she listened for, though something was missing. Then she knew it was the sound of fire and the fighting of fire. Tonight the dynamiting had ceased, there was no roaring of flames, no constant flicker of red light, no blistering heat, no shouting, no sounds of refugees in the streets. The city of St. Francis lay hushed and still.

How strange silence seemed by contrast. How quickly one became accustomed to the impossible. Would she as quickly grow used to a new love that might hurt her even more than the old?

She slept at last, but at dawn that Saturday morning everyone was startled awake by the wild shrieking of fire whistles and the sound of triumphant bugles from the camps. San Franciscans heard and understood. The puny men who had stood up against the enemy had held their line and bested the flames. The fire was over.

But the city was too weary to savor its triumph. Along the water front where the last stand had been made, men fell in their tracks and slept where they lay.

NINETEEN

THERE WAS NO BREAD LEFT FOR BREAKFAST, NOT EVEN A piece of stale pound cake. But Ah Foong managed scrambled eggs in his outdoor kitchen, with bits of bacon sprinkled through, and there was still coffee. Everyone came down for breakfast except Mrs. Renwick and Ritchie. Ritchie had not come home at all last night and Sara wondered about him.

Her old blinders were, she knew, gone forever. Both the blinders she had worn toward him and toward her own heedless conduct. She could never love him again, but she could pity him, as she might have pitied an unfortunate child who managed always to hurt himself. No one else in this house seemed concerned about him and Sara was not sure what loneliness would do to Ritchie. What Judith had said was true. He needed someone who believed in him as he could not fully believe in himself.

Judith came down looking pale, but with the change in her still evident. There was resolve in her manner now. Judith was no longer a bystander.

"Nick," she said, "you'll find out what's happening, won't you? So we'll know what there is we can do?"

"I'll be going out soon," Nick said. "I expect every able-bodied man in the city will be needed to help clear streets and dig out the ruins. We've a big job ahead. Thanks to you, Miss Varady, my hands are better today."

"But what can we women do?" Judith asked. "We'll be needed too."

"For one thing," said Miss Varady dryly, "you can go stand in a bread line if you want to. Ah Foong tells me supplies are already being sent into San Francisco and relief stations are opening in several places."

"Then perhaps I can volunteer as a helper," Judith said, and Sara added quickly that she would volunteer too.

Geneva offered her own help, though Nick shook his head and said she wasn't strong enough for the long hours of standing such work would entail.

"There will be plenty to do," Nick said. "There's no doubt about the fact that our home on Nob Hill is gone. For the moment we are in your debt, Miss Varady, and most grateful. Of course as soon as possible we will try to find quarters of our own."

"Don't think about that now," said Miss Varady regally. "You are welcome here. It is the least I can do."

This morning there was an air of hope abroad. The fire was out. It had done all the damage it could do. No one wasted time moaning over losses, over what was past. The future was what mattered—a new San

Francisco. The old phoenix trick for which the city was famous must be worked again. After all, the city had burned down and been reborn from the ashes several times in the past. Only this time the task was bigger than it had ever been before.

After breakfast Mrs. Jerome approached Miss Varady on the matter of a change of rooms. Sara, she explained, was content with the room that had once been her father's, but she herself would rather not stay there.

Miss Varady regarded her for a moment without expression and then summoned Ah Foong. "Show Mrs. Bishop to the little room on the third floor," she directed. "The north room. It won't be as comfortable," she added to Mary.

Mrs. Jerome said she didn't mind, she would be grateful. But Sara thought Ah Foong, whose face seldom revealed his thoughts, gave his mistress a slow look of surprise. At once Sara decided to go upstairs with her mother and see what the "little room" was like.

Ah Foong led the way, carrying her mother's few possessions. This room, like no other room in the house, was apparently kept locked. He produced a key to open the door, then pocketed it himself.

It was a bare, small room, rudely furnished, with peeling gray wallpaper that was more depressing than decorative. The single brass bed was narrow and Sara, bouncing experimentally upon it, found the mattress lumpy. The rest of the furniture consisted of a straight bureau across one corner, a single chair, and a small table. Though this room was at the side of the house where most of the vines had been cleared away, its one window was completely shut in by strangling green tendrils.

"This is a dreadful place," said Sara indignantly when Ah Foong had gone for fresh sheets and pillowcase. "Of course you can't stay here, Mama."

Her mother smiled wryly. "How like Hester to play such a joke. I've never been in this room before—in fact, when I lived here I was never permitted on the unused third floor at all. But I knew about this room. It's the one that's supposed to be haunted."

"Haunted!" Sara echoed. "Mama, you don't believe—"

"No, of course I don't," Mrs. Jerome said quickly. "But I know this house used to have a reputation for curious sights and sounds. And they were supposed to come from this room. I gathered that much from the servants—who were constantly changing. They weren't allowed up here either, but they gossiped. Ah Foong took care of this floor."

Sara looked about with more interest. "Did you ever hear or see anything odd?"

Her mother hesitated. "I'm not sure. I was so frightened, so worried the last few months I was at this house that I couldn't always tell what was real and what imagined. Sometimes I thought I heard someone crying up here. And once, when I was outdoors, I saw something like a hand pushing at the vines. But the wind blew the leaves and it might have been only their fluttering. Then of course there was the little white cat."

"In this house? I thought Miss Varady wouldn't have a cat."

"That's true. Yet there was a cat. I saw it myself once

or twice and I'm sure I heard it mewing. But when I asked Hester about it, she flew into a rage. She said there wasn't any cat and I must be demented. She looked at me as if she liked the idea of my being demented. So I never mentioned the cat again. But one of the servants told me it came out of this room."

"What did Papa think about all this haunting?" Sara asked, still incredulous.

"I don't believe the stories started until your father had gone. Hester behaved very queerly after he disappeared. Perhaps she herself caused the talk to start. His leaving for good was a terrible blow to her, even though I always felt she drove him away. She began to shut herself in and walk about the house endlessly, day and night. That was when Ah Foong started to sleep outside her door. I noticed that he still does."

Sara glanced about the depressing little room. "Anyway, ghosts or no ghosts, you can't stay in a hole like this."

"Yes I can," her mother said quickly. "Let well enough alone, Sara, or she'll think up something worse. She did it on purpose—because I didn't want to stay in the other bedroom. I'd rather have ghosts than memories any day. Ghosts can't hurt me. But of course we must arrange to leave as soon as possible. We can't possibly stay on in this house."

That was a matter on which Sara wanted to postpone discussion, and she found an excuse to get away. Going down to the second floor she met Allison again, climbing the stairs slowly and cautiously, an intent expression on her face, and a breakfast tray in her hands. The child flicked a quick glance at Sara, then returned her concentrated attention to balancing the tray.

"Come with me," she pleaded. "I got Ah Foong to let me take Mama's tray upstairs, but I'm afraid to go in there alone. She likes you, Sara, so maybe she won't be so mad about the plate if you're with me."

Sara went ahead to knock on Hilda Renwick's door. The "Come in!" that welcomed them was cheery enough and did not sound as though Mrs. Renwick had discovered the further tragedy of the plates.

"I've brought your breakfast, Mama," Allison said sweetly, putting one foot in front of the other with continued care until Sara took the tray from her and set it on a small table.

Mrs. Renwick, wearing a loose wrapper she had saved from the fire, stood at a window, looking out between partially opened shutters. This room was on the south side of the house, but a glimpse of Van Ness Avenue was possible and Mrs. Renwick seemed excited by whatever was going on in the street.

"Good morning, Sara. Good morning, Allison. How nice of you to bring my tray. Mercy, but I slept last night! Have you girls looked outside to see what's happened?"

Allison was not at the moment interested in the outdoors. She sidled across the room to where the Japanese plates were stacked, still wrapped in their pillowcases. But Sara went to the window and stood beside Mrs. Renwick.

The stretch of street they could see was alive with activity. Earthquake rubble was being shoveled away from street and sidewalks by dozens of willing hands. Across Van Ness dynamite had left blackened ruin, but

290 / Phyllis A. Whitney

the workers turned their backs on that, busy with a hundred tasks. On their own side a man and woman and small boy appeared to be putting together some sort of shed made of billboards and crinkly sheet iron. The woman held up a crudely lettered sign and Sara could see the words: OPEN FOR BUSINESS. Whatever the business was she couldn't tell, but there was laughter around the little shed and now and then someone stopped to look inside.

"See how the earthquake has wrenched the pavement down here," Mrs. Renwick said. "All this is low, sandy land and the quake damage is probably greater than on the hilltops. Your aunt's house is well built to have withstood the shock with so little hurt."

"Mama," Allison said, "if you don't come, your coffee will be cold."

Mrs. Renwick turned from the window and Allison pulled a chair up to the table. Her mother sat down, still musing aloud.

"Just think," she said, stirring her ration of sugar into creamless coffee. "Here we are actually living in Hester Varady's house. I wish Willie could see me now."

"Maybe Papa wouldn't like us to be here," Allison said.

Her mother shrugged. "I like it. And I mean to enjoy it until we find a place of our own. There are friends out of the city we might stay with, but I prefer it here in the midst of things. I wonder what's happened to Millie Matson? She rented a room with a family that lived on Leavenworth right down in the fire area. Well—Miss Millie ought to be busy now, what with none of us having more than a rag or two to our backs."

"We haven't any money either," said Allison. "Nick says we won't have a penny left when the company gets through paying insurance."

Mrs. Renwick was undisturbed. "Nick will manage." The idea of being penniless was not something she could easily visualize, having always lived in luxury. "Four lives I've lived," she went on, checking them off on her fingers for Sara and Allison. "First there was my life before I met William. But that never seems very important. I was such a silly child. Then I married William and he turned me into the exact pattern of what he wanted in a wife. I didn't know how held down I'd been until after he died. Then I went on a binge."

"Mama!" cried Allison, shocked. "That isn't a nice word."

"Nevertheless," her mother said, "that's what my letting down amounted to. A binge of doing only what I liked and getting fat and lazy. That was my third life. Now the fourth one is going to start and I'm very curious to know what it will be like."

"Maybe we'll have to take in boarders," said Allison. "If we can get a house to take them into."

"That's not a bad idea," said Mrs. Renwick. "I'll have to suggest it to Nick."

Apparently there was to be no immediate crisis about the plates and Sara decided she could leave Allison safely enough with her mother. But Allison saw her intention and jumped up from her chair to run across the room to where the plates lay.

"Wait, Sara!" she cried and then turned to her

mother with bleak tragedy in her voice. "Mama, have you looked at your plates?"

"Why no, I haven't," Mrs. Renwick said, draining the last drop of coffee with an air of satisfaction. "They're all right, aren't they?"

Carefully Allison lifted the wrapped plates and brought them to her mother. Pushing back her chair, Mrs. Renwick began to unwrap the pillowcase. One by one each red and gold plate emerged intact until she had four of them piled on the floor beside her chair.

"Isn't that nice," Mrs. Renwick said. "They came through beautifully. When we have a dining room again we can put them up on the wall."

Allison stared at her mother. "But you didn't count them!"

"Yes, I did. There are four. Let me see—you broke one a few weeks ago, didn't you? So that means another one must have been broken or lost while we were carrying them around night before last. I'm really not surprised under the circumstances."

"*I* broke it," Allison said grimly. "You trusted me with two plates and I broke one of them. I sat on it."

"What a shame," her mother said. "But it mustn't make you unhappy. I'm sure it was an accident and it's a wonder we saved any of them. In fact, this morning I'm not quite sure we should have tried. There were surely more important things to bring away from a fire."

Sara looked at Allison, expecting to see relief in her face. But Allison looked more stricken than before. Without a word she walked to the door and out of the room.

"Whatever's the matter?" Mrs. Renwick asked blankly of Sara.

"I'm not sure," Sara said. "I'd better go see," and she hurried after the little girl.

Allison's shoulders drooped and when Sara caught up with her she found to her dismay that tears were rolling down her cheeks.

Sara could only echo Mrs. Renwick. "Whatever is the matter?"

"She doesn't really care!" Allison stalked toward the stairs. "I thought she let me carry the plates because she—she trusted me and wanted me to help."

"Oh, no," Sara said soothingly, "you've got this wrong. Allison, listen to me—"

But Allison pulled herself out of Sara's grasp and ran blindly down the stairs and toward the back of the house. She'd be running to Comstock of course. Only Comstock would offer her loving comfort. There was no use following the child, Sara knew, or trying to argue her out of her notion at this moment.

As she went idly down the stairs, wandering aimlessly, she saw that Miss Varady stood at the library door watching her.

"That child was crying," her aunt said with an air of satisfaction. "I hope you smacked her good for whatever she was up to."

"Why should I smack her?" Sara asked in astonishment.

"There's no need to deny it to me," her aunt said. "I have no liking for children either, my girl. Indeed, Sara, I find that in a great many ways you and I are alike. This is gratifying. But I shall want to observe you for a longer period of time. And more closely."

She turned and went into the library, leaving Sara somewhat irritated by her words. Sara had never known anyone who treated others in so highhanded a manner. There was something a little insulting about Aunt Hester's intention to "observe" her. But she must keep her temper for now, if the future was to hold something brighter for her mother and herself.

Sara went to the front door and out upon the steps. In the well-built Varady house, with the front windows closed, outside noises penetrated only faintly. Now she discovered that all Van Ness stirred and echoed with activity. It was still too soon to attack the area of solid ruins, but this boundary was being cleared as quickly as possible. There was an air of cheer abroad that was surprising. Everyone talked to everyone else, continuing the easy comradeship disaster had engendered.

Sara sat down on the steps to watch, still uncertain of what her own contribution ought to be.

The little billboard shed nearby had been completed and Sara could see that a brick stove stood beside it. A huge laundry kettle heated over the bricks and the woman turned every now and then to stir the stew, or dish up a bowl of it for some hungry passerby. This, apparently, was not a free kitchen, but a new business enterprise. "Palace special!" the woman called and a man laughed and stopped to pay for a bowl of soup.

A group of three or four men, one of them incongruously dressed in loggers' boots and a top hat, with an assortment of extremes between, paused near her steps, and Sara could hear them talking about how Governor Pardee had closed all banks for three days, to give such institutions a chance to set their affairs in order and prevent any disastrous runs. In all likelihood this time would be extended. Money would be one of the scarcest items in San Francisco for a while. Though since there was little to buy, no one would suffer greatly from its absence.

Just the same, Sara thought, money would be important again soon enough and she wanted to find work. Aunt Hester might give Mary Jerome and her daughter shelter and care for their needs indefinitely, but Sara knew her mother would not consent to being dependent on Miss Varady for long. She didn't want that either. Her mother had been right when she had said that Hester Varady liked to own people. She could not own those who had an independent income.

Now, however, there was no insurance office to work in. Even if she could help Nick—which was hardly likely—he could pay her no salary. Yet in this new city which San Franciscans were already talking about there ought to be opportunities for an enterprising young woman. It was too soon to guess what they might be, but she would keep her eyes and ears open, be ready when her chance came. Judith and Geneva were not refugees in the sense that Sara and her mother were. No matter what happened, Nick would take care of Judith, and Miss Varady of Geneva. But Sara and Mrs. Jerome must work for themselves.

She looked up just then to see Ritchie crossing the street toward her. He no longer looked as dispirited as he had last night. "Good morning, Sara," he said cheerfully and dropped onto the steps at her feet. "Ah, it feels good to sit down. I had grass for a bed in Golden Gate Park last night. But they fed us well enough this morning from a soup kitchen, and I've been out having a look at the city. You've never seen such a tangle of wires, such heaps of brick! And the funny part is that the ruins aren't black the way you'd expect them to be. Everything is done in amazing color. Pink and purple and red. I suppose the heat was so terrific that it fused the brick. It's really something to see."

Sara watched him with a curious air of detachment as if he were a stranger she had just met. His clothes were soiled and the tears were longer and more jagged than before. But he had managed to clean himself up otherwise and comb his hair so that he looked a bit of the dandy in spite of his clothes.

"How is Judith this morning?" he asked. "Is she herself again?"

"I think so," Sara said. "She was talking at breakfast about volunteering to work at one of the relief centers that are opening up around town."

"Judith in relief work!" Ritchie laughed wryly. "I'll give her two hours at the most."

"Perhaps you underestimate her," Sara said.

He looked up quickly from his lower position on the steps. Whatever he saw in Sara's face must have puzzled him. For a while he was silent. Then he spoke a little awkwardly.

"Sara, I'm sorry about that night before the fire."

She felt no rancor toward him, only a curious detachment. "It doesn't matter now. Too much has happened since then."

"It matters to Nick," Ritchie said. "He'll never forgive either of us."

It was Sara's turn to be silent. There was no explanation that could be offered Nick. The truth he would hardly believe.

Ritchie sighed, sounding less confident now with his guard down. "Has Judith asked for me, Sara?"

She felt almost sorry for him. "I haven't heard her ask."

He tried to rouse himself, return to his more debonair manner. "Come to think of it—I don't know why she should." Then he tried a safer subject. "You should see the way the downtown section looks now, Sara. The buildings that were built of concrete and steel are still standing. Of course they're burned out inside, so they're only shells. But they've proved the case for themselves. All the trashy tinder that crowded about their feet is gone. It's as if a giant reached out to give San Francisco a clean start. Now there'll be a need for the sort of buildings I've made a hundred plans for."

"On paper," Sara said.

"Of course. And the paper has burned. But I have them in my head. I can plan them all again."

"But will you?" Sara asked. "Isn't this the same sort of make-believe you've gone in for all your life?"

He stared in astonishment. Sara Jerome had never spoken to him like this before.

"Don't you see, Ritchie?" she went on impatiently. "Judith doesn't want dreams. Why don't you wake up?"

She left him there on the steps, still surprised, and went into the house. Her sudden flare of impatience was for herself as well as for him. She must wake up too. But what was there to substitute for dreams?

TWENTY

ON THE SUNDAY AFTERNOON IMMEDIATELY AFTER THE fire, Judith surprised Sara by asking her to come for a walk.

"I want to stretch my legs," she said. "And I want to have a look at what has happened to San Francisco. Ritchie and Nick have been all around without hindrance, but they both discourage me when I say I want to see the ruins too. At least, Sara, we can climb to the top of Lafayette Square and have a view of what is left."

Sara too longed to stretch her legs and find out for herself what had happened in the fire.

On the low ground of Van Ness a few of the cheaper jerry-built houses which had crept in lately had suffered serious damage from the earthquake. Some of them had sagged, or had a roof fall in. But the more solid mansions had stood up well, both in the low areas and on the hills to the west. Obviously San Francisco could have recovered from earthquake damage with a laugh and a shrug. It was the fire which had caused the real destruction.

In the vicinity of California and Franklin the fire had crossed Van Ness and burned down a few blocks of Franklin Street. Otherwise this part of the western section was untouched.

They climbed to the square and picked their way among refugee camps, skirting tents and blanket-hung enclosures till they reached a vantage point of eucalyptus trees near the top of the hill. There, for the first time, they stopped to look back at the ruins of San Francisco.

Judith slipped a hand through Sara's arm and drew in her breath painfully. From Gough Street at their feet the streets ran away in the straight ruled lines that were typical of the city and followed the pattern of plain towns. Up and down the streets went, bowing to not even the steepest hill by going around it. In the blocks between the lines lay nothing but desolation. Rubble, broken bricks, and ruined walls; lone chimneys and the charred sticks of telegraph poles sticking up on all sides like spars and masts, made the scene look like the wreckage of a shipyard. The dome of City Hall had been shattered in the quake, yet the statue representing Liberty still posed upon its pinnacle.

Downtown the appearance was deceptive. A quick glance seemed to show tall buildings standing as they always had and it was hard to believe they were merely shells. Four square miles of ruins there were—the very heart and beauty of San Francisco.

Last Sunday had been Easter. A thousand years ago.

This morning, shorn of their finery, but of none of their courage, the people of San Francisco had met for church services wherever they could be held. There had been ministers preaching in every square, priests saying mass on the steps of ruined churches, children attending Sunday School beside the flower beds of Golden Gate Park.

Judith released a long-drawn breath and sat down on a bench. "Well," she said with a bite in her voice, "there's a city out there for Ritchie to rebuild. But of course he never will. He uses all his energy to avoid proving himself. If he would use a fraction of what he uses in running away to do what he might be capable of doing—" She broke off with an impatient sound.

Sara watched her, still feeling removed from all emotion, still uninvolved. You had to *want* something to be able to feel. And what was there she might dare to want?

"Perhaps this is your chance to get Ritchie to do what he really could do if he tried," she said.

"Do you think I haven't attempted that before this?" Judith asked. "I had such plans when I promised to marry him. I remember that day when I told you so highhandedly what I could do for Ritchie. And I couldn't have been more wrong."

"Perhaps the time wasn't right," said Sara.

Judith wore the same suit of cornflower blue that she had worn to escape the fire, and it was smudged now, with a long rip in the skirt that she had tried inexpertly to mend. She fingered the rough stitches absently. The old crystal calm behind which she had sheltered was gone and she had not regained it.

"Why are you talking to me like this, Sara? I thought you wanted Ritchie yourself."

Sara shook her head. "That's over. I don't believe Ritchie has ever loved anyone as he loves you. Or ever will again. You're the only one who can help him. Perhaps he's been through enough now to listen to you."

A wind from the bay caught at loose tendrils of Judith's hair and curled them above her forehead. It was chilly here. They must go down soon. But first there were certain things which must be said. Sara had not planned to say them. Had not, in fact, thought very much ahead. But now the moment was here and the words presented themselves.

Quietly she told Judith just what Ritchie had done on the eve of the earthquake; how he had planned in his mistaken way to make Judith notice him and perhaps value him more by getting Nick to create a scene.

Judith listened in surprise. "But how could he possibly think I might love him better under such circumstances? No one could reason that way."

"Ritchie could," Sara said. "He would rather have you angry and hurt, than to have you indifferent toward him as he thinks you are. There must be a sort of emptiness inside Ritchie that he keeps trying to fill. Because if he doesn't fill it he will be nothing."

Judith moved restlessly from the bench. "I'm cold. Let's go down. I don't want to talk about Ritchie. That's over and done with."

They walked home in silence. Judith did not speak again until they reached the steps of the Varady house. Then she touched Sara lightly on the arm.

"Thank you for telling me," she said.

Sara followed her silently into the house. Threads

had been left dangling and she had tried to tie them up —that was all.

Perhaps she could find something to read, she thought, and went to the library door. Nick stood beside the long table in the middle of the room sorting out the records and papers he had brought away from the office. His back was toward her and she would have turned away if a mirror across the room had not revealed her presence.

"Please come in, Sara," he said curtly.

Now that she had faced her own feelings about Nick, she did not want to be near him, knowing so well how he felt about her. But before she could turn away, he spoke again and she could only stand there listening, fixing her attention on his lean, strong hands as he sorted papers, so that she needn't watch his face.

"Everything is in a thorough mess," he went on more easily. "I'm trying to sort all this correspondence and the rest of the material into alphabetical headings under subject or name. That's the first step so we can see what we have. Later there will be a good many letters to write. Perhaps Mr. Merkel will bring over a typewriter from Oakland. Of course we can pay you nothing for this work at the moment. But since your aunt is taking care of you, you might be willing to give some time—"

"I don't mean to be dependent on Aunt Hester," Sara said quickly. "I want to find some sort of paying work for myself as soon as I can. But today at least I can help you with this."

She went to work on the opposite side of the table. Sometimes Nick talked as he sorted, but it was as if he were thinking out loud, more than speaking to her.

"It's a funny thing," he said. "Always before I've regarded insurance as the dullest business in the world. It seemed to require nothing but routine. Now, suddenly, it has stopped being statistics and has turned into people."

Sara sorted and said nothing. Nick put a typewritten sheet on the "D" pile and went on.

"Henry Dawson. I remember him very well. He has an invalid wife. They owned a building on Clay Street and lived on the top floor. I wonder if he got his wife out all right. There was a child too—a bright little boy of eight. They've lost everything material they had in the world. Everything but this insurance. And perhaps the records of that have been destroyed in the fire. This letter reminds me of Henry, so we'll find a way to get him that money."

As he spoke Sara could almost see the Dawsons. She glanced at Nick wonderingly.

"You've lost everything too. What about that?"

A look flashed into his face that she had never seen before. "No, I've gained. I've learned something. A man is what he is. It's what he can do with his own two hands and his own brain that matters. Nothing else. In the end that's all any of us has that can be counted on."

Sara went thoughtfully back to her sorting. What Nick had just said made all her longings for position and wealth seem empty, uncertain. But she did not want to be uncertain about all she demanded of life. What was she in herself? What could she become?

As they worked in silence; Mrs. Renwick wandered into her room, yawning, and stared at the heap of papers spread over the table.

"Hello, children. I envy you your industry. I am getting bored with my own idle company. When I put my head out a window I find that all San Francisco is pitching in except me. Is there anything useful I can do?"

"Of course, Mother," Nick said. "You can help right now if you like."

Sara showed her what they were doing and Mrs. Renwick went happily to work.

In a few moments they had two more visitors. Allison came into the room, propelling ahead of her a fat little girl with plump cheeks, short, pudgy legs, and stringy blond hair that hung down her back in a tangled mat.

Allison looked doubtful when she spied her mother, as if she would like to retreat. But the other child had a stolid air of not being easily budged. Having been pushed in here, she meant to stay and see what was going on. She regarded the room with round blue eyes.

"This is Miranda Schultz," Allison said hesitantly and introduced the three adults. Sara smiled at the plump little girl and Nick nodded to her in a friendly way. Mrs. Renwick stared.

"My papa," Miranda began at once, with an air of stating her own importance in the scheme of things, "is in prison."

Allison broke in hurriedly. "I think we'd better go look for Comstock now, Miranda."

Miranda stayed where she was, waiting for some recognition of her unique position. Nick seemed to have taken her statement in his stride, but Mrs. Renwick was plainly impressed.

"Does—does Miranda live near here?" she recovered sufficiently to inquire.

"Right now she lives in Lafayette Square," Allison said, taking the lead before Miranda, who was a slow starter, could speak. "Mrs. Schultz's delicatessen store was burned out in the fire. And her mother is afraid there won't be any insurance money because people in the park are saying that the companies will in—invoke the—the earthquake clause and never pay up." Allison stopped for breath and looked inquiringly at her brother. "That isn't true, is it, Nick?"

"I can't speak for all companies," Nick told Miranda gravely. "But I believe most will do their utmost to meet obligations."

"There—you see?" said Allison.

"Mama likes to worry about things," Miranda said placidly. "Of course she has a great deal to worry about. My papa—"

With a great show of enthusiasm, Allison waved her hands in a gesture that took in the room. "Look, Miranda! Did you ever see so many books? There are even more here than we had in our house up on Nob Hill."

Distracted by Allison's hand-waving, Miranda looked about, more in puzzlement than in awe. "Who'd ever read so many books?" she asked.

"I'll read some of them," said Allison. "And so will Nick and Sara."

"Don't you like to read, Miranda?" Nick asked.

"I don't like to read at all," said Miranda with conviction.

"But she likes to listen," Allison explained quickly. "I've been telling her stories and she loves to hear them. Don't you, Miranda?"

Miranda agreed, but was not to be outdone. "I can tell stories too. Mama says I'm a little pitcher when it comes to stories. Like the time I told company about the masher my Aunt Agnes—"

At this point Allison decided on action. She flung her own slight weight upon the firmly planted Miranda, jarred her loose from the spot to which she seemed rooted, and went out of the room, half pulling, half pushing her puzzled friend.

Mrs. Renwick forgot her sorting. "What are we to do?" she demanded of Nick. "Have you any idea why this child's father is in prison?"

"He strangled somebody," Sara offered. "Miranda feels that it was quite justified. Though the victim didn't really die."

"You'll have to speak to Allison, Nick," Mrs. Renwick wailed. "We can't have her running around with murderers' children!"

"I expect Miranda and Allison will be very good for each other," Nick said.

Mrs. Renwick threw up her hands. "You're confusing me terribly. I'm sure there is something extremely unwise here, but you've turned me all around."

"Don't worry, Mother." Nick smiled at her. "One doesn't inherit a tendency to murder. Allison has never had a satellite before. Let her enjoy the experience while it lasts. And she'll give Miranda a new experience too."

"Very well, Nick. Though I know exactly what William would have said about the matter." This reminded her of something and she turned to Sara. "Did you find out why Allison was so upset because I didn't scold her over breaking another plate?"

Sara nodded. "I can understand how she felt. After all, you did make rather a fuss when the first one was broken. And that gave Allison an exaggerated idea about the importance of those plates. When you actually let her carry them she felt you'd put a real trust in her. Then when it developed that you didn't mind another one getting broken, all the importance of your trust fell through. I'm afraid that means to Allison that you don't care about her."

"But that's ridiculous! Allison is more important to me than any plate."

"I think you should tell her that," Sara said.

She glanced at Nick and was disconcerted to find his dark gaze upon her, grave and puzzled. As if he wanted to thank her for understanding Allison, yet found it hard to believe that good might come from Sara Jerome. Sara flushed and turned hurriedly back to her sorting.

They worked on for a while without further talk, and after a time Allison reappeared in the doorway, without Miranda, beckoning to Sara. Her manner was one of exaggerated secrecy and Sara left her task and went into the hall.

"I've found something," Allison whispered. "Come see, Sara."

She led the way cautiously to a door beneath the stairs and pulled it open.

"Mostly it's locked with a padlock," she said. "But somebody left it open this time."

The closet was large and deep and there were shelves along the sides. Sara did not find their contents alarming. The rows of phials and bottles and canisters undoubtedly held Aunt Hester's medical supplies.

"Miss Varady knows a great deal about medicine and sickness," Sara said. "She bandaged Nick's hands when he was burned. This is where she keeps the things she needs for such purposes."

"Look!" Allison pointed to a bottle plainly marked with a skull and crossbones. "I'll bet she poisons people."

"Don't be foolish," Sara said. "That's disinfectant. It's marked that way so no one will make a mistake and drink it."

Allison was plainly disappointed at having her discovery fall so flat. She made one more effort to arrest Sara's attention.

"Well, then—look at those books! Aren't they sort of queer? Why should she keep them locked up?"

"They're medical books, probably," Sara said. She looked more closely and saw other titles as well. The collection was certainly on the esoteric side. A volume or two on spiritualism, a book of accounts by people who had seen visions, a short treatise on reincarnation and so on. These hidden titles gave Sara a slightly creepy feeling. She didn't like to think about Hester Varady sitting alone in this old house reading such queer subjects. They might do odd things to the mind. For Allison's benefit, however, she shrugged the books aside.

"Don't let your imagination run away with you, honey," she told the child as she closed the door upon books and medicine.

By Saturday evening, the fourth day after the earthquake, trolley cars, cheered by the populace, had begun to run again on Fillmore Street. And on Monday an overhead trolley was operating on Market. There was still no electricity, no gas, no running water in the houses. But water was available and there was no shortage.

During the week after the fire Judith and Geneva set off for a relief center and spent their day doling out bread and tinned milk, sorting clothing, assisting in the individual problems of those who came for help. Geneva came home at night looking wan, but happy, while Judith seemed to thrive on the work. Sara had intended to go with them, but what Nick needed done was in a sense relief work too, so for the moment she stayed with him.

Nick had managed to get in touch with Mr. Merkel over in Oakland and the company of Renwick and Merkel, composed of Nick, Mr. Merkel, and an indifferent Ritchie, had taken over Miss Varady's library to hold a council and prepare for the uncertain future. The moment they announced themselves open for business, Nick said, there would be lines outside the door down Van Ness.

The city's newspapers, burned out as they were, had moved temporarily to Oakland, and had missed only one day of publication. On the second day of the fire a joint edition had been printed from Oakland crying the first frightening news of the disaster. Now every edition carried personal items in which separated families tried to get in touch with one another.

While exact numbers would perhaps never be known, it was beginning to seem that, in spite of the size of the disaster, fewer had died than might be expected. The total was mounting toward five hundred, and perhaps three times that many had been injured.

During the following weeks help for San Francisco

began to pour in from the outside world. The Red Cross had set up relief agencies. Food was arriving by the carload. President Theodore Roosevelt had given a government sum to San Francisco's ex-Mayor Phelan and this was being wisely administered.

Already dynamite blasts were heard again, reminding wincing refugees of the days of the fire. But now the explosions were to clear the way for new buildings, or remove dangerously tottering wreckage. The sound of falling walls was common and there was the new invigorating clatter of preparation for building.

As Miss Varady had prophesied, business firms and professional offices opened wherever they could find space. Van Ness had changed overnight in character from a quiet residential street to one of professional and business activity. Fillmore, unharmed by the fire, boldly claimed itself the future rival of Market Street.

One day Sara came upon her aunt standing alone in the drawing room, her back to the clatter and dust of the street, staring at the painting of Consuelo Varady where it hung above the fireplace.

She did not turn when Sara came into the room, but she spoke her thoughts aloud.

"This is the end of the old life," she said. "We will never go back. Rincon Hill and South Park were already finished. And now Van Ness is doomed."

"Will you move away?" Sara asked. "Will you build elsewhere or buy a new place?"

Miss Varady held herself proudly erect. "I shall not. I shall stay here until I die. What becomes of the house afterwards will be up to my heir." She stared at Sara and then changed the subject. "How grubby you look, child. Is that gray suit the only thing you have to wear?"

Sara glanced down at the suit which had been her pride so short a time before. There was a rent in the skirt, one sleeve had been ripped at the elbow, and there were smudges everywhere. But she answered Aunt Hester cheerfully.

"Oh, no, I'm rich! I have two extra skirts and three shirtwaists. I had a suitcase packed to leave even before we knew how bad the fire would be."

"Leave? Where were you going?"

"To this house," Sara admitted. "I couldn't stay at the Renwicks' another day."

"Why not?" Miss Varady asked. "After all, you'd received no invitation to come here."

"I know. But I couldn't wait any longer. Something had happened."

"May I ask what?"

"I'd rather not talk about it," Sara said.

Miss Varady looked annoyed. "As you wish. I'd suggest, however, that you get into something more presentable if you have extra clothes."

"I'm saving my fresh things," Sara said. "I want to find work as soon as I can and I'll need them. My mother and I don't want to depend on your generosity any longer than is necessary."

What Miss Varady thought of this announcement, Sara could not tell. Her aunt returned to a study of Consuelo with an air that implied dismissal and Sara knew that for the moment the subject was closed.

By now the household had settled into something of a routine. Several of Ah Foong's relatives had remained to help out in the increased household. Sara came upon them dusting, polishing, scrubbing, and always Ah Foong was nearby, ready to give shrill directions in his native tongue.

Sara's mother continued to occupy the dismal little room at the top of the house. No ghosts had walked, no little white cat had mewed, and she was far happier than she would have been in the luxurious room which she had once occupied as a bride. She did not like their dependence on Miss Varady, however. Sara had promised to find work as soon as she could in this new San Francisco, but so far no such work had offered itself for either of them. Thus Sara had fallen into the regular habit of working with Nick and Mr. Merkel for a few hours every day.

Her relationship with Nick was for the most part stiff on both sides. He was courteous, but distant, and it was clear that he had neither forgotten nor forgiven. Sara, on her part, stood rigidly upon her dignity and spoke to him only on business matters. The one thing she must conceal at all costs was her true feeling about him.

The insurance work was both engrossing and heartbreaking. As Nick had been the first to realize, it had ceased to be statistics and had turned into human beings. Sara found her own interest and her emotions engaged and there were times when she almost forgot the unhappy situation between herself and Nick; times when he forgot, too, and they discussed individual problems with an earnest interest that was companionable, even while it had nothing of the personal in it.

Sometimes Geneva sat in on these discussions, but she had little head for business and was timid about expressing an opinion. Mostly she hunted for Mr. Merkel's misplaced spectacles, brought in cups of coffee or tea, and spoke soothing words to those who stood in line on the steps waiting for interviews.

It was far better, Sara found, to be busy than idle. Only in moments when she sat near Nick in the library taking down a record of some interview he might be holding with an unhappy refugee, did she feel truly alive these days. Listening to Nick's gentleness, as he dealt with the frightened and destitute, hearing the reassurances he uttered, the promises that might mean ruin to him, her eyes sometimes blurred so that she could hardly see the symbols she wrote. He was so good, so very dear. And he was taking the troubles of others onto his own strong shoulders in a way that began to concern her.

Since Renwick and Merkel could pay nothing for her services, Nick would not allow her to put in the long hours he did, so she still had time to herself to look for work that proved hopelessly elusive. There seemed to be nothing she could do that anyone wanted.

One evening after dinner she sat before the sectioned mirror at her dressing table and studied her face as if some answer to an epic question might be revealed in her own features. It seemed to her that she was growing into a different girl than the determined young woman who had so heedlessly engineered the move to San Francisco. She was not sure she was any wiser, but she felt older, and it seemed as though the change ought to be visible in her face.

She was pondering this when Ah Foong came rapping on her door. Miss Varady, he said, wanted her downstairs in the sitting room. She was to come at once.

Glad enough for a distraction, Sara left her room and hurried after Ah Foong.

TWENTY-ONE

Candles and lamps were now permitted at night in San Francisco and it was hoped that in another month electricity and gas would be available again.

Hester Varady's sitting room glowed in the light of several lamps and Mrs. Renwick, Judith, and Geneva were already there. Miss Varady was not usually given to social gestures, and Sara was somewhat surprised. A moment later Ah Foong had brought Mrs. Jerome from her third-floor room, and the women of the house were all present.

Geneva seemed pleased and a little excited. She hovered near the door, as if she awaited some signal from her aunt. Hester Varady, gowned tonight in rich cinnamon-brown taffeta, sat at a drop-front desk with pen and paper before her. She had evidently been making some sort of list. She turned in her chair to regard her guests with a disapproving eye.

"Geneva has suggested this gathering," she said, "and I believe it is a good idea. I regret to see my house guests looking as shabby as you ladies have unfortunately grown. I realize that unlike Geneva and me, you have lost most of your wardrobe, and she has suggested that I do something about your sad state. Very well, Geneva, bring in the things."

Geneva hurried off and returned a moment later, followed by Ah Foong. Each carried over their arms bright heaps of garments which they flung across the pedestaled table in the middle of the room. It looked as if there were clothes enough here to dress an entire household of ladies.

When Ah Foong had gone, Miss Varady signaled to Geneva and the girl picked up the top garment, shook it out for them to see. There was a strong odor of moth balls. The dress was of good material, but had an old-fashioned bustle.

"I suppose with the present earthquake fashions," Judith said doubtfully, "the dress could be worn. And we'll certainly be grateful for a change, Miss Varady."

Sara picked up the frock and held it out at arm's length. "The bustle doesn't matter. There's so much material here that we can take out the stitches and cut a new costume that will be close enough to today's styles to fool anyone. The waist can be kept almost as it is, with just a bit of remodeling. And all these yards of skirt goods can be used in a new way. I like these rich old-fashioned materials."

"Do you mean you could do something to renovate these things, Sara?" Aunt Hester asked.

"*I* couldn't. But I can cut and plan and make patterns, if the rest of you will sew." She began to be carried away by her own interest. "There isn't any limit to what can be made from this old stuff. There must be enough here for each of us to have a dress or two, if that's what you intend, Aunt Hester."

Miss Varady tapped the sheet of paper before her. "That is what I have in mind, Sara."

Tossing the frock she held back to Geneva, Sara pulled out another dress that caught her eye. It was of watered silk grosgrain in chrome yellow, taffeta lined. The fullness in back fell into trailing folds as Sara held it up for them to see.

Her mother's gasp made the others turn. Mrs. Jerome had put a hand before her eyes as if the glowing color of the dress blinded her.

"What is it?" Sara asked.

"Perhaps she has recognized the dress," said Miss Varady dryly.

Mary Jerome nodded. "Yes. It is one I wore many years ago."

Sara turned quickly to her aunt. "Are these Mama's dresses you are giving us? In that case, don't you think—"

Miss Varady did not let her finish. "Your mother didn't want them. She left them here. And they are not all hers. Most of them go back to an earlier period. My sister Elizabeth was extremely fond of clothes. She never had my taste or much flair for wearing them, but she had a large wardrobe. Too large to be taken with her on a sea voyage. I packed them away against her return. As you know, she and her husband were lost on the ocean. The garments have been carefully protected from moths and light. Most of them should be in excellent condition. You may select the colors you prefer, ladies."

There was a considerable flurry while choices were made. Only Sara's mother held back. When Sara paused in her excitement over this luxury, she saw tears in Mary Jerome's eyes. Quickly she went to her.

"If you don't want your things touched, Mama," she whispered, "I'll get them from Aunt Hester. I'm sure everyone will respect your feelings in the matter."

Mary Jerome shook her head. "I know I'm being foolish. There is just one dress. . . . That one Miss Renwick is holding now. . . ."

The gown in Judith's hands was of bright cherry-red corded silk, with a modest décolletage and little red velvet bows on each shoulder. Sara found it difficult to picture her mother as a young girl wearing this dress. But if she wanted it, she should have it.

"That is a dress Mama was fond of," Sara said to Judith. "Do you mind if she has it again?"

Judith would have handed the frock over at once, but Miss Varady spoke with a deliberate malice.

"I remember that gown very well. A Paris model, it was. One of Leland's first gifts after he married Mary. It was a dress which required an air to carry it off successfully. I told him he had dressed a wren in peacock's clothing. And I must say he agreed after he saw her in it. Let's not be foolish about it again, Mary. If Sara really has a gift for designing, she can plan something quite effective for Miss Renwick using the material and trimmings."

Mrs. Jerome sat very straight in her chair. "I don't want to wear the dress," she told Miss Varady. "I would merely like to keep it."

"We can't afford foolish sentiment at a time like this," said Miss Varady shortly. "The dress is yours, Miss Renwick."

With quiet dignity Mary Jerome crossed the room to where Judith stood uncertainly with the shining cherry silk in her hands. Gently Mrs. Jerome touched it, her fingers lingering on the bright material. Then she turned and went out of the room without a word for Miss Varady.

Judith held the dress out to Sara. "Of course your mother must have it."

But Miss Varady was too quick for them. She reached out and took the gown into her own hands.

"I have made my decision," she said. "When the time comes the dress shall be cut up for Miss Renwick. It no longer belongs to Mary Bishop. She forfeited all right to anything in this house long ago. In fact, Sara, I tolerate her presence only because you are her daughter."

Sara held back a surge of anger. Only tonight she had been considering her own growth. Now she must behave quietly and with dignity.

"Please let my mother have the dress, Aunt Hester," she said. Miss Varady tossed the dress onto the pile on the table. "Ladies I apologize for this intrusion of a strictly family matter. Please continue with your choices."

Sara stood where she was. A trembling had begun in the pit of her stomach. She wanted to strike out at her aunt, to storm and stamp and denounce. But Miss Varady disregarded her completely. She turned back to her list and began to check off items upon it. Sara might have been no more than a naughty child to be ignored.

Judith and Mrs. Renwick, unaware of the clash of forces beneath the surface, returned in some embarrassment to the frocks. Only Geneva sensed that Sara was shaken by an anger she was trying to control. With her back to Miss Varady, Geneva mouthed words of reassurance that only Sara could understand.

"Say nothing. Wait. I'll get the dress for you later."

Sara stared at her blindly, without comprehension. She would not permit her mother to be treated in so humiliating a fashion by Hester Varady. With an outward air of calm, in spite of inner trembling, she picked up the dress and walked toward the door with it.

Her aunt looked up and spoke sharply. "Sara! Come back here at once!"

Her voice was imperious, commanding. It brooked no disobedience, but Sara did not hesitate. She opened the door and walked out past Ah Foong, who lingered suspiciously close. Up the stairs she went, running now, to release her tension. An angry elation filled her. She had shown Hester Varady that she could not dominate Sara Bishop as she dominated everyone else in her life.

Mrs. Jerome's door was closed and Sara tapped on it lightly, slipped inside when her mother answered. Mrs. Jerome lay upon the bed, her face hidden in the crook of an arm, and Sara saw her slight shoulders quivering.

"Look what I've brought you!" Sara cried. "You didn't think I'd stay and let her give it to anyone else, did you?"

But her mother sat up and looked at Sara almost

fiercely. "It's not just the dress. It's this house and that dreadful old woman. The only way she can live is to crush everyone around her into obedience. There's no use fighting her—she always wins. There's no honor in her, no consideration for honesty or justice. She won't hesitate to use any weapon that presents itself, so long as she can get her way. Tomorrow I'm going out and look for a room. Then we can leave this house before something terrible happens."

"Rooms are the scarcest thing in San Francisco just now," Sara reminded her. "And we can't afford to move until I've found some sort of work. Besides, that isn't the way. I won't run away from her, Mama. I'm not afraid of her and I'm going to stay right here and stand up to her. In the long run I expect that's the only way to treat her. Look at Ah Foong. I believe he's the only human being she really has any use for. And he does as he pleases, even when he pretends to obey her."

Mrs. Jerome shook her head. "No, Sara. She'll tear you to pieces if you try to fight her. She's not only unscrupulous—she's dangerous. Sometimes I used to think she wasn't quite sane. She goes a little mad when anyone opposes her."

There was no use reasoning with her mother's feeling about Hester Varady. Sara changed the subject gently.

"Tell me about the dress," she said.

Mrs. Jerome lay back on the pillow, closed her eyes. "I wore it to the opera with Leland. We had a box that night and for once *she* stayed home. That was before she told your father that the dress was wrong for me. He thought it looked lovely on me. I—I felt almost beautiful that night. And not afraid of San Francisco, or even of Hester Varady. Afterwards, we went to a fine restaurant and he ordered for me from the French menu, and didn't mind that I'd been around so little. But she was waiting up for us when we got home. She hadn't known we were going to have an evening out together and she was furious."

Sara held her mother's hand comfortingly.

Mary went on, remembering. "She was waiting for us in the drawing room, sitting below that portrait of Consuelo the way she likes to do. She is prouder of family than anyone should be. When Leland helped me out of my cape she looked me up and down and asked me how I could possibly wear a dress to which I could do so little justice."

Sara's grasp on her mother's hand tightened. "What did my father say?"

"He didn't say anything. He knew better than to oppose her openly. But he began to look at me through her eyes. I could feel it, and straightaway I turned into a wren. I never wore the dress again. But I kept it in my wardrobe closet and sometimes I used to hide my face against it and live over every detail of that lovely night."

For the first time Sara turned in distaste from the memory of her father. If Leland Bishop could do such a thing to so gentle a bride as Mary Jerome must have been—

Her mother opened her eyes and saw Sara's expression. "You mustn't blame him. She made him the way he was when he was too young to help himself."

Sara could not excuse Leland Bishop so easily. Something of the cavalier image she had built of her father had begun to crumble in her mind. Sara sat on in thoughtful silence until Mary Jerome turned her head, listening.

"What was that, Sara?"

Sara could hear nothing. The evening was fog-filled and Mrs. Jerome had closed her windows against its raw dampness. A vine clattered against the pane, but there was no other sound that she could hear.

"It was inside the house. It sounded like—like a mewing, Sara."

Cold fingers seemed to touch the back of Sara's neck. The bare little room was suddenly oppressive, as if it held old secrets whose shadow lived on within its walls.

"Listen!" her mother whispered. "Sara, it's the little cat! The ghost cat."

Now Sara could hear it too. A faint, urgent mewing that seemed to come from anywhere and nowhere. But she did not believe in ghosts and she went to the door and opened it, to listen again. The mewing was more distinct now, and she smiled at her mother.

"That's no ghost cat. It's my friend Comstock. He has a talent for getting into places where he's not supposed to be."

She went into the hall, following the sound. No cat but Comstock mewed so expressively. Undoubtedly he was shut in somewhere and demanding to be let out. The sound came from Geneva's room, and Geneva was downstairs. Sara went to the door and was about to open it to release the imprisoned Comstock, when she heard someone coming up the stairs.

The stair carpet muffled footfalls, but the rustle of heavy taffeta was unmistakable. Hester Varady was ap-

proaching and it would not do for her to discover
Comstock in hiding on the third floor.

Sara went quickly away from Geneva's door and
started downstairs. If her aunt was looking for her, it
might be just as well to face her at once. The two
women met at the turn of the stairway on the second-
floor landing. Sara knew by Hester's bright, intense
look that she was bent on battle.

"I wish to have this matter out at once," said Miss
Varady. "I do not propose to be treated disrespectfully
in my own house, and by a chit like yourself."

Sara felt suddenly unsteady, unsure of herself with
that strange, deep-set gaze upon her. She remembered
her mother's words—that sometimes Hester seemed a
little mad.

"Defiance of my word in this house," her aunt went
on, "is something I shall not brook. You picked up
that dress and took it to your mother directly against
my wishes. Now you will fetch it downstairs and give it
to Miss Renwick as I directed."

Sara put a hand upon the rail to steady herself. She
wanted to drop her gaze, look away from her aunt, but
Hester's eyes held her own, commanded her. In a moment, Sara knew, she would go and do weakly what
her aunt directed. It was as if a dark sea were about to
close over her head and she could do nothing to save
herself.

On the floor above Comstock had grown impatient
again. His mew came plainly through the door, but
Miss Varady's concentration in bending Sara to her will
was so great that she did not hear the sound. Its reality, however, released Sara from the spell of Hester
Varady's will. She wrenched her gaze away from her

aunt's, heard the mewing again and spoke quickly, lightly.

"Aunt Hester, have you ever seen a little white cat walking about up on the third floor? I thought you didn't like cats, but there's one there. You can hear it mewing."

This was sheer inspiration, and she did not expect it to have so startling an effect. The blood drained from Hester Varady's face, leaving it parchment-pale, and now there was clearly a little madness in the burning eyes. She took Sara's wrist in a grip that made the girl gasp with pain.

"There is no cat!" Hester said. "No cat at all. Do you hear me?" The vise of her hand moved to Sara's shoulder, shook her roughly. "Never mention a white cat in this house again."

For an instant Sara thought her aunt might do her bodily harm. Then Hester raised her head, plainly listening, while Sara winced beneath the pain of her grip. But Comstock chose to be silent now. There was no mewing, nothing. Only the frightened thumping of Sara's own heart.

Miss Varady flung her back against the wall of the landing and went downstairs without another word. At least she had been distracted from Sara's possession of the cherry-red dress.

Sara stayed where she was for a moment, breathing heavily, truly frightened, as she could never remember having been frightened before, except in her dream. Her legs and arms seemed lead-heavy as she went upstairs again and opened the door of Geneva's room. Comstock flew out like a streak and vanished downstairs in leaps that hardly touched the steps. However he had come into Geneva's room, Comstock plainly did not like this house or the smell of Hester Varady's presence. He would probably return willingly enough to Ah Foong's cellar now and to pleasant tidbits of fish.

Sara had no heart for working on those frocks in Miss Varady's sitting room. Nor had she any wish to return to her big lonely bedroom. Tonight she did not want to be alone. Strangely she'd had no fear of dreaming in this house in the time she had been here. No memories had stirred in her. Not even her sense of recognition of the hallway had returned since she had slept under this roof. But Aunt Hester's blazing fury had frightened her. It was true that the woman could be dangerous.

She went to her room only to gather up her night things. Then she carried them upstairs to her mother's little room.

"Let me stay here tonight, Mama," she pleaded. "I —I don't want to be alone."

She did not tell her mother of the meeting on the stairs, and Mrs. Jerome, content with her daughter's desire to be here, asked no questions.

When her mother was in bed and the lamp turned off, Sara stood for a few moments looking out the little side window. So heavy was the overgrowth of vines, unshriveled here by the fire, that no curtain was needed. Yet anyone in the room could peer out between fluttering leaves.

How strangely menacing the fog seemed in this low area. Sara had loved to watch it from the hilltop as it rolled in through the bay in soft billows, engulfing water and shore, enveloping the buildings, one by one.

But from this house there was nothing to see. Here one had been enveloped, swallowed.

There were lights on in the house next door, dimmed by the gauzy gray veil. A length of electric wire between the two houses was strung with droplets of water shining like a strand of beads. The air was clammy cold and smelled dankly of wet ruins.

Shivering, Sara got into the narrow bed beside her mother. She lay close to her as she had done as a child, gaining comfort from her nearness. For a little while they talked in soft whispers. Desultory talk that followed no pattern.

"I miss the view we had at the Renwicks'," Sara said. "I don't like a house that crouches in a valley as if it had to hide. Someday I want a house with a view of the water and the hills. I like the wind to whistle around my ears."

Here the night was quiet, windless, thick with fog. Outside their room lay a strange obscurity in which normal sounds seemed muffled and unnatural.

"I wish we could lock the door," Mary Jerome said uneasily. "I think of that every night. If spirits ever do walk in this house, they'll surely come to this room."

Sara dared not let her thoughts follow such a course. She closed her eyes and tried to remember pleasant things. Her mother slept soon enough, quietly, deeply, and Sara lay very still so as not to disturb her.

The midnight hours ticked by and still Sara lay as if she waited for something. She did not really want to sleep. Sleep might bring her dreams again and she was glad enough to be wakeful. Because she was awake she heard the opening of a door somewhere deep in the house.

Who would be stirring at this hour and why?

As one might listen for a second shoe to drop, she waited to hear the door close again. But it did not. Somewhere a door had been opened and left ajar. Why? Because someone had slipped through, not wanting to make the second sound of closing it behind? Or because someone waited in its opening, breathing lightly in the darkness. Waiting. For what?

Whoever it was had not waited. The footfall in the hall outside their door was light, but Sara, tense with listening, heard it. She stiffened under the covers. She could not see the doorknob when it turned, but she heard its faint squeak. The door opened a crack and a thread of candlelight cut into the dark room.

As Sara waited, holding her breath, too frightened to move, the thread widened to a ribbon and a hand in a long white sleeve appeared in the opening. A hand which held a candlestick, a tall candle, spear-headed with flame.

This was the dream again. The glow of candlelight, the hand. But now there was no mirror into which Sara could look, as if into the past. This was real and she was awake. It was impossible to move her frozen body, to make a sound in her tightened throat. Her mother slept on, her breathing slow and steady.

The dark shadow of the door slowly narrowed, giving way to the glow of light. In the opening stood Hester Varady, a tall figure in her white nightgown. Her hair, long as Sara's own, hung over her shoulder in a rope-thick braid of iron gray. Her eyes stared, their look senseless, without focus. Sara wanted to cry out, but the muscles of her throat were inflexible bands and she could make no sound.

What did Hester Varady intend? Had madness finally banished all reason? Had she come here to wreak some punishment on them because they had dared to oppose her?

With a curious, balanced tread, Hester came into the room. Now her blank eyes seemed to search for something she did not find. The look glided over Sara without recognition, perhaps without knowing she was there, though the candle, held high, lighted the room's center and sent shadows trembling to the corners.

With sudden realization, Sara knew that her aunt was asleep. She had come up here walking quietly, steadily, as if with purpose. And she was not awake at all.

Now something almost frantic seemed to guide this unconscious searching. The woman turned hurriedly, holding the candle to every corner of the small room, as if something might hide there, escaping her. Words came like a rattle from between her lips.

"Callie! Where are you, Callie? Don't try to hide from me. Callie, I'll never let you get away. Answer me, Callie!"

The rattling mumble was horrible to hear. More dreadful than if Hester had spoken consciously. There was no governing intelligence behind the words. Something had been dredged up out of past depths that could not face consciousness and the light of day. What would happen if Hester wakened suddenly in this room, found Sara staring at her in the quiver of candlelight?

Before Sara could decide on any move, Ah Foong appeared abruptly in the doorway. He did not glance in Sara's direction, but put a hand upon Miss Varady's arm as if he knew exactly what to do. Hester offered no resistance as he led her out of the room.

Sara watched the light go flickering away through the dark hall. Then, her power of motion recovered, she slipped out of bed and closed the door softly, propped a chair under the knob. Her mother had not stirred and Sara was thankful for that. She crept close to her again in the bed, drawing warmth from her sleeping body. It was a long time before her chill went away.

Now she knew why Ah Foong slept on a cot outside Miss Varady's door. The need was not to protect her, but to watch her. Tonight perhaps he had slept too soundly. His mistress must have slipped past him so that he wakened to find her gone. And he had known just where to look for her.

Sara shivered in the warm bed, remembering the rattling words Hester Varady had spoken. Who was the "Callie" she searched for? And why in this room? Whose spirit was it that haunted this strange house?

TWENTY-TWO

AT BREAKFAST THE NEXT MORNING, AH FOONG, WITHOUT a glance at Sara, announced that Miss Varady was ill. She had a severe headache and would remain in bed today. Mrs. Renwick, who came downstairs to breakfast with the others these days, murmured that it was too bad, but otherwise a faint ripple of relief seemed to flow around the table.

Sara planned her day with a new sense of freedom. She had not told her mother what had happened in the night, though she had mentioned the name "Callie" to her casually, without result. Her mother had recalled no one of that name and had been puzzled by her inquiry. Sara meant to try the name on others in the household. Ah Foong, for instance, and perhaps Geneva.

When the breakfast dishes had been cleared away, Sara sought until she found him in the drawing room on his knees, polishing big brass andirons. He ignored her with elaborate unconcern and did not look up until she pulled over a hassock and dropped down beside him. There she could talk to him on his own level, and he had to recognize her presence. He did so wordlessly, with the most guileless of smiles.

"Does Aunt Hester walk in her sleep very often?" Sara asked directly.

He did not even blink. Nor did he pause in his busy polishing, though the brass under his cloth already shone.

"Ah Foong," Sara said. "I asked you a question. Aunt Hester came to Mama's room last night walking in her sleep. And you came after her and took her away. Does she do this often?"

He looked at her again, out of black-currant eyes in a seamy face. "You talkee fool talk," he said calmly. "Me no savvy."

By now she recognized that Ah Foong, when he chose, could put up a wall of obstinacy that was difficult to penetrate.

"Well then," she went on, "if you won't tell me about Aunt Hester, tell me who Callie is. Aunt Hester was calling for someone named Callie. Whom did she mean?"

The innocent smile stretched his lips again and this time he answered her glibly enough.

"Callie litty white kitty," he said. "Velly nice litty white kitty."

"A ghost kitty?" Sara asked.

Ah Foong closed his eyes. "You go 'way now. You fool ge'l. You talkee fool talk."

It was plain that Ah Foong intended to tell her

nothing. But now that she had a chance to talk to him without fear of discovery by her aunt, there were other topics she wanted to broach.

"All right then—we'll let Callie go for now. Ah Foong, did you know my father when he was a little boy?"

He looked pleased at the change of subject and nodded willingly. "Him velly fine litty boy. Boy mo' betta than ge'l. Too solly you mama makee ge'l."

Ah Foong gave the handle of the poker a last swipe with his cloth and stood up.

"Wait, please," Sara said. "Ah Foong, I know so little about my father. What happened to him in this house? Why did he go away?"

At once Ah Foong started for the door. "Velly busy, velly busy," he muttered and would have escaped if Sara had not flung herself after him and caught his blue sleeve in pleading.

"Tell me about him when he was a little boy, then. Surely you can talk about that."

He looked at her for a long moment, small and dignified, old and wise. Then he beckoned to her and went padding through the door. She followed him across the hall, watching his queue swinging jauntily against his blue linen back.

He led the way into the library, where Nick was already at work writing letters at the big table, his dark brows drawn together in concentration. Mr. Merkel came over from Oakland later these mornings to join him. Probably Ritchie was playing hooky again. Nick did not look up as they came in, and Ah Foong paid no attention to him.

Quickly the little Chinese brought a stepladder,

placed it before the bookshelves in one corner of the room and climbed its few steps. Reaching high, he pulled out several heavy volumes of history and handed them to Sara to hold. Then he dug deep into the hollow where they had been. In a moment he had a wooden cigar box in his hands. This too he handed to Sara, replaced the books and came down the ladder.

"Sodjers belong you papa," he said.

Wonderingly Sara opened the box. Packed in a nest of cotton were a dozen or more tin soldiers. One by one Sara took them out and set them on the library table at the far end from Nick. There were two minor cavalry officers, a number of foot soldiers with muskets on their shoulders, a drummer boy, and a red-coated general on a white horse. The paint had once been bright and the tin shiny. But the little soldiers had obviously fought hard campaigns, marched the years away. Now they were slightly battered, their colors dull.

Shaking his head, Ah Foong picked up the general. "Him enemy. Him Englis'. No gotchee Amelican boss sodjer now."

Sara could see her father more clearly than she had ever seen him before. Not the grown man who had taken his aunt's side in so unkindly a fashion over Mary's gown, but a little boy. A boy with fair hair playing in this very room, lining up his armies on the library table. She heard Geneva come in, was aware that the girl stood beside her, looking at the soldiers. But Geneva's quick perception must have told her that this was a moment of deep feeling, for she did not speak.

Ah Foong set the enemy general down gently, and

Sara, glancing at him, saw that there was moisture in his eyes, that his chin quivered as if he might cry at any moment. Lest he be disgraced, he went abruptly out of the room, his pigtail flying as he disappeared from sight.

"Did you see?" Sara asked Geneva. "Ah Foong had tears in his eyes. I thought the Chinese were never emotional!"

Geneva smiled. "Most of our notions about the inscrutable Chinese are mistaken. They are really a very emotional people. It's just because they're different in their customs that we think they're mysterious and not to be understood."

"But Ah Foong *is* mysterious," Sara said. "There are a good many things shut up inside his head that he doesn't choose to tell."

"I expect that's wise of him," Nick put in unexpectedly.

Sara put the soldiers back into their nest of cotton.

"I was looking for you, Sara," Geneva said. "If you're going to be home today, perhaps we could get started on a dress for Judith. I have all her measurements—if you care to work on it now. It seems that I'm not to go back to the relief center."

"Indeed not," Nick said.

Geneva had worked too hard for her slight strength and had fainted one day from being on her feet so long. Aunt Hester didn't seem to care what she did, but Nick insisted that she must not return.

Delighted at this opportunity to have Geneva to herself, Sara agreed to work on the dress.

Before they left the library, Geneva went to Nick's side for a moment. He took her affectionately into the circle of his arm and Sara slipped hastily out of the room. The sight of Geneva's love for Nick made her own feeling all the more difficult to bear. Yet how could she make herself stop loving when every new sight of him drew her all the more strongly?

At Geneva's request Ah Foong had laid a fire in Miss Varady's sitting-room grate. The two girls found it especially cozy here with Aunt Hester absent.

Judith's first choice had been the chrome-yellow gown and Sara and Geneva went to work snipping at the stitches, pulling the seams apart, so that as nearly as possible they could start anew.

"I've been happy about your coming here, Sara," Geneva confided shyly. "I like our being cousins. But I have the feeling that Aunt Hester has been purposely keeping us apart. Every time I try to be alone with you, she finds something for me to do, or interrupts in some way."

Now that she thought of it, Sara realized that this was so. She had not considered the matter before, being occupied with other things. It seemed rather pointless to keep the mild Geneva away from anyone, but Sara was beginning to learn that Hester Varady liked intrigue for its own sake. This made just one more touch in an evident pattern.

"I suppose you know that Aunt Hester walks in her sleep," Sara said, ripping a seam open with strong fingers.

"Oh, dear!" Geneva cried. "I was afraid she'd disturb your mother eventually in that room. She goes to the same place every time she gets away from Ah Foong. He's growing old and he doesn't always hear her. She has done that as long as I can remember. When I was a little girl it used to frighten me when I'd hear her walking about at night on my floor. But she never seems to wake up, and Ah Foong always gets her back to bed. I don't know what this house would ever do without him."

"Have you heard her speak?" Sara asked.

Geneva bent her head above the bright material of the dress. "A few times."

"Do you know who the Callie is she calls for? Ah Foong says Callie is a little white cat, but I don't believe him."

Quickly Geneva glanced toward the door, as if their aunt might come through it at any moment. Then she leaned toward Sara, lowering her voice.

"Don't mention that name out loud! I was curious about it too when I was small. I got up the courage to ask Aunt Hester who Callie was. I've never seen her so angry in her life. She was like a madwoman. She struck me across the face. It wasn't just a slap—it nearly knocked me down. I went about with my head ringing for days. I've never dared mention the name again. Whoever Callie was she must have been very upsetting to Aunt Hester. Let's not talk about it, Sara."

But this was exactly what Sara wanted to talk about. "Then you think she was a person—not a cat, as Ah Foong says?"

"Ssh! Don't speak so loudly. I don't know—I don't know anything about it. Except that there really was a cat—small and white. I ran after it once when I was little and Aunt Hester was angry. When I asked her if I could have the little cat, she told me I was making up stories. She said there wasn't any cat and I was never to say such a thing again. But I know what Ah Foong believes."

She tiptoed to the door, opened it softly and looked into the hall. Then she returned, assured of their privacy.

"He believes that the spirit of Callie—whoever she was—entered into a little white cat and that it will always walk about this house. I know too that the cat is the one thing that frightens Aunt Hester nearly out of her wits. But there's something else in this house, Sara —a strange thing I discovered a long time ago. I don't think even Aunt Hester or Ah Foong knows about it or it would have been removed. Perhaps there'll be a chance to show you someday."

"Why not today?" Sara asked. "This may be a better chance than we'll ever have again."

But Geneva looked frightened. She seemed to back away from her own suggestion, to be ready to disavow it. Before Sara could urge further, the door opened in the silent manner Ah Foong could always manage and he stood bowing to them in the opening.

"You come topside see Missy Valady," he told Sara.

"She must have found out that we were together," Geneva said in alarm. "Why did you tell her, Ah Foong?"

Ah Foong shook his head at Geneva, as if he reproached a child.

"Me no tellum. Miss Valady wantchee talkee Missy Sala."

Sara did not go readily. By the time she reached the foot of the stairs her heart was thumping again and she had to fight her own desire to retreat, to hide at all costs from the woman who waited for her upstairs.

Twice yesterday she had been terrified by Hester Varady. Once when her aunt's hand had gripped her shoulder and her eyes had burned so intently. And again in the eerie hours after midnight when Hester had walked in her sleep. Now Sara felt that she never wanted to be alone with her aunt again.

Nevertheless, her feet carried her up the stairs and her hesitant hand tapped on the door of the room she had never entered.

"Come in, Sara," Miss Varady said.

Sara opened the door.

"Close it quickly," said the woman in the big canopied bed. "Shut out the draft. Then come and sit here beside me. I want to talk to you, Sara."

Without will of her own, Sara closed the door and went to the indicated chair.

The room was even larger than the one Sara occupied and it had been furnished sumptuously with the gilt, the cupids, the damask of the courts of France. The bed was hung with faded draperies and carved cupid faces peeked coyly at the woman who sat against the pillows, ignoring them—or perhaps forgetting they existed. The seats of the gilt chairs were covered with pink satin and the rug which had once been gay with great roses had faded to a yellowish hue.

"Well," said Miss Varady sharply, "what do you make of it?"

"Why—it's a very beautiful room," Sara faltered.

"Should be," her aunt said. "Goodness knows it cost me a pretty penny. And believe me, *they* didn't get to sleep in it. It was mine from the beginning. And it always will be."

Sara stole an uneasy look at her aunt. Hester's face

was shadowed by the starched ruffles of a bedcap, and her dark eyes, with brown shadows smudged beneath them, seemed cavernous in the morning light. Did Aunt Hester know, Sara wondered, that she had walked in her sleep? Had she wakened when Ah Foong brought her back to her bed? Had he told her what she had done? Or was she unconscious of these nighttime excursions?

When Miss Varady broached the subject Sara had been summoned to discuss, she ignored both the incident on the stairs and the matter of Mary's dress.

"I have made up my mind about you, Sara," she announced flatly.

There was no telling whether this was good or bad, so Sara merely waited.

"I have observed you from the time I learned you had come to San Francisco," her aunt said. "All my life I have wanted an heir. Someone of my own blood. Someone of whom I could be proud. This was part of my family plan. Do you see those miniatures on the bed table? Look at them, Sara."

The painted portraits were small and set in oval black frames. Sara took them into her hands and studied the faces. One was of an elderly, mustachioed gentleman with eyes as deep-set and commanding as Aunt Hester's. The second portrait was of a younger man who wore sideburns and bore a family resemblance to the first. Though here force of character was less evident.

"The two Julians," her aunt said. "My father and my grandfather. The first Julian meant to found a dynasty and he would have done so if his wife had lived. But he could never bring himself to remarry after her death. All his hope for a family line depended on his son, the second Julian. But my mother was a puny thing, for all that she outlived her husband, and she bore him only two daughters. You can imagine the disappointment to my grandfather."

Sara, studying the strong face which the artist had portrayed, could well imagine it.

"In the end of course, Grandfather put all his hopes in me. He was proud that I was so much like him and he trained me from childhood to be head of the family. Even if the name died, he hoped the bloodline would continue. He would have preferred me to be a boy and he gave me the business training he might have given a boy, although neither he nor my father would hear of my interest in medicine. Grandfather was further disappointed that I did not marry. When he was dying he made me swear to raise Elizabeth's son to continue the line."

There was a burning quality in Hester Varady's voice. Sara could envision this handing down of the family scepter as the older Julian sought to assure continuance of the line that descended from him and his wife Consuelo. Hester in turn had inherited something of his own forceful purpose. And all this, Sara thought in dismay, might now be concentrated upon herself.

"Leland, your father, failed me," her aunt went on. "I had hoped to raise his child suitably. Your mother spoiled that. Geneva was a makeshift—the best I could manage. There was no other descendant, however remote. I gave her the Varady name in the hope that the possession of it would help her to develop the necessary iron in her soul. It is not, of course, her own name."

Aunt Hester paused and reached for throat lozenges on the bed table. Sara waited uneasily.

"Geneva," Miss Varady continued, "was an even greater disappointment than Leland. She is too much like my sister Elizabeth—soft, without character."

Sara could not feel that this was true of Geneva. In her quiet way the girl had character one learned to respect. But this was not something her aunt would appreciate. The likeness to Elizabeth would probably get in the way.

Unexpectedly, with perhaps deliberate intent to tantalize, Hester Varady changed the subject.

"Tell me," she said, "what is all this about Ritchie Temple being an architect?"

It was hard for Sara to turn her thoughts to Ritchie at such a moment.

"Why, he—he's always been interested in the subject," she said feebly.

"But what does he know about it?"

"He studied in Chicago. Ritchie says American architects should stop imitating Greece and Rome, or anything in Europe. He doesn't believe such styles fit our country. He wants to do something that would be truly American." This was a subject she knew, having listened to Ritchie for so long.

"Well, then, why hasn't he tried to do something about these beliefs?"

This was too complicated a subject to go into, since the answer lay deeply in Ritchie's own character. Sara chose a surface answer.

"It would cost too much to put up that sort of structure in San Francisco. Because the insurance is so high. All those little wooden buildings that invite fire."

"An invitation which has been accepted," Miss Varady snapped. "The tinder has been burned out. Now new buildings must go up."

"But neither the Renwicks nor Ritchie Temple will have the money to invest in such buildings," Sara pointed out. "Aunt Hester, how did you learn about Ritchie?"

"Through Judith Renwick. There is a woman with brains. She would be wasted on him, of course. But she is foolish enough to think she can do something to help him."

So Judith had listened, after all, Sara thought. It seemed strange that she should have talked to Miss Varady about the matter. Now her aunt was watching her with bright malice.

"You disappoint me, Sara. Perhaps I'm mistaken about you after all. I would have expected a more direct reaction a few moments ago when I changed the subject from the one you should obviously be interested in."

"I am interested," Sara said stiffly.

"I am sure you are." Aunt Hester nodded. "There's iron in you, my girl. The same iron that's in me, and that was in your great-grandfather, the first Julian Varady. You can go far, Sara. You can have exactly what you want of life if you are determined to have it. You are like me in that."

Sara thought about this for a moment. She was no longer sure, as she had once been, just what she wanted from life.

"Have *you* had everything you want just by being determined about it?" she asked.

Sara half expected anger, but it did not come.

"I was too young to be wise in myself. Just as you are too young. But you have an advantage I lacked. You will have my years and knowledge directing you. There will be no chance to make the mistakes that I made. It was no more than a foolish mistake and a lack of wisdom on my part that allowed Elizabeth and Martin to be thrown together. I never for a moment thought that so colorless a creature as Elizabeth could be my rival. But these gentle, helpless women seem to have an appeal for men. Had there been someone wiser to guide me—" She moved her hands in a gesture of futility.

"What do you want of me?" Sara asked directly.

Her aunt regarded her with satisfaction. "That is the approach I would take in your place. There need be no mincing of matters between us. We are enough alike to understand each other from the start. You are as eager for power and wealth as I ever was. I am going to make you my heir. My sole heir. You will divide with no one."

Sara could only stare at her, without fully comprehending. "But there is Geneva—" she began.

A flick of Miss Varady's hand dismissed Geneva. "I may fix a small sum upon her. In any event she will probably marry Nicholas Renwick and be impoverished for years to come, considering the unfortunate business he is in. Why should I leave my wealth to someone who would never appreciate it? You, Sara, will do something with what I give you. You can make this house a center of fashion, of importance and influence.

You must marry, of course. Suitably. Have you anyone in mind?"

Still dazed, Sara could only shake her head.

"That will be remedied. You are young and when you are properly dressed you will be one of the handsomest women in San Francisco. You lack grace and poise, it's true. But these things can be learned. And I will see that the eligible young men of the city meet you so that you can choose. Of course you must be in love. That is a Varady tradition. But there is no reason why you cannot fall in love with the right young man if you are thrown together."

Sara felt an almost hysterical desire to laugh. "But what if he shouldn't fall in love with me?"

"We will plan wisely," Miss Varady said. "We will find the young man to whom you will be irrisistible."

This was too much and Sara laughed out loud. "Aunt Hester, do you really think life can be managed like that? You sound like one of the Fates, weaving, planning, snipping."

Directness had not made her aunt angry, but laughter did. Hester Varady leaned across her pink satin quilt and took Sara's wrist in her metallic grip, silencing her.

"If I find that you consider this a laughing matter, I shall drop the entire plan. You will work with me seriously. You will do what I say or nothing will come of it."

With her aunt's cold fingers about her wrist, the matter no longer seemed funny.

"Very well, Aunt Hester," said Sara meekly.

"Good. Tomorrow I'll arrange to settle a generous monthly allowance upon you. I have money in banks outside San Francisco. Perhaps we can plan a ball to present you to society. Not crude Nob Hill society, but to members of San Francisco's best old families."

"Aren't the old families rather poor these days?" Sara asked. Somehow it was easier to talk about the inconsequential than to face the larger facts of what had happened.

"I am thinking of blood, not money," said Miss Varady. "I happen to have both. My wealth will be enough for you—and a husband. It is possible, Sara, that you do not realize how great that wealth is. I'm not exaggerating when I say that I am probably one of the wealthiest women in California today. I do not boast of this, naturally. It is merely a fact you should know. A society event will launch you as my accepted heir."

"But, Aunt Hester," Sara pointed out, "only a few weeks have gone by since San Francisco burned down. It doesn't seem that people will be thinking of parties for a long while to come."

"That's where you are wrong. Human beings are not wholly averse to disaster, Sara. There has been excitement to buoy everyone up about plans for rebuilding the city. The building itself, however, will be long and tiresome. I fancy that we will be weary of dust and the sound of donkey engines and pile drivers, before the year is up. The novelty of wearing what I've heard called 'earthquake fashions' will evaporate. In no time people will be yearning for amusement and gaiety. Do you follow me, Sara?"

Sara was doing her best, but the current was too swift. This was all too sudden, too unforeseen for her to grasp.

Miss Varady went on. "There will be a certain publicity value in giving the first real party to be held in San Francisco after the fire. It will make you known to those who should know you. I doubt if we'll have a single refusal. Well, that is all I have to say for the moment. And so far I have heard no words of gratitude from you."

Sara looked uneasily at the woman in the bed. It would be quite impossible to lean over and kiss her. One did not run up and kiss the cheek of one of the Fates, even if she were so inclined.

"I need some time to understand what has happened to me," Sara said.

Miss Varady nodded. "Yes, I'm sure you are overwhelmed. Of course your mother must move downstairs now to a more suitable room." If there was any recollection in her of her own intrusion last night in the upstairs room, Miss Varady did not betray it. "Run along now, Sara, and ask Ah Foong about a change of rooms for her."

Sara went out feeling that she was not the same girl who had entered this door an hour before. Anything she wanted she could have. *Three* dozen taffeta petticoats, if she chose, she thought, smiling wryly to herself. Sara Bishop would possess a Midas wealth and all the position and power it would give her. Yet somehow the taste was flat in her mouth.

She went upstairs to her mother's room, though she did not mean to tell her the entire truth as yet. She wanted to think this out for herself first, to understand exactly what was involved. Besides, her mother would only be dismayed. Wealth was never what Mary Jerome had wanted. But now at least Sara could tell her that she was to be moved to a more comfortable room on the floor below.

Her mother was not in, however. Sara found her door ajar, and Allison on her knees, peering under the bed.

"What's the matter?" Sara asked. "Have you lost something, Allison?"

The face Allison raised to her was tragic and tear-streaked. "Yes! I've lost Comstock. He isn't anywhere. This is the very last place there is to look."

At the moment, Sara could not take this seriously. "Oh, I'm sure he'll turn up. You know he likes to go out on the town. He'll come home as soon as he's had his fill of adventure."

But Allison shook her head. "I'll never see him again. I know what's happened to him. That old witch hates him. And now she's poisoned him and thrown away his body!"

"Allison!" Sara cried. "You read too many story-books. You mustn't say such things."

"I showed you where she keeps all her bottles," Allison said. "She has a whole closet full of poisons. And there are probably hundreds of bodies buried in the garden."

This was more than Sara felt able to cope with. She took Allison downstairs to talk to Nick. As always his untroubled air was quieting. No one could listen to him and believe in the phantasmagoria of the night.

He did not, he said, hold with Allison's notions about bodies in the garden. And he had seen that medicine cupboard of "poisons." Allison must come down to earth. In the meantime, he would inquire around about Comstock. There was nothing as yet to worry about.

Allison was somewhat soothed, but Sara, watching her, did not believe that the child's private convictions had changed.

TWENTY-THREE

THE NEXT FEW WEEKS WERE BUSY AND DISTURBING ONES for Sara. Not that there was any outward and immediate change in her way of life. Her mother was moved downstairs and given a comfortable, well-furnished room. But she was no happier in it than she had been in her cramped quarters on the third floor. Indeed, the move seemed to alarm her a little.

"What is behind it?" she demanded more than once of Sara. "Why should Hester Varady be suddenly kind to me? I don't trust kindness in that woman."

Miss Varady had as yet made no announcement to the effect that she meant to make Sara her heir. Sometimes Sara had the feeling that she had dreamed the whole thing. To have the dream come true would be rather alarming. The girl she had once been was a child who would have accepted the waving of a magic wand with unquestioning glee. The present Sara could not hold her hands out quite so guilelessly. Of course it would be pleasant to have the things she had always wanted. But she could not be indifferent to her mother's fears. Nor could she accept so callously the injury to Geneva. Indeed, she would not permit it.

Perhaps she ought to talk to her cousin and warn her of what Aunt Hester intended. She could assure the girl that no matter how highhanded their aunt was in this matter, when the time came Sara would share fairly and equally with her cousin. But she winced away from the hurt she must inflict by telling Geneva how Aunt Hester meant to treat her. Perhaps it would be better to let it come first from Miss Varady herself. Then Sara could step in quickly afterwards to reassure and comfort Geneva.

It was necessary for Sara to tell her mother that an allowance was now being given them, though she did not divulge the full sum for fear of disturbing her still more. During these past weeks money had not been important anyway. There was so little in San Francisco that it would buy.

But by the middle of June many things were returning to normal operation. The city had gas and electricity again, and of course water. Chimneys had long since been inspected and cooking indoors replaced the sidewalk kitchen. The smell of smoke which still saturated everything had grown more familiar than fresh air.

There was a ferment of building going on in the cleared lots on the east side of Van Ness. Little redwood shops were springing up and luxury items had begun to appear on their shelves. Already insurance money was dribbling in to some extent, and many who had never had ready money before, had the feel of it now in their pockets, or at least the prospect of it on which to borrow. Fillmore Street, with its crowds and its pennants and signs, had taken on the air of a mining town community and Van Ness, slightly more elegant and professional, ran it a close second.

Within the Varady house activity had speeded up. Lines of people stood outside for hours, waiting for an interview with Mr. Merkel or Nicholas Renwick. The front door stood open and the house was no longer quiet during the day. Miss Varady retreated to the drawing room and closed the door, or remained upstairs in her own room if the intrusion of business into her house disturbed her too greatly.

It seemed to Sara, however, that her aunt took these matters far better than might have been expected. Rules that had held before the fire were casually ignored these days. Barriers had been lowered in new comradeship and the rigid social pattern had blurred and run together. Everyone wanted to play his part in the recovery of the city. Even while the outside world commiserated and pitied, San Francisco was too busy to know that she was performing the impossible.

These days Hester Varady often drove out on some private business of her own. Sometimes dignified gentlemen visited her in the privacy of her drawing room and there was many a consultation held behind closed doors.

Miss Varady had given up any attempt to use her sitting room for her own purposes. It had been usurped by the women of the household, who were engaged in a frenzy of dressmaking. Here Sara was the acknowledged captain and the others did her bidding.

Their confidence was more than rewarded by the surprising creations born anew from old-fashioned garments which had belonged to Elizabeth and Mary Bishop.

Aunt Hester had insisted upon one change which Mary had been helpless to fight. She was to be known as Mrs. Leland Bishop now, and there was to be no argument about the matter. The others in the household complied readily enough and thought it a natural change.

As Sara knew, her mother had tried to rebel, to escape. Day after day she had gone about in the Western Addition, seeking work as a housekeeper. But in the sections which were unburned, there were plenty of servants. Until the wealthy who had been driven out re-established themselves in San Francisco, no one needed her services. In the end, she settled down to sewing under Sara's direction. Even Mrs. Renwick, who was hardly skilled with a needle, was put to work basting and sewing hems and seams. The Renwicks had still found no place to live which would come within their reduced means and Miss Varady in her role of Lady Bountiful would not hear of their leaving till they found something suitable.

Sara's planning and supervisory work did not take as much time or require the application of the actual sewing. Thus she had found it possible to work with Nick for a portion of each day. This had come about naturally and without strain. Whatever his private opinion of her, he needed her help. She typed a good many letters, taking time to run across the hall now and then to make sure the sewing went well. Nick was impersonally grateful for her help and always courteous. Sometimes she even worked with him in the evening, though he made it clear that he regarded her contribution as something she gave to the people of San Francisco, and not to him.

Sara, however, knew this was not altogether so. Being a woman, it was Nick whom she must serve first. In the beginning she had found it painful to be constantly near him, but now she discovered a certain peace in working beside him and giving herself to his need. She was learning to understand the problems which faced him as Geneva could not. There was a quiet joy in her when she could save Nick some laborious task, or anticipate some need before he was aware of it himself.

As Nick grew to depend on her, it became increasingly difficult to remember that behind his courteous manner he might be condemning her for what he regarded as unscrupulous behavior. Perhaps there were times when Nick himself forgot and accepted her in the old way. The thing Sara most dreaded was the moment when Aunt Hester would make her planned announcement. There was no telling how Nick would react to that. He might well consider that Sara had somehow tricked Geneva out of her inheritance. It was possible that the news might be one more thing added to his distaste for her. She wondered at times if she ought to tell him herself, so he would know the truth of the matter before Aunt Hester said anything. It would not, however, soften the facts to have them come from her, so she said nothing.

There was one night when they worked late after a strenuous and frustrating day. Even Ritchie had been kept busy all day long, running errands. Mr. Merkel had stayed to dinner and worked with Nick and Sara for an hour or two before returning to Oakland. Geneva, who liked to be near Nick in the evening, even when he had no time for her, brought in some hand sewing. She busied herself quietly until her eyes wearied. Then she said good night and went up to bed. Geneva was plainly concerned about the way Nick drove himself, but she would never utter a word of protest.

By now Sara knew just what confronted Nick. He worried constantly—not for himself, but about where he was to get funds for those who needed their insurance money so desperately. The sums he and Judith could put in were like grains of sand used to fill an ocean. Mr. Merkel felt that Nick was being unrealistic. He did not mean to stop the ocean with his private fortune. But he was fearful lest the law take it away from him. Nick's hope was for some postponement, for some arrangement by which partial payments could be made from time to time, so that the firm would not go under completely, yet the investors would get what was due them.

Today, however, the pressure had been especially heavy. There had been more harrowing hard-luck stories than usual, and Sara knew that while Nick could appear a rock of calm strength for those who needed him to lean upon, tonight he was hollow and spent with the effort of loaning that strength to others.

Having finished her letters, Sara was sealing and stamping envelopes so they'd be ready to mail in the morning, when Nick startled her by flinging down a ledger with a slam that shook the library table.

"There's no way out!" he said grimly. "We're cornered. Licked."

"It's eleven thirty," Sara said, "and you've worn yourself out. Why don't you stop and get some sleep? It won't look so bad tomorrow."

He gave her a haggard, derisive look. "Sleep? What's that? I can't remember when I've slept a whole night through."

"You won't solve anyone's problems if you drive yourself till you go to pieces."

He put his head in his hands unhappily. "When I go to bed, I see the faces and hear the voices of those I've talked to all day. In the days before the fire I used to be restless because I didn't have anything I could really put my heart into. Now my whole being is in this, but I can't rest for worrying about how it will all come out."

Sara took up the ledger and put it away. Then she plucked at Nick's sleeve.

"Come over here," she said, smiling, drawing him toward a big chair. "I remember one night in the library at the Nob Hill house. Tonight the situation is reversed."

He was too weary to oppose her, but sank into the chair, let her bring a pillow for his head, prop his feet on a stool.

"I'm going to read to you," she said, "the way I read to my mother sometimes till she falls asleep. Close your eyes and be still while I find a book."

She searched the bookshelves for her purpose. She wanted nothing serious. Aunt Hester's tastes did not run to light novels, but Sara found a copy of *Wuthering*

Heights and settled down with it under a green-shaded lamp.

There was gloom and violence in this tale of somber moors and unbridled passion, but it held the attention. In a little while she knew that Nick had begun to listen and relax, had been caught again by the illusion of life that Emily Brontë had wrought in this tale of Heathcliff and the woman named Catherine Earnshaw.

Now and then as she read, Sara stole a look at Nick. His hands had relaxed on the chair arms, his eyes were closed, but she could not be sure whether he slept or not. Finally she paused, weary herself, but ready to go on if he were not yet asleep.

With all her heart she longed to do more than read to him. She wanted to trace the new furrows in his lean cheeks with loving fingers, smooth cool hands across the place where his brows drew darkly together in worry and concern. If only she could put her arms about him, somehow infuse him with her own vitality and strength in this defeated moment.

He startled her when he opened his eyes and spoke to her suddenly. "Sara, tell me the truth about that night before the fire when Ritchie came to your room."

How often she had imagined herself telling him what had really happened, but the unexpected question left her helpless. After all, what could she say to him, how explain?

He was looking at her with a kindness she had not expected to see in him again. Her eyelids stung with the promise of tears and she was afraid she might cry. She could talk about this to Judith, but not to Nick.

Anything she might say could so easily sound like a made-up defense.

"It's for Ritchie to tell the truth," she said. "Ask him if you want to know. Close your eyes now and be quiet."

He did not protest and she began to read again, steadying her voice. When next she paused, she knew that he had fallen asleep. She covered him with a blanket, remembering the bright violet, red and orange squares of the afghan with which he had once covered her—a brightness long since ashes in the fire. For a trembling instant she was tempted to touch her lips lightly, tenderly to his cheek. But she dared not risk his wakening. She tucked the blanket gently about him and then went upstairs to get wearily into bed.

It was during the next evening as dinner was coming to an end, that Hester Varady, without any warning to Sara, and with her usual sense of the dramatic, made her announcement. She had her audience captive and could savor their reactions.

"I've had a few talks with my niece Sara lately," she told them, "and I would like you all to know the conclusion to which I have come. As soon as it can be arranged, I plan to change my will."

She paused, well aware that every eye was upon her. Sara listened in helpless dismay.

"I've decided that Sara is the one who can most properly carry on the Varady tradition and fortune. I intend to leave everything I have to her. Very shortly now I shall go about making her known in this town in her proper position as my heiress."

Sara could not look at her mother. She watched Geneva apprehensively and saw the flush creep into her face. It was wicked of Aunt Hester to do such a thing publicly without preparing Geneva ahead of time. The girl might not care about the money, but she was too sensitive to be so carelessly humiliated. Besides, this disinheritance might seem a frightening thing to her.

Before anyone could move or comment, Miss Varady signaled that the meal was at an end by rising from the table. Having taken everyone by surprise, she walked out of the room with a curious smile curling her lips.

Geneva turned away from the table, obviously fighting her own tears. Sara would have gone to her, if Nick had not reached her first. It was Nick who led her gently from the room, and Sara went instead to her mother.

Mrs. Jerome stood before one of the long dining-room windows, but she was not looking into the yard. Her head was bent and she had covered her face with her hands. She did not speak or move when Sara touched her arm.

"Please don't mind so much, Mama," Sara said. "It doesn't really matter. It isn't going to make any difference."

Mrs. Jerome shook her head. "It will make all the difference. You will be fully in her hands now."

"That's not true! I'm in no hands but my own, and I can stand up to her. I won't let Geneva be cut off as Aunt Hester plans. Isn't it possible to look at the good side—at what this may mean to us?"

But her mother could not see it like that. She moved away from Sara's pleading touch and went upstairs to her room.

Left alone, Sara had the feeling that every hand in

the house had turned suddenly against her. Most of all, she minded the cruel hurt to Geneva. When she went into the hall, she could hear the murmur of Nick's voice in the library and knew that he was talking to the girl in there. Perhaps he, if anyone, could reassure her, assuage her hurt. Though what he believed now of Sara Bishop, Sara hated to think.

Since there was nothing to do for the moment, she wandered into the empty drawing room and stood once more before the portrait of Consuelo. This, she thought wryly, should be her moment of triumph. Tonight she had been acknowledged without reservation as the direct descendant of Consuelo Olivero Varady. Yet there was no elation in her, no sense of accomplishment.

She knew she must see Geneva alone before she went to bed that night, but the soft drone of voices continued in the library and the evening wore on. Sometimes Nick's voice was raised for an instant, as if he argued or pleaded, but Sara could not hear his words.

In the end they came out of the library so quietly that Sara would not have heard them if Geneva had not called her name from the hall.

"I'm in here," Sara answered. "Geneva, I want to talk to you—" She broke off because the Geneva who stood in the doorway, with Nick's arm about her, was a girl whose eyes were shining, whose whole face was alight with happiness.

"Cousin Sara!" Geneva cried. "I want you to be the first to know. Nick and I are going to be married!"

Sara stared at her blankly.

"Oh, I know it's hard to believe," Geneva ran on. "I was so sure he was just sorry for me after what happened that I wouldn't believe it myself. But he has been planning this all along." She glanced up at Nick, shyly anxious even now, but seemed to find reassurance in his eyes.

Sara forced her lips into a smile, held out her hands as she went toward Geneva. But she could not keep her eyes from Nick's face and she saw that his own were a cool gray as they rested on her. Falteringly she tried to tell Geneva what she meant to do about the will; that she would never accept all of Aunt Hester's fortune when half should of course belong to her cousin. But Geneva brushed her words aside.

"The money doesn't matter," she said happily. "Truly I'm glad for you, Sara. And if she leaves it to you, it must all be yours." She glanced lovingly at the tall man beside her. "Nick and I won't mind being poor for a time. Except that it means we can't be married right away. But it's nice to be engaged. I want to tell the others, Nick. Do you mind? I want to tell Aunt Hester."

Sara, watching mutely, saw the lift to Geneva's chin as she spoke her aunt's name. The girl wore an armor to protect her now—the armor of Nick's love.

All this was something Sara had been through before, she thought dully, as she climbed the stairs to her room. What bad fortune dogged her steps that she must always love a man who cared for someone else?

Once more she sat before her mirror and this time she saw the change in her face. Hurt was stamped in every line and there was a lost, hopeless look in her eyes. At once she straightened and forced a smile to her lips. There—that was better! It would never do to go about wearing a look that would betray her feelings to the world.

Sternly she told herself that nothing had really changed. Geneva had always had a claim to Nick's affections. And Nick did not think highly of Sara Jerome. Yet somehow she had walked with her guard down straight to the very thing that could wound her most. Now there was left only what Aunt Hester could offer. Wealth and position, which she had once valued so highly and which now seemed so empty of meaning. Somehow, somehow, she must believe in them again if she were to save herself.

Dry-eyed she sat watching the too vulnerable face of the girl in the mirror. What had happened to the old Sara who would storm any citadel for what she wanted?

TWENTY-FOUR

ONE AFTERNOON A WEEK LATER THE WOMEN WERE SEWING and chatting in Miss Varady's sitting room. A signet ring of Nick's which he'd had fitted for her shone on Geneva's finger and she was abrim with happiness these days. Of them all, Geneva enjoyed these sewing sessions most. She was doing something she could do well, and enjoying the company of other women, as she had seldom been permitted to do before.

Allison and Miranda Schultz sat on the floor, using scraps to make clothes for dolls they did not possess. Miranda said she had seen some new dolls in a store on Fillmore Street, and Sara had promised to buy each child her own. Partly this was intended as consolation for Allison.

Comstock had never returned, never been found, and the child was inconsolable. She grieved as if for a member of her family and refused any suggestion that another cat be given to her. Once Sara had been startled to find the child ghoulishly digging among the neglected flower beds in Miss Varady's garden. "For bodies," she said, when Sara asked what she was doing. Sara felt a little squeamish. She could not imagine what would happen if Allison's ugly suspicions were proved true and Comstock was found in the garden.

This was all the more reason for encouraging the companionship of Miranda and finding things for the two children to do.

These days Judith was again in touch with old friends and often away on visits. But this afternoon she came into the sewing room, bringing a friend with her. Mrs. Blanchard was pretty and young and at the moment she wore refugee clothes which did not become her.

Introduced by Judith, she looked at the busy group in delight. "This is wonderful!" she cried. "I'm going to be the luckiest woman in San Francisco!"

Sara removed a heap of patterns from a chair and invited her to sit down. She didn't know what Mrs. Blanchard felt lucky about, but a new face was always welcome. Sara was eager for any distraction these days.

"You see," Judith explained to Sara's mother, "I've brought you a customer. Not the sort of charity customers we've been. But one who will pay you for making her some dresses. She can furnish the goods. Friends have sent her an assortment of material from New York. But there's no one here to make it up for her. Miss Millie is living on Octavia Street now, but she is so overworked that she cries at the thought of sewing one more dress. Besides, Mrs. Blanchard wants something with more flair than Miss Millie can manage. I've suggested Sara. So if you and Sara are willing to make the dress—"

Mary Bishop agreed with pleasure and Sara knew that her mother regarded this as a life line flung their way. Mary was still insisting that she would not touch anything Miss Varady settled on Sara, and that she would be out of this house the moment she could earn something for herself. Sara realized that it was because Judith knew this that she had brought Mrs. Blanchard here.

Sara was happy to throw her own energies into work she enjoyed and which would keep her from thinking about herself. It would be pleasant to design something from goods that would have no tendency to split with age, and which set no restrictions upon her by having been first cut into dresses. Indeed, with this slight opening of a door, she was almost regretful that there was no further need for her to earn her living.

It was agreed that if Mrs. Blanchard would bring in her materials tomorrow afternoon Sara would see what could be done to plan a new wardrobe.

That night at dinner Sara talked about what she meant to do, so that Aunt Hester would not think she was hiding anything. Apparently Miss Varady had no objection to her keeping busy in this manner. She had never been one for idleness herself, and Sara's lack of skill in housewifely matters had already become apparent.

There was one rather bad moment at dinner that night. After Miranda had gone, Allison had returned to the garden. When Sara called her for dinner, she pretended to be studying a sun dial—in the fog! Sara suspected that the child had been digging for "bodies" again. All through dinner Allison seemed deep in gloom, and more than once Sara caught her eye balefully upon Miss Varady. It was a relief when dessert came and Allison still held her peace. Perhaps they would get through without an explosion after all.

But they were not so fortunate. Allison waited her chance. When the desserts had been set at each place and there was a pause in the conversation she spoke out in a clear voice.

"Miss Varady," she said, "where did you bury his body?"

Hester Varady went as white as the napkin she raised to her lips. Into the room's stunned silence came the sound of breaking glass. Ah Foong, who never broke anything, had dropped a water pitcher with a resounding crash. Sara was not sure whether he'd dropped it purposely to cover Aunt Hester's reaction, or whether he himself had been startled into dropping it.

With false gaiety Sara stumbled into the breach. "Allison is talking about her cat, Comstock. She has a foolish notion—" but Allison's notion was too unpleasant to speak aloud at the dining table and Sara's voice trailed into uncomfortable silence.

With some presence of mind, Miss Varady recovered herself and regarded Allison coldly. "While I did not like your cat, or want him in this house, I can assure you that I had nothing to do with his disappearance. I have noted your activities in the garden and I forbid you to continue them. For lack of a gardener the place has already gone to seed. However, I don't wish to have it looking as if gophers had been burrowing through it. If I were your mother I would send you to bed at once for your rudeness."

Allison shoved back her chair. "My mother doesn't care what I do! She didn't even care when I broke another plate! You murdered Comstock and you buried him in the garden. I know you did!"

She flung down her napkin and ran to the door. Sara went after her, Hilda Renwick following.

"Allison, wait!" Mrs. Renwick called as Allison started up the stairs.

Allison paused to look at her mother, tears streaming down her face, while Sara hesitated in the hall. At the foot of the stairs Mrs. Renwick held out her hand.

"Allison dear, come down here, please," she said.

Allison shook her head. "You gave me those old plates to carry because you didn't care what happened to them any more. Just the way you don't care what happens to me!"

For once Mrs. Renwick did not give up in despair over her incomprehensible child. "Don't you know that you're more important to me than any plate could ever be?" she asked. "We'd been through a terrible experience and *you* were safe. So how could I care because a plate was broken?"

Allison gave her mother a long doubtful look, but she did not come downstairs. She turned instead and ran up to her room. Uncertainly, Mrs. Renwick glanced at Sara, then, as if at last she accepted and faced the difficulties and responsibilities of being Allison's mother, she followed the child.

Relieved, Sara went quickly back to the dining room. The others were talking again, behaving like civilized people who did not permit ragged emotions to run riot. But Sara knew that for a few scant moments something primitive and frightening had been loose in this room. Now, though Miss Varady's color was not entirely normal, and Ah Foong was still clearing up the mess on the floor, the emanation of ugly terror had vanished.

It was because of this incident and because of Nick's concern over Allison's digging obsession, that the picnic was planned. Nick suggested it to Allison the next day to give her something to look forward to. Miranda could come, of course, he said, and she and Allison could pick any place they wanted to visit. He and Geneva would take them next Sunday, if the day was fine. The automobile was in order again and no longer on civic duty, so they might take a trip anywhere they liked.

Nick was talking to his sister at the door of the library and Sara, coming down the hall just then, could not help hearing. Allison's choice surprised her.

"I want to go back to the ruins," the little girl said. "Nobody ever allows Miranda and me to explore. So we want to go back inside and see what it's like. Sara— wait!"

Sara paused unwillingly at the foot of the stairs. This picnic was not her affair and she did not want to remember another picnic to which she had been invited, when Geneva had not been present.

Nick shook his head at his sister. "Can't you make a better choice? It's terribly dusty, you know, and the burned-out stench gets worse when you leave Van Ness. I can't imagine a less appetizing place for a picnic. Why not go west away from the ruins?"

"You said I could pick," Allison said. "And that's where I want to go. Not just any ruins. Back to our old house. But if you don't want to go where I want, I don't care about a picnic. May Sara go too? I don't want to go without Sara."

Nick looked as if he wished he had never brought up the idea, but he was always gentle with his little sister.

"All right," he said, giving in helplessly. "We'll go where you want. And bring Sara, if she will come."

Sara was fairly caught. A picnic with Nick and Geneva was not an enticing prospect. It was only because of Allison that she agreed to go.

That night after Allison had gone to bed, Sara went up to her room. She didn't feel that the mere distraction of a picnic would be enough to swerve Allison from her gruesome activities. She turned on the light and stood beside her bed while the child blinked up in the glare.

"If Nick gives you this picnic exactly as you want it," Sara said, "and if I come, then you must promise to stop this ridiculous digging in the garden."

Allison's mouth trembled and a quiver of revulsion went through her. "I have stopped. I looked again today. There isn't any more reason to dig. I found it."

Sara stared in shocked silence.

After a moment Allison went tragically on. "It was Comstock. So she *did* poison him. And she buried his body in the garden, just the way I said. Sara, didn't you see her face at the table last night? After that I *had* to keep looking."

The child turned over in bed and burrowed into her pillow. Sara sat beside her, helpless to offer comfort. She felt cold with horror. This was like the witch picture Allison kept trying to paint.

"Did you tell anyone else about this?" she asked gently.

"I—I can't talk about it! But I will later. When I g-g-get used to it, I'm going to tell everyone in this house."

"Listen, Allison," Sara went on more urgently. "Promise me that you won't say anything for at least a week. Not to Aunt Hester, or to anyone else." She felt that she must talk to someone about this before Allison told her story—perhaps to Nick.

Allison promised readily enough. The subject was too painful to reveal for the time being. But now Sara could not go off and leave Allison alone with so great a tragedy in her keeping.

"Come sleep in my big bed tonight," she whispered. "Then you can talk, or cry, or anything you like. But you won't be alone and you won't be frightened."

Allison came eagerly. Her small body was cold at first under the covers. But gradually she drew warmth from Sara and fell asleep.

During the remainder of the week Allison was as good as her word. She told no one. And every night she stole secretly to Sara's room and slept in her bed.

Sunday was a beautiful day. The rains were over, and while there were cool mornings and cool nights, the fog rolled in through the Gate almost every afternoon, the middle of the day was often bright and sunny.

They drove from the house in the automobile, a well-packed lunch provided by Ah Foong resting at their feet. It promised to be a happy day. Allison had thrown off her private tragedy for the moment. It would return, but for a little while she had the flexibility of the child in a temporary forgetting.

By now the streets were cleared of rubble and the auto could travel without puncturing a tire every few blocks. It carried them into the wilderness of ruins and Allison constantly uttered exclamations of pleasure. How beautiful the colors were! Look at that rose and purple wall! This with a nudge for Miranda. Miranda remarked that there sure were an awful lot of bricks in San Francisco. But Allison was not concerned with the bricks.

"It's like pictures of Roman ruins. They're beautiful —so why aren't these?"

Geneva and Sara could not share Allison's objectivity. The wreckage tore at the heart in every block. All these had been loved homes. Fewer people had died in the disaster than might have been expected, but so many, many lives had been changed in one way or another in those three days of the fire.

The auto, as was its habit, coughed and died on a hill, and Nick set the brakes so they could get out and finish the trip on foot. Fortunately they had only a few more uphill blocks to go. It was strange, Sara found, not to know exactly where she was. There were no street signs, no recognizable landmarks. Each rubble-filled block looked like the next, and none of it looked like any place she had ever seen before. Only the contour of the hill gave them a clue. Even then Sara would have gone past the fallen walls and crumbling steps of the Renwick house if it had not been for Allison's scream.

"Look!" she cried. "There on our steps. Sara, it's a ghost!"

But it was not a ghost. There at the top, where the steps dropped off into nothing, sat Comstock, quietly washing his face and observing their approach with interest. Allison flew up the steps and Comstock rose calmly and allowed himself to be smothered in her embrace. He licked her ear in greeting, but seemed to take her appearance somewhat for granted, as if he had been waiting there for her certain arrival.

Geneva had tears in her eyes and Nick was smiling over the reunion. Miranda followed her friend with interest, but took care to avoid Comstock's claws. Comstock had never taken kindly to Miranda in the past and she did not trust him. Sara was the last one to climb the steps, lost in puzzled speculation.

If Comstock was alive—and very plainly he was— then what had Allison Renwick found in Aunt Hester's garden? This was a matter which called for investigation. There was something else too. If she had not poisoned and buried Comstock, why had Hester Varady turned white with shock at Allison's words? Why had the careful Ah Foong dropped a water pitcher?

When Allison could stop her joyful weeping she put the big cat down and examined him inch by careful inch. He had lost his fat, sleek look and was now a rangy denizen of this brick wilderness. Though he continually washed himself, his coat was reddish with brick dust.

When the wind blew over the hill dust swirled in eddies about their ankles. Miniature cyclones whirled among crumbling foundations, getting into the eyes and mouth. Oddly enough there were almost no ashes. Ash was light and had long ago been carried away by the wind.

"Yes, indeed," said Nick dryly, "this is a charming place for a picnic. I especially like the smell."

But Allison, having recovered Comstock, would not have her spirits dampened. When you went to the beach, she pointed out, you expected to get sand in your food, and the air was sometimes fishy. So now you took what happened when you picnicked in a ruin.

Of them all, it was Geneva who was most moved by these remains of the Renwick house. She slipped her hand through Nick's and leaned against his shoulder.

"I didn't know I'd feel like this. Now I'll not be able to remember it the way it used to be. I was happier in this house than I've ever been anywhere in my life."

"You'll remember it again," Nick said gently. "What is in your mind, in your heart *is* real, and you can keep it just as it was."

By now Allison was climbing down to explore the foundations, with Miranda following more cautiously. Sara was glad to join the two little girls. She did not want to stay and watch the affection so apparent between Geneva and Nick. Watching them hurt too much, though she was trying to live with her hurt.

After a moment Nick called to them. "Careful down there. Stay away from that side wall. It looks as though it might topple at any moment."

Sara saw the wall and led the children quickly away from danger. The wall did indeed seem to be leaning. Its upper portion had already fallen in, but the rest still stood high enough to be a threat and it slanted perceptibly toward them.

Allison regarded the wall with interest. "I'll bet I could run right along the top of that wall. I could jump down to it from the steps."

"You could do nothing of the kind!" cried Sara.

"Nick would pack you right in the car and take us all home if you so much as tried."

Allison gave up her adventuresome notion. The rest of the broken house seemed safe enough, for all the rough going underfoot. And there was a wonderful view.

Sara stood where a broken outline opened in a wall —surely a library window. She looked through the opening at the world. Her eyes swept past ruins to blue water and the green of the Contra Costa, the opposite shore. Over there green leaves fluttered and there would be flowers blooming as once they had bloomed here.

Nick called them back to lunch in a little while and the children at least returned with hearty appetites. Geneva had put the food out on a cloth spread upon the broad top step. She warned them that everything had to be covered until it was popped into their mouths because of the dust.

Comstock joined them with some show of interest and Allison squealed with joy every time he took a tidbit from her fingers. It was a gay meal, with Nick once more setting himself to amuse and entertain. Geneva sat on the step below him and leaned her head against his knee. It seemed as though she could not bear to be far away from him today. Not until after lunch, when he announced that he was going to nap in the sun with a newspaper over his face, did Geneva consent to leave him and join the others.

Nick was often tired these days, she said, as Sara and she climbed the hill for a view of the other side, the children and Comstock running on ahead.

Sara knew well how tired he was.

"When do you think you'll be married?" she asked, bracing herself to hear the truth.

Geneva shook her head sadly. "It's impossible for now. Nick can't afford a wife."

"But Aunt Hester—" Sara began, and fell silent. She had reason to know how little Geneva could count on help from Hester Varady.

"I don't want her aid," Geneva said. "I only want to be free of her." She broke off, sighing.

Sara spoke impulsively. "Aunt Hester is giving me an allowance now and it's quite a generous one. The money belongs to you as much as to me, no matter what she says. So why not let me help, so that—"

Geneva slipped a hand through her arm. "Nick wouldn't let me touch what was given to you. But you're truly kind, Sara."

Sara stiffened under Geneva's touch. No, she wasn't kind, really. Nor generous. In some strange way it was as if she tried to buy peace for herself by helping Geneva. And peace was not to be had that way.

They had reached the top of the hill and Allison was pointing out places of interest as much to Comstock as to the unresponsive Miranda.

"Look—there's a green place over on Russian Hill, where the fire didn't reach! On Telegraph Hill too. And up here on Nob Hill you can see the shell of the new Fairmont Hotel. It looks as if they've begun work on it again. The Flood mansion seems hardly touched, though you can see the inside's burned out. Geneva, do you suppose we'll build a new place and live up here again?"

"No, dear," Geneva said. "It costs far too much. Your brother is rather in trouble for money these days."

"Golly!" said Miranda, impressed for the first time. "Just like other people. Poor. Wait till I tell folks about that!"

"Well, I don't care!" Allison cried. "I've got Comstock!"

They stood for a moment longer looking over the miles of destruction before they turned downhill again. Geneva continued companionably, with her hand through Sara's arm. The two girls ran ahead.

"Have you ever felt afraid of your own happiness, Cousin Sara?" Geneva asked. "I feel that way sometimes. It's so wonderful to have Nick, to have him care about me. Sometimes I can't believe it's true. I keep feeling that it's a dream and one day I'll wake up and it will be over."

Sara shivered. "Don't talk like that. It's creepy. You'll be happy for years and years to come. Nick will get out of this present difficulty and—and—"

But she didn't want to finish. The prospect of Geneva's long years of happiness ahead as Mrs. Nicholas Renwick made her own life seem unbearably empty.

"I do think," Geneva went on, "that what has happened has been good for Nick. He is hardly the same person these days. Of course he's tired from working such long hours, but he's alive as he never used to be. He cares about what he's doing. I do believe he likes a really hard fight. Everything was too easy before, yet because of his family he couldn't strike out for himself."

Yes, Sara thought, all this was true. He had been talking to her more openly lately, since she was working with him and could understand the problems of his work. After the low ebb point of that night when he had felt beaten, he had come back to fight again, refusing to accept defeat.

"Today is good for him," Geneva murmured. "I can never get him to relax."

Nick was sitting up when they reached him and Geneva returned to his side as if she had been away too long. Now he had further plans for the day.

"If you and Miranda have had your fill of ruins, Allison," he said, "how would you like a drive? I told Ah Foong we might not be home for dinner, and he will let Miranda's mother know. Since we're on an outing, we might as well make it a real one."

Allison was delighted and Miranda acquiescent. They drove along the beaches where the air was brisk and clean again and the wind free of dust. When the afternoon waned, they had dinner at the Cliff House and watched the sun drop into the ocean.

As they ate, Miranda further displayed a talent for gossip which Sara had already noted in the child. For Allison's sake, she had tried to like the little girl. After all, Miranda did have an unhappy background and there was much to be excused. But her desire for attention which she often gratified by picking up unpleasant remarks she had heard and repeating them slyly to the objects of the criticism, made her increasingly hard to endure.

This time she fixed Geneva with her pale, unblinking stare and asked how a person could be like a jellyfish.

Miss Varady had said that Geneva's backbone was just like a jellyfish—and how could that be?

Seeing Geneva's flush, Sara felt like shaking the child.

Nick said, "I believe the Lord made backbones flexible so there'd be a little give and take in them. I like the kind Geneva has. The cast-iron sort is unnatural and difficult to live with."

Even Allison, who seldom championed Geneva, was annoyed with Miranda. When her friend opened her mouth, Allison said, "Oh, hush up or I'll pinch you!" and Miranda subsided sulkily. Sara wondered if the end of a beautiful friendship was in sight.

After dinner, when they returned to the car, Sara glanced up at the urns and statues around the balustrade of the Sutro place high above. She remembered the moment when there had been a slight quake and Nick had pulled her back from the wall. How little they had seen ahead that day. How long ago it seemed. Another lifetime, and Sara Bishop was no longer the same girl who had wandered on the heights that day.

On the way home Sara took the back seat with the two little girls, while Geneva sat in front with Nick. A big moon had come up to light their way and Geneva leaned back in the open tonneau to look up at it.

"A happy day," she said softly. "One of my happiest ever."

Allison chattered most of the way home, but Sara was exceedingly quiet. When Miranda had been dropped off—her mother now had a room on Gough Street, though Miranda preferred the tent—they went on to Van Ness.

Allison was the first one out of the car, the first one

in the house. She had wrapped her sweater around Comstock and scooted up the stairs as if by moving fast enough she would prevent Miss Varady from seeing him.

Sara followed more slowly, but she went straight to Allison's room.

TWENTY-FIVE

Allison let Sara in and closed the door hurriedly after her. Comstock once more occupied his favorite place in the middle of the bed. He was really working at the brick dust now with some hope of winning out against it.

"I'm going to keep him right here," Allison announced the minute Sara was in the room. "You can't make me take him downstairs to Ah Foong's place. I won't let him be frightened into running away again."

"Of course not," Sara said. "Aunt Hester will have to get used to him till Judith and your mother find a place to live. But that isn't what I came to talk about. Allison, what was it you found when you dug in the garden?"

Allison looked faintly surprised, as if she had not given the matter a thought since being reunited with

Comstock. "Why, I don't know. I just thought it was —wait, Sara. I've got it right here."

"Right here!" Sara echoed in dismay.

Allison opened the drawer of a bureau and brought out a folded newspaper. Sara could only watch in horrid fascination as the child set the package calmly on the bed and began to unwrap it.

"You see," said Allison, when the contents lay revealed. "It's an animal skeleton. So that's why I thought of course it was Comstock."

The sight was less gruesome than Sara had expected. The little white bones were very dry and clean. They were more pitiful than horrid. But even if Comstock had not been sitting on the bed beside the package, Sara would have known that these small bones could not belong to the big cat.

"Wrap them up," Sara said. "They do look as if they might have been a cat. But only a small one. Not a big animal like your Comstock."

"What shall I do with them?" Allison asked.

Sara hesitated. She had no desire to keep them in her own possession. And there seemed no point in following the matter up with Aunt Hester. Anyone had a right to bury a dead pet in a garden. If these bones had once been a cat . . . a little white cat—?

"Give me the package," Sara said abruptly. "I'll get rid of it. Will you be all right in your own bed tonight, Allison?"

The little girl smiled at her shyly. Her bangs had been blown askew by the wind, but she hardly looked like the pale child Sara had first met a few months before. There was color in her face today and she was far sturdier.

"I'll be fine. Tonight I'll have Comstock for company. Sara—" Allison faltered. "Thank you, Sara."

Sara gave the child a quick kiss on the cheek, touched and pleased. She said good night and went out, carrying the folded newspaper package. In the hall she stood for an uncertain moment, wondering what to do with it. A whimsical notion seized her and she ran upstairs to the third floor.

No one was about in the hall and she went quietly to the door of the little room her mother had occupied. Ah Foong must have forgotten to lock it, for it was open now and she slipped inside. A tall bureau stood across one corner of the room. Sara went to it and pulled open the bottom drawer. She thrust the little package of bones in and closed the drawer.

It was then that a strange, eerie thing happened. Until this moment the little heap of bones had filled her with no sense of horror. But here in this room, sudden cold seemed to touch her. A shivering panic pulsed through her in wave after wave. There was something almost tangible lurking here—almost a pressure in the air that frightened her. She was suddenly, sharply, aware of old suffering, of pain and despair. As if the long ago events which had taken place here had set a stamp upon the room.

She had never felt this before—not even on that frightening night when Aunt Hester had come through the door walking in her sleep. It was as if by bringing that little package of bones into the room she had freed old sorrow locked up here.

Cold perspiration broke out upon her body and panic ruled her. She fled from the room. Fled wildly, heedlessly. Had she met anyone on the stairs she would have had no explanation of her conduct. She knew only that she must get away before the past reached out and trapped her so she could not escape.

Dinner was over and she went into the sitting room to find the air charged with excitement. The women were all listening to Judith and only Mary Bishop looked up at her daughter. Sara slipped into the room and sat down near her mother. Her heart was quieting now. She would be all right here where there was lamplight and talk and laughter.

"It came out of a clear sky," Judith was saying. She sat on the small sofa, looking as beautiful as a queen, but no longer remote. She was warm tonight, glowing with a new happiness.

"Tell us how it happened!" Geneva cried.

Judith took a deep breath and tried to speak calmly. "Miss Varady is going to commission Ritchie as the architect for a new building she plans to put up on one of her Market Street lots. She likes his ideas of a modern office building and he is to have the job."

"All he has ever needed was the chance," Mrs. Renwick said. "I've always been fond of Ritchie."

There was a buzzing again, but Sara took no part in it. She was remembering the Ritchie she had known in Chicago. The boy with dreams in his eyes and a charming way of getting whatever he wanted with as little effort as possible. No, it was not just an opportunity that Ritchie had needed. Judith had found a way to give him more than that.

"They're in the drawing room, talking about plans and building problems," Judith went on. "Labor is difficult now. There have been so many strikes. But Miss Varady is determined and I imagine she will see this through. She has interested others who are going in with her on it. Though she will be in control. Nick's with them too, representing the insurance side. And also the good common sense that Ritchie sometimes lacks."

"This will mean a lot to Nick," Geneva said. "The beginning of new business. Where Aunt Hester goes others will follow."

As the talk surged around her, Sara's composure gradually returned. This was reality, life. It hardly seemed possible that for a shaken moment upstairs she had been so completely at the mercy of something intangible. It had been like having the mirror dream escape the confines of its glass world to run loose outside. A terrifying conception from which she winced away. She had not dreamed in this house. She would not dream.

When Ritchie and Nick came in everyone grew excited all over again. Judith ran to fling her arms about Ritchie's neck in a gesture Sara had never seen her give spontaneously before. Ritchie looked a little cocky and overconfident. Probably he would never change. But now perhaps he would be pushed into building out of more than cardboard.

No one noticed Sara and she slipped out of the room, feeling lonely and a little lost. She was truly glad about what had happened. Judith and Ritchie belonged together and they had found each other. But there was an emptiness of aching in Sara and she could not stay and watch the happiness of others.

Self-pity made her impatient, however. She was young and life lay ahead of her. It would hold a great deal that she didn't dream of now. She was telling herself these things stanchly as she started upstairs, when she looked up to see Aunt Hester waiting for her on the landing.

"Have you heard the news?" her aunt asked.

Sara nodded. "It's fine that you're offering Ritchie an opportunity like this."

"I'm not doing it out of generosity," Hester said dryly. "This young man will give me just what I want. The most beautiful and modern office building in San Francisco. The Varady Building. A suitable monument to a great name. One day, Sara, it will belong to you."

Sara could find no words. Once Ritchie had put a little cardboard building on her desk, and now she would own such a building of his designing in steel and concrete. The dream was too vast for comprehension.

Her aunt put a sudden hand on Sara's arm. "Listen. Do you hear something?"

Sara listened and heard the sound quite plainly—the distant mewing of a cat. It was Comstock in Allison's room and Allison had to be protected.

"Why, no," Sara said. "I don't hear a thing. What is it, Aunt Hester?"

Her aunt brushed a hand over her eyes and leaned heavily on Sara's arm. "Help me to my room. I'm tired tonight. I am getting old."

Sara helped her aunt upstairs and into her room. At her bidding, she jerked the bellpull for Ah Foong, who as usual would take up his post outside Miss Varady's door when she was ready to retire. There had been no further mewing and Aunt Hester had rallied. As they waited for Ah Foong, she watched Sara with eyes that seemed to glitter in the lamplight.

"I *am* old. Older than I thought. But you are young, Sara. You will go on in my place. You will do the things I might have done. I will be young again through you and this city will be ours for the taking, girl. You'll need only to put out your hand."

There was something so intense in her manner that Sara listened uneasily. "I don't think I can understand this yet. I'm not used to the idea of having anything I want. Besides, I don't want a city. What I want—" She broke off because she could never have the thing she wanted most.

"Yes?" Miss Varady said. "What do you want, Sara?"

She could only shrug helplessly. "I don't know—ah, the things any girl wants, I suppose."

"Yes, of course. As I did when I was your age and so much like you. You shall have them too. *We* shall have them. The ball I am planning will launch you. We'll wait no longer. I'll set the date a month ahead to enable us to get ready. It's to be a fancy dress party, Sara. Something San Francisco will love after the grim time we've been through. So you must start thinking about what you will wear."

Ah Foong knocked on the door to announce that he was at his post, and Aunt Hester, suddenly weary again, dismissed Sara.

When she was back in her own room, Sara stood before a window, looking out between half-opened shutters. There were still lights across Van Ness in the new little shops that had been thrown up so quickly. Everyone worked all hours now, with so much to be done.

But the sight of the street made her feel hemmed in, restricted. She longed for her high tower, with the wind rattling the panes, and the marvelous view spread out on all sides. Up there she might have comprehended the things her aunt planned. Here, somehow, her view was too narrow. She was an earth creature who could not scan the heights. She could not even remember what her tower had looked like, how it had felt to view the city of San Francisco from its windows. The tower she saw now in her mind was a heap of rubble, the roofs and pinnacles of San Francisco were no more.

Geneva's soft-spoken words whispered through her mind unbidden. For Geneva this had been one of the happiest days of her life. But Geneva had Nick. And what had Sara Bishop? The prospect of wealth such as she had never dreamed possible. Anything, Aunt Hester had said—anything she might want.

Well, she knew now what she wanted. To love and to be loved. Nothing else mattered as much as that. Some women were lucky and had it. Some were not. Or was it wholly a matter of luck? Aunt Hester had lost what she had wanted. But she had made mistakes. Sara, she'd said, need make no such mistakes. Hester Varady would have the wisdom to help her.

Fancy dress! So a girl who was to be presented to eligible young men could be at her most beautiful best. She would find exactly the right costume to give her the air of confidence she would need, the poise she often lacked. She was no wren like Geneva. Among these young men there would surely be one . . . She turned away from the window, closing her eyes, trying to imagine what he would be like. But another face came between—a face she did not want to see. Nick Renwick's face.

She got into bed at last, knowing only that the emptiness must be filled. It was the most imperative thing in her life. There were women who *had* to love. She was one of them.

It was two days later that Geneva came looking for her in the sitting room one morning and drew her out of her mother's hearing.

"This is our chance," Geneva whispered. "Aunt Hester is off on a business appointment and Ah Foong is busy in the kitchen."

Sara, who didn't know what she was talking about, looked puzzled.

"Don't you remember?" Geneva asked. "I said there was something I could show you. You wanted to know about the person named Callie. This one thing is all I know."

Sara remembered with a full return of interest and followed Geneva quickly upstairs. Her cousin led the way toward the little upper bedroom, and Sara had a momentary qualm. That package of bones still lay hidden in the bureau drawer, and she didn't want to repeat her feeling of panic in that room.

"Fortunately," Geneva said, "Aunt Hester hasn't ordered the room to be locked again. I came up here first to see."

They reached the door and Geneva pushed it open without hesitation. Nevertheless, like Sara, she paused an instant on the threshold, as if she wanted to sense the climate of the room before she entered it. Had Geneva too, on some past occasion, felt the miasma of grief that shrouded the place?

However, there seemed to be nothing here today. It was only a small empty room. Geneva went straight to the bureau and, for a startled moment, Sara thought she meant to open its drawers. But instead she pulled the bureau itself out from its corner.

"I'll tell you how I found this," Geneva said, with a smile that was not altogether happy. "As a child I was curious about this third floor. Oh, I was curious about lots of things I never dared ask about. But once I came up here and went through all the rooms. Of course, since this one was locked, it was the one I most wanted to get into. When no one caught me the first time, I tried again, and one day I found the door open."

She glanced over her shoulder at Sara, her hands still on the bureau's top.

"Well, go on!" Sara cried.

"It was a disappointment. There was nothing here—as you can see. Just bare, ugly furniture and an unmade bed. But while I was poking around I heard someone coming up the stairs. The rustling skirts told me it was Aunt Hester and I was terrified. I pulled the bureau out a crack and crawled behind it. I stood there absolutely still, holding my breath."

"With your feet showing underneath?" Sara asked.

"Of course. I never thought of that. So she saw me as soon as she came into the room and pulled me out by the ear. She was terribly angry. She talked about sending me back to the convent where I'd stayed as a baby and I began to hope she really would. But of course she didn't. She wanted to keep a hold on me for some reason, though I knew then as I know now that she really disliked me."

"But what did you find?" Sara asked.

"Come here. Wait—I'll pull it out a little farther. There, you can get behind it where I stood. I had a good few minutes of staring at the back of that bureau while I waited to see if Aunt Hester might go past the door without coming in."

Sara squeezed her larger person into the corner. At first she saw nothing but the oval wooden back of the mirror. Then she remembered that Geneva had been a child, with a considerably lower eye level. Enough light filtered into the corner from the window so that Sara could see plainly the scratching on the back of the bureau. Someone had taken a pin or a sharp-pointed instrument and scratched letters, words, into the wood. She bent to read them.

I am Callie. Callie. Callie. I am Callie. I am Callie Bis—

That was all. The last word had never been finished. Had the woman who once lived in this room been afraid of losing her identity? Had she tried to make this pitiful record of who she was? And had her name been Callie *Bishop?*

Sara wriggled out of the corner and pushed the bureau back.

"That doesn't tell us very much, does it?" she said carefully.

Geneva's eyes were wide, a little frightened. "It points to possibilities. I've thought and thought about them. But mostly I end by feeling terribly sorry for *her* —whoever she was. I think Aunt Hester must have kept her shut up in this room for a time. I don't know why, and I don't know what happened to her. But sometimes I used to go to sleep at night weeping for her. I had the feeling that she was young and lonely and unhappy, like me. No one else knows that scratching is there, or it would have been rubbed away, I'm sure. Let's go down, Sara. I don't like this room."

The chill was there again. The cold, creeping thing that stole up from the ankles and traced the spine. They hurried from the room together and downstairs to the more beneficent climate of the lower floors.

Sara's mother had left the sitting room and they could have it to themselves. More sewing remained to be done on Mrs. Blanchard's dresses and Geneva went to work on them again.

Sara watched her, puzzling. "How is it that when you've had to lead an unhappy childhood in this house, with no one to love you and a gloomy atmosphere around you—how could you grow up a sweet and gentle person?"

"Why, Sara, how nice of you to say such a thing!" Geneva was pleased and surprised. "But of course I did have someone to love me and whom I could love. Ah Foong. Even though I was a girl, and not a preferred boy, he was always good to me. And he never let Aunt Hester punish me too severely, or for too long a time."

"Just the same," said Sara, "if I'd been in your place I'm sure I'd have grown up wild and unruly and hating everyone."

Geneva smiled. "You heard Miranda quoting Aunt Hester. Every now and then my aunt says that I'm too much like her sister Elizabeth. I have a feeling, even though Aunt Hester would never admit it, that Elizabeth Varady Bishop was my grandmother." She listened a moment, then went on, lowering her voice. "Perhaps 'Callie' is the missing name on the roster."

"You mean—" Sara hesitated, not quite daring to put it into words.

"That Callie Bishop was my mother. The daughter of Elizabeth and Martin. Your father Leland's sister. I am almost sure of it."

"It may be that you're right," Sara murmured.

This was the thought that had come to her mind too. But then why had Geneva's identity been kept a secret? Unless there was some shame connected with it —something Aunt Hester feared would disgrace the Varady name. Aunt Hester was capable of going to fantastic lengths to keep that name unsullied if she thought it was in danger.

Geneva's needle moved carefully in and out of the goods she sewed. "Ah Foong was kind to poor Callie too. I think it was he who gave her the little white cat."

TWENTY-SIX

IN THE DAYS THAT FOLLOWED SARA CONTINUED TO PON-
der the mystery of the woman named Callie. If she had
been the daughter of Elizabeth and Martin, Leland's
sister, why was her presence not admitted on the family tree? Why did Sara's own mother have no knowledge of her husband's sister? Certainly she had not
been imprisoned in that room all her life. From what
Sara's mother had said, no particular mystery connected with the room became evident until after Leland Bishop had disappeared. Was that because he
would never have permitted his sister to be locked up
there had he been in the house?

In any case, where did Geneva fit into the picture?
Aunt Hester had admitted that she had given her the
name of Varady. Could this be because a child had
been born to Callie out of wedlock? However, it
seemed unlikely that Hester would keep the girl locked

up in this house because of such a thing. She would have been more likely to pack her off in a hurry. What, eventually, *had* been Callie's fate? Had she, like her brother, been driven from the house to die in some distant place? If they were both really dead.

Round and round, fruitlessly, until Sara almost wished that Geneva had never revealed the pitiful words scratched on the back of that bureau upstairs.

Fortunately, there were other things to think about these days. Ritchie's ring was back on Judith's finger. They were going to be married and move into a place of their own the very moment she found something suitable, but modest. With the fee that Miss Varady was paying him as an architect, and with Judith's own jewels to sell, they would be able to manage if they were careful, until Ritchie established himself. Mrs. Renwick and Allison were to come with them. Nick's problems were so serious now that no extra burden must be put upon him. Nick himself had no choice, for the moment, but to stay where he was, retaining the library office in Miss Varady's house and struggling to keep afloat.

For Geneva's sake and because she could not escape the urgings of her own conscience, Sara had broached the matter of Geneva's marriage to her aunt. It would be easy, if Aunt Hester wished to make it possible for Geneva to marry Nick. Miss Varady, however, had snorted indignantly.

"Because I rather like that young man, I have already offered to give him a wedding in this house and settle some small income on his wife until he recovers his losses. But do you know, he turned me down! A stiff-necked fellow, this Nicholas Renwick. Of course Geneva doesn't know. I'd not giver her the satisfaction of realizing I had made such an offer."

Sara did not tell Geneva. She had the feeling that her cousin might be more hurt by Nick's willingness to postpone the wedding, than by her present conviction that Aunt Hester was merely acting like herself.

Plans for the costume party were now well under way. Invitations had gone out ahead of time, because those who came might have difficulty in planning suitable dress. Sara had finally settled the matter of what she would wear.

One afternoon she was sitting in the drawing room with her aunt, helping to address invitations, when the matter of her costume had come up. Sara had been toying with the idea of a Marie Antoinette dress, when she happened to look up at the portrait above the mantel. Consuelo Varady's eyes seemed to catch hers significantly.

"Of course, Aunt Hester," Sara cried. "There is the dress I want to wear. I have Consuelo's comb, and if I could find a lace mantilla—"

Aunt Hester put her pen down and fixed her attention on the portrait for a moment. Then she rose with an air of making up her mind.

"Come along, Sara. We'll see what we can find upstairs."

She led the way to her own great bedroom, with its cupids and gilt. In one corner stood a handsome Japanese screen painted with a delicate flower design. Aunt Hester folded it out of the way, revealing a great Spanish chest hidden in the corner. The dark wood of the chest, with its deep carving, would not have suited this room, but it was plain that Aunt Hester set high stock in it.

"I've always meant to show you these things, Sara," she said, slipping a big key into the lock and raising the heavy lid.

The odor of moth balls was strong as Miss Varady folded back layers of tissue paper uncovering the bright garments which lay within the chest.

"Were these Consuelo's?" Sara asked.

Her aunt shook her head. "I only wish we could go that far back. There are a few of my mother's things here, but most of these are mine. When I was a girl I liked to fancy that I resembled Consuelo—as you do now, Sara. My father had a dress made for me to match the one she wears in the picture. I've old mantillas here too. And shawls. Everything you need."

The dress her aunt took from the trunk spilled golden light into the room. There was a tight, rounded bodice and a skirt that ended in flounces. A fragile shawl, delicately embroidered with flowers, had yellowed to the color of old ivory and its fringe was deep and thick. The mantilla was of white lace, yellowed too, like the shawl. This was fiesta garb of the finest.

"Put them on," Aunt Hester said. "Let me see how you look."

Sara carried the things eagerly to her room, excitement tingling through her. She could manage the dress and shawl, but not the mantilla. Whirling this way and that before the triple mirrors on her dressing table, she made the golden flounces spin out in a great wheel about her. Then she ran back to her aunt's room to show herself off and ask for help with the mantilla.

She expected approval, admiration. But Hester Varady did not look altogether pleased.

"You *are* a big girl, aren't you, Sara? Of course I am no puny little woman myself. But in my day a girl was taught how to carry herself. Back with your shoulders. If you are big, act big! Don't droop and step on those flounces. Here, let me show how the comb and mantilla go."

There were several dress rehearsals after that, until Sara began to gain more confidence in the wearing of such a costume. In her mind she could see just how she ought to look, just how she should carry herself. But to make this picture real was more difficult than she had expected.

Only Geneva was told the secret of her dress, and Geneva helped her confidence a great deal. She was always ready to admire and applaud. And she sighed wistfully because she was not the type for clothes like these. Ah Foong was bringing her the trousers and tunic of a Chinese lady to wear that night. A lady of China was supposed to behave in a most demure manner, and that suited Geneva exactly.

Allison, of course, could not attend a grown-up party, and was once more bewailing her lack of years. Mrs. Renwick, on better terms with her daughter these days, though still a little afraid of her, suggested that she might invite Miranda to stay overnight. They could sit up later than usual and peek over the banister to watch the guests.

So it was that on the night of the party Miranda came over for an early supper with Allison. They got into their nightgowns and wrappers, and were encamped in the hall above before the first guest arrived.

They had a special box seat to view the household as each member came downstairs. Mrs. Renwick, with considerable enjoyment and a lack of elegance, had dressed herself as an Irish washerwoman. Ritchie was a grandee of old California—and looked handsome enough to break a good many hearts. Sara was glad her own was immune. Geneva looked entrancing as a little Chinese maiden and Judith, as Juliet, was breathtaking. Sara had cut Judith's blue velvet dress, with its high waistline and high-bosomed bodice, from an old gown that had belonged to Elizabeth Varady.

In spite of all Sara's pleading, her mother would not be a guest at the party. Mary Bishop did not care for fancy dress, and would, she said, feel uncomfortable in it. Besides, Ah Foong, for all that he had help, would be overworked tonight. She would remain back of the scenes in a capacity she knew something about. Aunt Hester was indignant. This was Sara's introduction to society and her mother should be there to play a mother's role. Mary said merely that she would be happier if her daughter saw nothing at all of society.

Before her mother withdrew to the rear of the house, Sara presented herself at her door. "Am I all right, Mama? Do you think I seem a little like that painting of Consuelo?"

Mrs. Bishop looked at her daughter critically. "You're lovely in that dress. With your dark skin and hair you look quite authentic. But you seem to have gone so far away that I can't reach you any more."

"I'm right here," Sara assured her. She kissed her mother's cheek and hurried downstairs to join her aunt.

Hester Varady wore severe black tonight—the black

of the Spanish duenna. A red rose in her hair, high piled on a comb, made the one spot of dramatic color in her costume.

Only Nick's costume remained a mystery to everyone but Geneva up to the last minute. In fact, if it had not been for Geneva, he would not have come to the party at all. He had little heart for frivolity these days. His costume, easily thrown together at the last moment, was the hit of the evening and caused many a sympathetic chuckle of recognition. He wore a battered top hat, a red flannel nightshirt tucked into blue denim overalls, and a pair of loggers' boots on his feet. Nick, quite evidently, was a refugee. It was amusing to see those huge boots circling the drawing room floor in a waltz, tenderly careful not to tread on the brocaded slippers of the little Chinese maiden in his arms.

Sara's own appearance was outwardly all that she could have hoped for. Her mirror told her she was glowingly handsome. The draping of the lace mantilla over the high comb was as right as Aunt Hester could make it. It was her aunt's idea that they should stand together near the fireplace, with the portrait above them. As Hester received the guests and presented Sara, the pointing up of their heritage would thus be evident.

The younger women, as they arrived, were polite, but somewhat distant. Hester they accepted because they had grown up accepting her name and position. That she was an eccentric made no difference—she had the right to be one. But this sudden appearance of a handsome young niece, who would undoubtedly be a rival, was to be regarded with caution and little show of cordiality.

Sara was aware that a good deal of buzzing went on behind their fans. She did not really care. It was only the men who mattered tonight—the eligible young man whom her aunt had promised she should meet. They were here—scions of many an old San Francisco family—and they at least were attentive. Sara never wanted for a partner and she loved to dance. Their compliments and openly expressed admiration went to her head a little. True, she was unaccustomed to gay repartee, and she was ignorant of many things they talked of so casually. She had made no visits to Menlo Park, knew nothing of society life "down the peninsula." She had never been to New York, nor had she made the Grand Tour abroad.

Nevertheless, she laughed, flirted and was very gay. She danced with this young man, then that one. Each time she wondered if he would be the one—the one who would quickly and certainly draw her to him, make her heart stop its futile longing for Nick. But so far no electric response had occurred. As the evening wore on she sometimes wondered if the flattery of her partners was a little forced and insincere, if it was wearing a little thin.

At length there was a break in the dancing and the musicians rested. When the men had withdrawn to the library, which had been turned into a gentlemen's smoking room for the evening, Sara found a chance to slip away unnoticed. She had clumsily torn a rip in the hem of her gown and it needed to be pinned. Then too she wanted to escape the company of the rather distant and superior young women of her own age.

As she neared the second floor she had the queer sense of stepping into another world. Below was light and gaiety, the sound of voices, laughter. But above, the house brooded, rejecting festivity, waiting to be done with pretense so that the prevailing mood of gloom could be restored.

Sara shivered at her own fancy and hurried her steps. The children had gone from their post at the head of the stairs. Since it was late, they would be in bed by now. Allison's door stood open and a soft murmur of voices drifted out. She and Miranda were probably chattering as little girls always did when they visited together at night.

Before Sara reached her own door, however, she heard clumping steps behind her and turned to see Miranda, not in bed with Allison after all, but plodding determinedly up the stairs on short fat legs.

"Miss Sara," Miranda said, "I gotta tell you something."

Sara had no heart for listening to young Miss Schultz's gossip tonight, but she knew from experience that it was not easy to swerve Miranda from a set course. She waited at her door, trying to look as if she were in a great hurry.

Miranda did not notice, concerned solely with her own important mission. She exuded a strong odor of tobacco that set Sara sniffing suspiciously.

"Where have you been?" Sara asked.

"In the library," Miranda admitted readily. "The gentlemen are all smoking, and they're more interesting to listen to than the ladies. I hid behind the portieres and they didn't see me. Just now I sneaked out behind their backs."

"Little ladies—" Sara began somewhat primly, but Miranda was not interested in the conduct of little ladies. Her eyes had a gleam in them that meant she had a tidbit to impart.

"The gentlemen were talking about you, Miss Sara," she announced with a sly eagerness.

Sara knew she should hush the child and see that she went to bed at once. Instead, she waited, seized by an enormous curiosity.

Aware of her captured attention, Miranda went complacently on. "One of the gentlemen said, 'Can you imagine that ox of a girl trying to be a graceful Spanish belle?' And they all laughed. Then another one said your looks were on the f-f-florid side, but he said it didn't really matter when you'd have all that Varady money someday."

Sara stared at the child, shocked and dismayed. In spite of herself her voice trembled as she spoke sharply to Miranda.

"That's quite enough! You had no business hiding down there and listening." She wanted to go on angrily, but the words choked in her throat and she turned away.

Even though she didn't care about the young men, she had wanted so much to be attractive tonight, to be accepted. But they had only sneered behind her back, only been attentive because of the Varady wealth. And Sara was sick with shame.

"Go away!" she said to Miranda. "Go to bed!"

Miranda looked mildly astonished at her ingratitude. "I thought you'd like to know what they were saying. That's why I stayed and listened. Was your mother really a barmaid, Sara?"

Sara had opened her door, but she swung about and stared at the child. "What are you talking about?"

"One of the gentlemen said your father picked your mother up in a saloon before he married her."

"That's ridiculous!" Sara cried. Her disappointment in the evening, the raw wounds Miranda's words had opened, the months of emptiness, surged up in a wave of anger. This attack on her mother was too much! She would go downstairs and end this farce. She would tell those little, little men exactly what she thought of them and their cheap gossip. How dared they link Mary Bishop's name with a saloon? Before she could reach the stairs, however, a quiet voice stopped her.

"Wait a minute, Sara."

Nick, without his top hat now, stood in the door of his sister's room, and Allison was beside him, tall in her long nightgown. They must have heard every word Miranda had spoken.

New shame added itself to Sara's misery. It was bad enough to have failed in her pretense of being a San Francisco belle. But to have Nick Renwick know what was being said of her was more than she could bear.

"Miranda," Nick said in a tone that brooked no argument, "you are to go into Allison's room at once and get to bed. Close the door, Allison."

Miranda obeyed with more alacrity than usual and Allison took her roughly by the arm, yanking her into the room. Then Allison ran to Sara, crushing the golden folds of her dress in an anguished embrace.

"Don't you believe that Miranda! She tells fibs all the time. You are the most beautiful lady in San Francisco tonight. And the nicest too. Don't listen to such silly talk, Sara!"

Sara hugged the child, but couldn't speak. Nick

drew his sister gently away, sent her to her room. Then he took Sara by the arm.

"This won't do, you know. No matter what some bad-mannered young puppy says—and they're not all like that—you are the star of this party. You can't go back looking woebegone and defeated."

"I'm not going back," Sara said miserably.

"Of course you are. What you need is a breath of fresh air. Then you'll be fine again." He led her toward the rear of the hall and she had no strength left to resist him.

As they passed the stairwell Sara saw, as if through a distant haze, that Aunt Hester was coming up the stairs, probably looking for her. But Nick ignored her aunt and took Sara to the small room at the rear of the hall. There he opened the door and drew her onto the balcony. Here there was moonlight, calm and serene.

"Take a few deep breaths," he said. "And think about what Allison just told you—that you're one of the prettiest, nicest girls in San Francisco."

She tried to obey, drinking in the brisk, refreshing air. But tears came, though she wanted to fight them back. "Nicest," Nick had said, in spite of all the things he thought of her!

He drew her into the curve of his arm. "Go ahead and cry," he said, soothing her as gently as if she were Allison's age. She sensed again the tenderness in him she had felt that night in the Renwick library. If only she could cling to him, pillow her head against his shoulder, *belong* in his arms.

"You're going down again in a little while," he told her. "You're going to show everyone what you really are. Tonight you dressed up and tried make-believe.

But you don't need make-believe, Sara. You're someone special in your own right."

She no longer cared what anyone downstairs thought. She cared only about Nicholas Renwick. She looked up at him with tear-wet eyes.

"Did you ask Ritchie? Did he tell you what really happened that night?"

"Hush," Nick said. He drew her head onto his shoulder, mantilla and all, and she felt his hand warm through the lace. "I haven't asked Ritchie. I don't need to. I felt pretty sick when I knew he was there in your room. I thought you'd chosen your own blind course to get what you wanted. Because I'd grown fond of you, that was all the more difficult to take. But I've come to think differently now. Whatever your course was, you've changed it and that's what matters. Believe in yourself, Sara. Allison and I believe in you."

"But there's Aunt Hester's will and what you think about that—" Sara faltered.

"I think you've been caught in an unhappy position you didn't intend," Nick said. "I was angry because Geneva was being hurt. But not angry with you."

She raised her head from his shoulder and looked at him, and she could not keep all that she felt from her eyes. He bent and kissed her lightly, quickly, before he let her go.

"Geneva will be wondering what has become of me. Powder your nose and come downstairs soon, Sara."

His words put Geneva gently between them in her rightful place. He touched Sara's shoulder in a light caress and went away, leaving her alone on the balcony.

She stood where she was for a moment longer, staring into dark hollows of the garden where the moon did not reach. Then a whisper of heavy black skirts rustled behind her and Aunt Hester stepped onto the balcony.

"I've been blind, of course," her aunt said. "I should have realized the truth before this—"

With difficulty Sara returned to the present. She had no wish to talk to her aunt at this particular moment.

"There's nothing to realize," she said and turned toward the door.

Miss Varady's hand on her arm stopped her. "So Nicholas Renwick is the man you love?"

She wanted to deny it, to wrench herself free, but Hester's fingers did not loosen.

"Yes," Sara said helplessly. Concealment was no longer possible. Now it was in the open.

"At your age I'd have loved him myself," said Hester Varady. "Of course you can have him if you want him."

Again Sara tried to turn away and again her aunt's cold fingers held her back.

"Geneva is nothing." Hester's tone was low. "She is no more than Elizabeth was. Once *I* was bound by foolish pride. You must not be. He is in love with you. As Martin was once in love with me. Don't lose him, Sara."

In revulsion Sara drew herself from the older woman's touch. "There's nothing I can do," she said. "Nothing I want to do. He will marry Geneva and that is as it should be."

"Do you think he will be happy with Geneva when he loves you? Don't you understand why he postponed his opportunity to marry the girl?"

"Geneva loves him," Sara said dully. "He is everything in life to Geneva. And he loves her. I've no doubt of that at all."

"Then you're a fool. I can see that I will have to help you. Well, it's chilly here and I must return to my guests. Come downstairs soon, Sara, before your absence causes talk. And straighten your comb and mantilla before you come."

Miss Varady went through the little door and Sara listened to the sound of her footsteps in the long hall. Then she drew the fringed shawl more closely about her and stepped into the room off the balcony.

The flash of recognition came so suddenly that it was like a streak of lightning through her consciousness.

This was the room. The room of her childhood dream. Once it had stood crowded with furniture, used as a storeroom. Now it was empty and moonlight lay in a pool upon the bare floor, shutting the stormy darkness of another time into the corners.

The mirror had stood there, facing the balcony door. And she, a small child in a long nightgown, had crouched in terror behind a chair in the corner.

Fear was upon her again. She pressed her hands against her eyes, shook her head, brushed at her face as if cobwebs clung to it. The knowledge this room held was an almost tangible thing. It had set its stamp here just as it had marked that other room upstairs. And Sara could not stay to face it. She did not want to know whatever the room had to tell her. She fled down the corridor and did not pause until she reached her own room.

There she rinsed her face with water, brushed a powder puff over her nose and rubbed lip salve over pale lips. In a little while the trembling stopped and she was ready to go downstairs.

Her distress in the room off the balcony was greater than any she might feel toward human company. Besides, she no longer dreaded those who had ridiculed her. She could remember the feeling of Nick's arm about her, the words he had spoken, and they gave her strength to face anyone.

Now since the "puppies" no longer mattered and she no longer tried to please them, they began to look at her with new eyes. She was polite, but a little disdainful of their attentions.

Once Nick came across the room to dance a waltz with her. The music was *Over the Waves* and it was a lovely, dreaming moment to dance in his arms. She floated enchanted, not thinking for a little while.

"You're doing fine, Sara," he told her. "We're proud of you. Now that you've forgotten you need to impress anyone, you're being what you can be."

The only moment that spoiled her dance with Nick was when she caught Aunt Hester's watchful gaze upon her. Hester Varady looked so pleased and approving that Sara stiffened in Nick's arms. She did not dance with him again.

When refreshments had been served, when the last guest was gone and the party finally wound to its close, Sara went to bed, stretching out her weary body and thinking long thoughts of all the evening. Thoughts that were neither happy nor unhappy, but which only searched for answers.

She had the queer feeling that she was two people. One part of her was the self Nick said she could be. The growing-up self who no longer sat at the center of the world, considering all that happened in the single light of its concern to her. This newer self was discovering other worlds as important as her own.

But there was someone else whose persistent presence she could not ignore, or escape. The other self looked only at its own unhappiness and pain.

Nick had held her in his arms, this other self insisted. He had kissed *her*. Nick loved her and not Geneva.

TWENTY-SEVEN

Just three members of the household came down to breakfast the next morning—Allison, Nick, and Sara. The others stayed in bed to sleep late after the party.

Nick greeted Sara pleasantly, but gave no evidence of recalling their moments together on the balcony.

This morning Allison was cross and yawny. Her own late hours had not left her with a cheerful disposition.

"Where is Miranda?" Nick asked. "Still asleep?"

Allison made a scornful sound as she poured syrup on the pancakes Ah Foong set before her.

"I chased her home. I pulled her out of bed the minute I was awake this morning and made her go home."

"In that case," Nick said calmly, "you owe her an apology. We don't invite a guest to spend the night and then push her out before breakfast. That's hardly the way to treat a friend."

"She's not my friend!" Allison cried, with a quick look at Sara. "Not after what she did last night. I was beginning to get tired of her anyway. She's a stupid, really."

"How do you suppose Miranda feels?" Nick asked.

Allison looked confused. "I was thinking about how Sara feels," she said.

"I feel fine," said Sara. "You don't think I really cared last night what those young men said about me? I'll never see them again. What they think doesn't matter."

"But last night you cared!" Allison was further bewildered by this adult inconsistency. "I *know* they hurt your feelings last night. I pinched Miranda good for what she did after I got her into my room."

"You shouldn't have done that," Sara said. "Nick's right. You'll just have to get Miranda back and make it up to her."

"But then I'll have her on my hands forever!" Allison wailed.

"You can drift apart a bit more gradually," Nick suggested. "And next time you'll be more careful about picking someone for a bosom friend."

"But why," Allison demanded, looking at Sara again, "did you cry last night when you don't care a bit this morning?"

Sara looked at her plate. She couldn't explain that something had happened to make her feel better about the party, and Allison finally gave up.

Now events began to move quickly in the expanded Varady household. Judith found the place she was looking for and plans for the marriage were made with unusual dispatch. Judith wanted only a quiet wedding ceremony with relatives and a few friends present. Ritchie, busy now on the Varady Building, agreed to whatever she liked.

Sara and Geneva went with her one day to look at the place she was fixing up for her married life with Ritchie. It was the upper floor of a coach house belonging to a mansion farther west in the unburned section. The big house had stood empty, waiting for a buyer at the time of the fire. Since then it had been divided into separate rooms and small apartments, rented out to refugees. Judith had seen the coach house, empty of carriage or automobile. The man who had lived there as a caretaker was leaving and they could have the place.

The upper floor which had been used by the coachman's family would be perfect, Judith pointed out to Sara and Geneva. There was a small living room and the other two rooms could be used for bedrooms, so that Mrs. Renwick and Allison could have one together. There was even a bath and a tiny kitchen. Since the place was partly furnished, not many new things would be needed right away.

On the morning of the wedding, the first week in August, the house was filled with activity. Sara hovered wistfully near Judith, as if something of the other girl's happiness might be contagious. There was a moment when the two were alone in the room Judith occupied at Miss Varady's, and Judith spoke unexpectedly.

Sara was folding a delicate blue chiffon negligee she had designed and her mother had made for Judith's trousseau. She fingered the material with a pang she could not suppress. Judith crossed the room suddenly and held out her hands.

"Wish me luck, Sara! You *do* wish me luck, don't you?"

Sara dropped the froth of chiffon into a suitcase and took Judith's hands gravely.

"I wish you a great deal of happiness," she said.

"I believe you do." Judith held her hands a moment longer. "I don't suppose you know how much I owe you, Sara."

"Owe *me?*" Sara echoed in astonishment.

"Yes—you. That night after the fire was over, when I played the piano so wildly, you came and stood beside me listening. I spoke out against Ritchie that night. And you said, 'Yes, that's the way it is with Ritchie. That's the way it has always been.' Your words kept coming back to me, Sara. I'd always wanted perfection in the man I loved. I never meant to fall in love with Ritchie, but when I did, I tried to change him into something he could never be. And there was no peace for either of us until I could face what was real. I had to learn how to be to him what he needs me to be. You helped me to that, Sara."

Sara went back to her folding of Judith's things. There was nothing she could say. She sensed a certain faintly wry quality behind Judith's words. Perhaps that wry touch would always be present in Judith's love for Ritchie. But seeing him clearly and still loving him, she could deal with life as it really was.

Judith and Ritchie were married in a makeshift little church which had sprung up mushroom-fashion on the edge of ruins. After the wedding they went down the peninsula on a brief honeymoon in a house loaned them by friends who were away. In the meantime Mrs. Renwick and Allison moved into the new place with the air of intrepid explorers adventuring into a new continent.

Never in her life had Hilda Renwick so much as boiled a potato. Ah Foong was consulted frequently and Allison developed an unexpected talent for concocting delicacies, though she took little interest in everyday menus.

The Varady house seemed suddenly hollow and empty. Nick alone stayed on, having arrived at a business arrangement with Miss Varady so that he and Mr. Merkel rented the library-office and Nick paid a nominal sum besides for his room and board. Ritchie still dropped in frequently to discuss plans with Miss Varady, but the women were so busy housekeeping that Sara saw little of them. Only Allison came back to visit Sara at first. But even she came less often as she made friends in the new neighborhood. There was a boy living in the big house, she reported. Not a silly goof like that grocer's boy, Bernard, but someone who liked to read books and talk about them. Allison's appearances at Miss Varady's became infrequent, and Sara missed her.

Once Judith invited Nick and Geneva for dinner—it was not an apartment to accommodate much company at one time. Geneva came home looking wistful. Perhaps she and Nick could find a place like that, she mused to Sara. Such a lovely view of the bay! Cramped quarters and inconveniences didn't matter when two people could be together and there was a view to be shared. Nick, however, had decided that he could not afford even that sort of place for the present. Sara listened with outward sympathy and kept her own hurt fiercely to herself.

In general life had settled once more into orderly routine in San Francisco. There were still reminders of disaster on every hand, and would be for a long time to come. Everyone dated time as being "before" or "after" the fire. The earthquake was, as far as possible, ignored. Nevertheless, the earth itself reminded them from time to time. It had remained uneasy ever since the quake and Nick said it had so jolted itself that time would be needed before it could settle down to its new shape. They could expect minor shakes for a while.

The insurance companies were still struggling to keep afloat. Most of them meant to keep faith with the public, but policyholders did not always understand the problems involved. Records had been destroyed in every line of business, but this was particularly a handicap in insurance. Claimants had lost their own records and some could not even remember what insurance they held. Thanks to Nick's rescued wastebasket, his company held some advantage, though details were far from complete.

In August a meeting was held in which the insurance problems were thrown open to a public hearing and discussion. Out of this grew a plan which in the long run might work out to everyone's satisfaction. Certainly the claimants would get less and wait longer if they went to law and sued for what was owed them. By the new plan they would get fifty cents on the dollar in six months, instead of waiting another five years. The rest would be paid them in shares of stock in the company. Since buildings were going up on every hand, and all must be insured anew, this would not prove a bad plan in the long run.

Nick began to look less harried and Sara could see

hope in every glance Geneva turned upon him. It would not be long, she knew, before they would be married and would move away from the Varady house.

Sara was far from happy these days. She found it painful to be near Geneva. She had grown sincerely fond of the girl and yet it was Geneva who stood between her and Nick. This was a constant reminder of the very things Sara tried to thrust from her thoughts.

At least it helped to be breathlessly busy. Judith's friends had brought other women who wanted Sara's touch when it came to dresses. Something of a small business was growing up under Sara's direction. Mary Bishop was happy and more hopeful than ever before. She liked to sew and the way things were going she said it might even be possible to hire a helper to work with them. Geneva still assisted because she wanted to, but she refused to share in whatever money came in.

Aunt Hester, aware of the commercial project which had found its inception under her roof, had accepted the matter calmly. After all, it was Sara's mother who actually received the money. Perhaps if one of the "eligible young men" were still in attendance, this work might have been considered unsuitable. But though two or three "admirers" had actually been heard from since the party and had requested Miss Bishop's company at one affair or another, Sara had dismissed them without a second thought, and Aunt Hester had not objected. In one sense this made Sara uneasy, remembering her aunt's words about Nick.

Always these days Sara knew that Aunt Hester watched her and was dissatisfied; that her aunt expected some definite action which Sara had no intention of taking. Sometimes she almost wished that Nick would marry Geneva quickly and take her away from this house. Only then would the tension Sara felt between herself and Hester Varady be relieved.

In the meantime she continued to work at Nick's side whenever she could, involved now in what he was doing. They were in complete accord these days, though he never showed by so much as a flicker that he felt anything more than liking and friendship toward her. At least it was comforting to be near him, to know that he trusted her and even relied on her when his days became too crowded and hectic.

One evening after a long session of work in the office, he sent her sternly off to bed. She was, he said, working herself to a frazzle and he would have no more of that. There was her own dress-making enterprise which needed her attention. Someday she might want to consider that work seriously. No matter how much he could use her, she was not to spend any more of her time and energy in this room. These problems were his and he could cope with them perfectly well.

The strain had begun to tell with Sara and she felt close to tears.

"But this is what I *want* to do," she protested. "You can't dismiss me as if I were an office girl. I'm more than that now."

He looked at her with the air of a man who held himself in with difficulty.

"Sara, I don't want to argue with you about this. There are going to be a number of changes in the near future. Geneva and I will be married very soon. She's unhappy with these postponements and I don't blame her. I can't give her the home I would like to give my wife, but we will manage. We both want to move from this house as soon as we are married. And we'll move the office too. So you see, Sara, it will no longer be convenient for you to help us. This week I intend to find a girl to come every day and take the secretarial work off our hands."

He did not look at her, but Sara never took her eyes from his face as she listened, scarcely believing. His brows were drawn together over his eyes, and the furrows about his mouth seemed deeper than ever.

"So I *am* being dismissed?" Sara asked.

"You may take it like that if you wish," he said bleakly.

She turned without a word and ran upstairs. He had put it clearly enough at last.

In her room she moved about unhappily, not knowing where to turn, or what to do. Somehow she must find it in her to be strong. She must face Geneva's marriage to Nick without flinching, no matter how terribly torn she was. Whatever must be faced, she must learn to face with courage.

But not tonight. There was no strength in her tonight, no courage. She couldn't lie down on the bed—she would never sleep. For this one night she must let grief in, give herself up to it. Then never again!

There were tears on her cheeks as she pulled open a drawer of her bureau. A fluff of white chiffon lay within. It was a copy of the lovely negligee she had designed for Judith, but hers was white to contrast with her black hair. She had made it secretly and without reason, her own awkward stitches pulling at the thin material, hindering her from creating perfection. That moment of envy when she had handled the few articles Judith had been content with for a trousseau had been too much for her. As she had once yearned childishly for taffeta petticoats, she had yearned for this filmy thing she held in her hands. Yearned because it was a symbol of hope. It was as though by making this frivolous garment for her own future trousseau she could put meaning into her days.

She shook it out so that the pale material shone like moonlight. The gown wasn't finished. The lace around the hem was still pinned into place. But she put it on over her plain cambric nightgown and pulled the pins from her hair so that it rippled heavy and black over her shoulders. The mirrors in the dressing table gave back her reflection and she knew she was beautiful. But for whom, for what?

She went to stand before the water color of a San Francisco scene her father had painted so long ago.

"Did you ever love my mother as I love Nick?" she questioned. "Was this the way my mother loved you?"

The incongruous memory of Mrs. Renwick talking to Japanese plates on a dining room shelf came to her mind and she laughed at herself, with a touch of hysteria in the sound.

If only one could make time pass swiftly and not live through every long minute of every hour! With the passing of time would come a lessening of pain. But how did you hurry time in the dark hours of the night?

She heard Nick when he came upstairs and went to his own room. She sat on the edge of her bed and told herself that tomorrow she would find a room so that she and her mother could be out of this house before Geneva's marriage. What did she want of Aunt Hester's wealth? What would it give her that would have meaning for her? Her mother had been right all along.

Nick! Nick! her heart mourned, and time would not pass.

Perhaps it would help if she went downstairs to the room where she had worked with him so often. There might be comfort for her just to be near his things, to touch what had recently been touched by Nick's own hands.

She let herself out of her room softly, so as not to waken Ah Foong outside Aunt Hester's door, and fled downstairs with the white stuff of her gown floating in a whisper about her.

In the library she closed the door and turned on a single light, looked about her. Evidently Nick had read a while before turning in. There was a smell of tobacco smoke in the air, though he never smoked while he was working. His pipe protruded from an ash tray near the big chair, and a book lay face down on the cushions.

For an instant she had the queer feeling that time had stood still and she was back in the library at the Renwick house. Once before she had come upon Nick's pipe and book—but then she had not known him. He had been merely a question to wonder about. If only that question had gone unanswered, she thought—and then repudiated the notion. She would not wish Nick out of her life, out of her heart, no matter what lay ahead.

The pipe bowl was still warm and she held it for a moment in her hands, as if to drive away her own chill. Then she picked up the book. Once more it was Marcus Aurelius and she smiled wryly, remembering the way she had tossed a copy of it aside that other time. Now she turned the pages, read snatches here and there as if she might find Nick himself in these pages, learn to know him better. A passage caught her eye and she read it thoughtfully.

Thou must be like a promontory of the sea, against which though the waves beat continually, yet it both itself stands, and about it are those swelling waves stilled and quieted.

That was Nick! He was just such a promontory as this, and if only she could reach the haven of his shore all her own storms would be stilled, quieted. But the shore was far away and forbidden to her poor strength as a swimmer.

The door opened quietly behind her and she froze with the book in her hands.

"Sara!" Nick said. "What are you doing here? I came down for my book and saw the light—"

She was hardly aware that the book slipped from her fingers as she turned to face him. She knew only that he was there, that he was a part of her heart—and she of his. It was written in his eyes and she knew the truth was in her own.

She ran to him across the room in her filmy gown, and his arms opened to her, held her to his heart.

"Sara, Sara! he whispered against her hair and she wept brokenly, her cheek wet against his own. "Hush," he said, as weeping shook her. "Hush, darling."

He picked her up in arms that were strong enough to carry her lightly and bore her to the big chair. But this time he sat in it holding her against him, with her head in the hollow of his shoulder.

"I love you," he said gently. "Never doubt that, my dear. But I must tell you something, Sara, if you will listen."

Her head moved in assent against his shoulder. "I want to listen. Help me, Nick."

His hand touched the silky darkness of her hair and the touch was more than words.

"We must help each other," he said.

His voice went on softly, gently, and Sara listened, quiet now, though she knew there must be hurt in the listening.

"The first visit I ever had with Jenny was in this room. She perched on a ledge over there below the bookshelves, and I sat on a stepladder and we talked for nearly an hour, while old Merkel finished his business with Miss Varady across the hall in the dining room."

Sara did not stir in his arms. The velvet material of his smoking jacket was warm beneath her cheek. She could see the picture he was weaving and she did not shrink from it. Whatever the truth, she must know it, face it.

Miss Varady, he said, had invited Mr. Merkel to dinner, as she sometimes did, to talk business more comfortably than she could at the office. And on this occasion she had chosen for the first time to ask his younger partner as well—Nicholas Renwick. Geneva of course had dinner with them. She had been quiet and shy all through the meal, scarcely speaking a word, plainly afraid of her aunt's displeasure should she make a mistake of any kind. Nick's heart had gone out to her in pity. And when the other two had retired to the drawing room for their talk, he had set himself to draw out the timid young girl.

The library had given them a background in which they could both feel comfortable. When Nick had asked if she were lonely in this big house, Geneva made a gesture with two small hands that took in the bookshelves about her.

"How can I be lonely when the world comes in?" she had said.

So they had lost themselves in talking about a world which came in through these books, and Geneva had forgotten to be timid and self-conscious.

"I began to see her occasionally after that," Nick went on. "I was alone too, in spite of a family about me. I enjoyed being with Jenny and I somehow expected our friendship to remain as it was. I'm not sure when I realized she had grown to love me and that she was gently offering me the gift of her love. I've had no great opinion of myself in the scheme of things, Sara. It has never seemed to me that Nick Renwick was doing much that mattered one way or another, until lately perhaps since the fire. To bring happiness to someone like Jenny who had been starved for love all her life, seemed important to me. I had—I have—a great affection for Jenny Varady."

Sara lay quiet against his shoulder, listening. She could see Geneva as he pictured her. She too could love the gentle little person Geneva was and know in her own heart that she would never want to hurt her.

"I wanted you to know how it is, Sara," he went on, his arms tightening about her. "The thing you must understand, darling, is that I could never live with myself if I failed Jenny. She deserves only love and kindness from me. Can you understand this and forgive me?"

She sat up in his arms and framed his face with her hands, kissed him with a tenderness she had not known she could feel. For the first time she knew with all her heart that love had to be more a giving than a wanting, or it was nothing.

"I do understand," she told him softly. "Good night, Nick."

For just an instant he held her close, his face against her hair. Then he let her go. She went out of the room and back upstairs. Ah Foong slept without stirring, but beyond his cot her aunt's door stood ajar. A flash of warning ran through Sara and she turned from her own door, hurried down the hall to her mother's room. She could not bear to face Hester Varady now. It was better not to be alone.

"Mama," she whispered, grateful for the darkness of the room which hid her face, "may I come in with you tonight?"

"Of course, dear," Mary Bishop said. "Is it the dream again?"

Sara flung off the filmy negligee and crept beneath warm blankets, went close to her mother. Now she could talk—a little wildly, perhaps, governed only by a desire to escape from this house and the pain it held for her. To escape from Hester Varady.

"You were right from the beginning, Mama. Aunt Hester can never bear the slightest opposition to her wishes. Sometimes I'm afraid of what she might do if she's balked. We must move soon. No matter how small the room—anything will do." She could not speak of her love for Nick. All that must be hidden away forever.

Her mother asked no questions, but only comforted with crooning sounds, as if Sara were still a child.

Sara slept at last, through the early hours and late

into the morning. When she wakened her mother was gone from the room and the sun was well up over Van Ness Avenue.

Sara lay in bed thinking, groping. There was a soreness in her, a knowledge of pain to be faced. But now she felt strong and able to face it. Now, at length, her course was clear. She knew what must be done.

She got out of bed and returned to her own room without meeting anyone in the hall. As she dressed, she made her plans. Last night she had sought her mother's room for comfort and protection. But now in the light of morning she knew that she could never be at peace with herself until she had faced her aunt, stood up to her will. Hester Varady must be made to understand that Nick would marry Geneva and that Sara would never in any way interfere.

She went downstairs to a quiet breakfast alone. There was no need to rush heedlessly, to hurl herself into action, as she had sometimes done in the past.

When Hester Varady drove away from the house in the carriage, Sara did not hear her go. She did not know that her aunt had taken Geneva with her.

TWENTY-EIGHT

NOT UNTIL AFTER BREAKFAST DID SARA LEARN THAT HER aunt had gone out on a business appointment. Building had begun on several of her lots and Miss Varady liked to make tours of the work and see that everything moved to her satisfaction. It was odd that she had taken Geneva with her. Unusual.

They stayed away for lunch and into the afternoon.

Fog came rolling in through the Gate at an earlier hour than usual that day, inching its way into the sun-lit area, swallowing ships and islands, obscuring the water, edging bit by bit into the streets of San Francisco. This was no high fog that touched the hills and the tallest rooftops, but one that crawled on its belly through every street and into every cranny. The eucalyptus trees beside the Varady house creaked and dripped with moisture. A fog silence fell upon the city. Only the bay was alive with sounds of warning.

Sara heard her aunt's carriage return and she waited without haste for Miss Varady to settle herself in her room. She was quite sure now and unafraid.

Before she could see her aunt, however, Ah Foong came to summon her. His face looked more seamed and ancient than ever and his shoe-button eyes were uneasy. For a moment Sara thought he might let down his guard and speak to her of the forbidden. But in the end he only told her to "hully up" because her aunt wanted her right away.

Sara wished this particular interview could have been held elsewhere than in Hester's great, incongruous bedroom, with its peeping cupids and frivolous gilt. This room seemed too filled with reminders of what had never come to pass.

Her aunt sat at an ornate writing desk, inlaid with mother-of-pearl, a pen in her hand. As Sara came in she turned her chair about and her look of satisfaction, of triumph, was one Sara did not like to see.

"Sit down," Miss Varady ordered. "In that chair facing the light where I can see you. I've several things to say to you, my girl. For one thing, I've not been pleased with the limp-willed course you've taken lately. You remind me of Geneva. Of Elizabeth."

"There is something I want to say, too," Sara told her, determined to remain undaunted.

The heavy-lidded eyes watched her darkly, but this time Sara did not flinch before them.

"What you have to say can wait," Miss Varady told her. "I heard you go downstairs last night, though Ah Foong did not. He is getting old and useless, I'm afraid. I heard nothing but talk, and then you came scuttling upstairs like a frightened rabbit, and went straight to your mother's room. So I suppose you have muddled the whole thing and failed again."

Sara spoke firmly, still unafraid. "You might as well understand that whatever it is you are trying to accomplish through me is impossible. My mother and I intend to find a place of our own in the next few days. Then we will be off your hands for good."

Aunt Hester dismissed this nonsense with a scornful gesture. "Don't waste my time with such talk, Sara. I shall stand for no interference with my plans this time. As I've told you, you are the girl I once was. But now Nicholas stands in Martin's place, Geneva in Elizabeth's. And this time there will be no bungling as there was before. You shall have what you want, Sara. What *I* want!"

Sara longed suddenly to get out of the room, to remove herself from something monstrously unhealthy and distorted. But she managed to keep her voice steady when she spoke.

"Nick belongs to Geneva and she belongs to him," she said. "Nothing you can say or do will change that, Aunt Hester. They will marry and be happy together. You can't live over the past again and remake it as you wish."

"You mean you don't want Nicholas Renwick?"

Sara answered her evenly. "I don't want him at the cost of hurt to Geneva."

"So! You are exactly the fool I'd begun to think you. I suspected as much and I knew I must take steps to help you. Now I have done so."

The triumph in her eyes was ugly to see.

"What do you mean?" Sara asked, alert now to the warning.

"I have told Geneva the truth," Miss Varady said.

Sara left her chair and stood above her aunt. "What do you mean by that? What truth?"

"That Nicholas is in love with you, not with her. That she is in the way, cheating him and herself if she tries to hold him."

Never before had Sara touched Hester Varady of her own volition, but now she took her aunt's arm, shook it roughly.

"Where *is* Geneva? What have you done to her?"

"How dare you touch me!" Hester cried. She flung off Sara's hand and rose from her chair. "I have done nothing to her. How do I know where she is? She was sniveling there in the carriage in her usual way. When we stopped at a crossing, she got out with no apology and ran away into the fog."

"You mean you let her go off alone, shocked with grief like that?"

"I scarcely had a choice. I stopped the carriage of course. But by the time I'd sent the coachman after her, she'd disappeared. He couldn't hunt for her all day while I sat there waiting. She'll bring herself home in her own good time when she comes to her foolish senses."

Sara gave her aunt no second thought. She ran from the room and down the stairs to the library. Nick was there, talking to a client, when Sara burst into the room. He saw her face and turned the man over to Mr. Merkel, came into the hall.

"Sara, what has happened?"

"It's Geneva! Aunt Hester told her—that—you and I—" She choked, and went on again. "Geneva left the carriage and went off on foot. We've got to find her, Nick. We've got to undo this right away."

Nick wasted no time on words. He strode down the hall to the back door and Sara followed. The coachman remembered that Miss Geneva had left the carriage in the downtown area below Nob Hill. Nick started the auto and Sara went with him when he drove away.

Fog writhed through San Francisco's streets, as if possessed by a life of its own. The noise of the motor warned pedestrians away, but now and then some figure would loom up abruptly in the mist and Nick would swerve the wheel.

"Where are we to look?" Sara asked, peering anxiously ahead through the windshield. The wind whipped at her hair, tore strands of it loose, and she pushed it back impatiently so that it would not interfere with her vision.

"If she was near Nob Hill, I know where she might go," Nick said.

Sara knew too. Geneva, distraught and grieving, might return to what remained of the place where she had once spent happy times; a place that had been more a home to her than her own.

Where street lights burned, the fog thickened to a yellowish glow. The lamps wore a cloudy nimbus about them that made the streets all the more ghostly. Away from the light there was no color anywhere. Fog had turned the world to gray.

Now it became so difficult to drive that Nick left the automobile at a curb and they got out to climb on foot. There was some building going on up here, but ruins still crowded on all sides, looming eerily in the fog like the remains of a ghost city.

"Here we are," Nick said. "Step carefully." He took Sara by the arm.

Beneath their feet uncertain steps led upward, their summit hidden by the gray veil. The two mounted slowly a step at a time, lest they slip off the edge, where the iron rail had been twisted askew. If Geneva were anywhere near, they would not see her unless they were almost upon her.

In the distance foghorns wailed and the sound of boat whistles made a remote clamor. But nearby it was still.

"Jenny!" Nick called. "Jenny, I've come to take you home."

A gust of wind thinned the mists at the top of the steps and it seemed to Sara that a figure moved in the obscurity.

"There's someone up there. Go after her, Nick!"

"Wait for me, Jenny!" he called again.

But the figure at the top of the steps fled away from them—though there was nowhere to flee. A muffled sound reached them, as if someone had leaped into space and landed on some ledge, sending a brick or two flying. Sara remembered in fear the leaning brick wall that Allison had wanted to climb the day they had picnicked here.

Now Nick had disappeared too in the fog and Sara stood helplessly on the steps, her heartbeats thudding in her ears. She heard the light, heedless patter of footsteps, as if the runner gave no thought for the insecure path beneath her feet. Nick called again, his voice a command.

"Wait, Jenny! Stay where you are. I'm coming after you."

Only then did Geneva's words come back to them. "No, Nick! Don't! The wall is shaking—you mustn't, Nick!" Her voice was lost in the roar of falling bricks.

The sound echoed dully against surrounding walls, went reverberating down the hill, fog-deadened.

Sara could hear herself screaming senselessly, helplessly.

There were still rumblings of lesser volume, and then a sound as if someone clambered through the wreckage. Sara fled down the steps to where the fog was thinner and she could climb from the sidewalk to the grounds of the Renwick place. She made her way around by the side, found a low spot where she could lower herself into the rubble that had once been a house.

Nick heard her and called. "I've found her, Sara. Come quickly—I need you."

She scrambled over the heaps of brick, stumbled to her knees, rose and stumbled again. She followed the sounds until she stood beside him. He was working with all his might to pull away loose brick and Sara saw a small hand, its fingers curled inward. She knelt beside Nick to help as best she could.

At least Geneva had been flung from the top of the wall, so that she had been caught only by the edge of the avalanche. If she had dropped straight down she would have been buried completely. In minutes they had her head and shoulders free of the loose brick. She had fallen face down. Blood streaked her turned cheek and her soft brown hair was matted with blood and dust and bits of debris.

Sara did not know until later that her own hands were bleeding, her nails broken. She worked frantically with Nick until Geneva lay free of the burden that had crushed her. The girl did not cry out, or moan, and Sara could not tell whether she lived or not. Nick stripped off his coat and improvised a stretcher so that he and Sara could carry her without jarring. The weight in the coat-stretcher was so slight that it was no burden. They stepped carefully over rubble and did not rest until they had reached the side yard, where they lowered the girl gently to the blackened stubble of grass.

Only then did she open her eyes and look at them. Sara took her handkerchief and wiped the streak of blood from Geneva's cheek, but the girl looked only at Nick, her lips curving faintly.

"Jenny, darling!" He bent above her, kissed her, touched her matted hair. "You're going to be all right, Jenny. The auto is only a few blocks away and I'm going to get it. Sara will stay with you. I'll be back in a jiffy. Then we'll take you home to your own bed where you'll be warm and comfortable."

Geneva formed a word with her lips. "Nick—"

He kissed her again. "I love you very much, Jenny. You've got to be good now. Be quiet so you'll get well soon. I need you, Jenny."

Again the faint smile curved her lips. Nick gave Sara a quick look of warning and hurried off at a run to get the car.

The slash on Geneva's cheek was bleeding again and once more Sara wiped at it futilely. The cut was so little beside all the rest that might be wrong with Geneva's small body.

"How did you find me?" Geneva's lips formed the words weakly.

"Aunt Hester told me what she had done," Sara said. "And we came at once. You mustn't believe any of her lies. Nick loves you—that's the only truth. That's what you must hold to now, little cousin."

Geneva closed her eyes briefly, then opened them again. Her voice was stronger.

"Aunt Hester told me a great many things. We aren't cousins, after all, Sara. Callie Bishop was my mother, but she wasn't Leland's sister, as we thought. She was his wife. His first wife. So you and I are sisters—half sisters. I like that very much. It's nicer than being cousins."

Sara could feel tears sting her eyes. But for the moment she could think only of Geneva's plight.

"You mustn't talk. You must have your strength."

"It doesn't hurt to talk," Geneva said. "I must—while I can. You needn't worry—there isn't any pain. I can't seem to feel my legs or the rest of my body. It's better this way, Sara—it's the only way. After what Aunt Hester told me I knew I could never marry Nick."

"Of course you'll marry him!" Sara cried. "You mustn't ever doubt that he loves you."

"I know he loves me." Geneva closed her eyes, sighing faintly. "I knew that was a lie when Aunt Hester spoke it. I'm sorry if you love him too. But there's something else. She told me about the insanity that ran in my mother's side of the family. My mother—Callie—died in Aunt Hester's house. She had to be kept locked up in that little room—or else sent to some dreadful madhouse. Aunt Hester said that meant

I should never marry and have children. And about this, Sara, she was right."

Sara was shaken by Geneva's words, by the shock of what had happened. The only reality in this world of fog and nightmare was the sound of the automobile coughing as it climbed the hill. In a few moments Nick was with them again, his voice forcedly cheerful.

"We'll get you home safely in no time at all, Jenny. Grit your teeth, darling. We'll lift as gently as we can."

But Geneva raised one arm from her torn sleeve and slipped it about Nick's neck as he bent over her. "No," she said. "Not right away. I waited for you, Nick. Stay with me for a little while."

Nick bent over her and Sara stumbled to her feet, found her way to the auto. The engine was still running, so that Nick wouldn't have to crank it again. Sara stood with one hand on the vibrating door, the sense of unreality upon her. Surely in a few moments Nick would come hand in hand with Geneva out of the ruins, just as they had done that day of the picnic. Geneva—her sister. Older by two years, but still her *little* sister. She couldn't find and lose a sister as quickly as this.

But when Nick came toward her out of the fog, carrying Geneva in his arms, she knew the one, irrevocable truth that no one would ever be able to shake or change.

He scarcely saw Sara as she opened the door of the tonneau for him. With gentle hands he laid Geneva upon the seat. Sara got in and sat on the floor, so that Geneva would not slip off with the movement of the car. All the way back to Van Ness she held her sister's hand, though she knew Geneva would never know, or care.

Hester Varady stood in the lower hallway when Nick came in with Geneva in his arms. She started to speak, to question, but he brushed past her. And Sara, following him up the stairs, had no word or look for her aunt.

TWENTY-NINE

SARA COULD EAT NO DINNER THAT NIGHT, THOUGH AH Foong, old and more crumpled than ever, brought a bowl of soup to her room. His eyes were no longer shoe-button black, but rheumy with age and with sorrow. Sara put her hand upon his blue sleeve for a moment.

"Geneva was my sister," she said. "She told me this afternoon. Ah Foong, why didn't you let us know before?"

The old Chinese only shook his head and went away. Through all the long years his allegiance had been given first to Hester Varady, and he was too old to change.

When Ah Foong had gone, Mary Bishop came to sit beside Sara's bed to offer comfort. But tonight there was no comfort Sara could get from her mother. She did not know the truth. Perhaps she had never known that her husband had been married to another woman before he had married her. She had not known the identity of the Callie whose name was only whispered in this house.

Tonight Sara dreaded sleep. Too much that was terrible had happened. She could not bear to dream through it all again. When her mother went away she fought to stay awake, but her own emotional exhaustion betrayed her and at length she slept.

Slept deeply, soundly, until the cold thing gripped her again and in her dream she stood with bare feet in an impossibly long corridor. Closed doors like blank faces stretched into the endless distance. Step after inevitable step she must move down the long hall with the sound of storm all about her. She knew that rain blew against windows, pounded on the roof. Trees outside moaned and threshed their branches about. She had always loved storms and there was a moment of exultation when she started down the hall to a room from which she could look out upon the storm. What other room would she choose save one which opened upon a small balcony?

With the abrupt transition that was possible in a dream, the hall was gone and she was in the small crowded room, with furniture piled untidily about her. There—there near one wall, reflecting door and balcony—stood a long wardrobe chest with a mirror down its side.

Terror gripped her. She could hear voices—angry voices. These had never come into the dream before. And she could see the faint, advancing glow of light. Closer and closer it came, until the moment when she knew she would see the hand come into the mirror—a pale hand, carrying a tall candlestick. Outside gray light pressed against the windows, but the storm had turned the afternoon dark and a candle was needed. Then the hand vanished and the light with it. Dim figures moved in the mirror and again came the sound of a strange crackling.

She could feel horror grip her throat, stifle the screams she wanted to utter. She fought now, struggled against the web of dream that bound her to this freezing fear. She fought like a swimmer who struggles wildly against drowning, fought so fiercely that she tossed about the bed and her own violent movement jerked her awake. For the first time that she could remember she had not carried the dream through to the final moment of horror when memory put down its curtain and refused her the knowledge of whatever had happened.

She sat up on the edge of her bed, trembling with cold and dread, yet not abjectly ruled by her own fear as she had always been before. This time she must follow the dream through to the end before it could fade. This time she must hunt it down, no matter what terror it held for her.

She troubled with no wrapper or slippers, but ran barefoot down the hall as she had done that long ago time as a child. She could hear again the sounds of storm shaking the house, though the night was still and windless, with fog dampening all the city. The door of the little room stood open and she pushed her way in, stood in the corner where once she had hidden trembling as a child. The mirror was there—there where it reflected the balcony. She could see it as clearly as though it had been real.

But this time it was no hand with a candlestick she saw, but the scene on the balcony beyond—the scene which her dream had always refused to make clear. A man and a woman struggled together in the mirrored reflection, their angry words lost in the storm sounds outside. The woman screamed and struck out at the man, pushed wildly. There was the ripping, crackling sound of splintered wood as the balcony rail gave way. The cry that rang down through the years of memory made Sara clap her hands over her ears, though the real night beyond the long-repaired rail was quiet and heavy with fog.

But Sara knew the truth now. The man had gone through the flimsy wood, crashing to the flagstones of the walk below. The storm had washed over the sound of his fall, and over the screaming of the woman who had thrust him to his death.

Then the picture was gone. There was no mirror. The room stood empty about her. She knew now what had happened to Leland Bishop. She knew again her love for her father, knew the horror her young mind had rejected, thrust away to the very deeps of her being.

The knowledge left her empty and sorrowful. Until this moment there had always been the possibility that her father still lived, that somewhere, sometimes she would find him. Now, for these few moments, her loss was as keen as though his death had just occurred.

But she roused herself, shook off new sorrow. Now she must deal with the present. She was filled with a purpose that warmed her, that sent the blood tingling through her body, banishing the clammy cold. The present meant Aunt Hester, and she knew what she must do.

She hurried upstairs to the little room with the bureau in it. The bureau on whose wood poor Callie had scratched her name, fighting perhaps to recover a sense of her own being which Aunt Hester tried to take from her. The bottom drawer stuck, but Sara pulled it open with a clatter. Inside lay the bundle of bones, wrapped in newspaper. Sara took it into her hands and hurried to the stairway.

At her aunt's door it was necessary to slip past Ah Foong, lest he try to stop her. But again he slept soundly and well. She opened the door and stepped into the room. Here the shutters had been closed against the fog.

Miss Varady stirred in her great bed and spoke in the darkness.

"Who is it? Who is there?"

Sara knew where the candlestick stood. Candlelight would be best for her purpose. She set her package down and found the matches, struck one and lit the candle.

"How dare you—" Miss Varady began.

Sara set the candle close to the bed, so that its light fell upon her aunt's face. And she stood beside it, sharply aware of her own youth and strength, of the frailty of the woman who struggled to sit up against her pillows. Why had she ever feared this old woman?

"Today you sent Geneva to her death," Sara said. "It was your hand which thrust her from that wall just as surely as though you had been there. It was you who pushed my father from that balcony so that he died on the flagstones below."

Hester spoke between tight-drawn lips. "You've gone mad!"

"Oh, no, I haven't. I was there in that little room. I saw what happened. I saw it all. Though I couldn't remember until tonight. You hated my father, didn't you? You wanted him to die."

Hester Varady stared at her for an angry moment. Then her hand began to move toward the bellpull. Sara snatched up the newspaper bundle and flung it beside her aunt on the covers of her bed. The paper rustled open and the little white bones shone in the candlelight.

Hester forgot the bellpull. She put a hand to her throat as if she were choking and moved desperately away to the other side of the bed.

"It was only a little cat," Sara said. "A little white cat. And you had to kill that too. Because Ah Foong said Callie's spirit had come back to inhabit its body. But you couldn't get rid of the cat as you did the others. It still walks the corridors, doesn't it?"

"Take that away!" her aunt cried. "Take it away at once!"

"Only if you'll tell me the truth. All the truth. What happened after you pushed my father from the balcony?"

The woman in the bed turned her face from the sight of the packet and Sara closed the wrapping of newspaper.

"It wasn't I who thrust your father from that balcony." Her aunt's voice trembled and she steadied it with an effort. "It was Geneva's mother—that miserable Callie. She was always an unbalanced creature, emotional and unpredictable. Pretty enough, I suppose, as a wretched little barmaid in a saloon down on the Coast when Leland found her. He felt she needed rescuing. Besides, he knew nothing would upset me more than to bring such a person home to my house. So he married her in his irresponsible way and tried to install her here as his wife. I managed to hush it up so that it never got into the newspapers and I hustled them both out of town at once. Before their baby was born he left her and I managed to get him a quiet divorce."

Hester paused and rubbed a hand over her eyes as if there were sights she too wanted to wipe away.

"Go on," Sara said.

"I was not pleased by Leland's second marriage, but it was better than the first. I let them live in this house. I let their child—you—be born here. We didn't hear from Callie again for a long while. Leland had settled some money on her, thanks to me. But he was back again in his shady schemes for making a fortune and Callie stumbled onto them. She began to follow him and make threats, I found he was paying her money to hold her tongue and I knew that couldn't go on indefinitely. I told him to have her come here. I was going to talk to her myself and put a stop to what she was doing. She might frighten your father, but she couldn't frighten me."

"Where was Geneva all this time?" Sara asked.

"Callie had her. She brought her here to the house that day and Ah Foong took Geneva into the kitchen to free the mother for the interview. But Callie came early and she was in a state of nervous emotion bordering on hysteria. She got away from Ah Foong and came upstairs looking for Leland. There was a terrible wind that afternoon and a rainstorm. Your mother had gone to nap in her own room and there at the front of the house she heard nothing of what happened. You were supposed to be having your nap too.

"Callie met Leland in the hallway and began to shriek at him. To keep her away from your mother, he took her to the back of the house—that little room near the balcony. Ah Foong came to tell me what was happening."

"And you came along the hall with a candle," said Sara.

Hester's heavy lids drooped over her eyes. "Yes. By the time I reached the room they were out on the balcony. Callie was half crazy and threatening to fling herself over the railing if Leland would not comply with her wishes. I thought it might be convenient if she did and I stayed where I was, watching them from the door of the room."

"With that tall candlestick in your hand," Sara whispered.

"Small as she was, Callie had the strength of madness that day. When he put himself between her and the balcony rail she flung herself upon him, fighting and struggling. I don't think for a moment that she intended what happened. But the rail gave way and he went through to those stones below."

A shudder ran through Hester's body. She opened her eyes and stared at Sara.

"Is this what you wanted to know?"

"It's not all," Sara said. "What did you do about—about my father?"

"Ah Foong helped me that night. First Callie had to be taken care of. She had gone clean out of her mind. I gave her something to put her to sleep and Ah Foong and I got her upstairs to that small bedroom where we locked her in. I'd sent the servants out that day, so there was no one to see. Ah Foong hitched up the carriage and we took Leland away. You need not know where. He had died at once. His body was never found. It was the only thing to do. I could not have such a scandal as would have stained the Varady name forever."

Sara felt a little sick, listening. "And Callie?"

"Her case was hopeless. We managed to keep her quiet most of the time. There are drugs. She was better here than in the type of institution which care for such cases. She was very ill. Her death came only a few months after your mother had left this house. Fortunately she had no relatives to look for her. In the meantime I had put the child in the capable hands of convent nuns. She was well cared for until I brought her here. I told her nothing, hid her identity. I could take no chance on anyone else knowing."

"And today she died too," Sara said softly.

"I did not intend that," Miss Varady said and Sara saw that she looked suddenly old and withered and helpless.

"I was there in the room when it happened," Sara mused. "I must have seen the whole thing."

"I was afraid you had," Miss Varady said. "When I found you there you were shivering and crying. It was a good thing your mother was so busy nursing you in the days that followed that she didn't know what was going on. You were down with fever and in a delirium for days. When it cleared up you didn't remember anything you had seen. But you began to have those dreams at night."

"I won't have them any more," Sara said. "I'm free of them forever." She held up the packet in her hands. "What of the little cat?"

"Ah Foong is an old woman! He gave the cat to her up in that room. I suppose it kept her quiet a bit."

"And after Callie's death?"

"Get out!" Miss Varady cried. "Get out of my room. You have tormented me enough."

There was no reason to stay. When Sara turned to the door she found Ah Foong waiting for her. She did not know how long he had been there, or how much he had heard, but this house held no secrets from him. As she went out, she put the little packet into his hands, and he took it without question. It would be buried again. Silently in the night. As the body of Leland Bishop had once been buried in some unknown spot.

Sara returned wearily to her room and sat for a while by the window looking out upon the fog-laden quiet of Van Ness Avenue. It was too bad that the fire had not flared out to take this house as well as the rest. It was an ill-fated house where no one could ever be happy. She would be glad to get away from it.

In the days following Geneva's funeral, Sara walked from house to house in Pacific Heights until she found rooms she and her mother could move into.

She saw little of Nick in the days before she left Miss Varady's and she tried to keep away from him in his grief. The very sight of her would, she knew, be an unhappy reminder. He too sought other quarters and he and Mr. Merkel rented a single office room above a store on Fillmore Street.

Nick left the house before Sara and her mother and he said good-by to her sadly, impersonally. Since Geneva's death he had changed. He held his grieving to himself and withdrew from the society of others. More than ever now he was immersed in his work. Sara did not blame him for avoiding the sight of her. But when she gave him her hand in parting, she tried to offer some small word of comfort.

He only said, "Good luck, Sara," and turned soberly away.

She knew then how irrevocably Geneva's death had set itself between them. He blamed himself and perhaps he blamed her too. Under the circumstances he could take no happiness for himself with another woman.

Hester Varady made no comment upon any of these changes. She had aged in the span of a few weeks and often she did not come down for meals, but had Ah Foong bring a tray to her room. She still kept her business appointments, but her interest had obviously faded.

When Sara left she tried to say good-by to her aunt, feeling a certain pity for her, in spite of all that had happened. But Hester refused to see her, and only Ah Foong stood on the steps to say farewell, his eyes rheumy as he watched her go. Had she dared, Sara might have kissed his cheek, but she knew he would resent so personal a gesture.

In the new place Sara flung herself into the work of designing dresses for the ladies of San Francisco. Her growing reputation stood her in good stead and it was not necessary for her mother to seek outside work. Mary was kept busy enough with her needle and she worked happily, glad to be free of Hester Varady and her house of dark memories. To please her mother, Sara used the name *Jerome* as a label in her designing of dresses.

There was a weary numbness in Sara these days. She helped her mother in the simpler phases of the sewing, forcing herself to learn what she had always scorned before. They could not afford assistance now and she must fill in where she could. The purchase of a sewing machine had been their one important expenditure.

These days Sara wanted only to work until she dropped. When she was tired enough hurtful thoughts would not come at night. But sometimes, no matter how exhausted she might be, they forced themselves upon her. An old treadmill of futility. If Geneva had lived and refused to marry Nick, perhaps Sara and he might eventually have come together.

Or if Geneva had lived and married Nick, there would have been a certain peace for Sara. She could have turned to the making of a life for herself knowing that at least everything was right with Geneva and Nick. There would have been none of this soreness of blame, this grieving for Geneva herself.

Then one day when a woman put on a dress Sara had designed for her, and posed before a mirror, looking fashionable and lovely, Sara experienced a brief upsurge of happiness that astonished her. Afterward she felt a little guilty, as if she had no right to be happy ever again. But words Nick had once said to her returned and she found a meaning in them she had not seen before.

He had said that happiness was not a goal in itself, but only a by-product of other things. This surge of satisfaction over her own creative effort was exactly that. And remembering Nick's words, she was grateful.

When the fateful year of '06 had worn its way to an end San Francisco put on as big a celebration as that celebrating town had ever produced. By New Year's Eve there was no longer any doubt that the city was on its feet again. And its citizens bade an uproarious farewell to a year of disaster and rebirth, greeting 1907 with hope and joy. San Francisco had done the impossible—let the rest of the world take note!

Sara spent the evening quietly with Allison, so the other Renwicks could attend a party. Even Hilda Renwick was willing to go out these days. Allison was Sara's one link with Nick. The child seemed unconscious of the fact that they never saw one another and she talked casually about her brother. Sara never asked questions, but she listened eagerly, fed herself on these crumbs whenever they came her way.

She did not go near Hester Varady at all that Christmas, or on New Year's Day. This was something she could not bring herself to do. Then the holidays were over and she was so hard at work again she hardly noted the passing of time.

One beautiful spring Sunday the telephone range and the unexpected sound of Nick's voice came over the wire. Sara was so startled that she could hardly speak. He sounded awkward himself, but he came to the point quickly enough.

"I've promised Allison a trip to Sutro Heights this afternoon, Sara. Would you care to come along?"

She held back, remembering other invitations, afraid to open wounds that were at least quiet, if not healed.

"I suppose Allison wants me—" she began faintly, "and—"

"I want you," Nick said. "Please come, Sara."

She put the phone down with a hand that was shaking.

THIRTY

THAT DAY AT SUTRO HEIGHTS WAS A BEGINNING. Geneva's death had made them strangers and there must now be a groping toward reacquaintance. There was a certain contentment for Sara in being with Nick again, but she was glad for Allison's presence, which postponed any need for serious talk.

After that there were other times, and Allison was not always along. Sometimes Nick would take Sara to a concert, or a play, with a quiet dinner in some small restaurant. Eventually words came more easily between them, and they could at last speak of Geneva, talk out some of the soreness that lay in them both.

There had been too much of the futile round in which each blamed himself and wondered what would have happened if he had done this differently, or that. When they could cease reproaching themselves and speak of Geneva as she had been, they could face what Geneva in her goodness would have wanted.

It was even possible now to speak with more tolerance of Hester Varady. Not because what she had done could ever be forgiven, but because she was now a pitiable shadow of herself. By this time Sara had brought herself to visit Aunt Hester on several occasions. She had never fully recovered from the events that had surrounded Geneva's death and it seemed to Sara that her aunt was fading almost before her eyes. She stayed in bed most of the time, watched over and waited on by Ah Foong. She would have nothing to do with doctors and took no interest in prescribing for herself, as once she would have done.

One Sunday afternoon, shortly before Nick was to call for Sara, Ah Foong appeared at the door to fetch her to Aunt Hester's bedside. It was plain that he was worried and when Sara had left word with her mother for Nick to come to the house on Van Ness, she went back to Miss Varady's with Ah Foong.

The house was more gloomy and shut away than ever these days. Sara could never walk into it without a shiver. As she followed Ah Foong upstairs to the familiar bedroom, the house seemed once more to lay a heavy hand upon her spirit. It was as if it brooded on defeat and failure, even as its mistress must have brooded.

But when Sara stood beside Hester's bed she could feel only pity for the shriveled old woman who lay there. Nevertheless, there was still life in the sunken, burning eyes, and a sudden strength in Miss Varady's voice when she spoke.

"Sit down," she said in the old curt way. "I wanted you here so I could tell you about my will."

"You mustn't trouble yourself, Aunt Hester," said Sara gently.

"Don't mollycoddle me! I want you to know that I'm not leaving a cent to you, Sara Bishop. Every penny of my wealth is going to Ah Foong. What do you think of that, my girl?"

Sara had only a sense of relief, of fitness. Ah Foong deserved this. He could be a king in Chinatown now. Or he could go back to his homeland and take care of a thousand-thousand relatives. But she knew Aunt Hester wanted the satisfaction of a last triumph, and she groped for words which might give her that meaningless pleasure.

"Aunt Hester—" she began, but her aunt's gaze swept past her to the door and there was sudden terror in her eyes. She struggled to sit up in the bed.

"Do you hear the mewing, Sara? It's that cat again! The little white cat. Don't let it come near me!" Her voice rose shrilly.

Sara leaned above her, took Hester's cold, parchment hands into her own warm clasp. "Don't be frightened. It's only Comstock out there—not the little white cat. And you've never been afraid of Comstock."

Time had stopped for Hester Varady and she could believe. The fear went out of her, as irritation took its place. "You must speak to Allison. I won't have that creature—"

"I'll tell her," Sara promised. "Of course you needn't have Comstock in your house."

The dry cold hands relaxed in her own. "That's all, Sara. I just wanted you to know that you need expect nothing at all in my will. You've disappointed me, just as the others have. Go away now and let me sleep."

Sara slipped quietly out of the room. Ah Foong was in the hall and he looked at her anxiously.

"She's all right," Sara assured him. But she knew how low the flame flickered, how little time was left for it to burn.

"Mista Nick waiting," Ah Foong said and Sara went down, grateful to find Nick in the hall.

He had a cab at the curb and she did not speak until they were in it together. When she told him what had happened, he listened in sympathy.

"You've done what you could," he said. "Let's not talk about her now. I want to show you something, Sara."

He took her hand into his and it was the first time he had touched her so, since that day in the library.

At the place where Broadway steepened, Nick stopped the cab and dismissed it. The climb up Russian Hill was difficult and they went up hand in hand. At the very top they could stand and look out upon the wonderful view. A view that was not merely of bay and hills and far shores, but of a city rebuilding itself.

Of course there were patches of rubble—the scars would show for years to come. But everywhere new houses, new buildings shone in the sunlight. Sara could see the great shaft of the Varady Building rising above the others, almost completed now. She could look at it with a feeling of admiration for what Ritchie had built and only good will toward him and Judith. All soreness lay in the past.

"I want to build a house up here," Nick said. "Only a small one that I can afford. But there will be a view. I hope you will like that, Sara. I hope you will want to share it."

The moment had come as simply as that and she reached out for it as simply, lifting her face for his kiss. How very much she wanted to share with Nick, she meant to spend the years in proving.

They walked about for a while looking for the perfect site. When they found a place where new grass had covered black stubble, they sat down on the hillside in the sun and the wind.

San Francisco lay below them. The hills stood tall and firmly rooted. Surely they had never swayed or trembled. Surely fire had never ravaged their very crowns.

"Before long you'll never know there'd been a fire," Sara said softly.

Nick held her hand. "Those who were here will always know. It changed us all. We were never the same people afterwards. I'm rather proud of us for what we did."

But Sara was no longer thinking of the fire, or of the men and women who had done the incredible. She was thinking only of Nick whose hand was strong about her own. Nick who had changed her more than had the fire.

In through the Gate stole the fog, unhurried and lazy, sure of its way as it puffed its soft gray breath through the streets of San Francisco.

Born in Japan of American parents, Phyllis A. Whitney is the bestselling author of over 35 books. She is recognized as one of America's most successful writers of romance and suspense. Her most recent novel, RAINBOW IN THE MIST, was a *New York Times* hardcover bestseller. Ms. Whitney lives in Virginia.